GIANT DAYS

VOLUME FIVE

BOOM! BOX

Ross Richie CEO & FOUNDER

Matt Gagnon EDITOR-IN-CHIEF

Filip Sablik PRESIDENT OF PUBLISHING & MARKETING

Stephen Christy PRESIDENT OF DEVELOPMENT

Lance Kreiter VP OF LICENSING & MERCHANDISING

Phil Barbaro VP OF FINANCE

Bryce Carlson MANAGING EDITOR

Mel Caylo MARKETING MANAGER

Scott Newman PRODUCTION DESIGN MANAGER

Kate Henning OPERATIONS MANAGER

Sierra Hahn SENIOR EDITOR

Dafna Pleban EDITOR, TALENT DEVELOPMENT

Shannon Watters EDITOR

Eric Harburn EDITOR

Whitney Leopard ASSOCIATE EDITOR

Jasmine Amiri ASSOCIATE EDITOR

Chris Rosa ASSOCIATE EDITOR

Alex Galer ASSOCIATE EDITOR

Cameron Chittock ASSOCIATE EDITOR

Matthew Levine ASSISTANT EDITOR

Sophie Philips-Roberts ASSISTANT EDITOR

Kelsey Dieterich PRODUCTION DESIGNER

Jillian Crab PRODUCTION DESIGNER

Michelle Ankley PRODUCTION DESIGNER

Grace Park PRODUCTION DESIGN ASSISTANT

Elizabeth Loughridge ACCOUNTING COORDINATOR

Stephanie Hocutt SOCIAL MEDIA COORDINATOR

José Meza SALES ASSISTANT

James Arriola MAILROOM ASSISTANT

Holly Aitchison OPERATIONS ASSISTANT

Sam Kusek DIRECT MARKET REPRESENTATIVE

Amber Parker ADMINISTRATIVE ASSISTANT

BOOM! BOX™

GIANT DAYS Volume Five, June 2017. Published by BOOM! Box, a division of Boom Entertainment, Inc. Giant Days is ™ & © 2017 John Allison. Originally published in single magazine form as GIANT DAYS No. 17-20. ™ & © 2016 John Allison. All rights reserved. BOOM! Box™ and the BOOM! Box logo are trademarks of Boom Entertainment, Inc., registered in various countries and categories. All characters, events, and institutions depicted herein are fictional. Any similarity between any of the names, characters, persons, events, and/or institutions in this publication to actual names, characters, and persons, whether living or dead, events, and/or institutions is unintended and purely coincidental. BOOM! Box does not read or accept unsolicited submissions of ideas, stories, or artwork.

A catalog record of this book is available from OCLC and from the BOOM! Studios website, www.boom-studios.com, on the Librarians page.

BOOM! Studios, 5670 Wilshire Boulevard, Suite 450, Los Angeles, CA 90036-5679. Printed in China. First Printing.

ISBN: 978-1-60886-982-4, eISBN: 978-1-61398-653-0

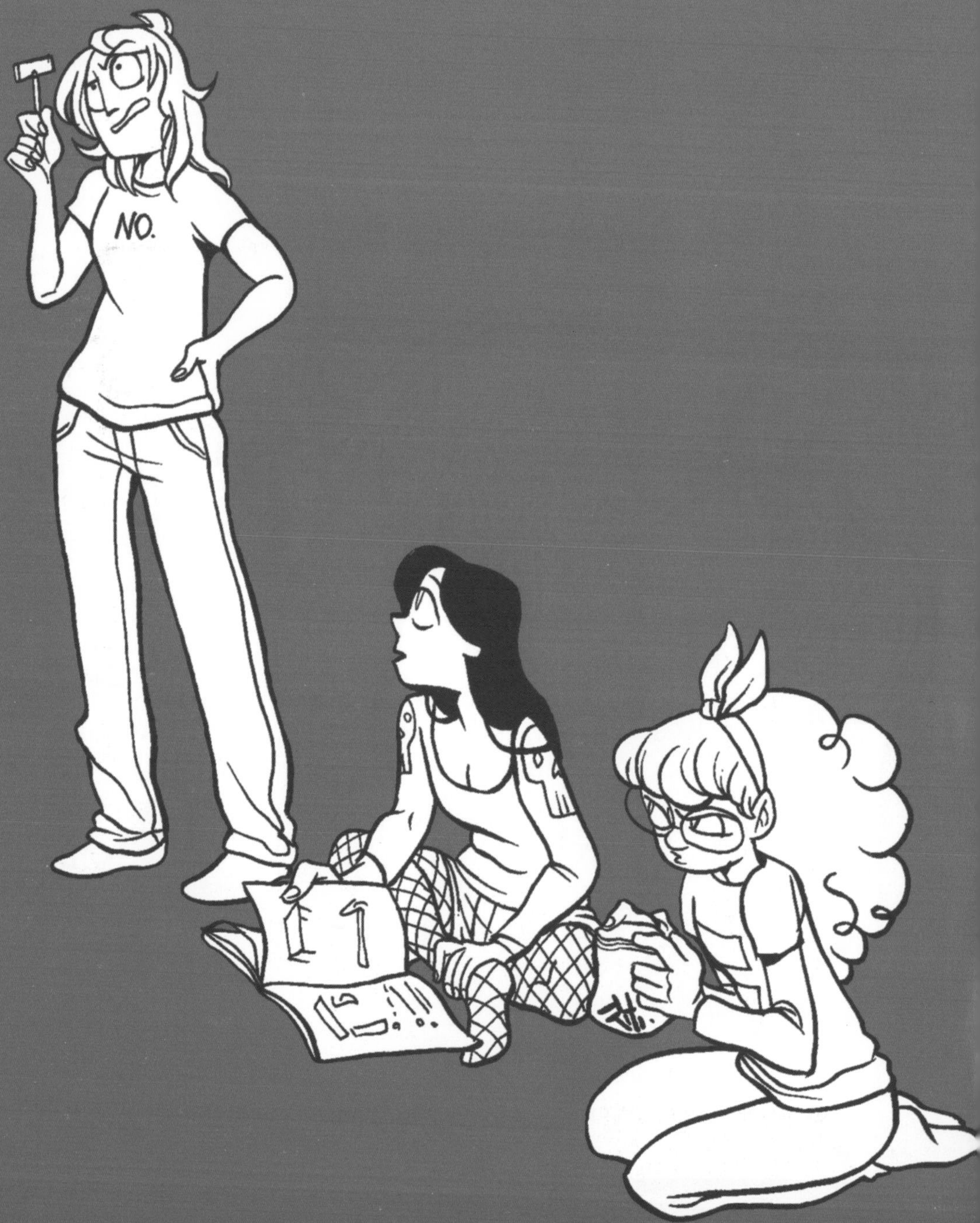
NO.

GIANT DAYS

CREATED & WRITTEN BY
JOHN ALLISON

ILLUSTRATED BY
MAX SARIN

INKS BY
LIZ FLEMING

COLORS BY
WHITNEY COGAR

LETTERS BY
JIM CAMPBELL

COVER BY
LISSA TREIMAN

DESIGNER
MICHELLE ANKLEY

ASSOCIATE EDITOR
JASMINE AMIRI

EDITOR
SHANNON WATTERS

CHAPTER SEVENTEEN

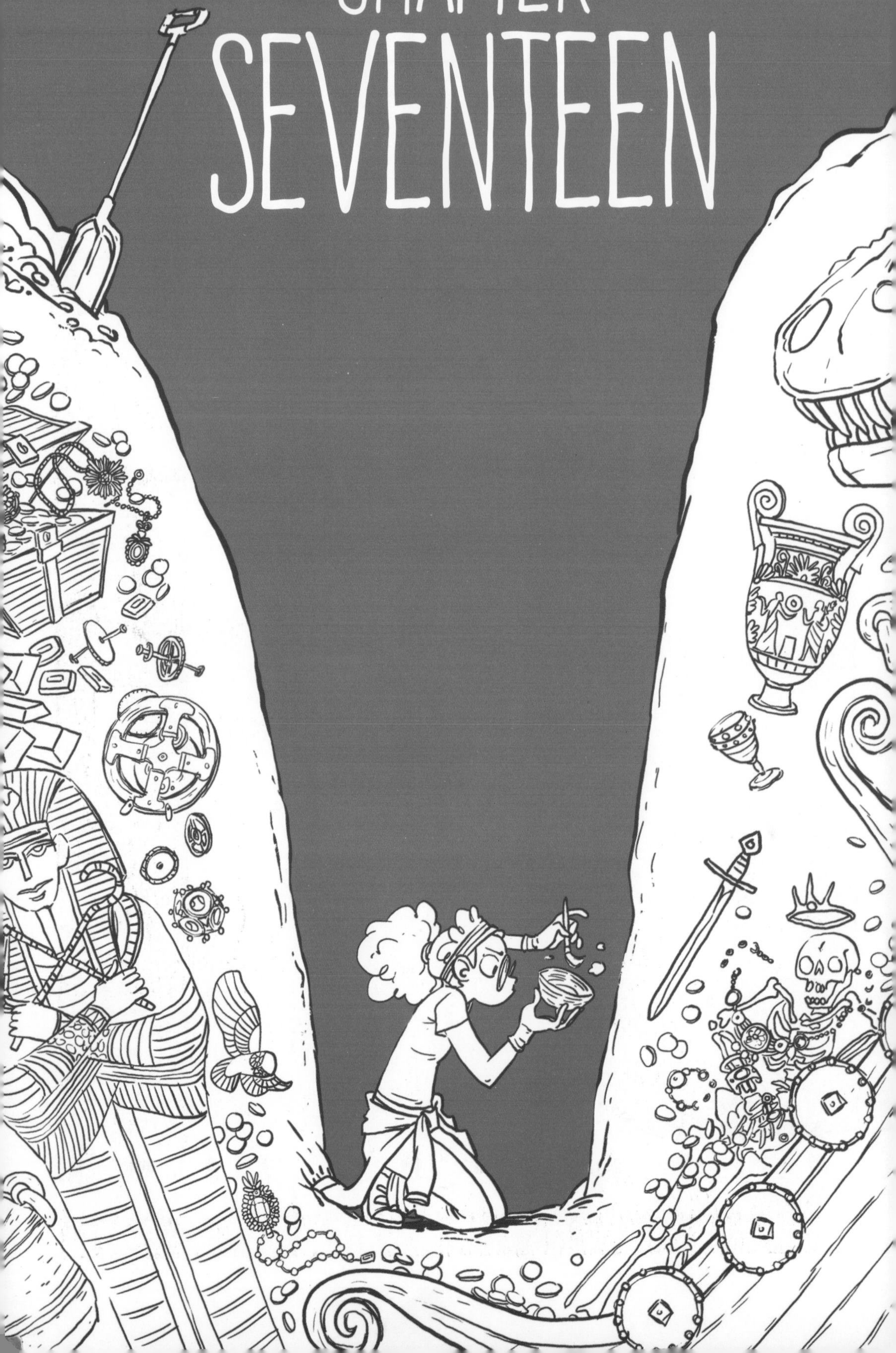

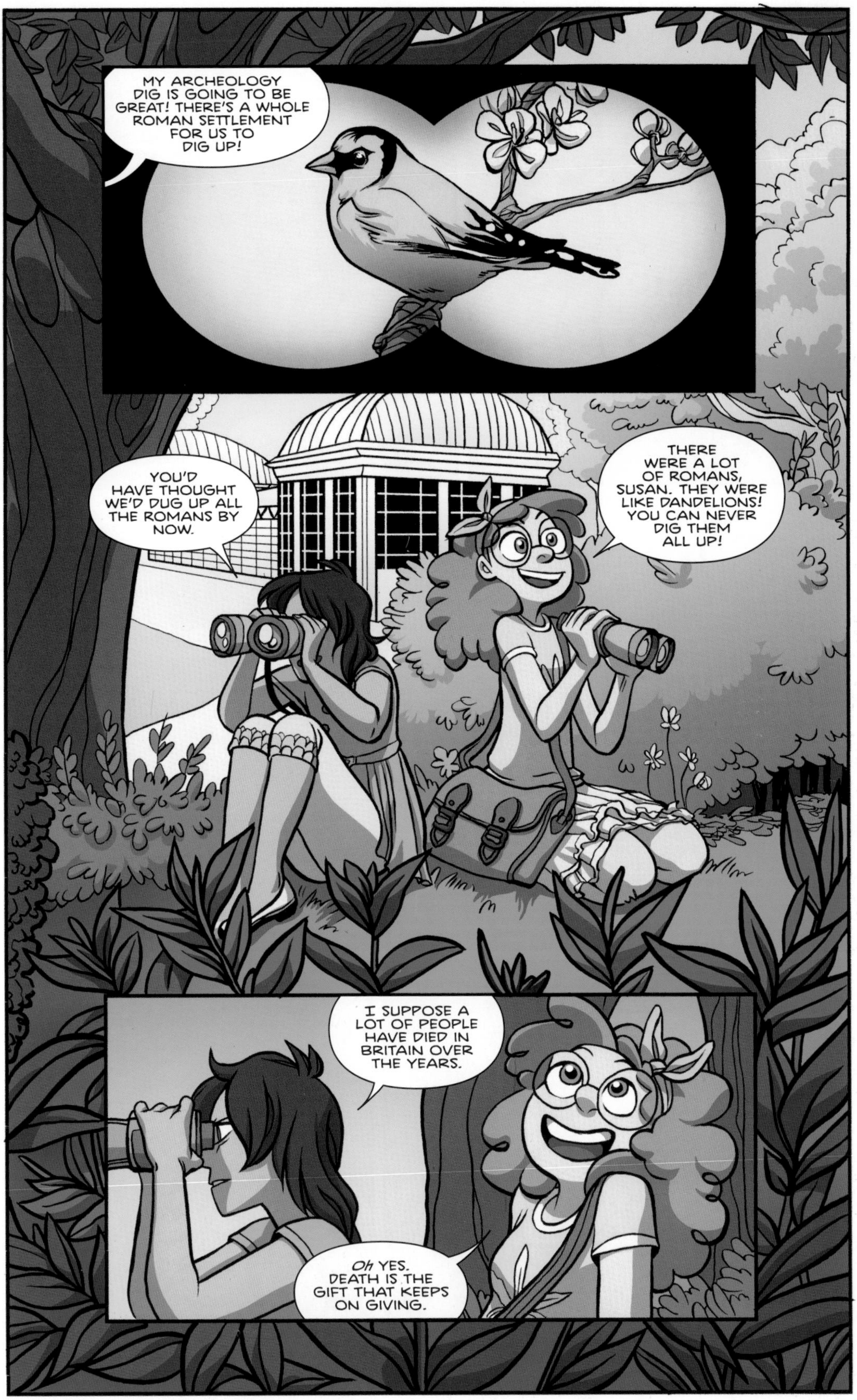

MY ARCHEOLOGY DIG IS GOING TO BE GREAT! THERE'S A WHOLE ROMAN SETTLEMENT FOR US TO DIG UP!
YOU'D HAVE THOUGHT WE'D DUG UP ALL THE ROMANS BY NOW.
THERE WERE A LOT OF ROMANS, SUSAN. THEY WERE LIKE DANDELIONS! YOU CAN NEVER DIG THEM ALL UP!
I SUPPOSE A LOT OF PEOPLE HAVE DIED IN BRITAIN OVER THE YEARS.
Oh YES. DEATH IS THE GIFT THAT KEEPS ON GIVING.

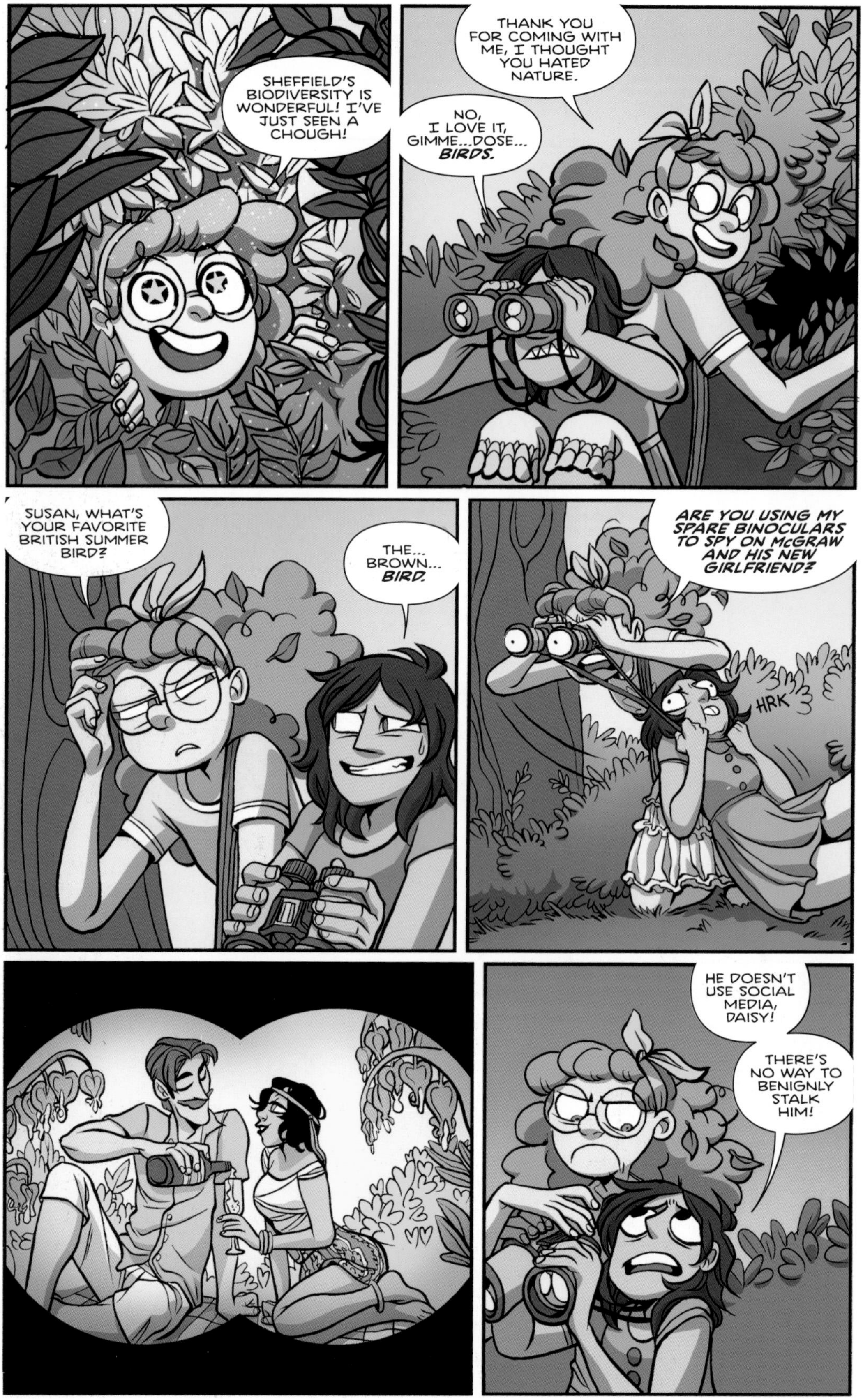
SHEFFIELD'S BIODIVERSITY IS WONDERFUL! I'VE JUST SEEN A CHOUGH!
THANK YOU FOR COMING WITH ME, I THOUGHT YOU HATED NATURE.
NO, I LOVE IT, GIMME...DOSE... BIRDS.
SUSAN, WHAT'S YOUR FAVORITE BRITISH SUMMER BIRD?
THE... BROWN... BIRD.
ARE YOU USING MY SPARE BINOCULARS TO SPY ON McGRAW AND HIS NEW GIRLFRIEND?
HRK
HE DOESN'T USE SOCIAL MEDIA, DAISY!
THERE'S NO WAY TO BENIGNLY STALK HIM!

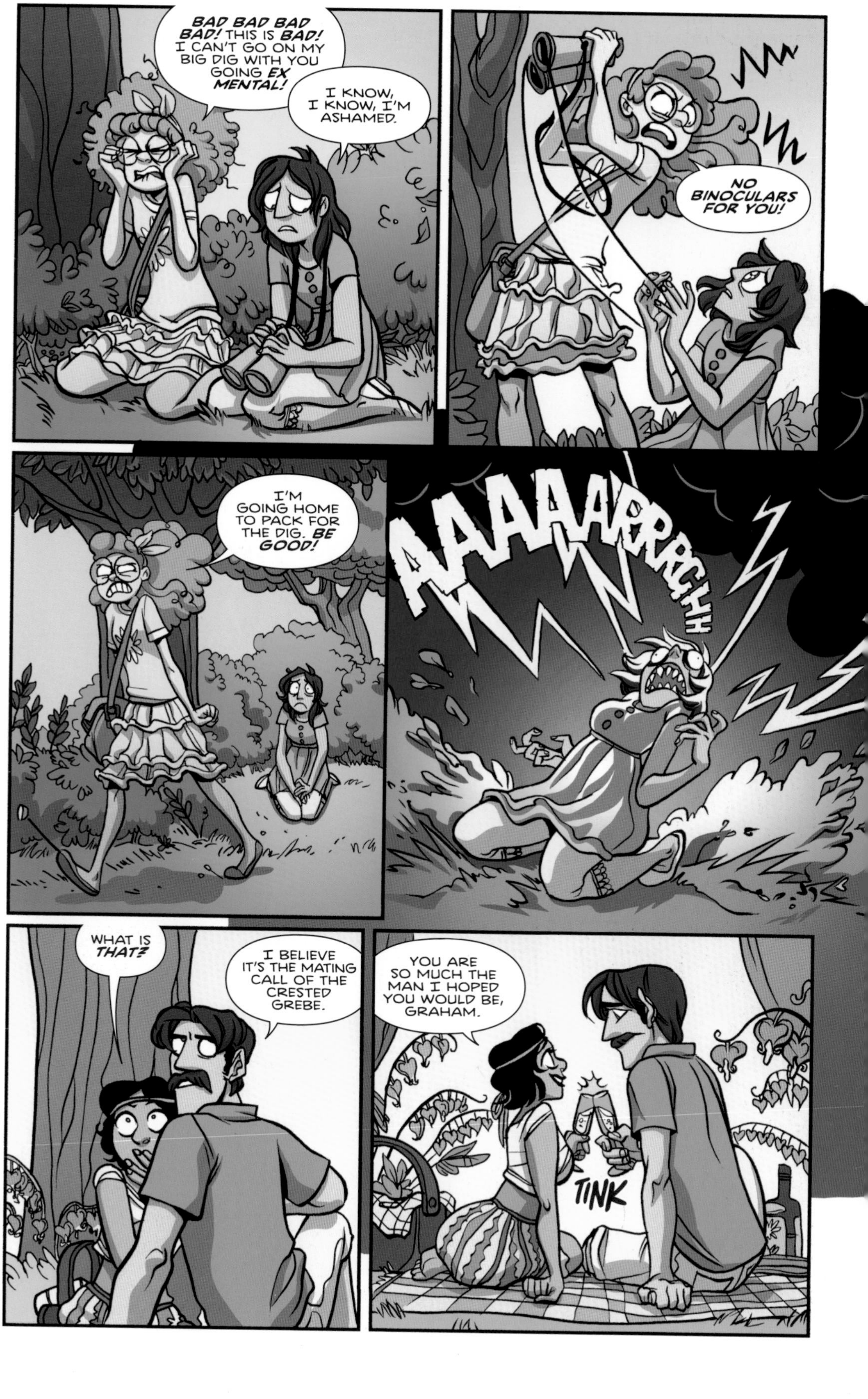
BAD BAD BAD BAD! THIS IS BAD! I CAN'T GO ON MY BIG DIG WITH YOU GOING EX MENTAL!
I KNOW, I KNOW, I'M ASHAMED.
NO BINOCULARS FOR YOU!
I'M GOING HOME TO PACK FOR THE DIG. BE GOOD!
AAAAARRRGHH
WHAT IS THAT?
I BELIEVE IT'S THE MATING CALL OF THE CRESTED GREBE.
YOU ARE SO MUCH THE MAN I HOPED YOU WOULD BE, GRAHAM.
TINK

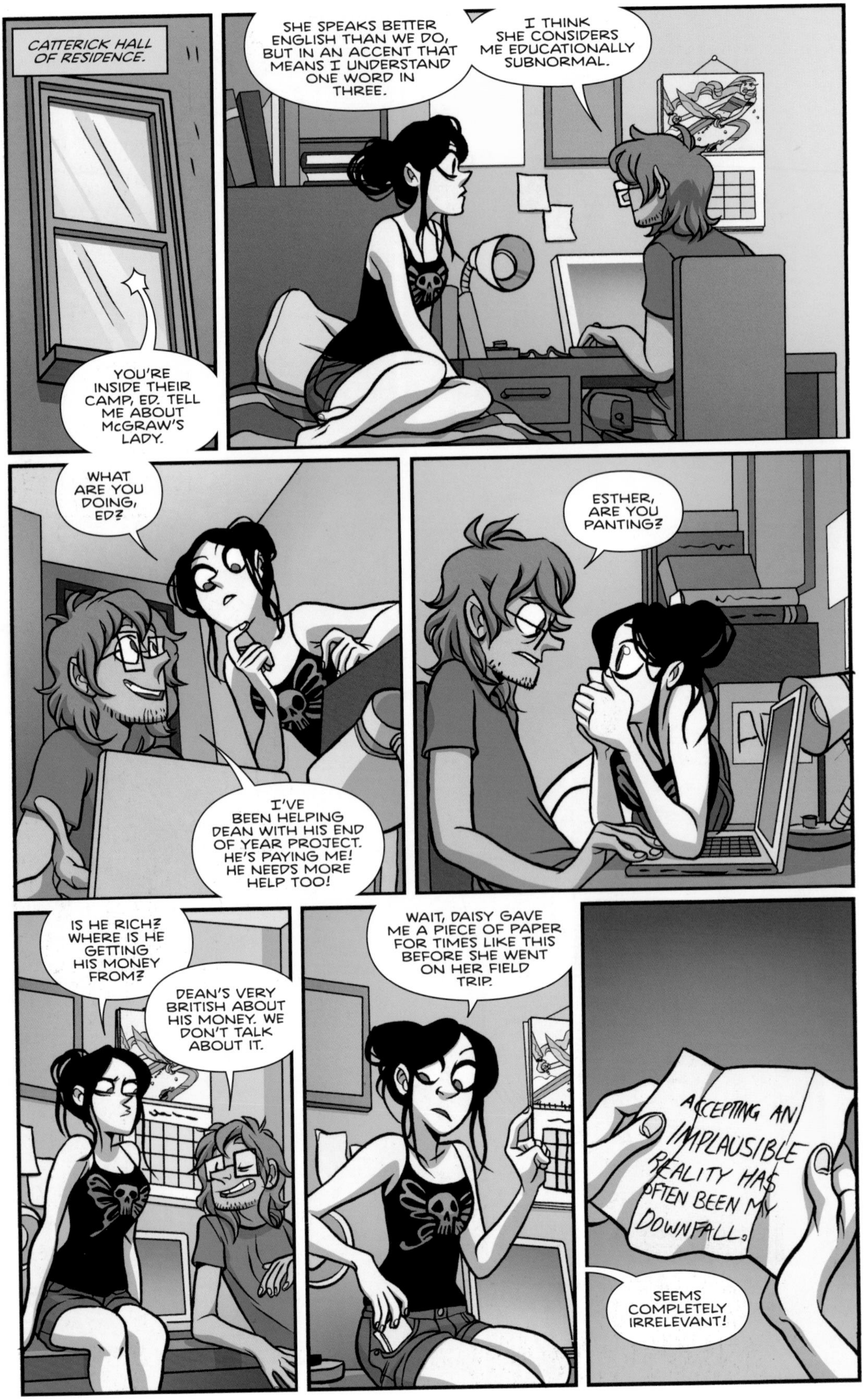

CATTERICK HALL OF RESIDENCE.
YOU'RE INSIDE THEIR CAMP, ED. TELL ME ABOUT McGRAW'S LADY.
SHE SPEAKS BETTER ENGLISH THAN WE DO, BUT IN AN ACCENT THAT MEANS I UNDERSTAND ONE WORD IN THREE.
I THINK SHE CONSIDERS ME EDUCATIONALLY SUBNORMAL.
WHAT ARE YOU DOING, ED?
I'VE BEEN HELPING DEAN WITH HIS END OF YEAR PROJECT. HE'S PAYING ME! HE NEEDS MORE HELP TOO!
ESTHER, ARE YOU PANTING?
IS HE RICH? WHERE IS HE GETTING HIS MONEY FROM?
DEAN'S VERY BRITISH ABOUT HIS MONEY. WE DON'T TALK ABOUT IT.
WAIT, DAISY GAVE ME A PIECE OF PAPER FOR TIMES LIKE THIS BEFORE SHE WENT ON HER FIELD TRIP.
ACCEPTING AN IMPLAUSIBLE REALITY HAS OFTEN BEEN MY DOWNFALL.
SEEMS COMPLETELY IRRELEVANT!

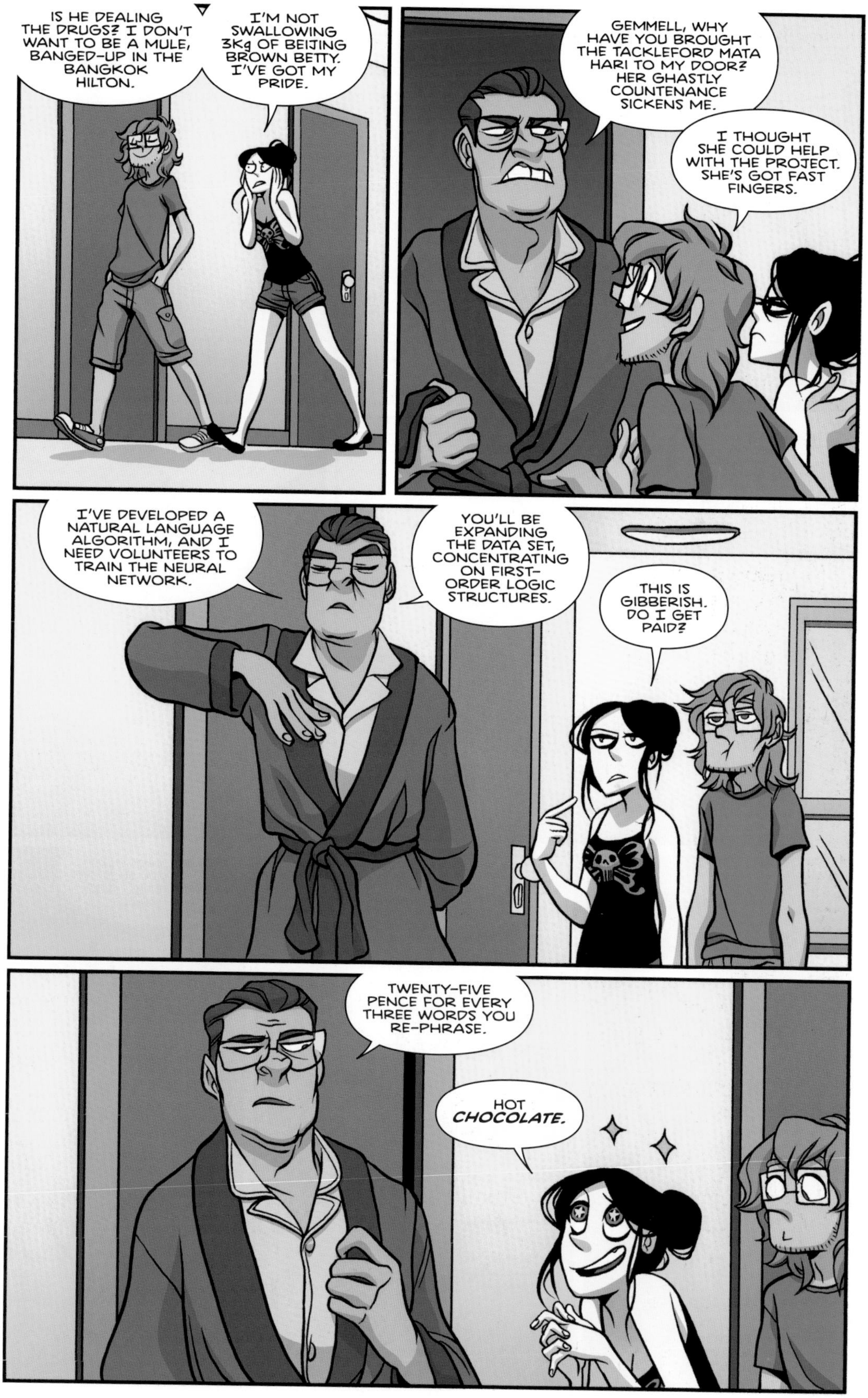
IS HE DEALING THE DRUGS? I DON'T WANT TO BE A MULE, BANGED-UP IN THE BANGKOK HILTON.
I'M NOT SWALLOWING 3Kg OF BEIJING BROWN BETTY. I'VE GOT MY PRIDE.
GEMMELL, WHY HAVE YOU BROUGHT THE TACKLEFORD MATA HARI TO MY DOOR? HER GHASTLY COUNTENANCE SICKENS ME.
I THOUGHT SHE COULD HELP WITH THE PROJECT. SHE'S GOT FAST FINGERS.
I'VE DEVELOPED A NATURAL LANGUAGE ALGORITHM, AND I NEED VOLUNTEERS TO TRAIN THE NEURAL NETWORK.
YOU'LL BE EXPANDING THE DATA SET, CONCENTRATING ON FIRST-ORDER LOGIC STRUCTURES.
THIS IS GIBBERISH. DO I GET PAID?
TWENTY-FIVE PENCE FOR EVERY THREE WORDS YOU RE-PHRASE.
HOT *CHOCOLATE.*

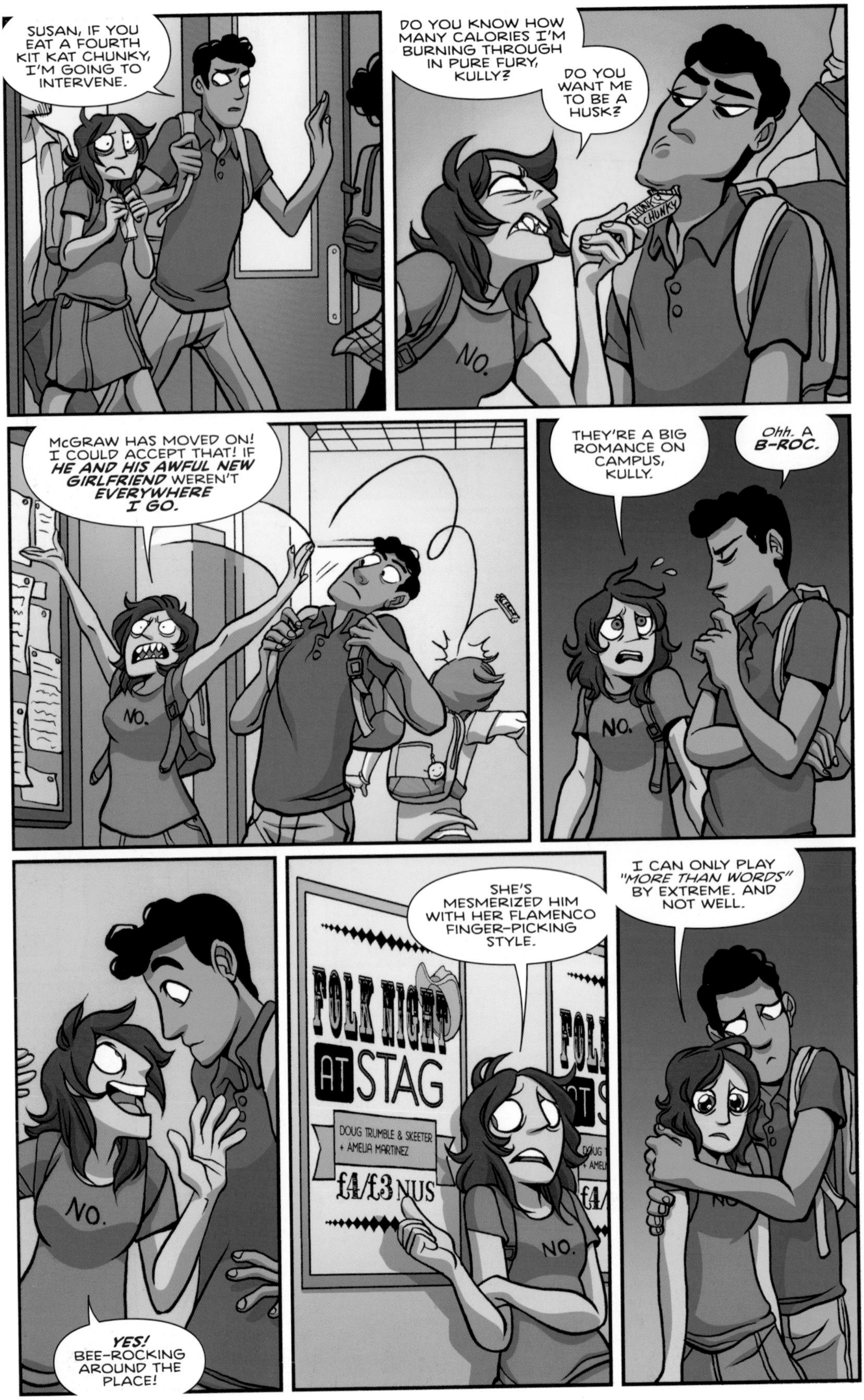
SUSAN, IF YOU EAT A FOURTH KIT KAT CHUNKY, I'M GOING TO INTERVENE.
DO YOU KNOW HOW MANY CALORIES I'M BURNING THROUGH IN PURE FURY, KULLY?
DO YOU WANT ME TO BE A HUSK?
CHUNKY
NO.
McGRAW HAS MOVED ON! I COULD ACCEPT THAT! IF HE AND HIS AWFUL NEW GIRLFRIEND WEREN'T EVERYWHERE I GO.
THEY'RE A BIG ROMANCE ON CAMPUS, KULLY.
Ohh. A B-ROC.
YES! BEE-ROCKING AROUND THE PLACE!
FOLK NIGHT AT STAG
DOUG TRUMBLE & SKEETER + AMELIA MARTINEZ
£4/£3 NUS
SHE'S MESMERIZED HIM WITH HER FLAMENCO FINGER-PICKING STYLE.
I CAN ONLY PLAY "MORE THAN WORDS" BY EXTREME. AND NOT WELL.

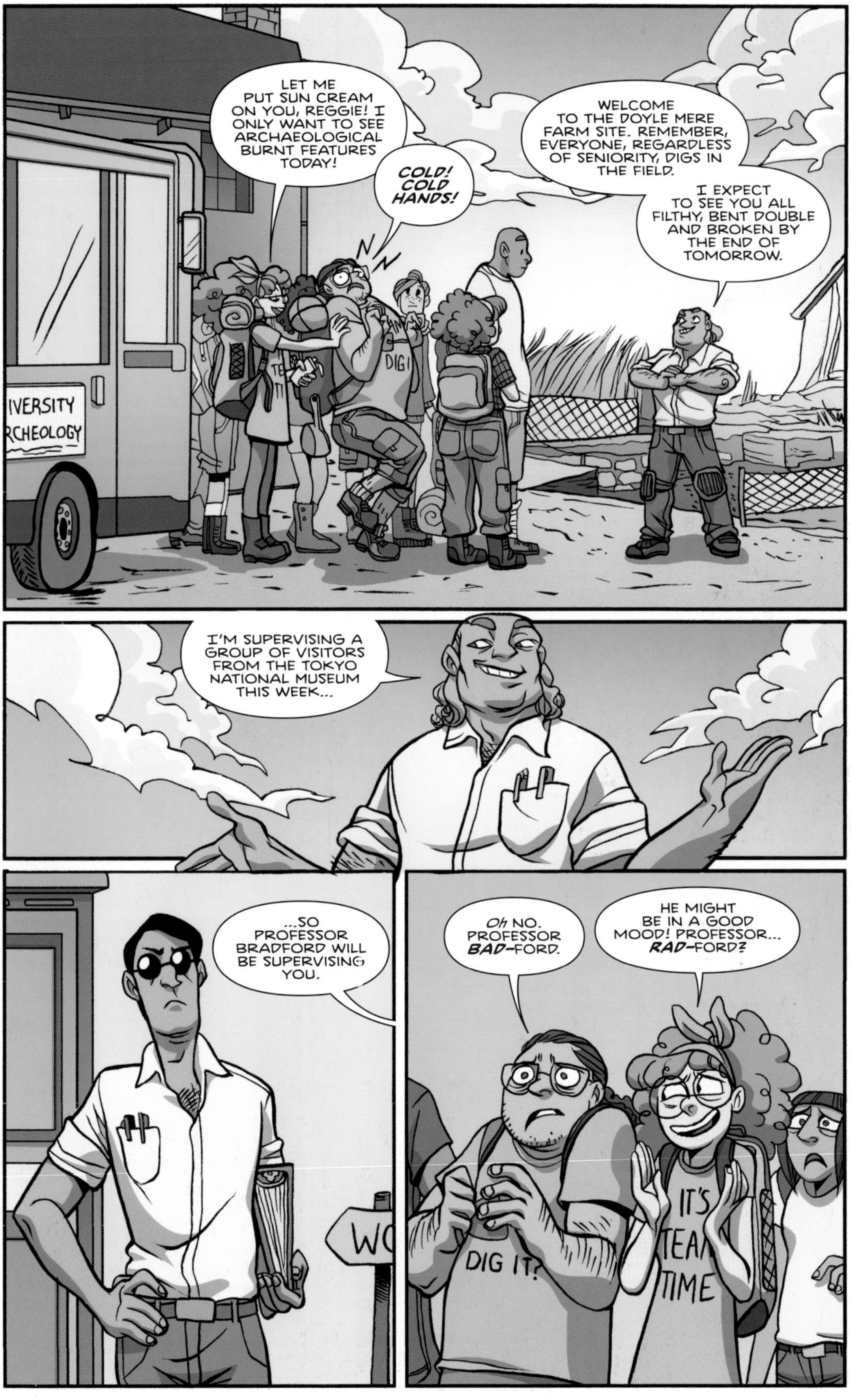
LET ME PUT SUN CREAM ON YOU, REGGIE! I ONLY WANT TO SEE ARCHAEOLOGICAL BURNT FEATURES TODAY!
COLD! COLD HANDS!
WELCOME TO THE DOYLE MERE FARM SITE. REMEMBER, EVERYONE, REGARDLESS OF SENIORITY, DIGS IN THE FIELD.
I EXPECT TO SEE YOU ALL FILTHY, BENT DOUBLE AND BROKEN BY THE END OF TOMORROW.
IVERSITY
RCHEOLOGY
DIG
I'M SUPERVISING A GROUP OF VISITORS FROM THE TOKYO NATIONAL MUSEUM THIS WEEK...
...SO PROFESSOR BRADFORD WILL BE SUPERVISING YOU.
WO
Oh NO. PROFESSOR ***BAD*-FORD.**
HE MIGHT BE IN A GOOD MOOD! PROFESSOR... ***RAD*-FORD?**
DIG IT?
IT'S TEA TIME

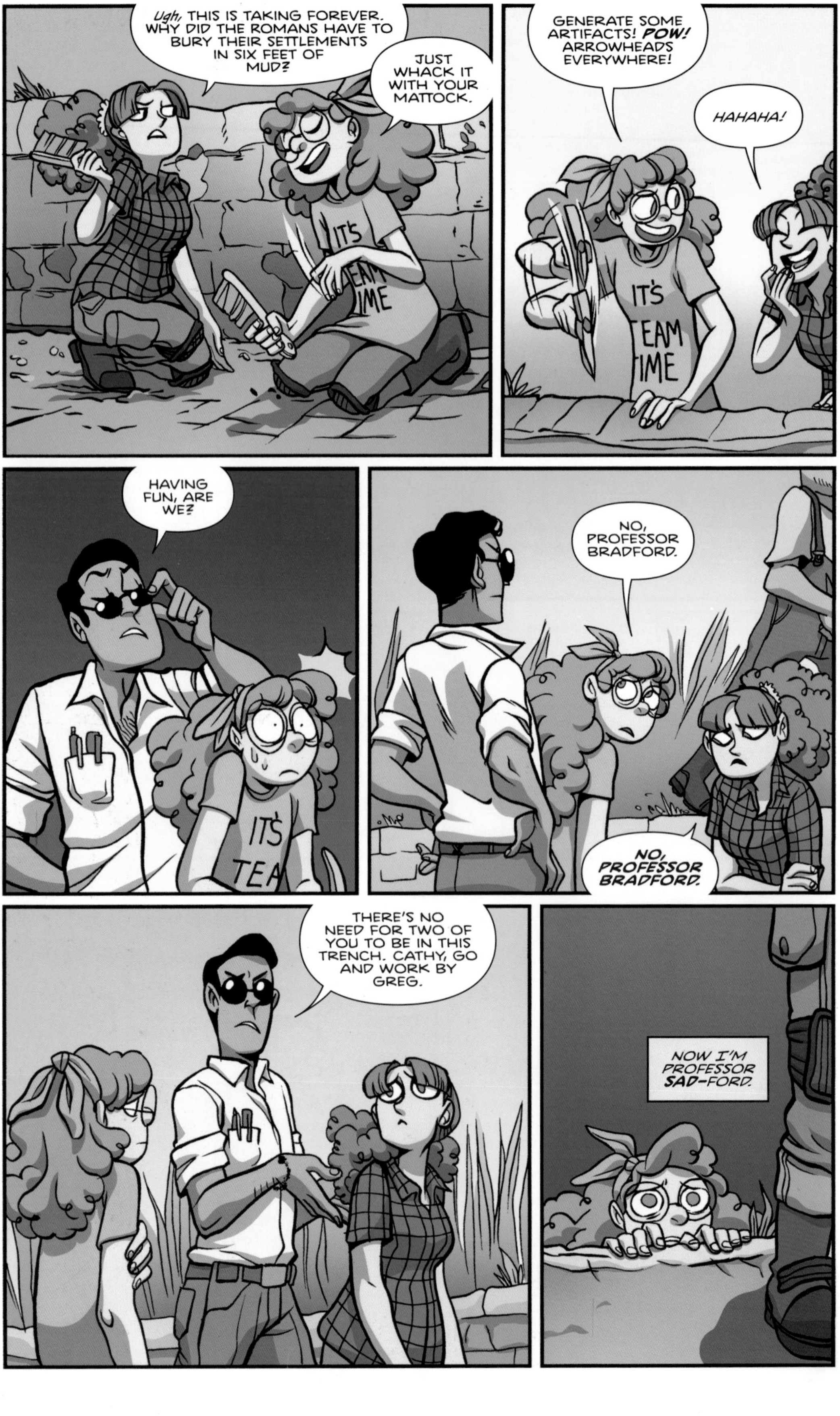
Ugh, THIS IS TAKING FOREVER. WHY DID THE ROMANS HAVE TO BURY THEIR SETTLEMENTS IN SIX FEET OF MUD?
JUST WHACK IT WITH YOUR MATTOCK.
IT'S TEAM TIME
GENERATE SOME ARTIFACTS! POW! ARROWHEADS EVERYWHERE!
HAHAHA!
IT'S TEAM TIME
HAVING FUN, ARE WE?
IT'S TEA
NO, PROFESSOR BRADFORD.
NO, PROFESSOR BRADFORD.
THERE'S NO NEED FOR TWO OF YOU TO BE IN THIS TRENCH. CATHY, GO AND WORK BY GREG.
NOW I'M PROFESSOR SAD-FORD.

OKAY, MAD SNACKS AND REFRESHMENTS HAVE BEEN SECURED. SHOW ME WHAT TO DO.

RIGHT, SO ALL YOU HAVE TO DO IS REWRITE THREE WORD PHRASES.

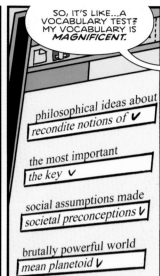

SO, IT'S LIKE...A VOCABULARY TEST? MY VOCABULARY IS *MAGNIFICENT*.

philosophical ideas about
recondite notions of ✓

the most important
the key ✓

social assumptions made
societal preconceptions ✓

brutally powerful world
mean planetoid ✓

I'M UP TO A POUND! WILL I EVER ACTUALLY RECEIVE THIS POUND?

IF YOU CLICK THE BUTTON IN THE CORNER, YOU CAN MAKE IT PAY OUT TO YOUR PAYPAL ACCOUNT.

THIS IS EASY! IT'S FUN!

I'M UP TO £45.00 ALREADY! I'M GOING TO BUY A CROWN!

I WISH DAISY HADN'T GIVEN ME THIS PIECE OF PAPER.

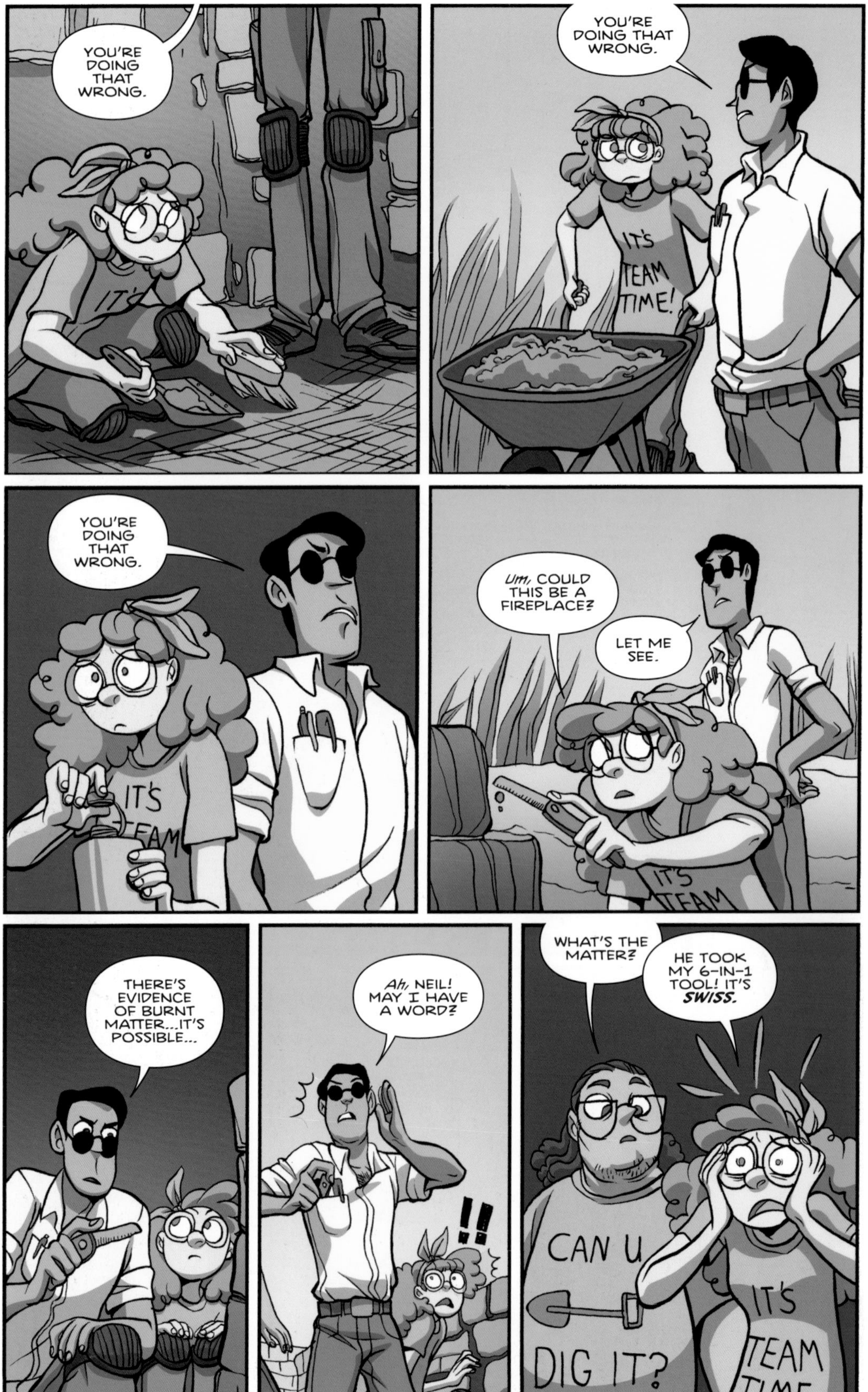
YOU'RE DOING THAT WRONG.
IT'S
YOU'RE DOING THAT WRONG.
IT'S TEAM TIME!
YOU'RE DOING THAT WRONG.
IT'S TEAM
Um, COULD THIS BE A FIREPLACE?
LET ME SEE.
IT'S TEAM
THERE'S EVIDENCE OF BURNT MATTER...IT'S POSSIBLE...
Ah, NEIL! MAY I HAVE A WORD?
!!
WHAT'S THE MATTER?
HE TOOK MY 6-IN-1 TOOL! IT'S SWISS.
CAN U DIG IT?
IT'S TEAM TIME

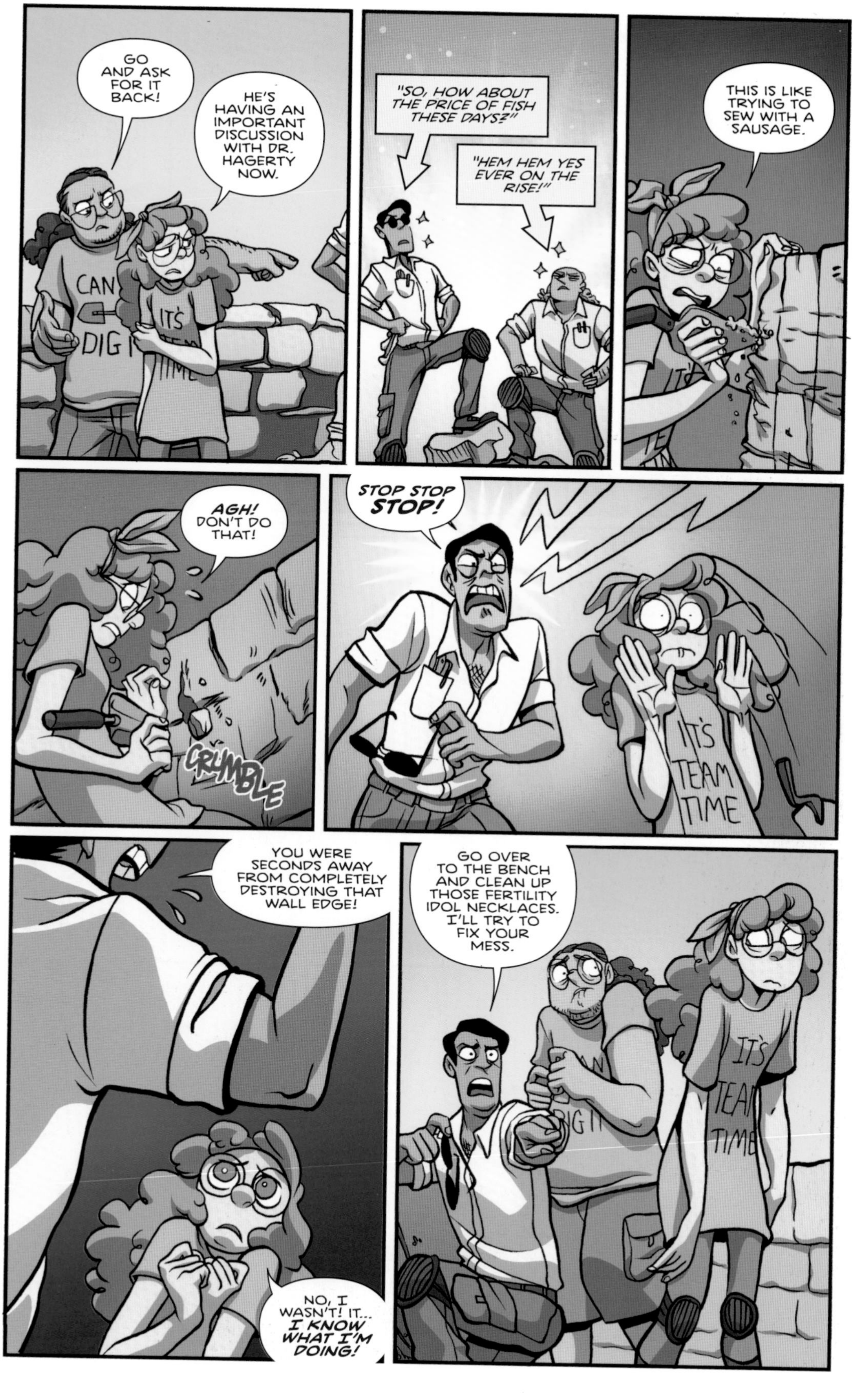
GO AND ASK FOR IT BACK!
HE'S HAVING AN IMPORTANT DISCUSSION WITH DR. HAGERTY NOW.
CAN DIG!
IT'S TEAM TIME
"SO, HOW ABOUT THE PRICE OF FISH THESE DAYS?"
"HEM HEM YES EVER ON THE RISE!"
THIS IS LIKE TRYING TO SEW WITH A SAUSAGE.
AGH! DON'T DO THAT!
CRUMBLE
STOP STOP STOP!
IT'S TEAM TIME
YOU WERE SECONDS AWAY FROM COMPLETELY DESTROYING THAT WALL EDGE!
NO, I WASN'T! IT... I KNOW WHAT I'M DOING!
GO OVER TO THE BENCH AND CLEAN UP THOSE FERTILITY IDOL NECKLACES. I'LL TRY TO FIX YOUR MESS.

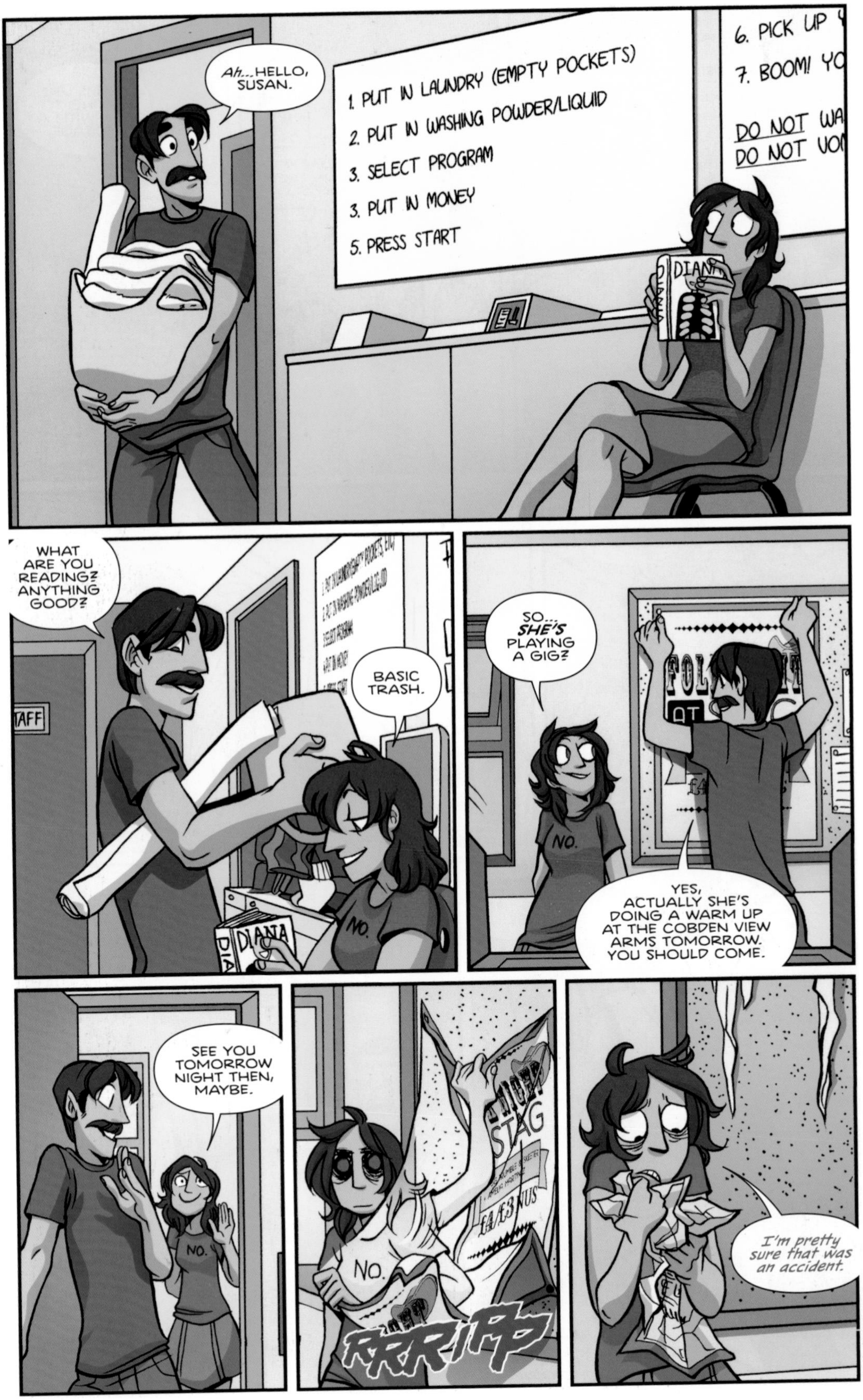

Ah... HELLO, SUSAN.
1. PUT IN LAUNDRY (EMPTY POCKETS)
2. PUT IN WASHING POWDER/LIQUID
3. SELECT PROGRAM
3. PUT IN MONEY
5. PRESS START
6. PICK UP
7. BOOM! YO
DO NOT WA
DO NOT VO
DIANA
WHAT ARE YOU READING? ANYTHING GOOD?
BASIC TRASH.
STAFF
SO... SHE'S PLAYING A GIG?
NO.
YES, ACTUALLY SHE'S DOING A WARM UP AT THE COBDEN VIEW ARMS TOMORROW. YOU SHOULD COME.
SEE YOU TOMORROW NIGHT THEN, MAYBE.
STAG
RRRIPP
I'm pretty sure that was an accident.

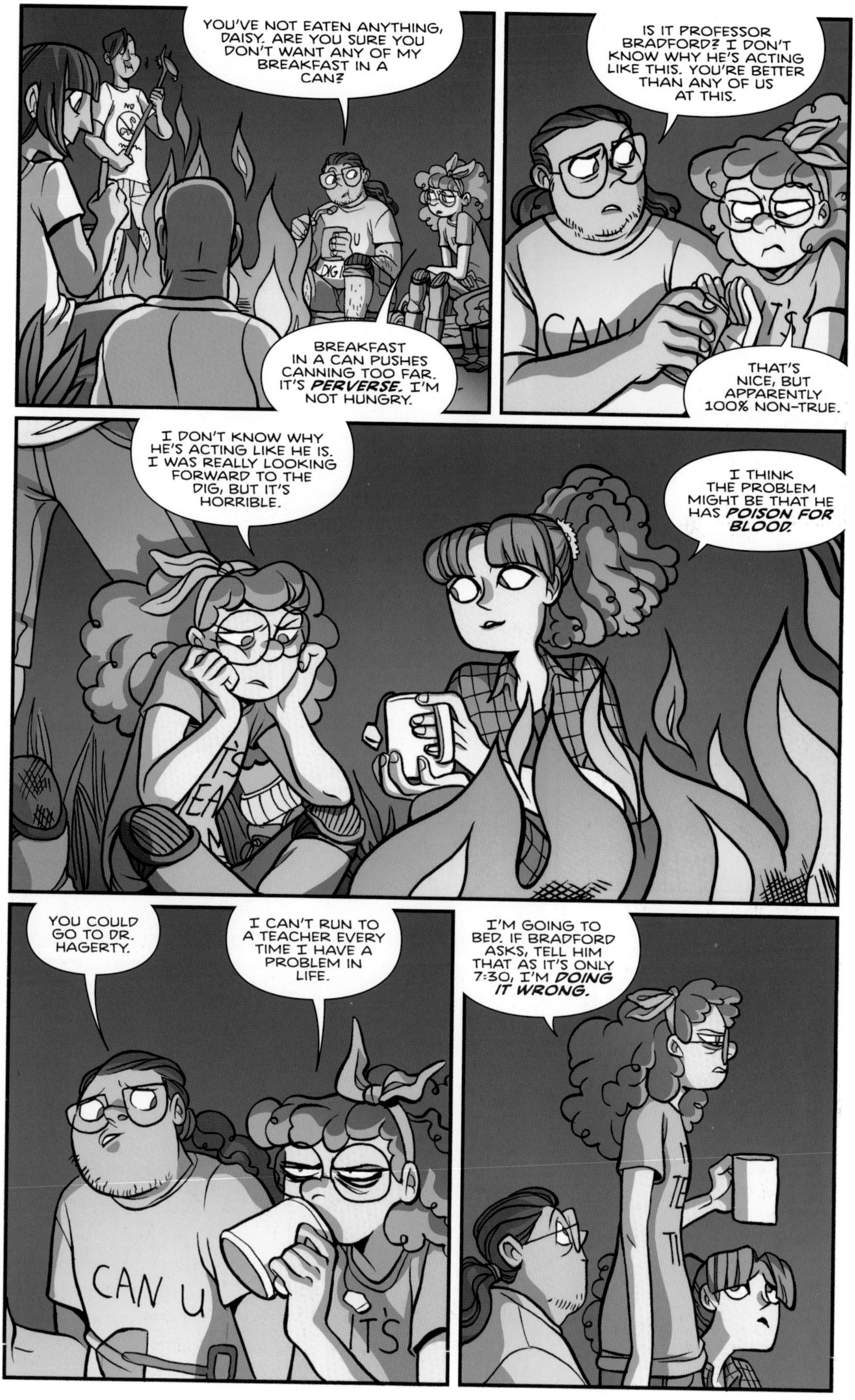
YOU'VE NOT EATEN ANYTHING, DAISY. ARE YOU SURE YOU DON'T WANT ANY OF MY BREAKFAST IN A CAN?
BREAKFAST IN A CAN PUSHES CANNING TOO FAR. IT'S *PERVERSE.* I'M NOT HUNGRY.
IS IT PROFESSOR BRADFORD? I DON'T KNOW WHY HE'S ACTING LIKE THIS. YOU'RE BETTER THAN ANY OF US AT THIS.
THAT'S NICE, BUT APPARENTLY 100% NON-TRUE.
I DON'T KNOW WHY HE'S ACTING LIKE HE IS. I WAS REALLY LOOKING FORWARD TO THE DIG, BUT IT'S HORRIBLE.
I THINK THE PROBLEM MIGHT BE THAT HE HAS *POISON FOR BLOOD.*
YOU COULD GO TO DR. HAGERTY.
I CAN'T RUN TO A TEACHER EVERY TIME I HAVE A PROBLEM IN LIFE.
I'M GOING TO BED. IF BRADFORD ASKS, TELL HIM THAT AS IT'S ONLY 7:30, I'M *DOING IT WRONG.*
CAN U
IT'S

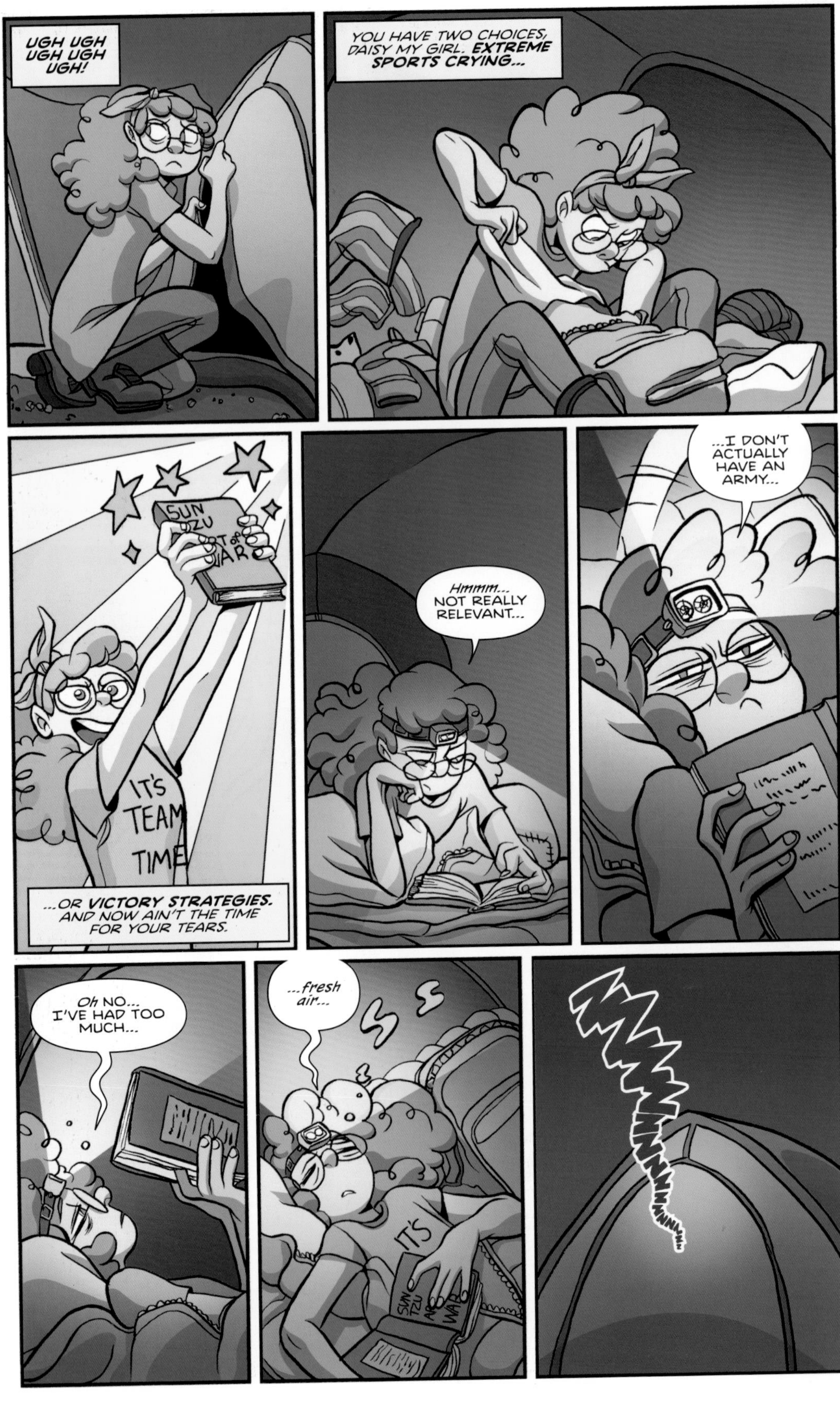
UGH UGH UGH UGH UGH!
YOU HAVE TWO CHOICES, DAISY MY GIRL. EXTREME SPORTS CRYING...
SUN TZU ART of WAR
IT'S TEAM TIME
...OR VICTORY STRATEGIES. AND NOW AIN'T THE TIME FOR YOUR TEARS.
Hmmm... NOT REALLY RELEVANT...
...I DON'T ACTUALLY HAVE AN ARMY...
Oh NO... I'VE HAD TOO MUCH...
...fresh air...
IT'S
SUN TZU ART WAR

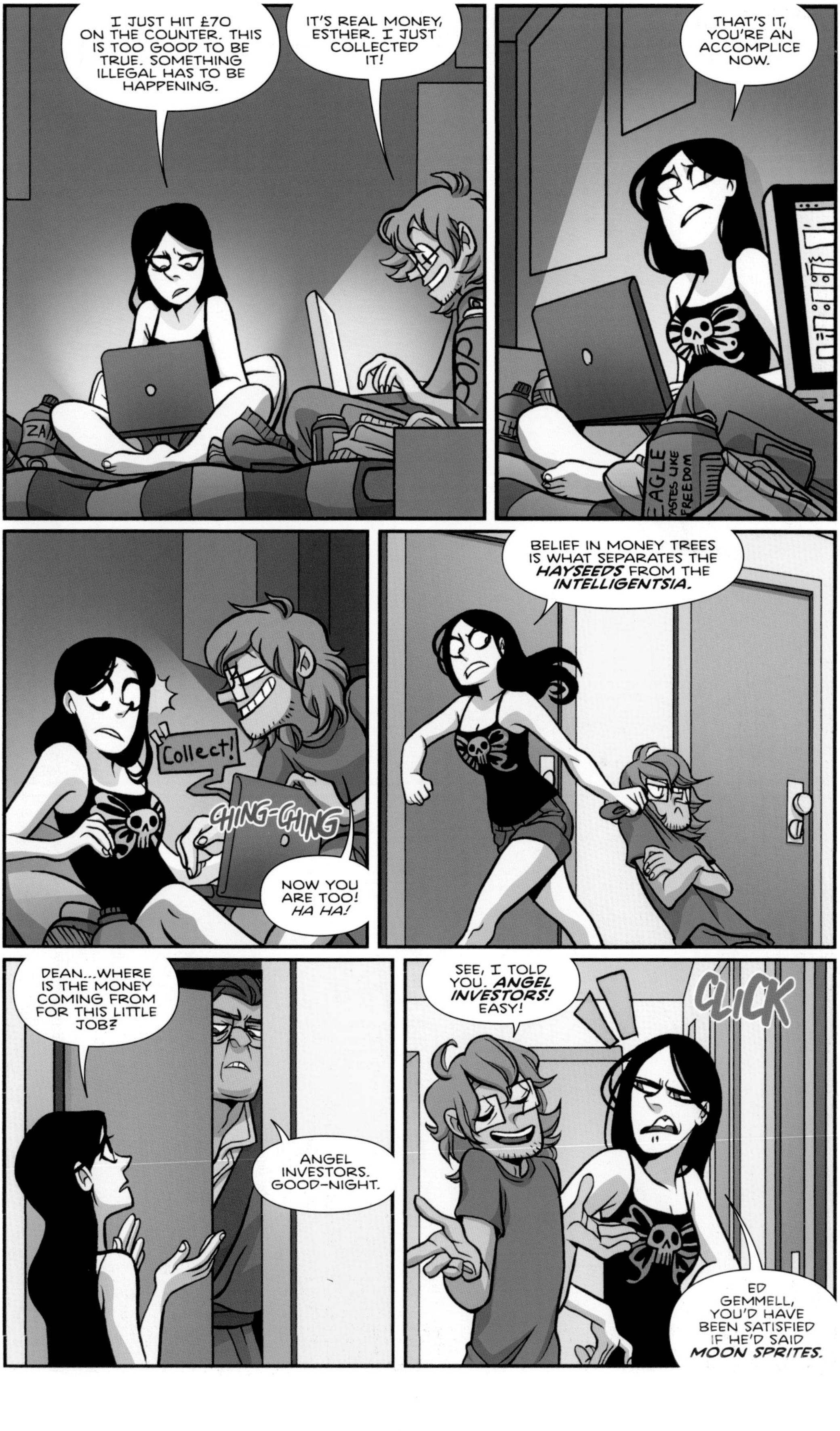
I JUST HIT £70 ON THE COUNTER. THIS IS TOO GOOD TO BE TRUE. SOMETHING ILLEGAL HAS TO BE HAPPENING.
IT'S REAL MONEY, ESTHER. I JUST COLLECTED IT!
THAT'S IT, YOU'RE AN ACCOMPLICE NOW.
EAGLE TASTES LIKE FREEDOM
Collect!
CHING-CHING
NOW YOU ARE TOO! *HA HA!*
BELIEF IN MONEY TREES IS WHAT SEPARATES THE ***HAYSEEDS*** FROM THE ***INTELLIGENTSIA.***
DEAN... WHERE IS THE MONEY COMING FROM FOR THIS LITTLE JOB?
ANGEL INVESTORS. GOOD-NIGHT.
SEE, I TOLD YOU. ***ANGEL INVESTORS!*** EASY!
CLICK
ED GEMMELL, YOU'D HAVE BEEN SATISFIED IF HE'D SAID ***MOON SPRITES.***

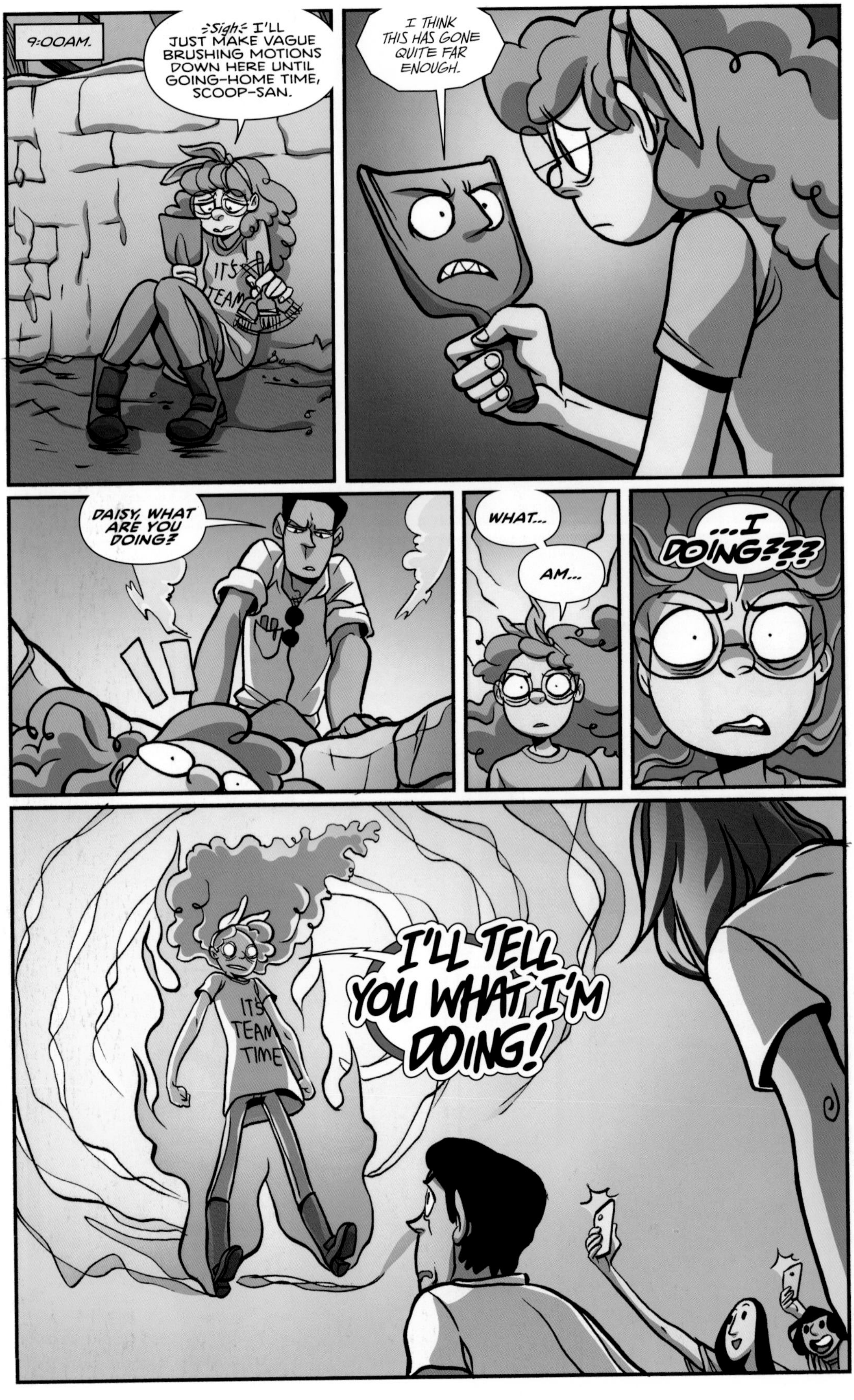

9:00AM.
Sigh I'LL JUST MAKE VAGUE BRUSHING MOTIONS DOWN HERE UNTIL GOING-HOME TIME, SCOOP-SAN.
IT'S TEAM
I THINK THIS HAS GONE QUITE FAR ENOUGH.
DAISY, WHAT ARE YOU DOING?
WHAT...
AM...
...I DOING???
IT'S TEAM TIME
I'LL TELL YOU WHAT I'M DOING!

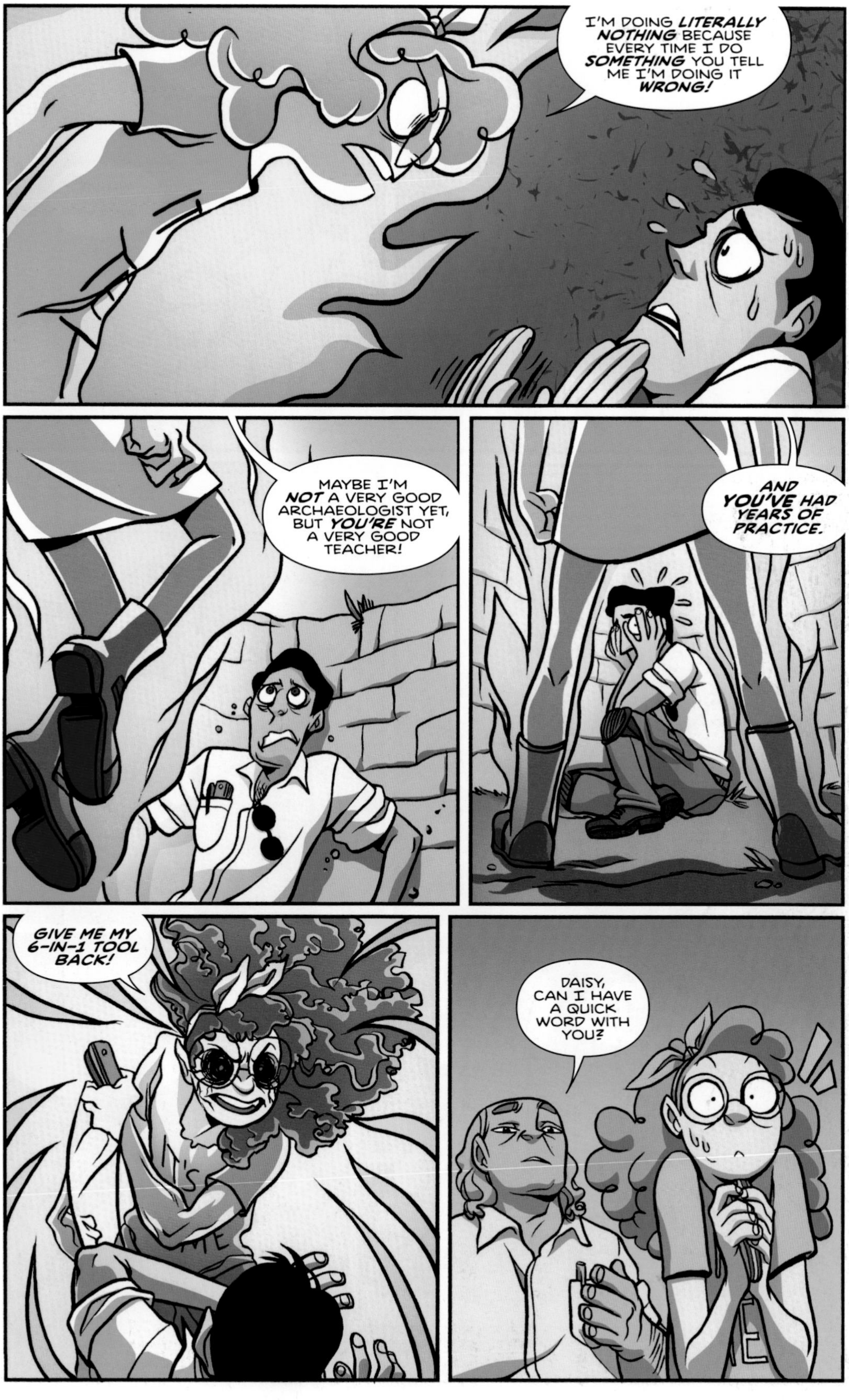
I'M DOING LITERALLY NOTHING BECAUSE EVERY TIME I DO SOMETHING YOU TELL ME I'M DOING IT WRONG!
MAYBE I'M NOT A VERY GOOD ARCHAEOLOGIST YET, BUT YOU'RE NOT A VERY GOOD TEACHER!
AND YOU'VE HAD YEARS OF PRACTICE.
GIVE ME MY 6-IN-1 TOOL BACK!
DAISY, CAN I HAVE A QUICK WORD WITH YOU?

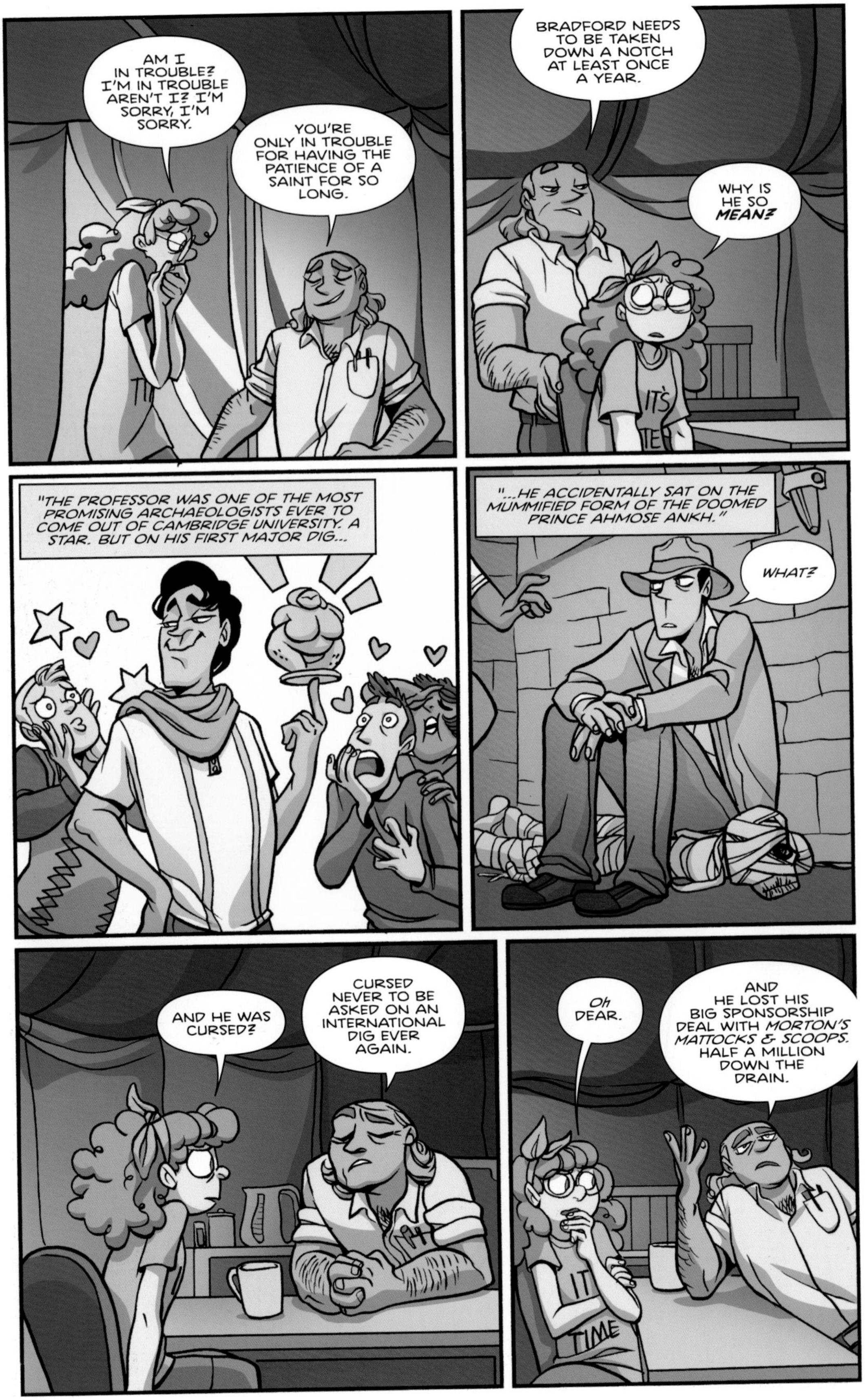

AM I IN TROUBLE? I'M IN TROUBLE AREN'T I? I'M SORRY, I'M SORRY.
YOU'RE ONLY IN TROUBLE FOR HAVING THE PATIENCE OF A SAINT FOR SO LONG.
BRADFORD NEEDS TO BE TAKEN DOWN A NOTCH AT LEAST ONCE A YEAR.
WHY IS HE SO MEAN?
"THE PROFESSOR WAS ONE OF THE MOST PROMISING ARCHAEOLOGISTS EVER TO COME OUT OF CAMBRIDGE UNIVERSITY. A STAR. BUT ON HIS FIRST MAJOR DIG...
"...HE ACCIDENTALLY SAT ON THE MUMMIFIED FORM OF THE DOOMED PRINCE AHMOSE ANKH."
WHAT?
AND HE WAS CURSED?
CURSED NEVER TO BE ASKED ON AN INTERNATIONAL DIG EVER AGAIN.
Oh DEAR.
AND HE LOST HIS BIG SPONSORSHIP DEAL WITH MORTON'S MATTOCKS & SCOOPS. HALF A MILLION DOWN THE DRAIN.

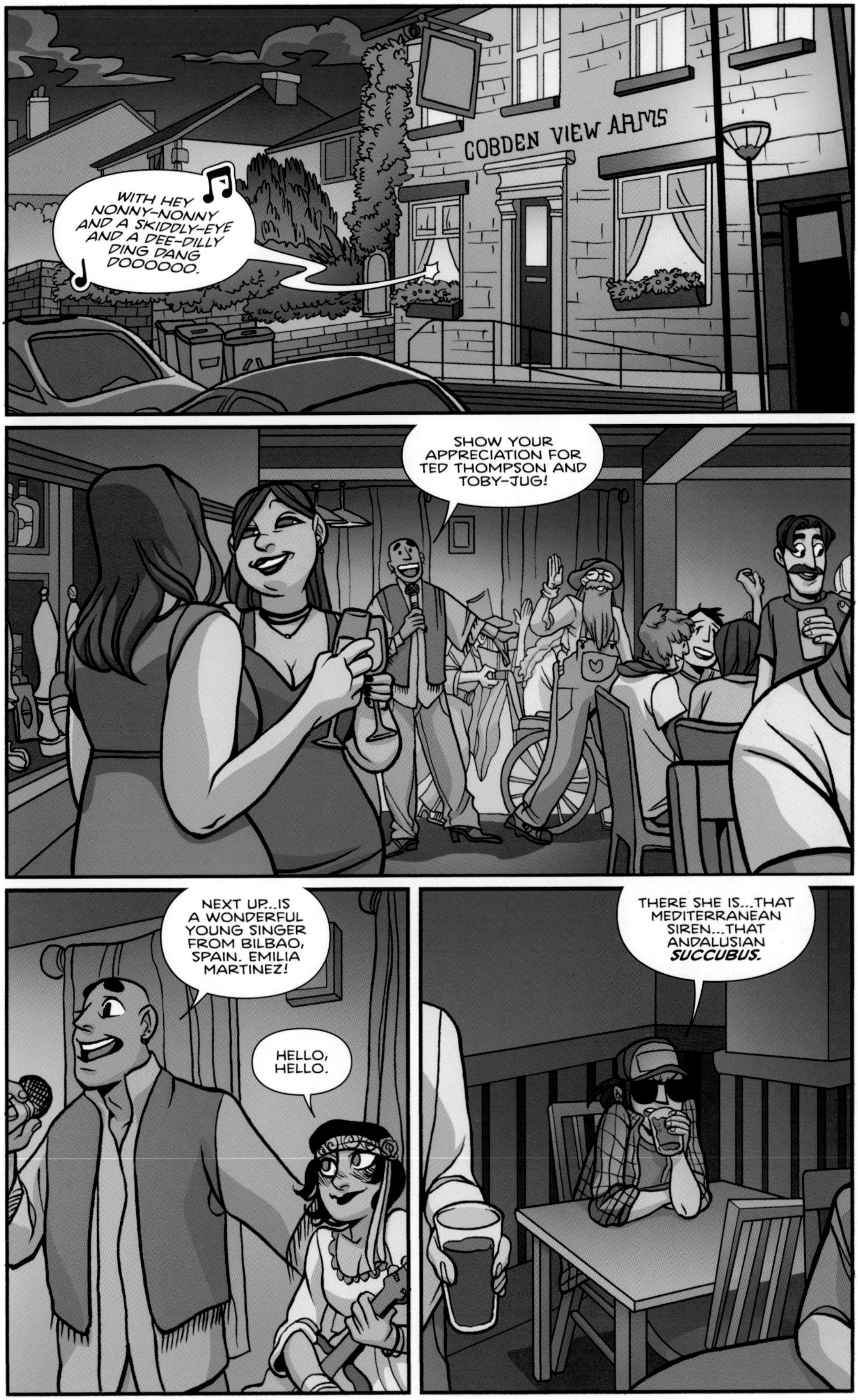
COBDEN VIEW ARMS
WITH HEY NONNY-NONNY AND A SKIDDLY-EYE AND A DEE-DILLY DING DANG DOOOOOO.
SHOW YOUR APPRECIATION FOR TED THOMPSON AND TOBY-JUG!
NEXT UP...IS A WONDERFUL YOUNG SINGER FROM BILBAO, SPAIN. EMILIA MARTINEZ!
HELLO, HELLO.
THERE SHE IS...THAT MEDITERRANEAN SIREN...THAT ANDALUSIAN ***SUCCUBUS.***

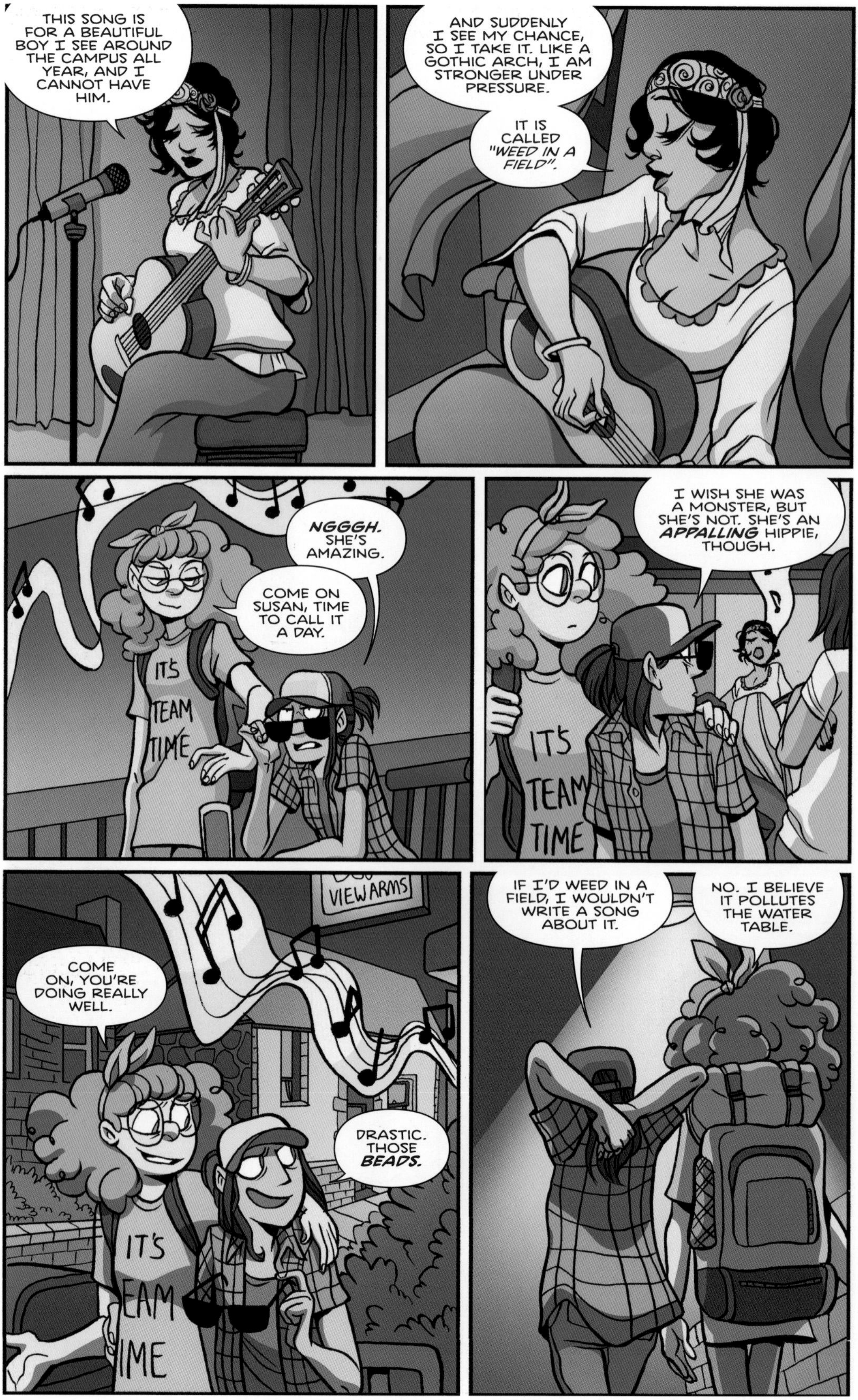
THIS SONG IS FOR A BEAUTIFUL BOY I SEE AROUND THE CAMPUS ALL YEAR, AND I CANNOT HAVE HIM.
AND SUDDENLY I SEE MY CHANCE, SO I TAKE IT. LIKE A GOTHIC ARCH, I AM STRONGER UNDER PRESSURE.
IT IS CALLED "WEED IN A FIELD".
NGGGH. SHE'S AMAZING.
COME ON SUSAN, TIME TO CALL IT A DAY.
IT'S TEAM TIME
I WISH SHE WAS A MONSTER, BUT SHE'S NOT. SHE'S AN APPALLING HIPPIE, THOUGH.
IT'S TEAM TIME
VIEW ARMS
COME ON, YOU'RE DOING REALLY WELL.
DRASTIC. THOSE BEADS.
IF I'D WEED IN A FIELD, I WOULDN'T WRITE A SONG ABOUT IT.
NO. I BELIEVE IT POLLUTES THE WATER TABLE.

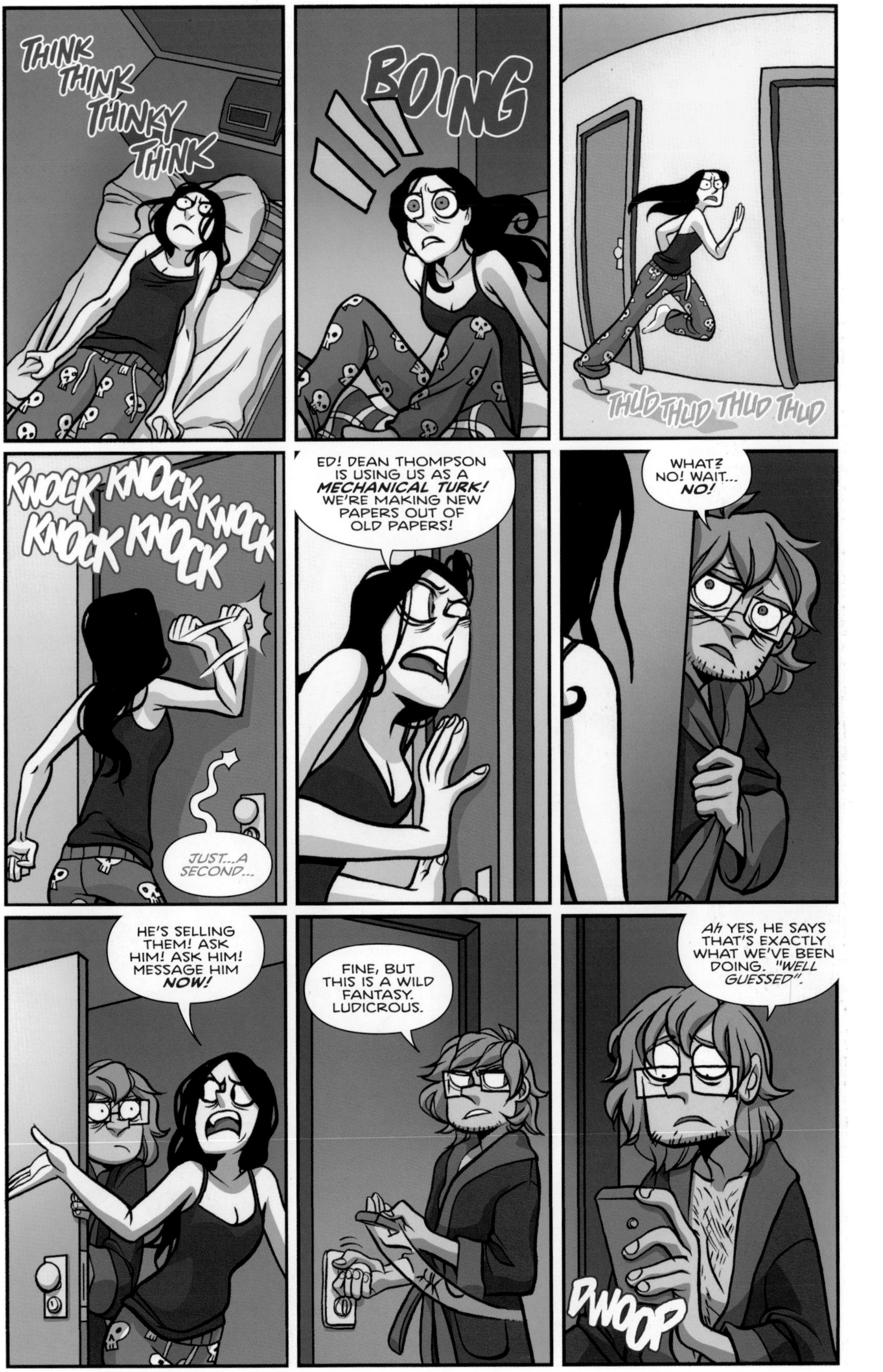
THINK THINK THINKY THINK
BOING
THUD THUD THUD THUD
KNOCK KNOCK KNOCK KNOCK KNOCK
JUST...A SECOND...
ED! DEAN THOMPSON IS USING US AS A MECHANICAL TURK! WE'RE MAKING NEW PAPERS OUT OF OLD PAPERS!
WHAT? NO! WAIT... NO!
HE'S SELLING THEM! ASK HIM! ASK HIM! MESSAGE HIM NOW!
FINE, BUT THIS IS A WILD FANTASY. LUDICROUS.
Ah YES, HE SAYS THAT'S EXACTLY WHAT WE'VE BEEN DOING. "WELL GUESSED".
DWOOP

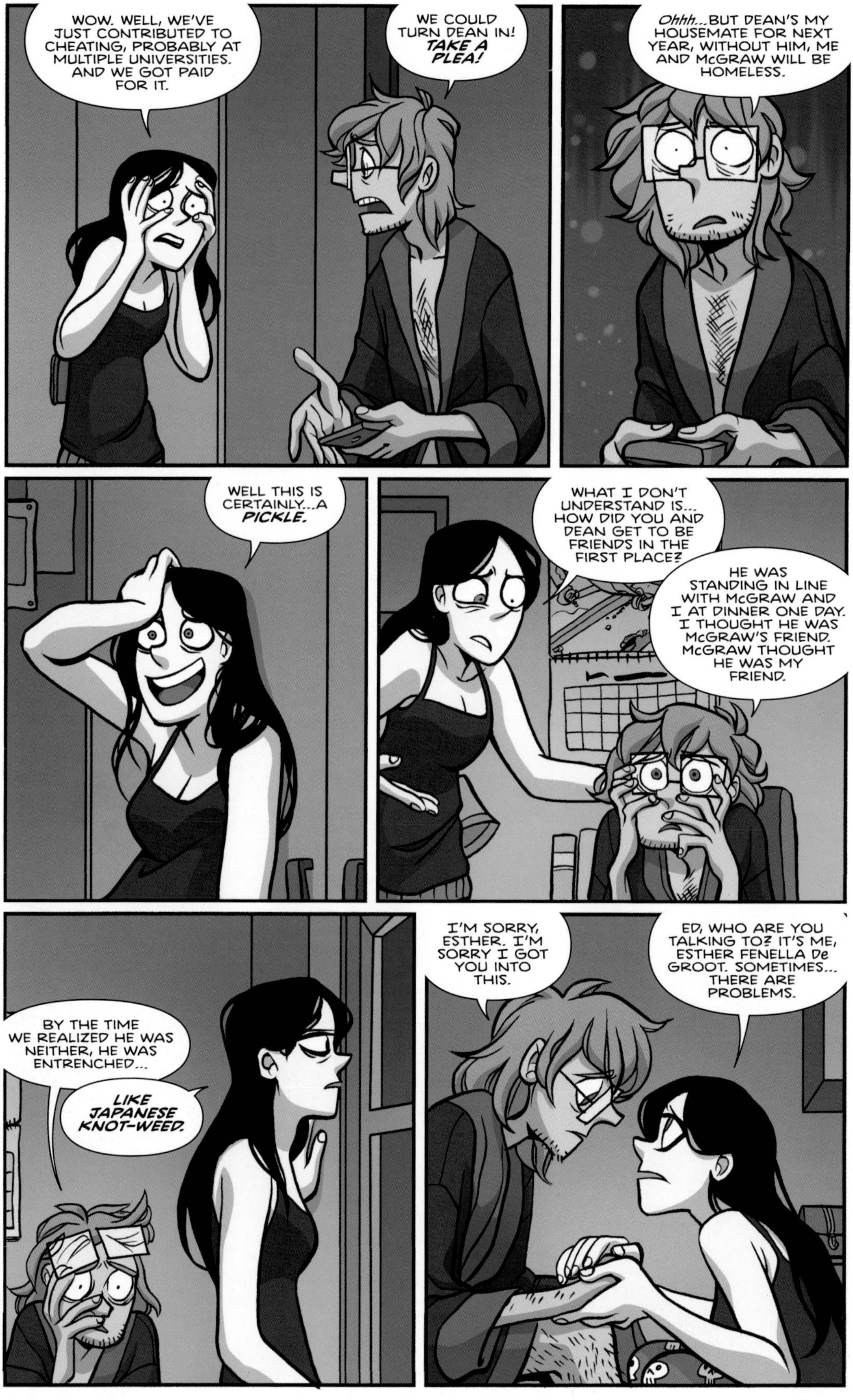
WOW. WELL, WE'VE JUST CONTRIBUTED TO CHEATING, PROBABLY AT MULTIPLE UNIVERSITIES. AND WE GOT PAID FOR IT.
WE COULD TURN DEAN IN! *TAKE A PLEA!*
Ohhh... BUT DEAN'S MY HOUSEMATE FOR NEXT YEAR, WITHOUT HIM, ME AND McGRAW WILL BE HOMELESS.
WELL THIS IS CERTAINLY...A *PICKLE.*
WHAT I DON'T UNDERSTAND IS... HOW DID YOU AND DEAN GET TO BE FRIENDS IN THE FIRST PLACE?
HE WAS STANDING IN LINE WITH McGRAW AND I AT DINNER ONE DAY. I THOUGHT HE WAS McGRAW'S FRIEND. McGRAW THOUGHT HE WAS MY FRIEND.
BY THE TIME WE REALIZED HE WAS NEITHER, HE WAS ENTRENCHED...
LIKE JAPANESE KNOT-WEED.
I'M SORRY, ESTHER. I'M SORRY I GOT YOU INTO THIS.
ED, WHO ARE YOU TALKING TO? IT'S ME, ESTHER FENELLA De GROOT. SOMETIMES... THERE ARE PROBLEMS.

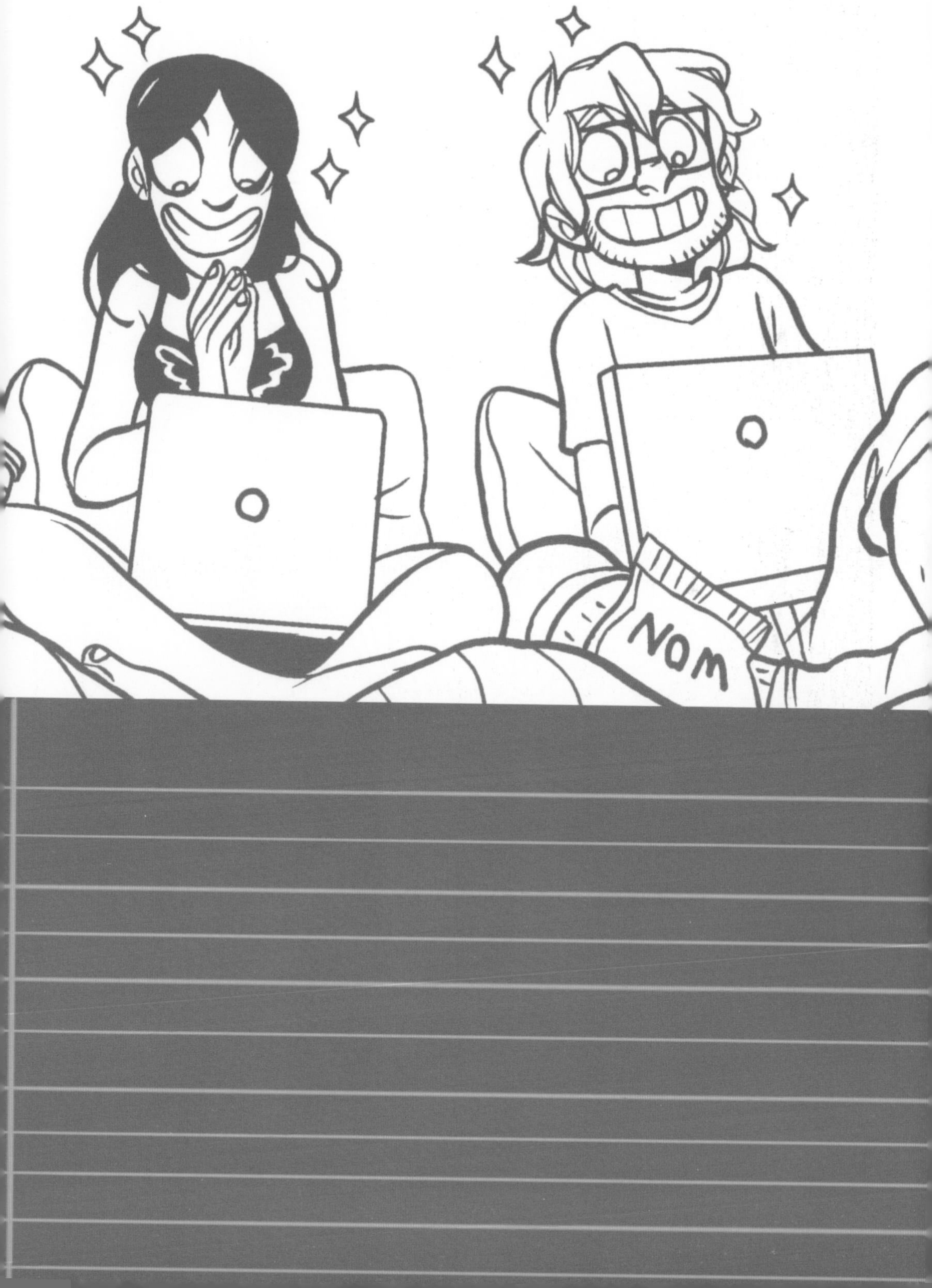
NOM

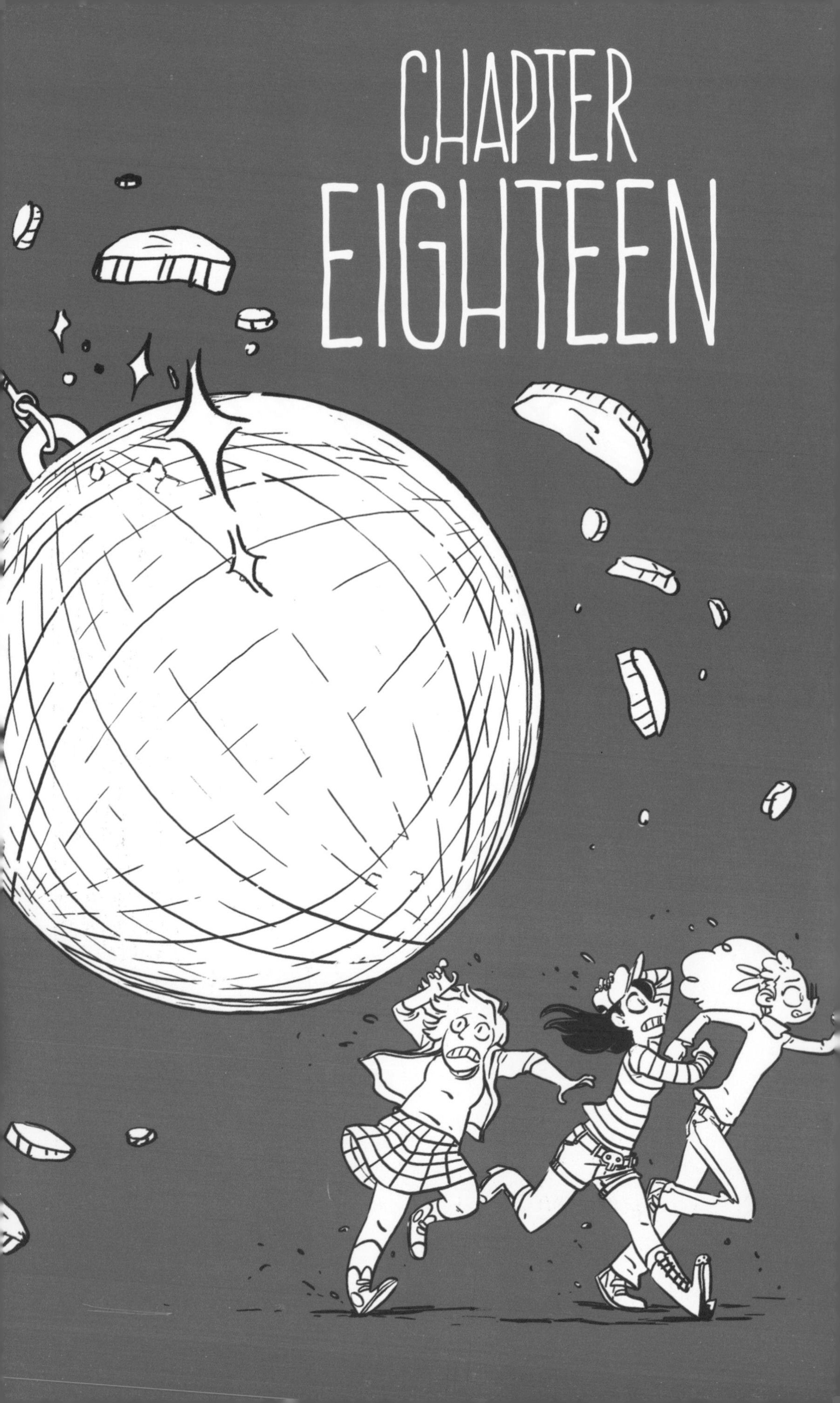
CHAPTER
EIGHTEEN

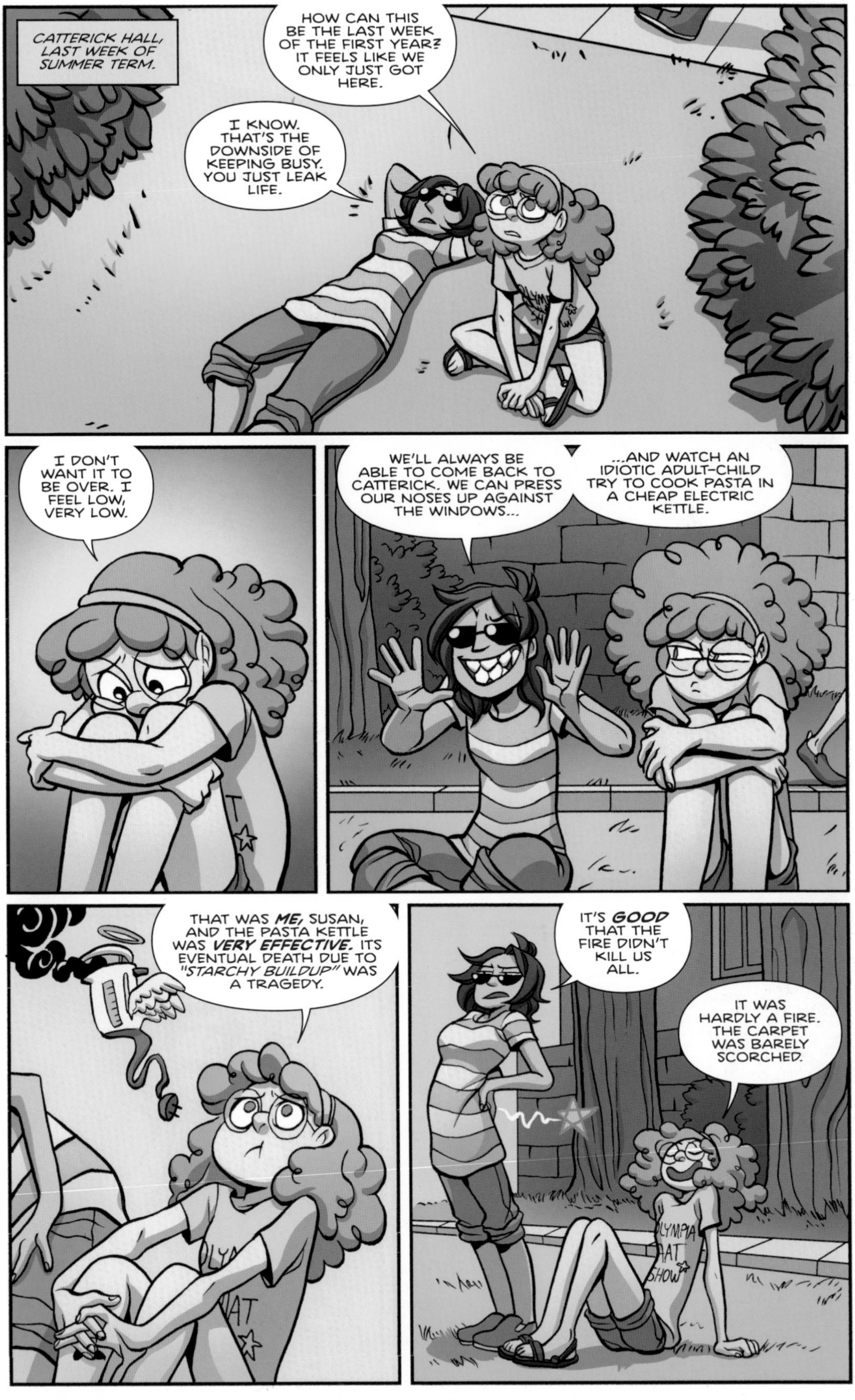
CATTERICK HALL, LAST WEEK OF SUMMER TERM.
HOW CAN THIS BE THE LAST WEEK OF THE FIRST YEAR? IT FEELS LIKE WE ONLY JUST GOT HERE.
I KNOW. THAT'S THE DOWNSIDE OF KEEPING BUSY. YOU JUST LEAK LIFE.
I DON'T WANT IT TO BE OVER. I FEEL LOW, VERY LOW.
WE'LL ALWAYS BE ABLE TO COME BACK TO CATTERICK. WE CAN PRESS OUR NOSES UP AGAINST THE WINDOWS...
...AND WATCH AN IDIOTIC ADULT-CHILD TRY TO COOK PASTA IN A CHEAP ELECTRIC KETTLE.
THAT WAS ME, SUSAN, AND THE PASTA KETTLE WAS VERY EFFECTIVE. ITS EVENTUAL DEATH DUE TO "STARCHY BUILDUP" WAS A TRAGEDY.
IT'S GOOD THAT THE FIRE DIDN'T KILL US ALL.
IT WAS HARDLY A FIRE. THE CARPET WAS BARELY SCORCHED.
OLYMPIA HAT SHOW

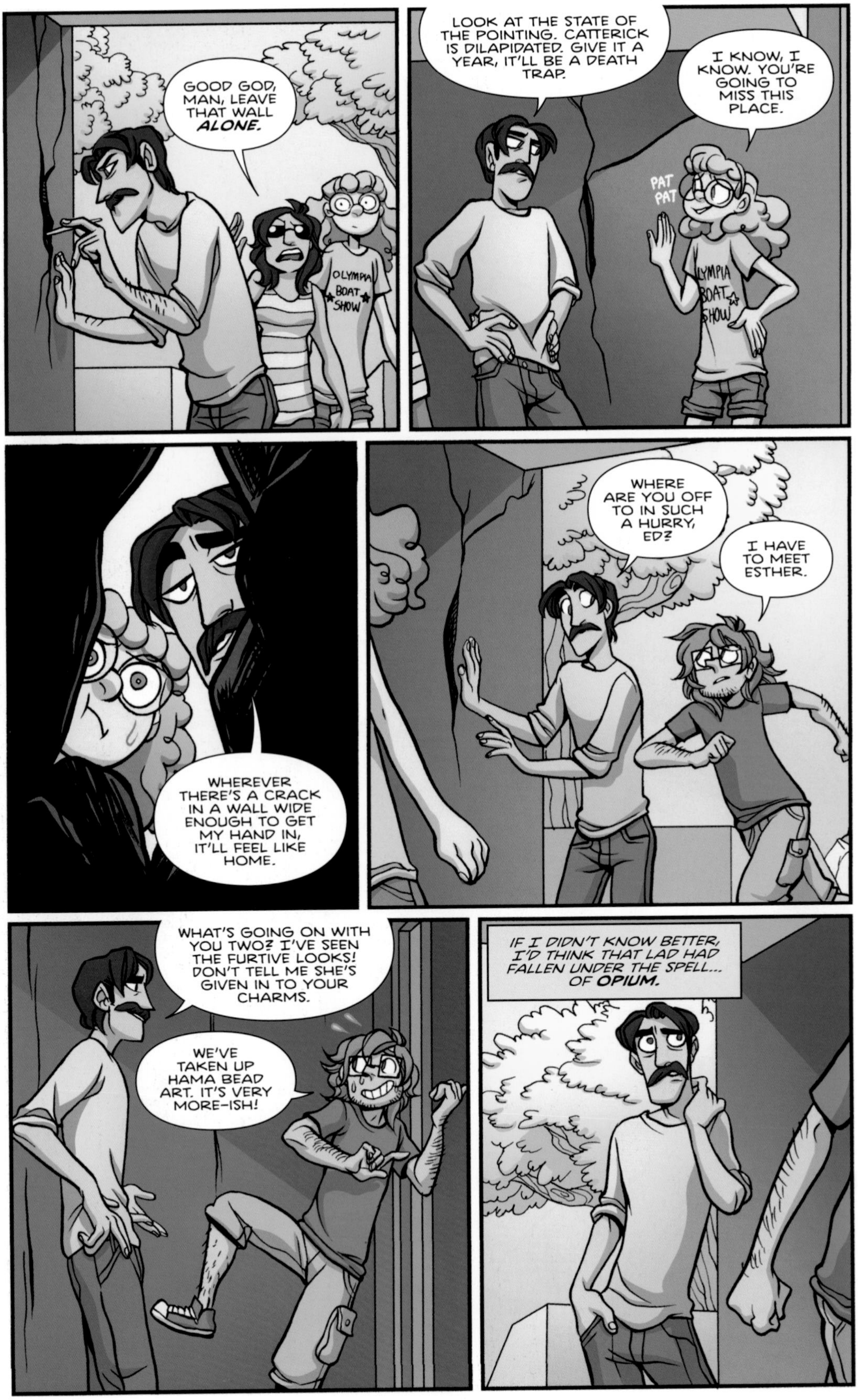
GOOD GOD, MAN, LEAVE THAT WALL ALONE.
OLYMPIA BOAT SHOW
LOOK AT THE STATE OF THE POINTING. CATTERICK IS DILAPIDATED. GIVE IT A YEAR, IT'LL BE A DEATH TRAP.
I KNOW, I KNOW. YOU'RE GOING TO MISS THIS PLACE.
PAT PAT
OLYMPIA BOAT SHOW
WHEREVER THERE'S A CRACK IN A WALL WIDE ENOUGH TO GET MY HAND IN, IT'LL FEEL LIKE HOME.
WHERE ARE YOU OFF TO IN SUCH A HURRY, ED?
I HAVE TO MEET ESTHER.
WHAT'S GOING ON WITH YOU TWO? I'VE SEEN THE FURTIVE LOOKS! DON'T TELL ME SHE'S GIVEN IN TO YOUR CHARMS.
WE'VE TAKEN UP HAMA BEAD ART. IT'S VERY MORE-ISH!
IF I DIDN'T KNOW BETTER, I'D THINK THAT LAD HAD FALLEN UNDER THE SPELL... OF OPIUM.

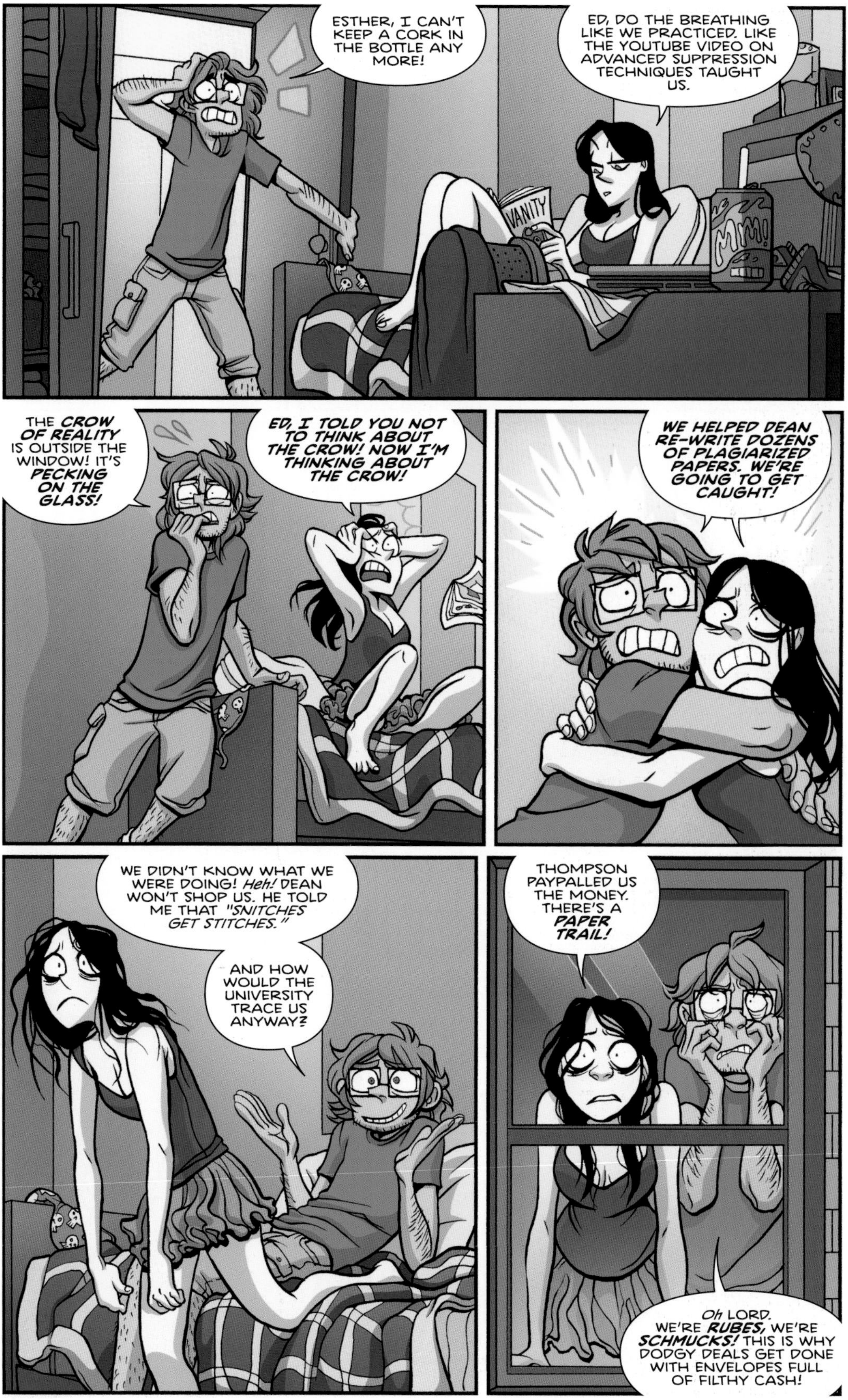
ESTHER, I CAN'T KEEP A CORK IN THE BOTTLE ANY MORE!
ED, DO THE BREATHING LIKE WE PRACTICED. LIKE THE YOUTUBE VIDEO ON ADVANCED SUPPRESSION TECHNIQUES TAUGHT US.
VANITY
MM!
THE CROW OF REALITY IS OUTSIDE THE WINDOW! IT'S PECKING ON THE GLASS!
ED, I TOLD YOU NOT TO THINK ABOUT THE CROW! NOW I'M THINKING ABOUT THE CROW!
WE HELPED DEAN RE-WRITE DOZENS OF PLAGIARIZED PAPERS. WE'RE GOING TO GET CAUGHT!
WE DIDN'T KNOW WHAT WE WERE DOING! Heh! DEAN WON'T SHOP US. HE TOLD ME THAT "SNITCHES GET STITCHES."
AND HOW WOULD THE UNIVERSITY TRACE US ANYWAY?
THOMPSON PAYPALLED US THE MONEY. THERE'S A PAPER TRAIL!
Oh LORD. WE'RE RUBES, WE'RE SCHMUCKS! THIS IS WHY DODGY DEALS GET DONE WITH ENVELOPES FULL OF FILTHY CASH!

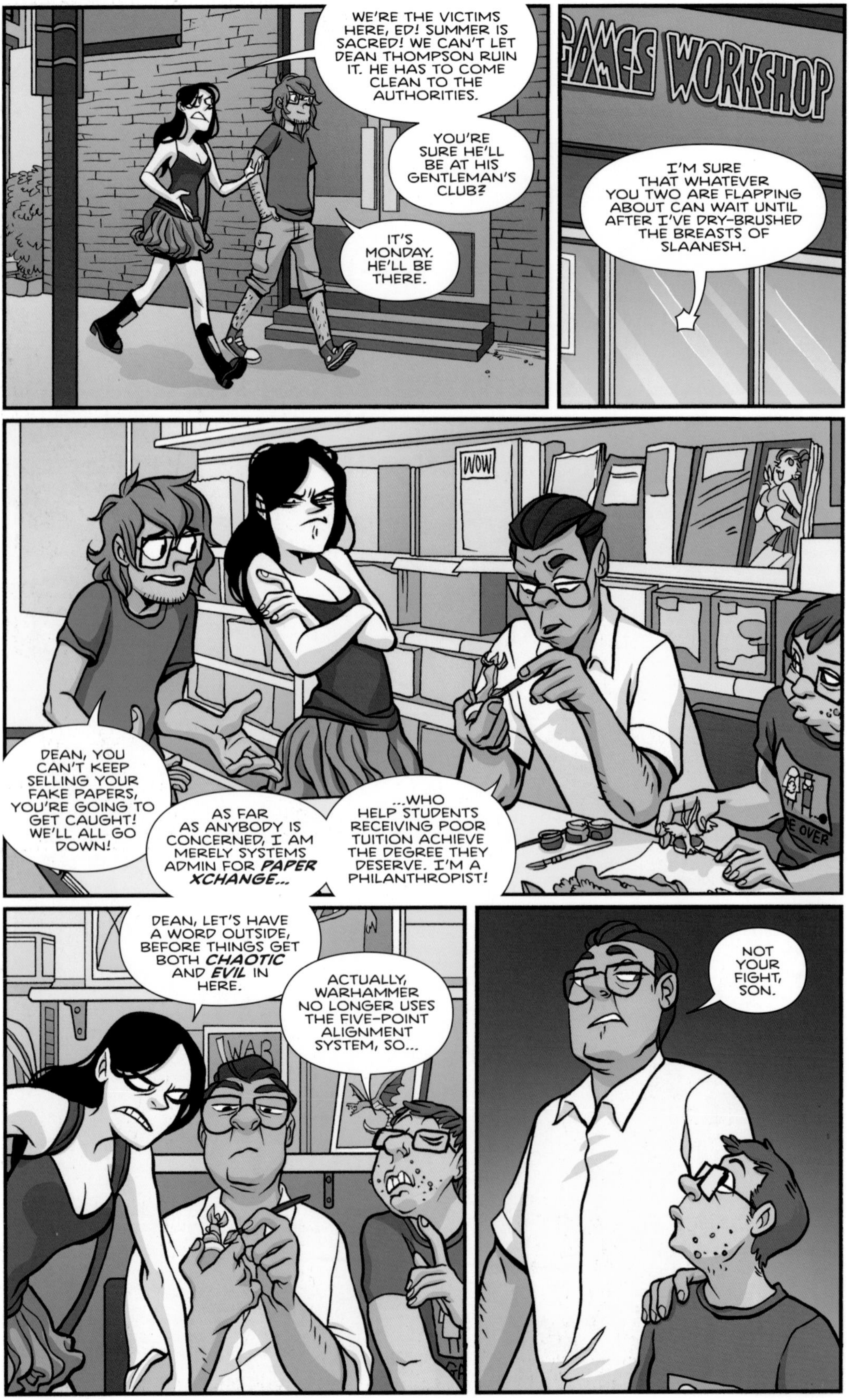

WE'RE THE VICTIMS HERE, ED! SUMMER IS SACRED! WE CAN'T LET DEAN THOMPSON RUIN IT. HE HAS TO COME CLEAN TO THE AUTHORITIES.
YOU'RE SURE HE'LL BE AT HIS GENTLEMAN'S CLUB?
IT'S MONDAY. HE'LL BE THERE.
GAMES WORKSHOP
I'M SURE THAT WHATEVER YOU TWO ARE FLAPPING ABOUT CAN WAIT UNTIL AFTER I'VE DRY-BRUSHED THE BREASTS OF SLAANESH.
WOW
DEAN, YOU CAN'T KEEP SELLING YOUR FAKE PAPERS, YOU'RE GOING TO GET CAUGHT! WE'LL ALL GO DOWN!
AS FAR AS ANYBODY IS CONCERNED, I AM MERELY SYSTEMS ADMIN FOR *PAPER XCHANGE...*
...WHO HELP STUDENTS RECEIVING POOR TUITION ACHIEVE THE DEGREE THEY DESERVE. I'M A PHILANTHROPIST!
DEAN, LET'S HAVE A WORD OUTSIDE, BEFORE THINGS GET BOTH ***CHAOTIC*** AND ***EVIL*** IN HERE.
ACTUALLY, WARHAMMER NO LONGER USES THE FIVE-POINT ALIGNMENT SYSTEM, SO...
NOT YOUR FIGHT, SON.

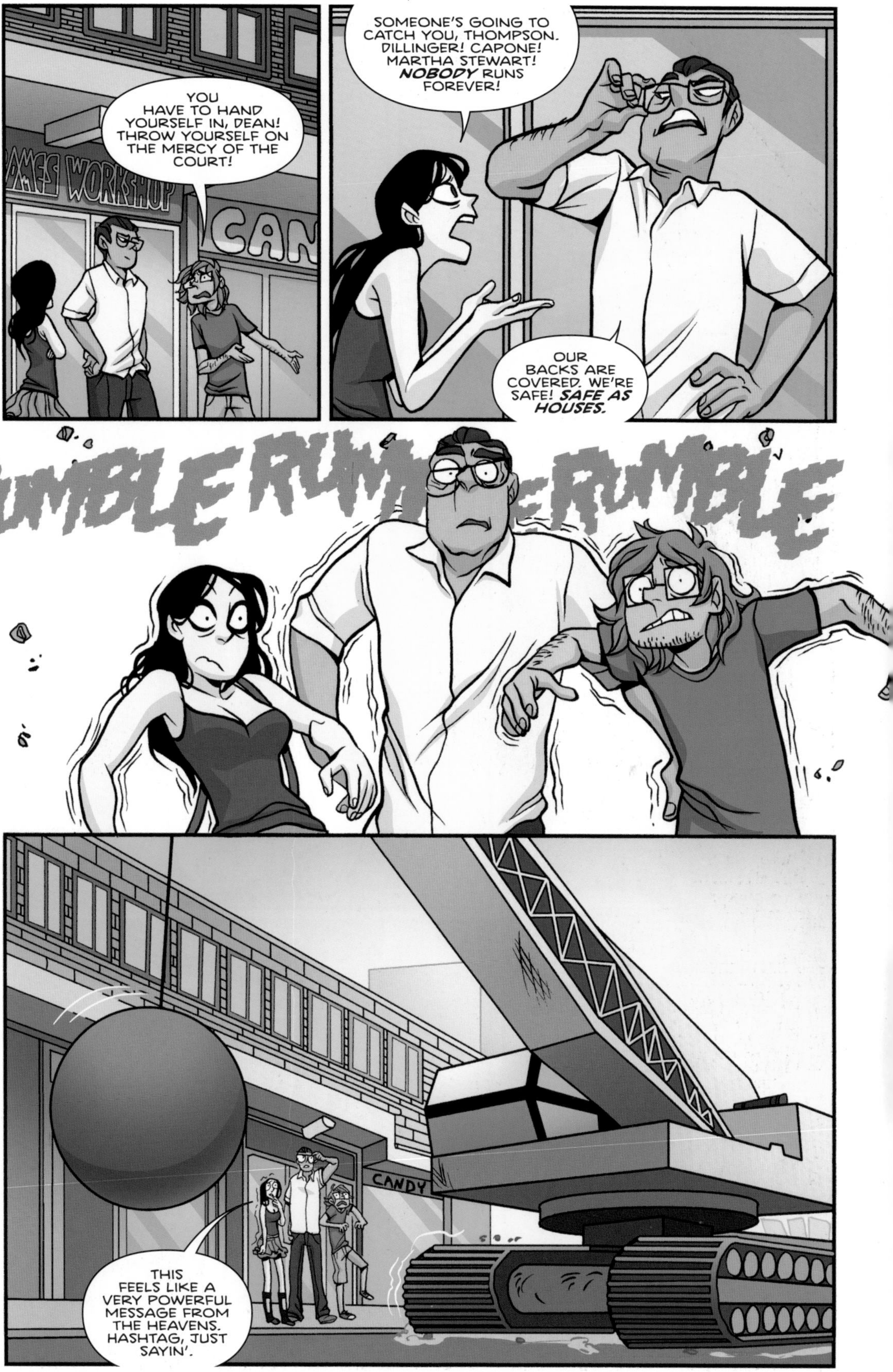
YOU HAVE TO HAND YOURSELF IN, DEAN! THROW YOURSELF ON THE MERCY OF THE COURT!
SOMEONE'S GOING TO CATCH YOU, THOMPSON. DILLINGER! CAPONE! MARTHA STEWART! NOBODY RUNS FOREVER!
OUR BACKS ARE COVERED. WE'RE SAFE! SAFE AS HOUSES.
RUMBLE RUM
E RUMBLE
CANDY
THIS FEELS LIKE A VERY POWERFUL MESSAGE FROM THE HEAVENS. HASHTAG, JUST SAYIN'.

WHO ARE YOU TEXTING? ARE YOU CUTTING A DEAL WITH THE D.A.?

TEXTING SUSAN! SHE CAN HELP US! SHE'S AN EXPERT ON CRIMINAL LOWLIFES!

SHE'LL JUDGE US, ESTHER.

I'D RATHER BE JUDGED BY SUSAN THAN AN ACTUAL JUDGE.

Flying you up to its nest...

THIS IS NO TIME TO SAUNTER DOWN *WHIMSY STREET*!

WHAT DID SHE SAY?

HA HA!

VWOOP

11:41 AM

Messages SUSAN

IT YOU

Send

QWERTYUIOP
ASDFGHI
ZXCVBN

.?123 SPACE REPL

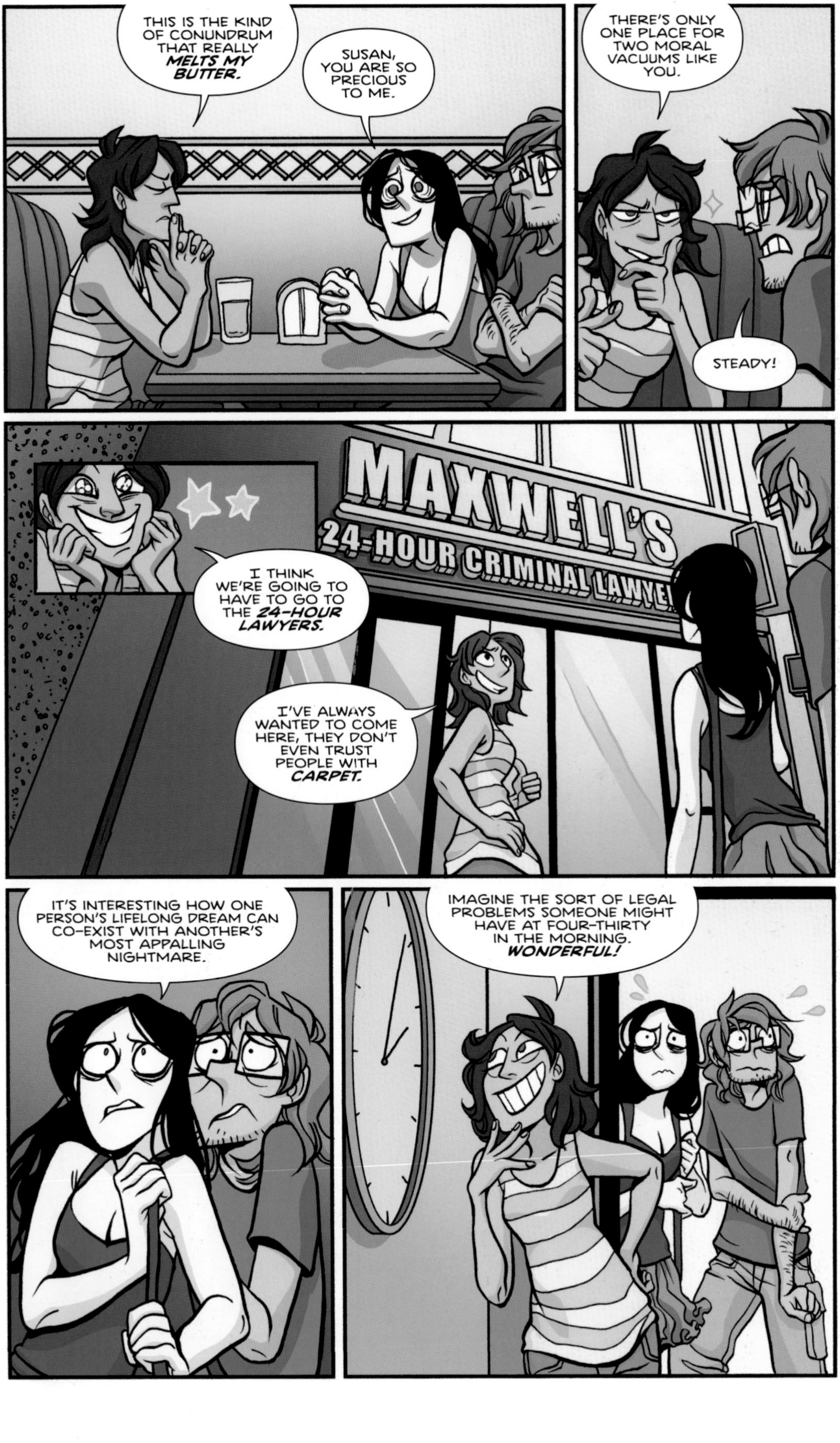
THIS IS THE KIND OF CONUNDRUM THAT REALLY ***MELTS MY BUTTER.***
SUSAN, YOU ARE SO PRECIOUS TO ME.
THERE'S ONLY ONE PLACE FOR TWO MORAL VACUUMS LIKE YOU.
STEADY!
MAXWELL'S
24-HOUR CRIMINAL LAWYE
I THINK WE'RE GOING TO HAVE TO GO TO THE ***24-HOUR LAWYERS.***
I'VE ALWAYS WANTED TO COME HERE, THEY DON'T EVEN TRUST PEOPLE WITH ***CARPET.***
IT'S INTERESTING HOW ONE PERSON'S LIFELONG DREAM CAN CO-EXIST WITH ANOTHER'S MOST APPALLING NIGHTMARE.
IMAGINE THE SORT OF LEGAL PROBLEMS SOMEONE MIGHT HAVE AT FOUR-THIRTY IN THE MORNING. ***WONDERFUL!***

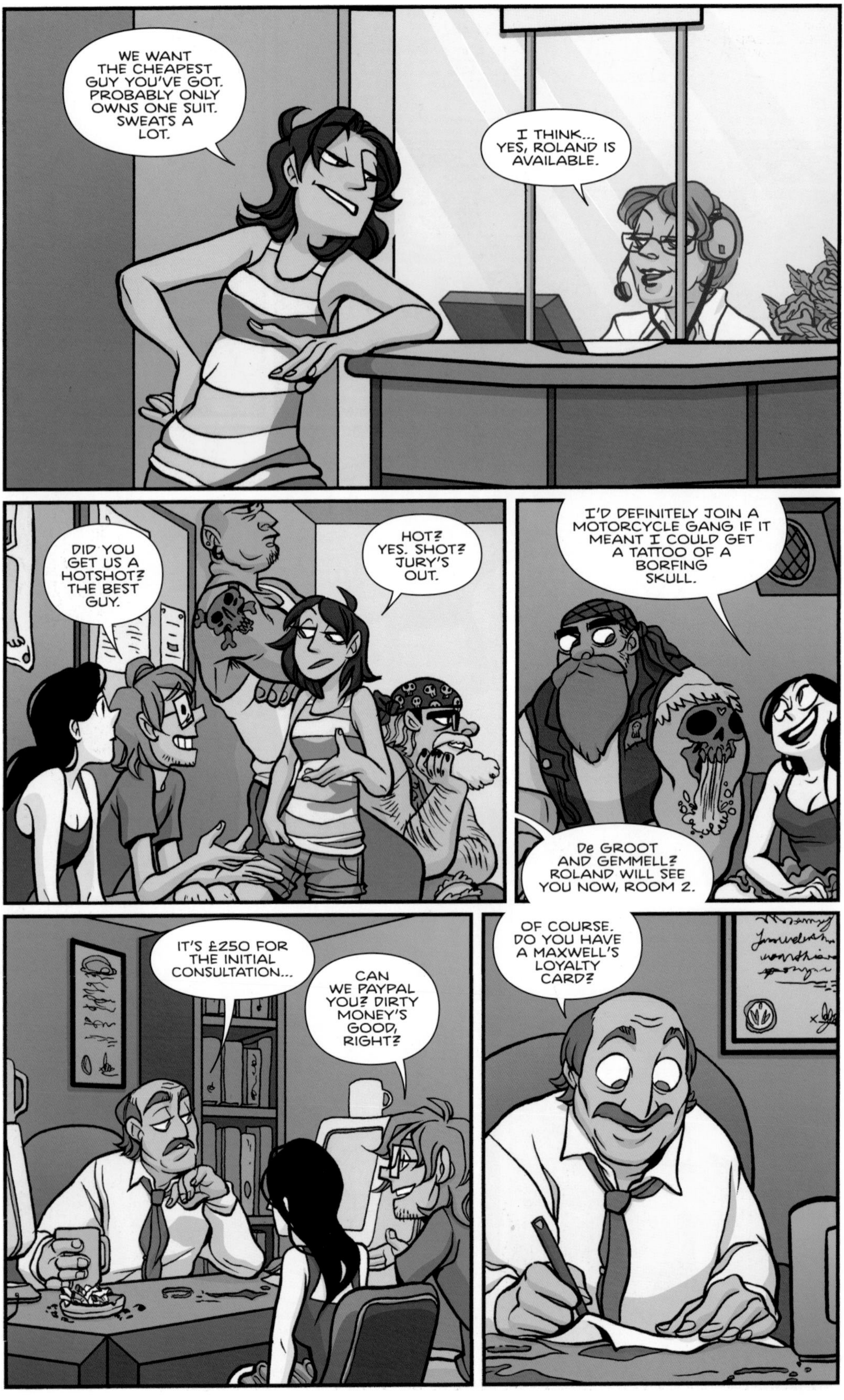
WE WANT THE CHEAPEST GUY YOU'VE GOT. PROBABLY ONLY OWNS ONE SUIT. SWEATS A LOT.
I THINK... YES, ROLAND IS AVAILABLE.
DID YOU GET US A HOTSHOT? THE BEST GUY.
HOT? YES. SHOT? JURY'S OUT.
I'D DEFINITELY JOIN A MOTORCYCLE GANG IF IT MEANT I COULD GET A TATTOO OF A BORFING SKULL.
De GROOT AND GEMMELL? ROLAND WILL SEE YOU NOW, ROOM 2.
IT'S £250 FOR THE INITIAL CONSULTATION...
CAN WE PAYPAL YOU? DIRTY MONEY'S GOOD, RIGHT?
OF COURSE. DO YOU HAVE A MAXWELL'S LOYALTY CARD?

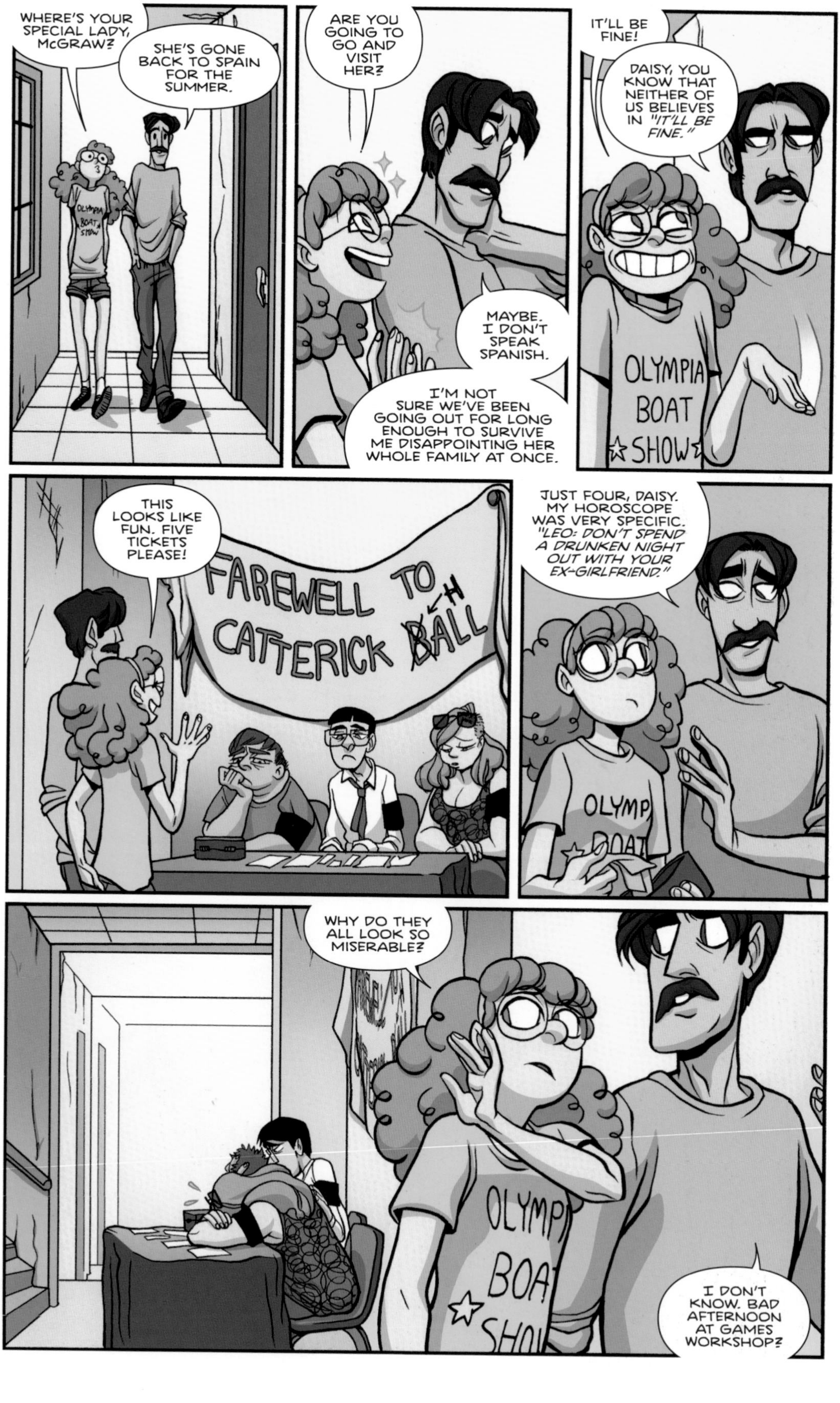
WHERE'S YOUR SPECIAL LADY, McGRAW?
SHE'S GONE BACK TO SPAIN FOR THE SUMMER.
OLYMPIA BOAT SHOW
ARE YOU GOING TO GO AND VISIT HER?
MAYBE. I DON'T SPEAK SPANISH.
I'M NOT SURE WE'VE BEEN GOING OUT FOR LONG ENOUGH TO SURVIVE ME DISAPPOINTING HER WHOLE FAMILY AT ONCE.
IT'LL BE FINE!
DAISY, YOU KNOW THAT NEITHER OF US BELIEVES IN *"IT'LL BE FINE."*
OLYMPIA BOAT SHOW
THIS LOOKS LIKE FUN. FIVE TICKETS PLEASE!
FAREWELL TO CATTERICK BALL H
JUST FOUR, DAISY. MY HOROSCOPE WAS VERY SPECIFIC. *"LEO: DON'T SPEND A DRUNKEN NIGHT OUT WITH YOUR EX-GIRLFRIEND."*
WHY DO THEY ALL LOOK SO MISERABLE?
I DON'T KNOW. BAD AFTERNOON AT GAMES WORKSHOP?

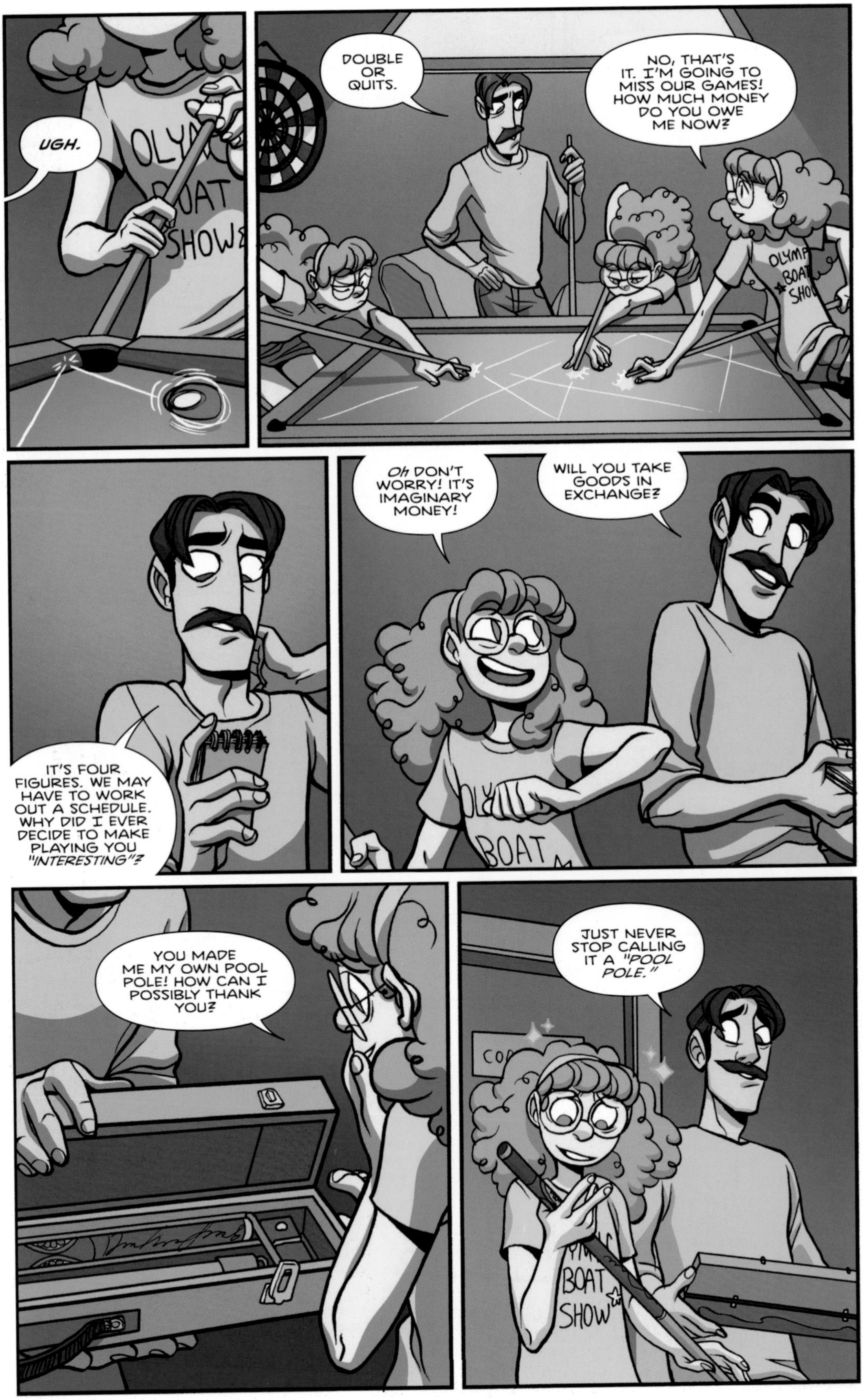
UGH.
DOUBLE OR QUITS.
NO, THAT'S IT. I'M GOING TO MISS OUR GAMES! HOW MUCH MONEY DO YOU OWE ME NOW?
OLYMP BOAT SHOW
IT'S FOUR FIGURES. WE MAY HAVE TO WORK OUT A SCHEDULE. WHY DID I EVER DECIDE TO MAKE PLAYING YOU "INTERESTING"?
Oh DON'T WORRY! IT'S IMAGINARY MONEY!
WILL YOU TAKE GOODS IN EXCHANGE?
YOU MADE ME MY OWN POOL POLE! HOW CAN I POSSIBLY THANK YOU?
JUST NEVER STOP CALLING IT A "*POOL POLE.*"
BOAT SHOW

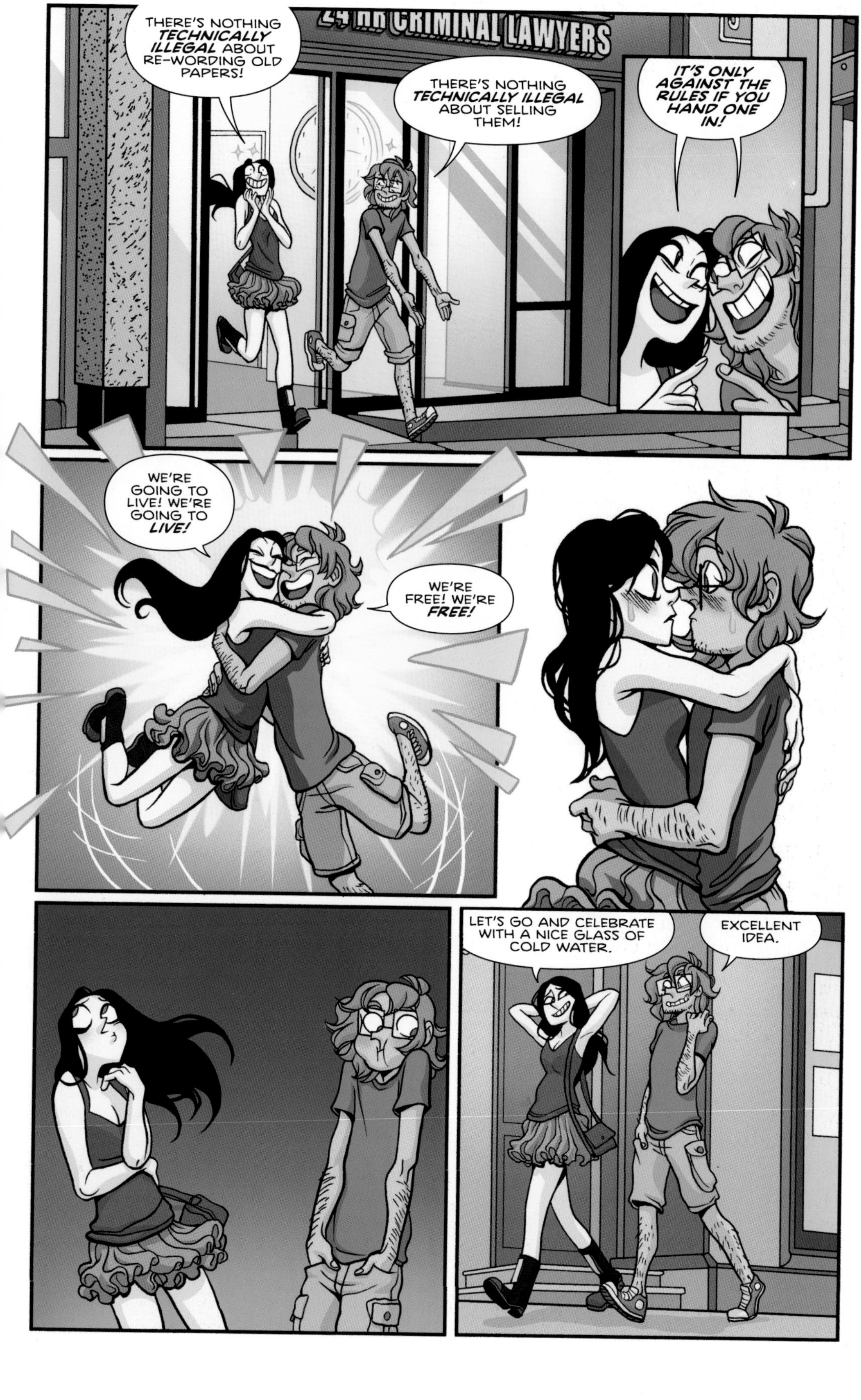
24 HR CRIMINAL LAWYERS
THERE'S NOTHING *TECHNICALLY ILLEGAL* ABOUT RE-WORDING OLD PAPERS!
THERE'S NOTHING *TECHNICALLY ILLEGAL* ABOUT SELLING THEM!
IT'S ONLY AGAINST THE RULES IF YOU HAND ONE IN!
WE'RE GOING TO LIVE! WE'RE GOING TO *LIVE!*
WE'RE FREE! WE'RE *FREE!*
LET'S GO AND CELEBRATE WITH A NICE GLASS OF COLD WATER.
EXCELLENT IDEA.

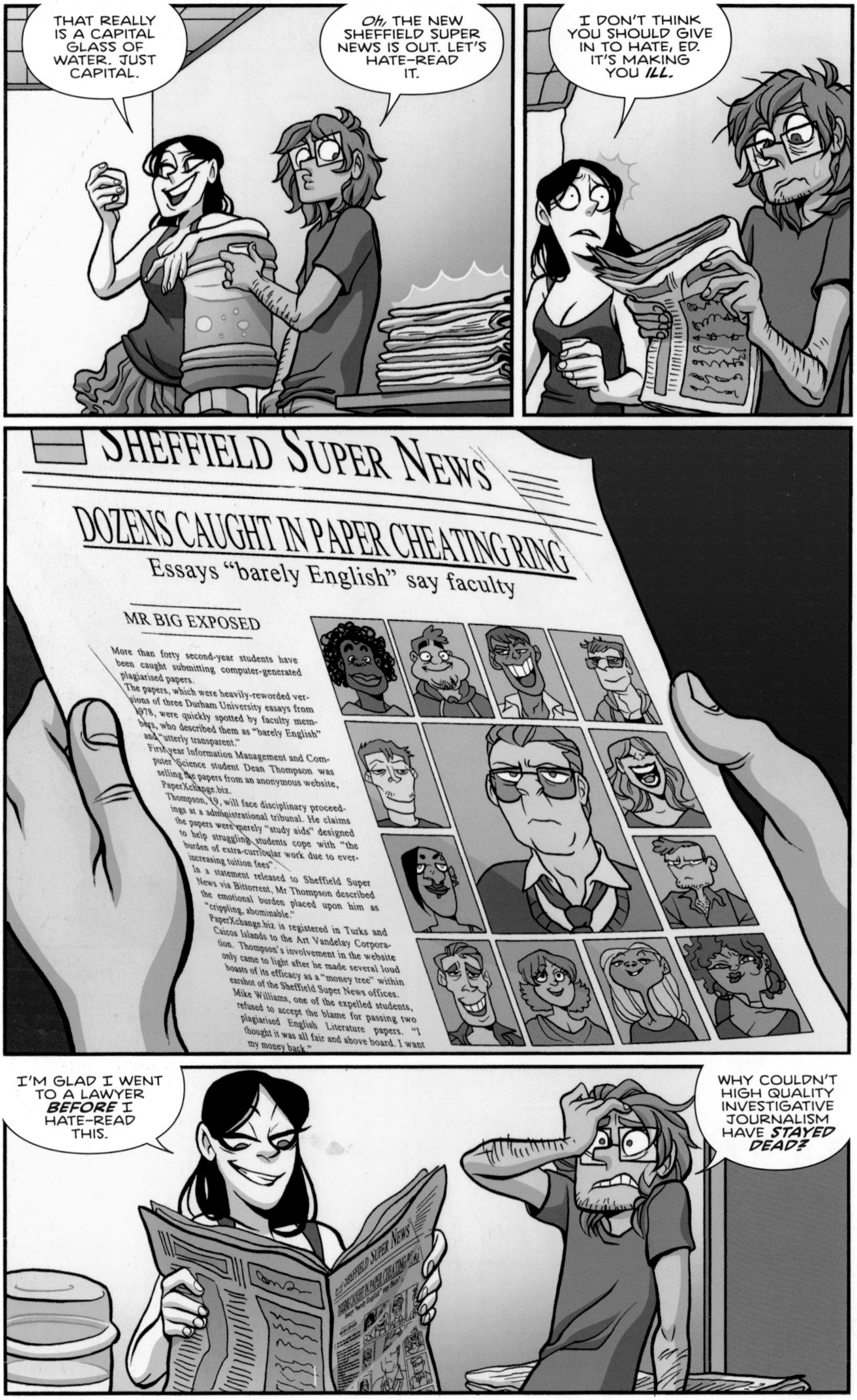

THAT REALLY IS A CAPITAL GLASS OF WATER. JUST CAPITAL.
Oh, THE NEW SHEFFIELD SUPER NEWS IS OUT. LET'S HATE-READ IT.
I DON'T THINK YOU SHOULD GIVE IN TO HATE, ED. IT'S MAKING YOU ***ILL.***
SHEFFIELD SUPER NEWS
DOZENS CAUGHT IN PAPER CHEATING RING
Essays "barely English" say faculty
MR BIG EXPOSED
More than forty second-year students have been caught submitting computer-generated plagiarised papers.
The papers, which were heavily-reworded versions of three Durham University essays from 1978, were quickly spotted by faculty members, who described them as "barely English" and "utterly transparent."
First year Information Management and Computer Science student Dean Thompson was selling the papers from an anonymous website, PaperXchange.biz.
Thompson, 19, will face disciplinary proceedings at a administrational tribunal. He claims the papers were merely "study aids" designed to help struggling students cope with "the burden of extra-curricular work due to ever-increasing tuition fees".
In a statement released to Sheffield Super News via Bittorrent, Mr Thompson described the emotional burden placed upon him as "crippling, abominable."
PaperXchange.biz is registered in Turks and Caicos Islands to the Art Vandelay Corporation. Thompson's involvement in the website only came to light after he made several loud boasts of its efficacy as a "money tree" within earshot of the Sheffield Super News offices.
Mike Williams, one of the expelled students, refused to accept the blame for passing two plagiarised English Literature papers. "I thought it was all fair and above board. I want my money back."
I'M GLAD I WENT TO A LAWYER ***BEFORE*** I HATE-READ THIS.
WHY COULDN'T HIGH QUALITY INVESTIGATIVE JOURNALISM HAVE ***STAYED DEAD?***

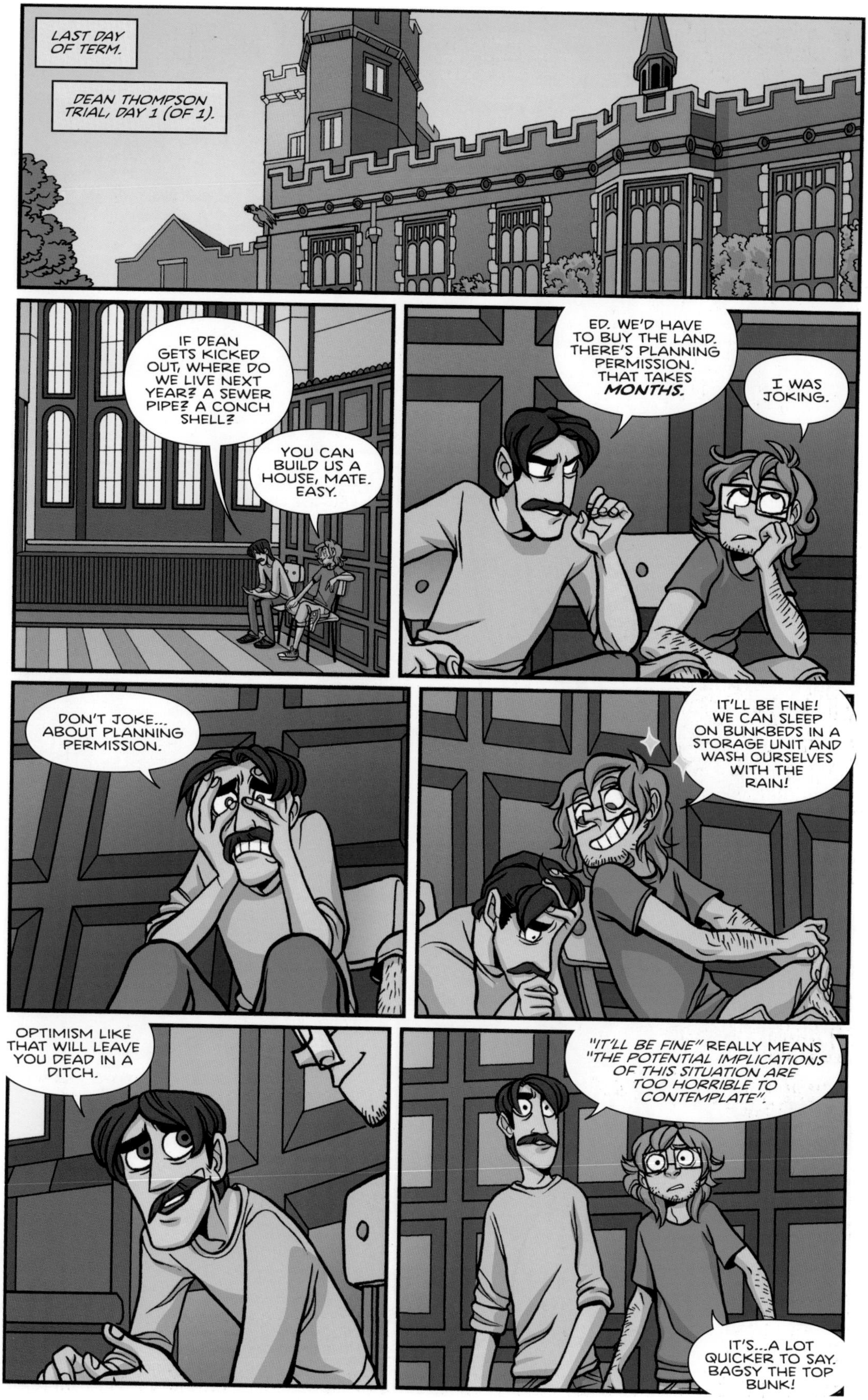
LAST DAY OF TERM.
DEAN THOMPSON TRIAL, DAY 1 (OF 1).
IF DEAN GETS KICKED OUT, WHERE DO WE LIVE NEXT YEAR? A SEWER PIPE? A CONCH SHELL?
YOU CAN BUILD US A HOUSE, MATE. EASY.
ED. WE'D HAVE TO BUY THE LAND. THERE'S PLANNING PERMISSION. THAT TAKES MONTHS.
I WAS JOKING.
DON'T JOKE... ABOUT PLANNING PERMISSION.
IT'LL BE FINE! WE CAN SLEEP ON BUNKBEDS IN A STORAGE UNIT AND WASH OURSELVES WITH THE RAIN!
OPTIMISM LIKE THAT WILL LEAVE YOU DEAD IN A DITCH.
"IT'LL BE FINE" REALLY MEANS "THE POTENTIAL IMPLICATIONS OF THIS SITUATION ARE TOO HORRIBLE TO CONTEMPLATE".
IT'S...A LOT QUICKER TO SAY. BAGSY THE TOP BUNK!

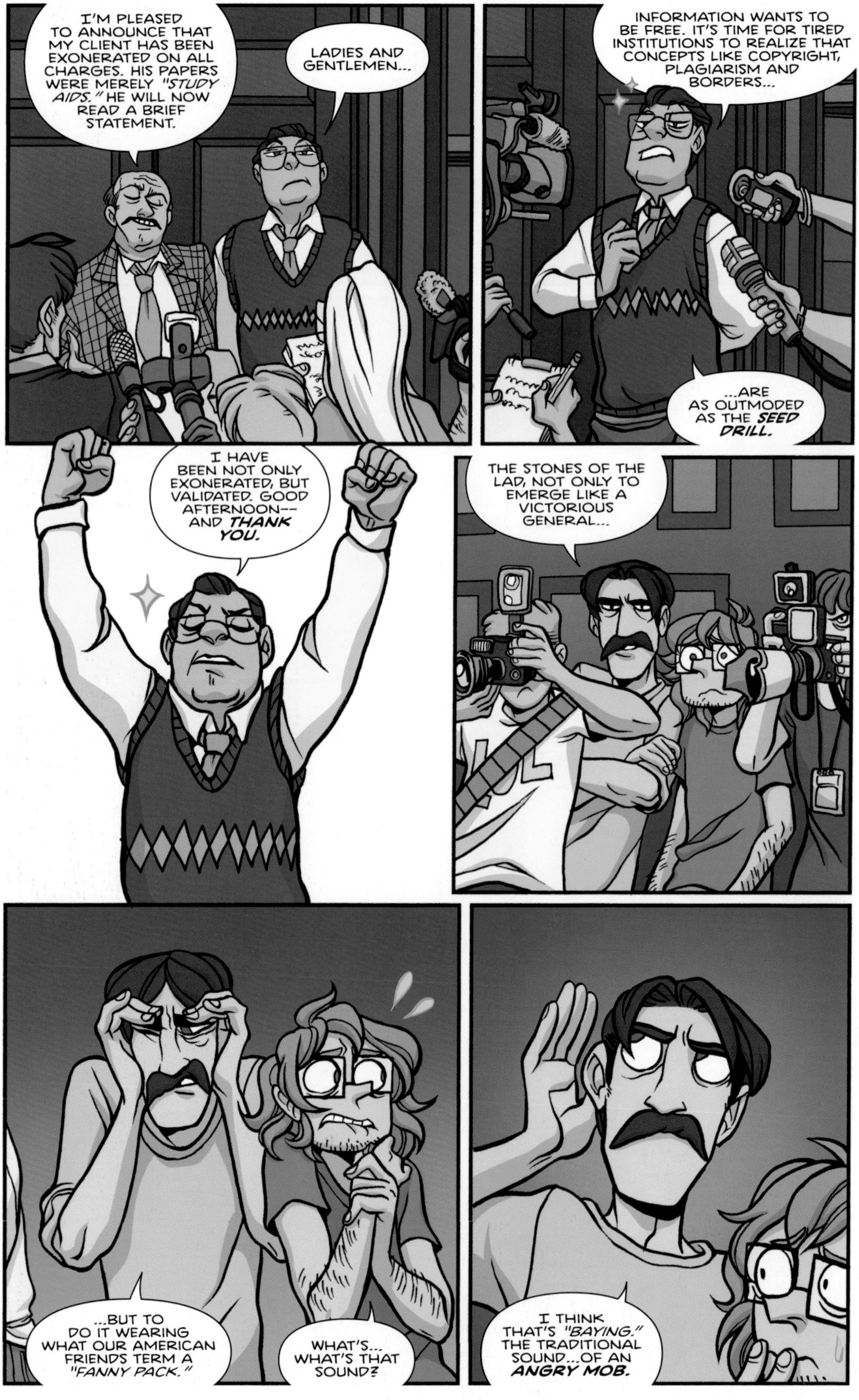
I'M PLEASED TO ANNOUNCE THAT MY CLIENT HAS BEEN EXONERATED ON ALL CHARGES. HIS PAPERS WERE MERELY "STUDY AIDS." HE WILL NOW READ A BRIEF STATEMENT.
LADIES AND GENTLEMEN...
INFORMATION WANTS TO BE FREE. IT'S TIME FOR TIRED INSTITUTIONS TO REALIZE THAT CONCEPTS LIKE COPYRIGHT, PLAGIARISM AND BORDERS...
...ARE AS OUTMODED AS THE SEED DRILL.
I HAVE BEEN NOT ONLY EXONERATED, BUT VALIDATED. GOOD AFTERNOON-- AND THANK YOU.
THE STONES OF THE LAD, NOT ONLY TO EMERGE LIKE A VICTORIOUS GENERAL...
...BUT TO DO IT WEARING WHAT OUR AMERICAN FRIENDS TERM A "FANNY PACK."
WHAT'S... WHAT'S THAT SOUND?
I THINK THAT'S "BAYING." THE TRADITIONAL SOUND...OF AN ANGRY MOB.

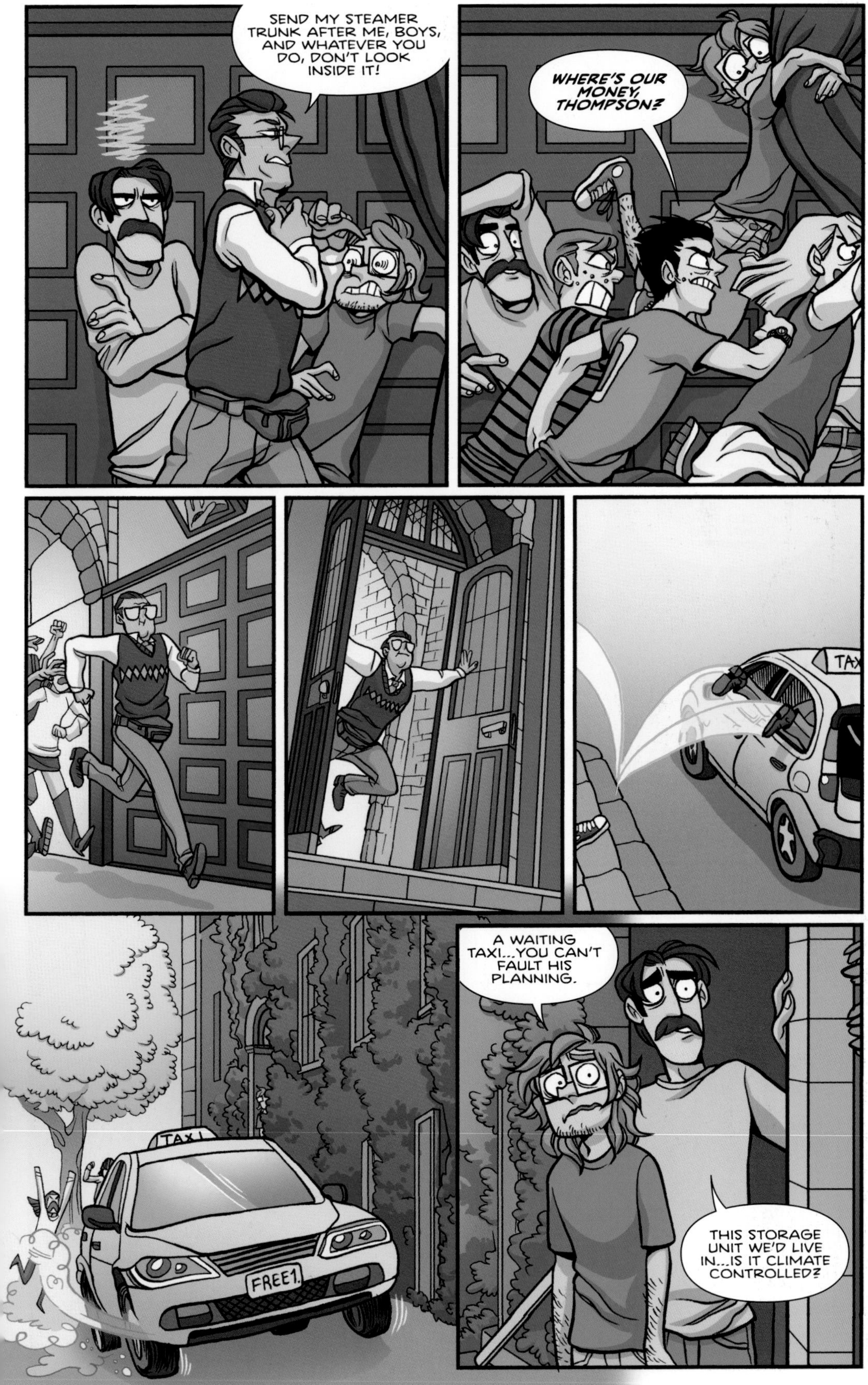
SEND MY STEAMER TRUNK AFTER ME, BOYS, AND WHATEVER YOU DO, DON'T LOOK INSIDE IT!
WHERE'S OUR MONEY, THOMPSON?
TAXI
TAXI
FREE1
A WAITING TAXI...YOU CAN'T FAULT HIS PLANNING.
THIS STORAGE UNIT WE'D LIVE IN...IS IT CLIMATE CONTROLLED?

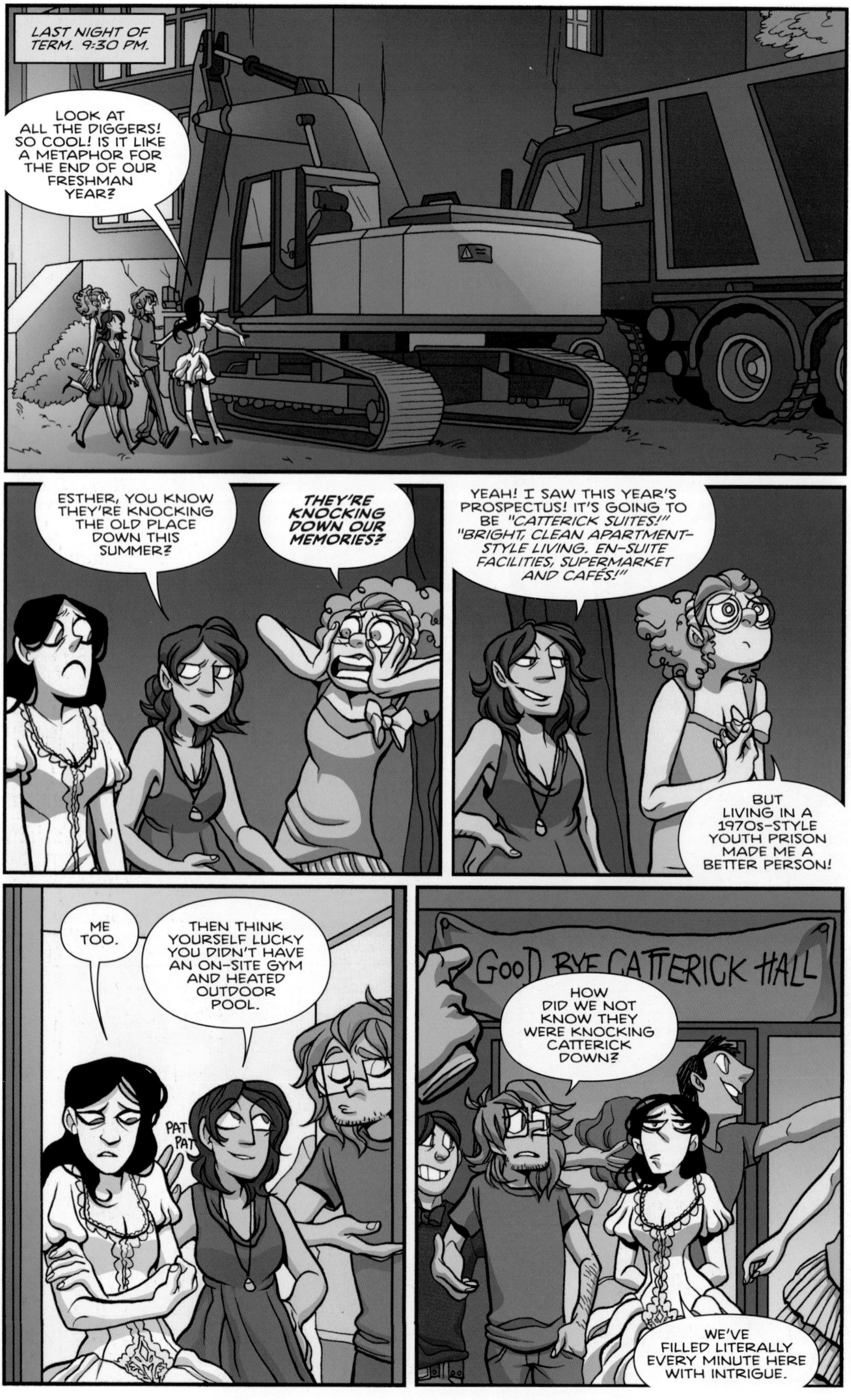
LAST NIGHT OF TERM. 9:30 PM.
LOOK AT ALL THE DIGGERS! SO COOL! IS IT LIKE A METAPHOR FOR THE END OF OUR FRESHMAN YEAR?
ESTHER, YOU KNOW THEY'RE KNOCKING THE OLD PLACE DOWN THIS SUMMER?
THEY'RE KNOCKING DOWN OUR MEMORIES?
YEAH! I SAW THIS YEAR'S PROSPECTUS! IT'S GOING TO BE "CATTERICK SUITES!" "BRIGHT, CLEAN APARTMENT-STYLE LIVING. EN-SUITE FACILITIES, SUPERMARKET AND CAFÉS!"
BUT LIVING IN A 1970s-STYLE YOUTH PRISON MADE ME A BETTER PERSON!
ME TOO.
THEN THINK YOURSELF LUCKY YOU DIDN'T HAVE AN ON-SITE GYM AND HEATED OUTDOOR POOL.
PAT PAT
GOOD BYE CATTERICK HALL
HOW DID WE NOT KNOW THEY WERE KNOCKING CATTERICK DOWN?
WE'VE FILLED LITERALLY EVERY MINUTE HERE WITH INTRIGUE.

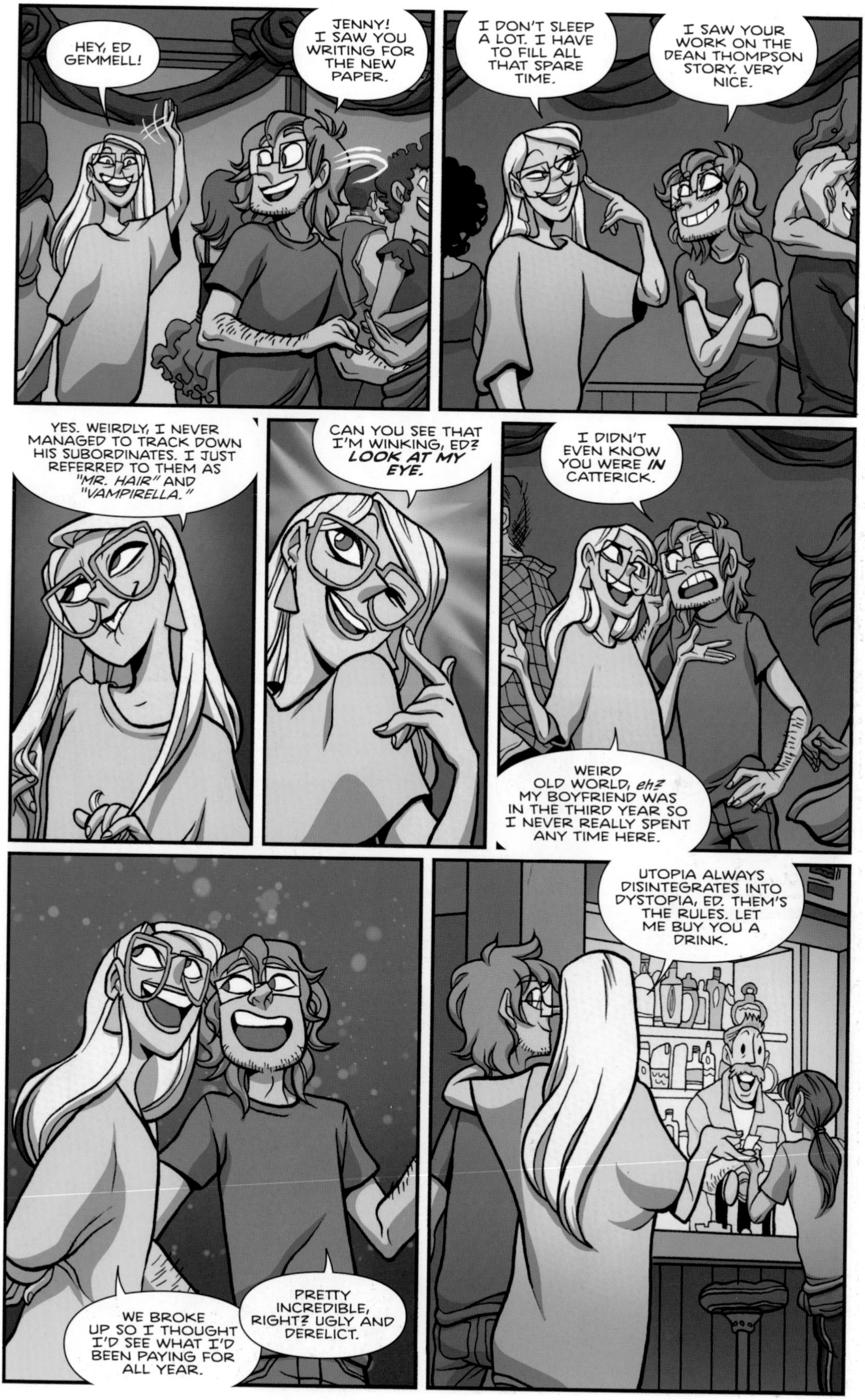
HEY, ED GEMMELL!
JENNY! I SAW YOU WRITING FOR THE NEW PAPER.
I DON'T SLEEP A LOT. I HAVE TO FILL ALL THAT SPARE TIME.
I SAW YOUR WORK ON THE DEAN THOMPSON STORY. VERY NICE.
YES. WEIRDLY, I NEVER MANAGED TO TRACK DOWN HIS SUBORDINATES. I JUST REFERRED TO THEM AS "MR. HAIR" AND "VAMPIRELLA."
CAN YOU SEE THAT I'M WINKING, ED? *LOOK AT MY EYE.*
I DIDN'T EVEN KNOW YOU WERE *IN* CATTERICK.
WEIRD OLD WORLD, *eh?* MY BOYFRIEND WAS IN THE THIRD YEAR SO I NEVER REALLY SPENT ANY TIME HERE.
WE BROKE UP SO I THOUGHT I'D SEE WHAT I'D BEEN PAYING FOR ALL YEAR.
PRETTY INCREDIBLE, RIGHT? UGLY AND DERELICT.
UTOPIA ALWAYS DISINTEGRATES INTO DYSTOPIA, ED. THEM'S THE RULES. LET ME BUY YOU A DRINK.

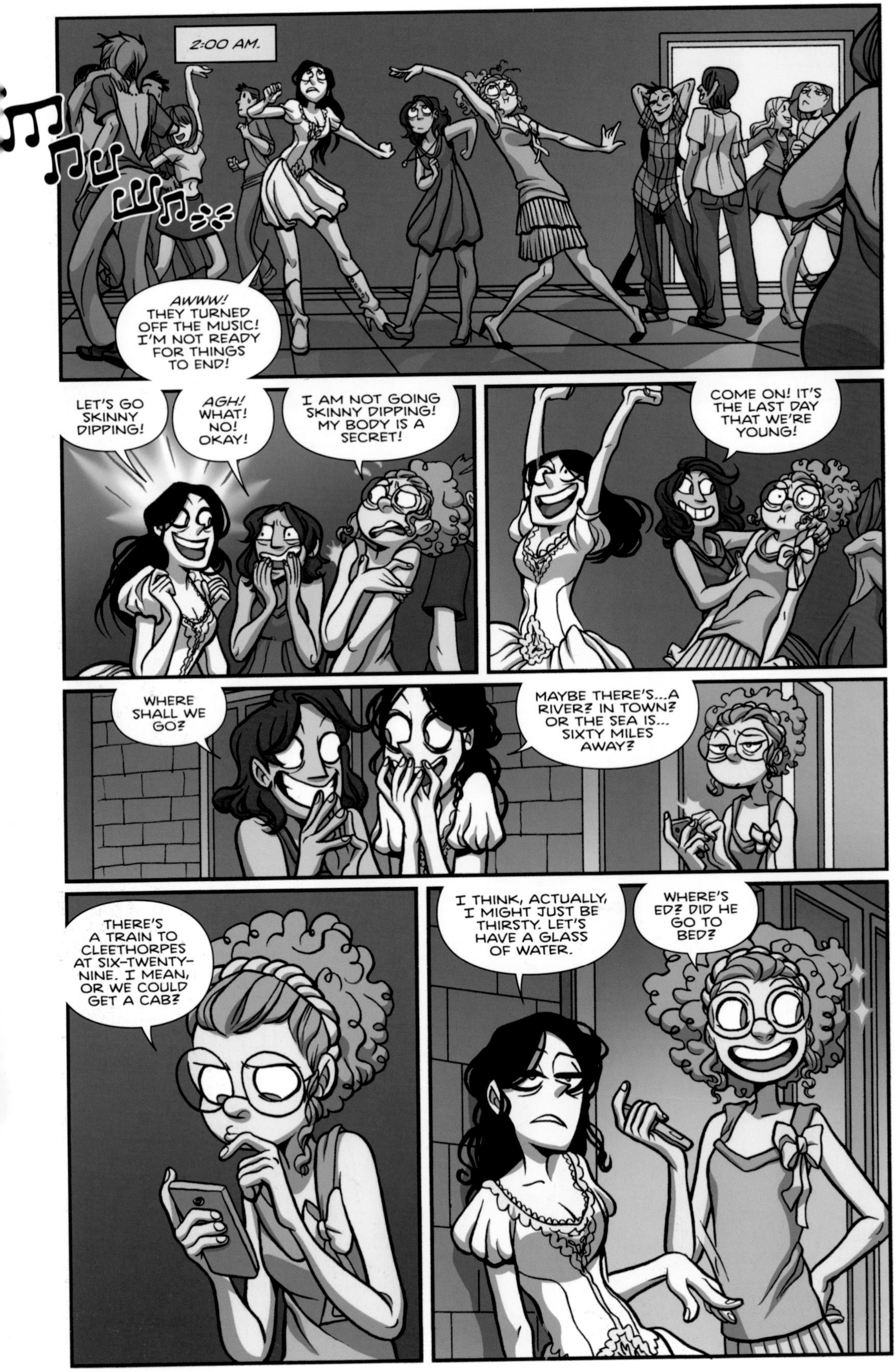
2:00 AM.
AWWW! THEY TURNED OFF THE MUSIC! I'M NOT READY FOR THINGS TO END!
LET'S GO SKINNY DIPPING!
AGH! WHAT! NO! OKAY!
I AM NOT GOING SKINNY DIPPING! MY BODY IS A SECRET!
COME ON! IT'S THE LAST DAY THAT WE'RE YOUNG!
WHERE SHALL WE GO?
MAYBE THERE'S...A RIVER? IN TOWN? OR THE SEA IS... SIXTY MILES AWAY?
THERE'S A TRAIN TO CLEETHORPES AT SIX-TWENTY-NINE. I MEAN, OR WE COULD GET A CAB?
I THINK, ACTUALLY, I MIGHT JUST BE THIRSTY. LET'S HAVE A GLASS OF WATER.
WHERE'S ED? DID HE GO TO BED?

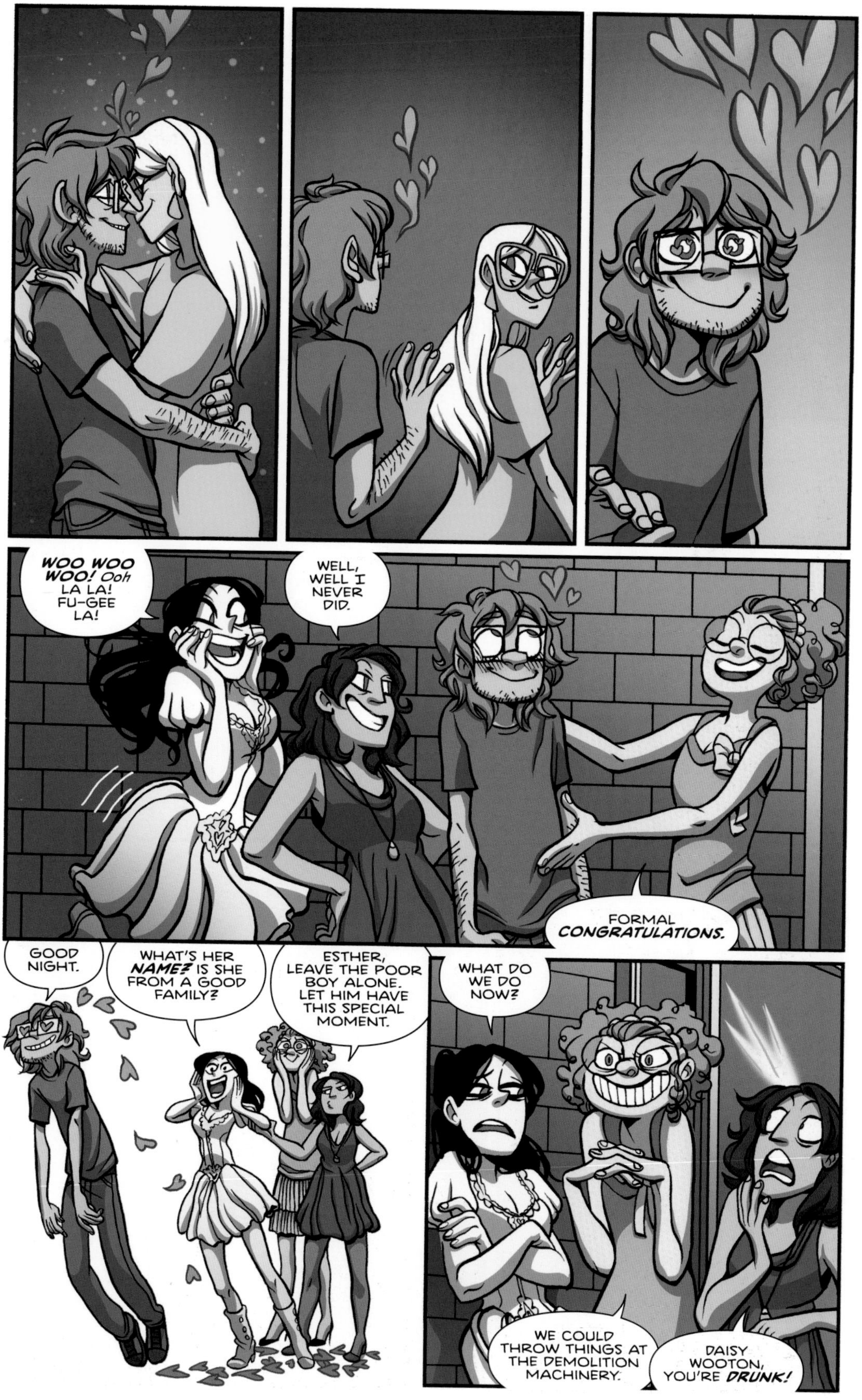
WOO WOO WOO! Ooh LA LA! FU-GEE LA!
WELL, WELL I NEVER DID.
FORMAL CONGRATULATIONS.
GOOD NIGHT.
WHAT'S HER NAME? IS SHE FROM A GOOD FAMILY?
ESTHER, LEAVE THE POOR BOY ALONE. LET HIM HAVE THIS SPECIAL MOMENT.
WHAT DO WE DO NOW?
WE COULD THROW THINGS AT THE DEMOLITION MACHINERY.
DAISY WOOTON, YOU'RE DRUNK!

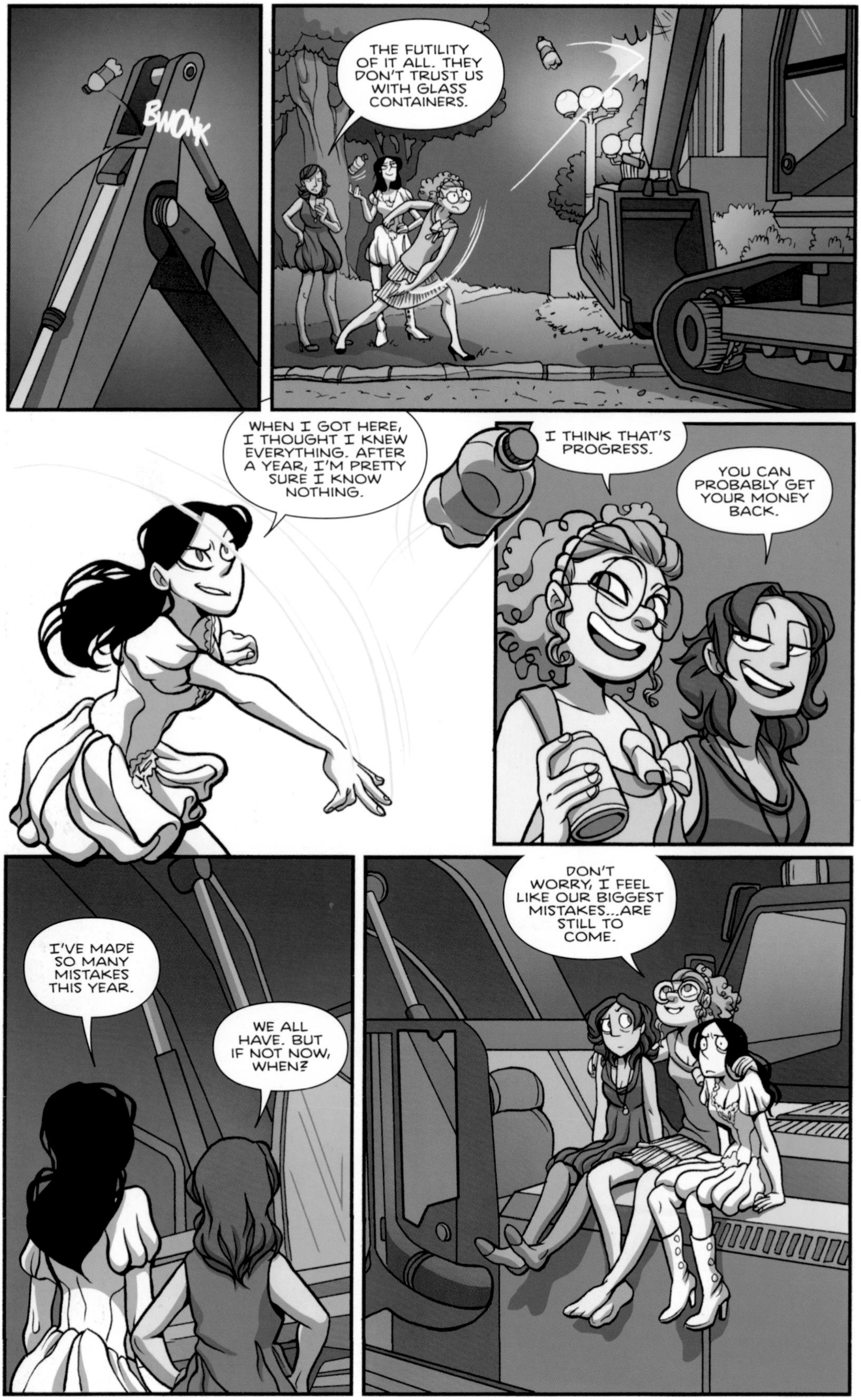
BWONK
THE FUTILITY OF IT ALL. THEY DON'T TRUST US WITH GLASS CONTAINERS.
WHEN I GOT HERE, I THOUGHT I KNEW EVERYTHING. AFTER A YEAR, I'M PRETTY SURE I KNOW NOTHING.
I THINK THAT'S PROGRESS.
YOU CAN PROBABLY GET YOUR MONEY BACK.
I'VE MADE SO MANY MISTAKES THIS YEAR.
WE ALL HAVE. BUT IF NOT NOW, WHEN?
DON'T WORRY, I FEEL LIKE OUR BIGGEST MISTAKES...ARE STILL TO COME.

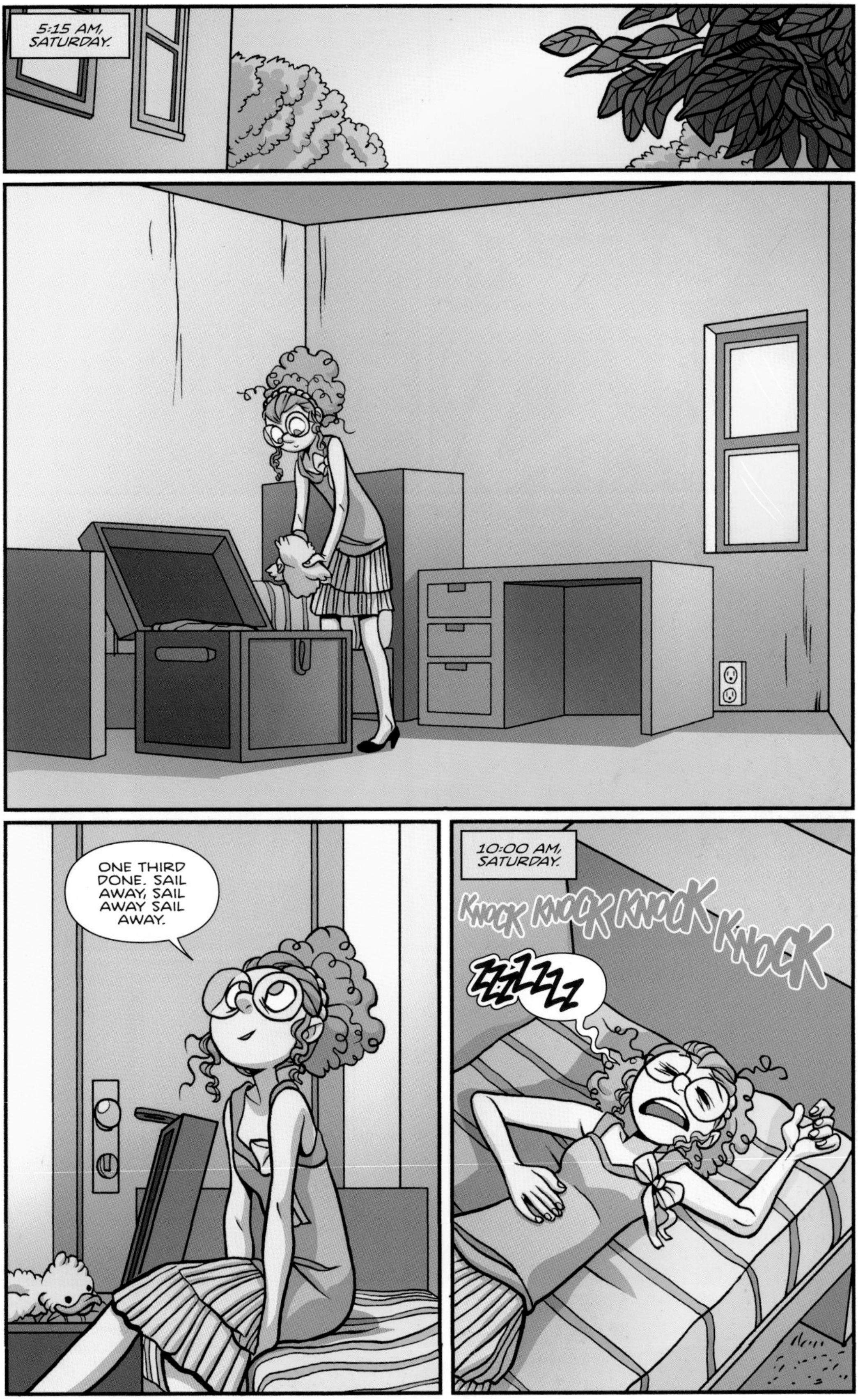
5:15 AM, SATURDAY.
ONE THIRD DONE. SAIL AWAY, SAIL AWAY SAIL AWAY.
10:00 AM, SATURDAY.
KNOCK KNOCK KNOCK KNOCK
ZZZZZZZ

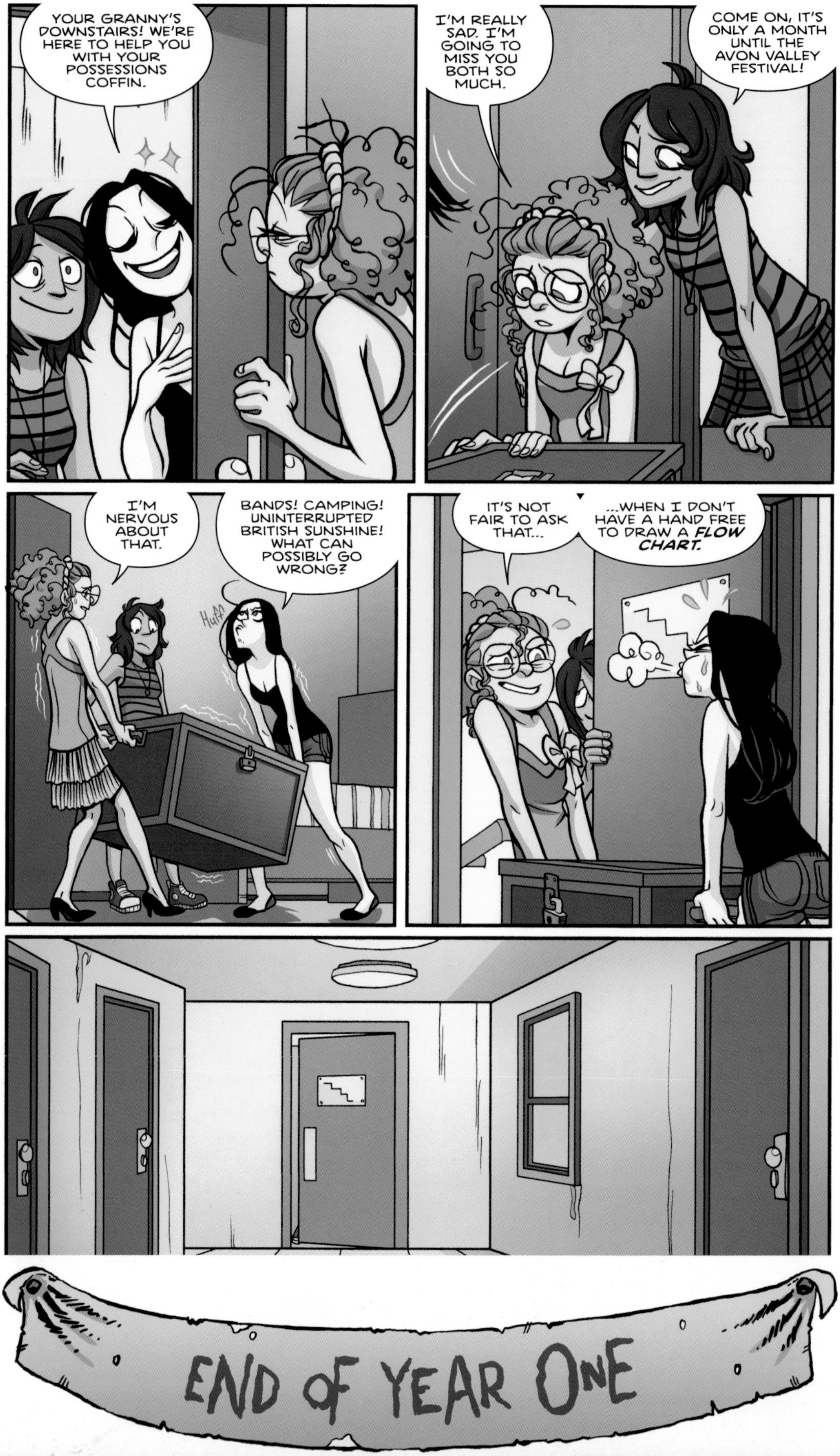
YOUR GRANNY'S DOWNSTAIRS! WE'RE HERE TO HELP YOU WITH YOUR POSSESSIONS COFFIN.
I'M REALLY SAD. I'M GOING TO MISS YOU BOTH SO MUCH.
COME ON, IT'S ONLY A MONTH UNTIL THE AVON VALLEY FESTIVAL!
I'M NERVOUS ABOUT THAT.
BANDS! CAMPING! UNINTERRUPTED BRITISH SUNSHINE! WHAT CAN POSSIBLY GO WRONG?
Huff
IT'S NOT FAIR TO ASK THAT...
...WHEN I DON'T HAVE A HAND FREE TO DRAW A *FLOW CHART.*
END OF YEAR ONE

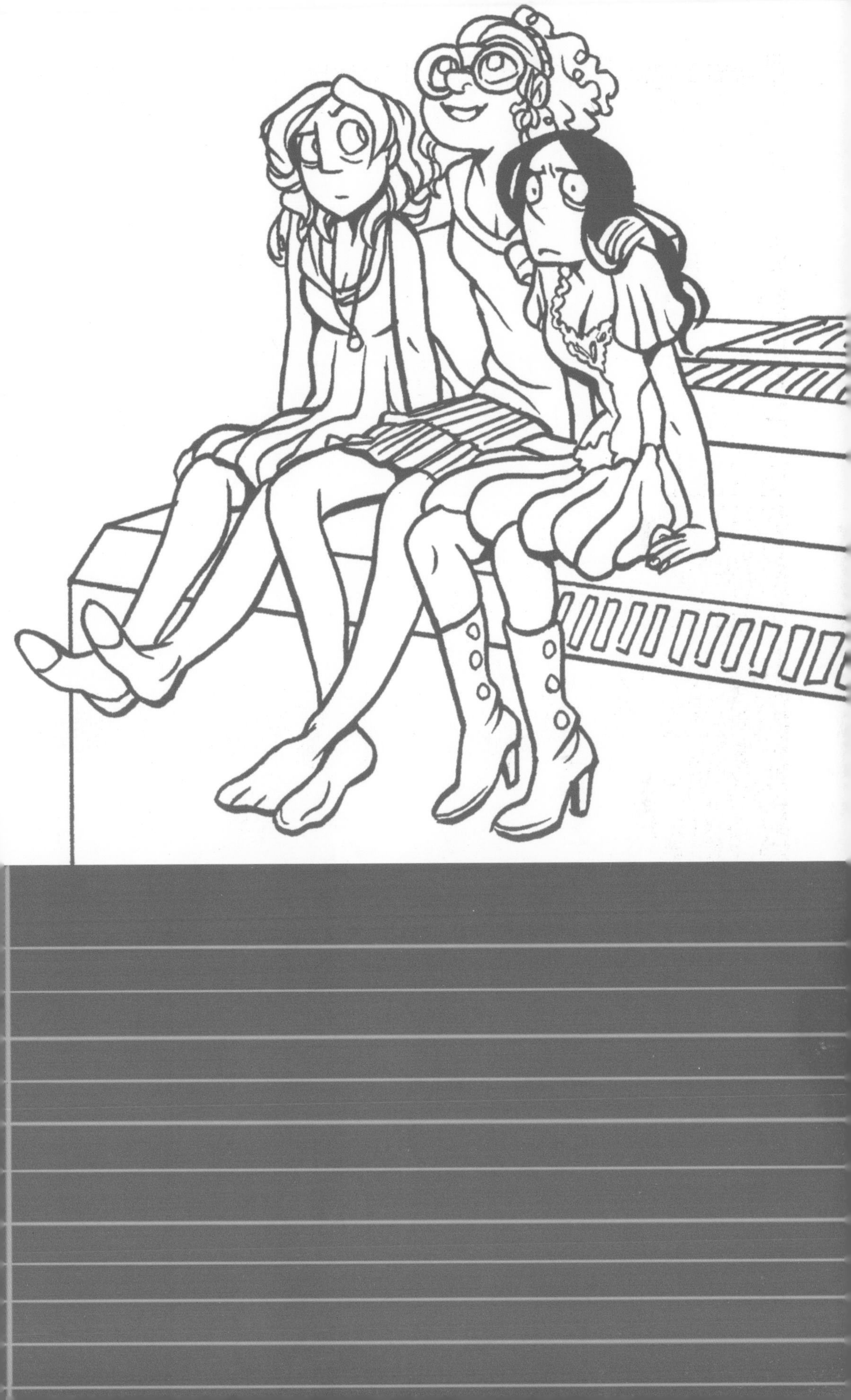

CHAPTER NINETEEN

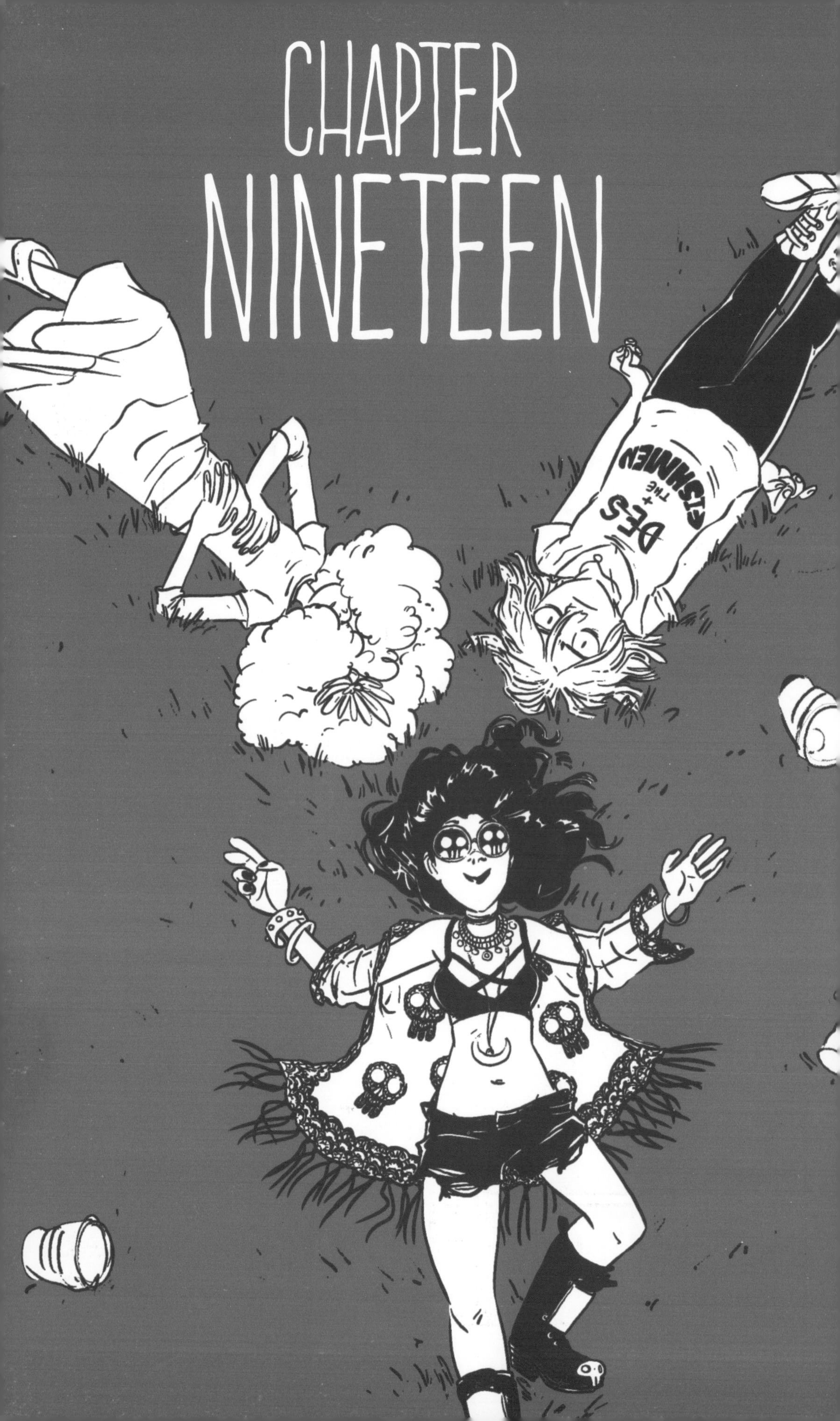
DES + THE FISHMEN

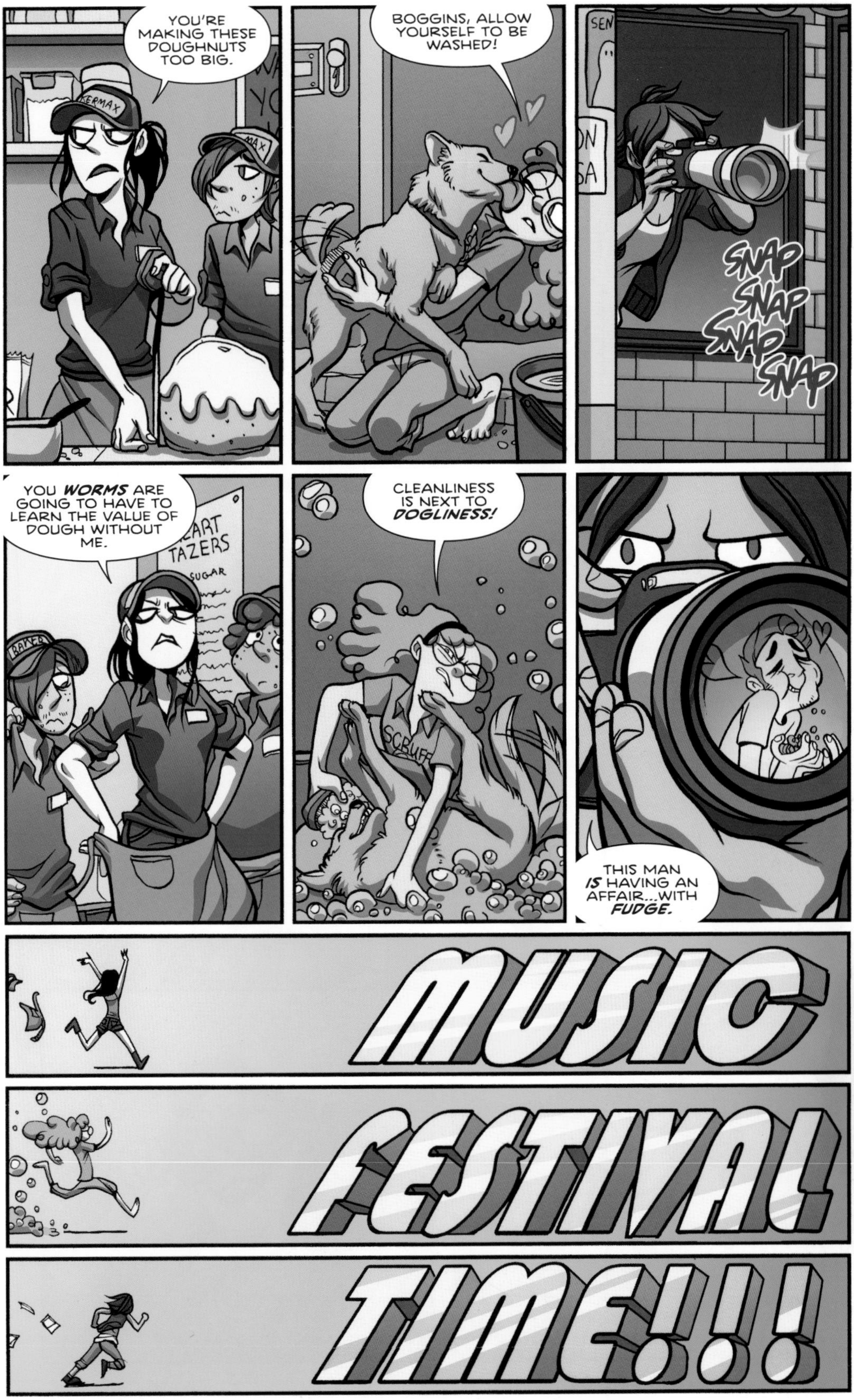
YOU'RE MAKING THESE DOUGHNUTS TOO BIG.
BOGGINS, ALLOW YOURSELF TO BE WASHED!
SNAP SNAP SNAP SNAP
YOU **WORMS** ARE GOING TO HAVE TO LEARN THE VALUE OF DOUGH WITHOUT ME.
HEART TAZERS
SUGAR
CLEANLINESS IS NEXT TO ***DOGLINESS!***
SCRUFF
THIS MAN ***IS*** HAVING AN AFFAIR...WITH ***FUDGE.***
MUSIC
FESTIVAL
TIME!!!

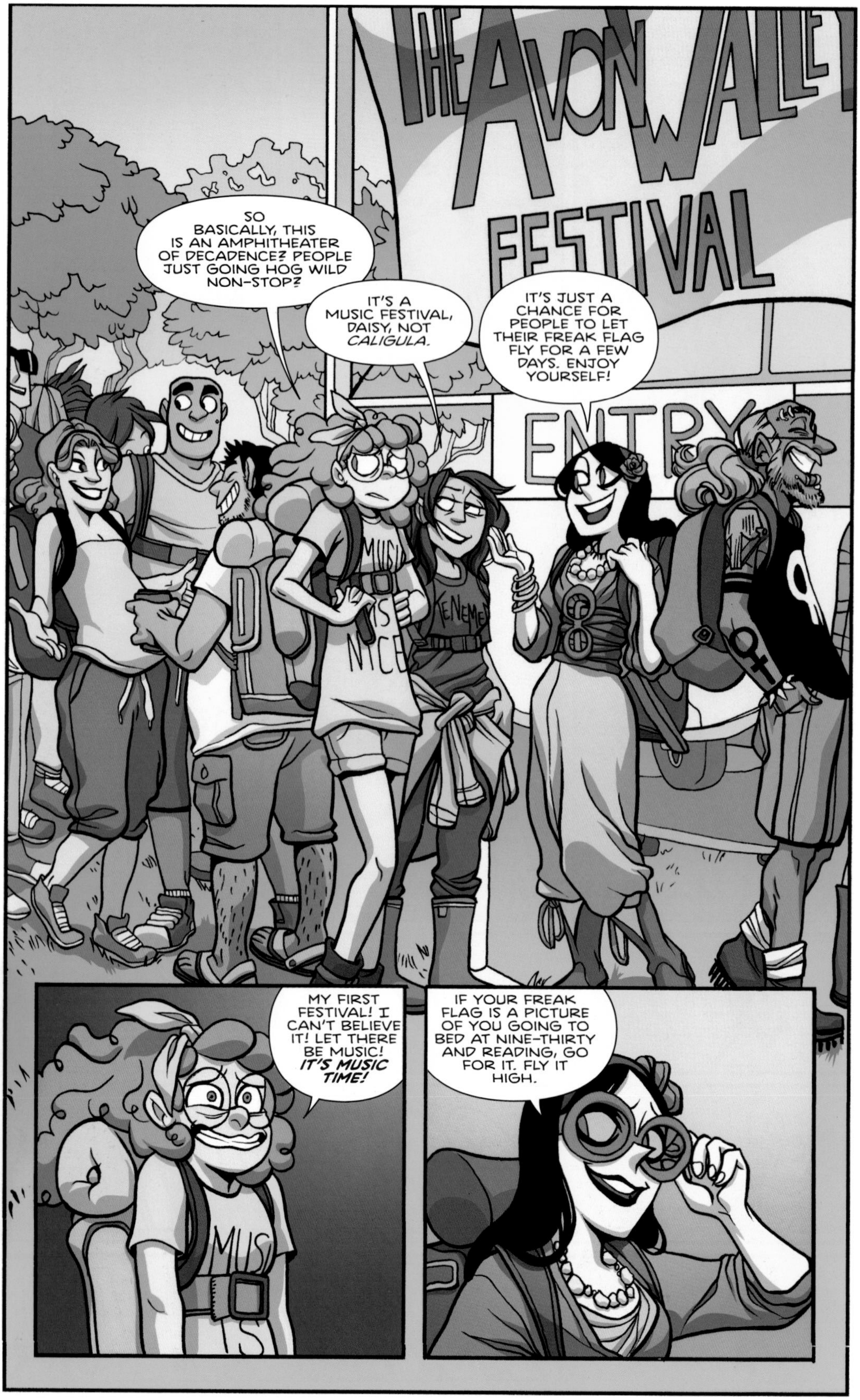
THE AVON VALLEY FESTIVAL
SO BASICALLY, THIS IS AN AMPHITHEATER OF DECADENCE? PEOPLE JUST GOING HOG WILD NON-STOP?
IT'S A MUSIC FESTIVAL, DAISY, NOT *CALIGULA.*
IT'S JUST A CHANCE FOR PEOPLE TO LET THEIR FREAK FLAG FLY FOR A FEW DAYS. ENJOY YOURSELF!
ENTRY
MY FIRST FESTIVAL! I CAN'T BELIEVE IT! LET THERE BE MUSIC! ***IT'S MUSIC TIME!***
IF YOUR FREAK FLAG IS A PICTURE OF YOU GOING TO BED AT NINE-THIRTY AND READING, GO FOR IT. FLY IT HIGH.

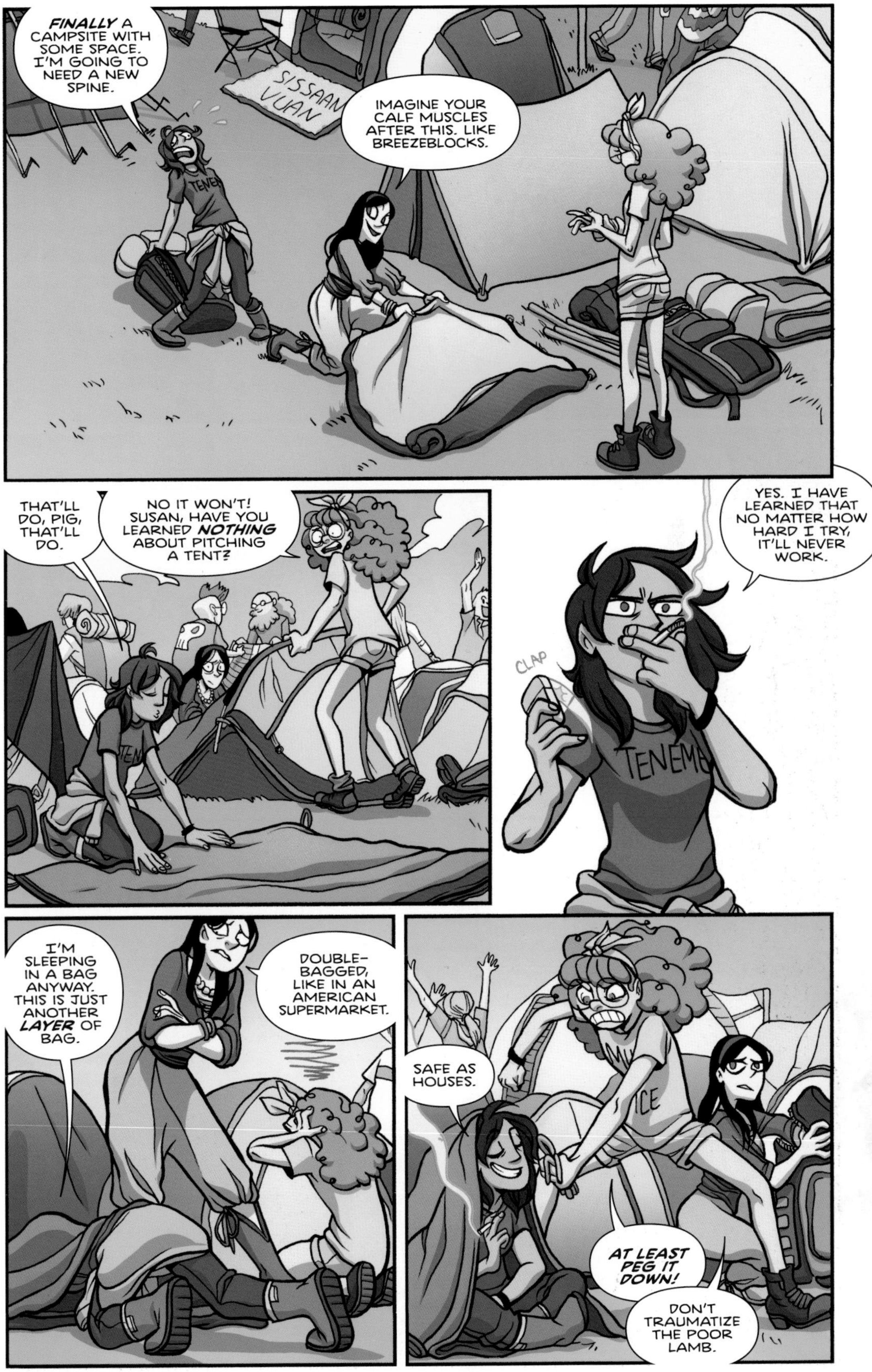
FINALLY A CAMPSITE WITH SOME SPACE. I'M GOING TO NEED A NEW SPINE.
SISSAAN VUAN
IMAGINE YOUR CALF MUSCLES AFTER THIS. LIKE BREEZEBLOCKS.
THAT'LL DO, PIG, THAT'LL DO.
NO IT WON'T! SUSAN, HAVE YOU LEARNED NOTHING ABOUT PITCHING A TENT?
YES. I HAVE LEARNED THAT NO MATTER HOW HARD I TRY, IT'LL NEVER WORK.
CLAP
I'M SLEEPING IN A BAG ANYWAY. THIS IS JUST ANOTHER LAYER OF BAG.
DOUBLE-BAGGED, LIKE IN AN AMERICAN SUPERMARKET.
SAFE AS HOUSES.
AT LEAST PEG IT DOWN!
DON'T TRAUMATIZE THE POOR LAMB.

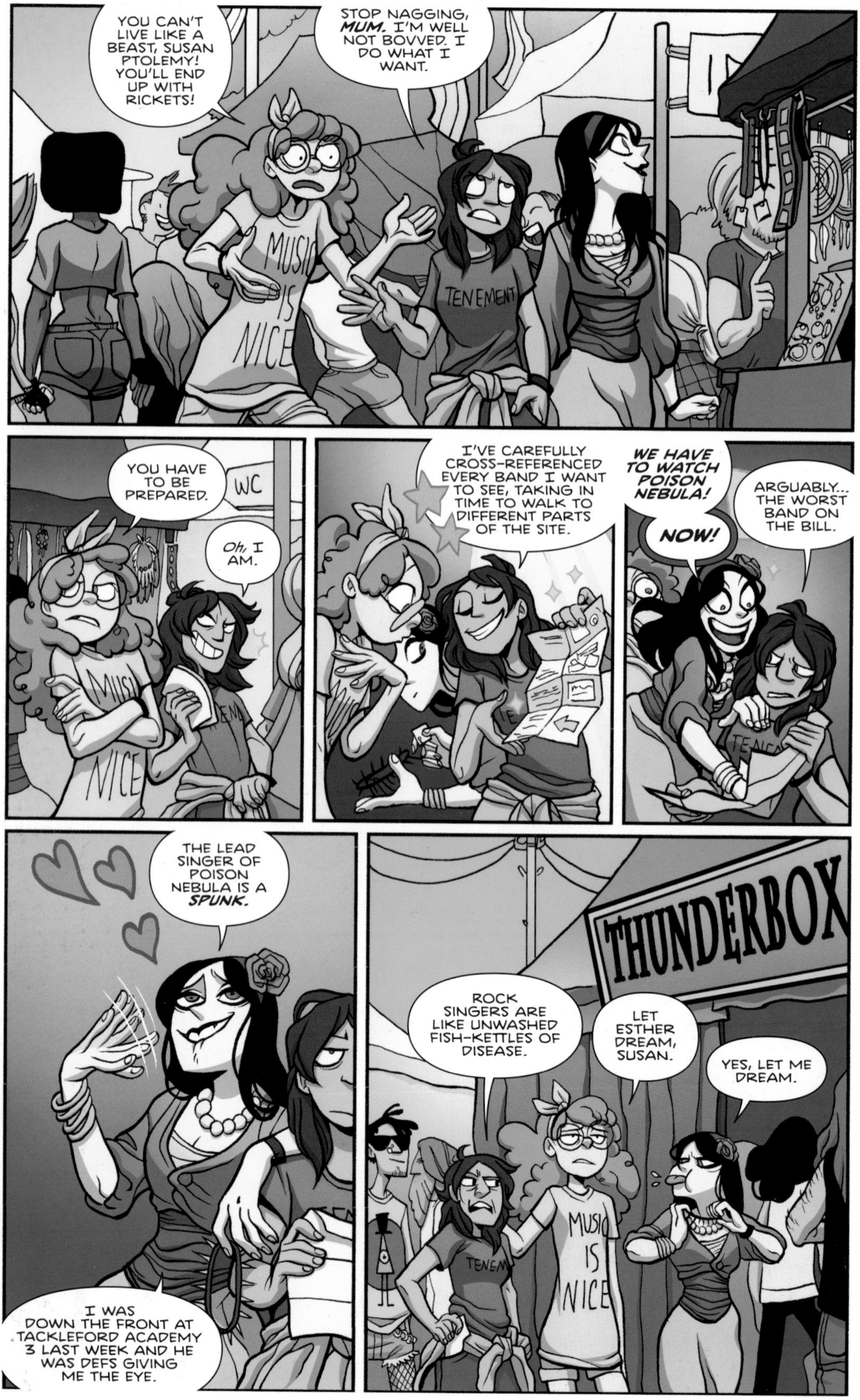
YOU CAN'T LIVE LIKE A BEAST, SUSAN PTOLEMY! YOU'LL END UP WITH RICKETS!
STOP NAGGING, *MUM.* I'M WELL NOT BOVVED. I DO WHAT I WANT.
YOU HAVE TO BE PREPARED.
WC
Oh, I AM.
I'VE CAREFULLY CROSS-REFERENCED EVERY BAND I WANT TO SEE, TAKING IN TIME TO WALK TO DIFFERENT PARTS OF THE SITE.
WE HAVE TO WATCH POISON NEBULA!
NOW!
ARGUABLY... THE WORST BAND ON THE BILL.
THE LEAD SINGER OF POISON NEBULA IS A *SPUNK.*
I WAS DOWN THE FRONT AT TACKLEFORD ACADEMY 3 LAST WEEK AND HE WAS DEFS GIVING ME THE EYE.
THUNDERBOX
ROCK SINGERS ARE LIKE UNWASHED FISH-KETTLES OF DISEASE.
LET ESTHER DREAM, SUSAN.
YES, LET ME DREAM.

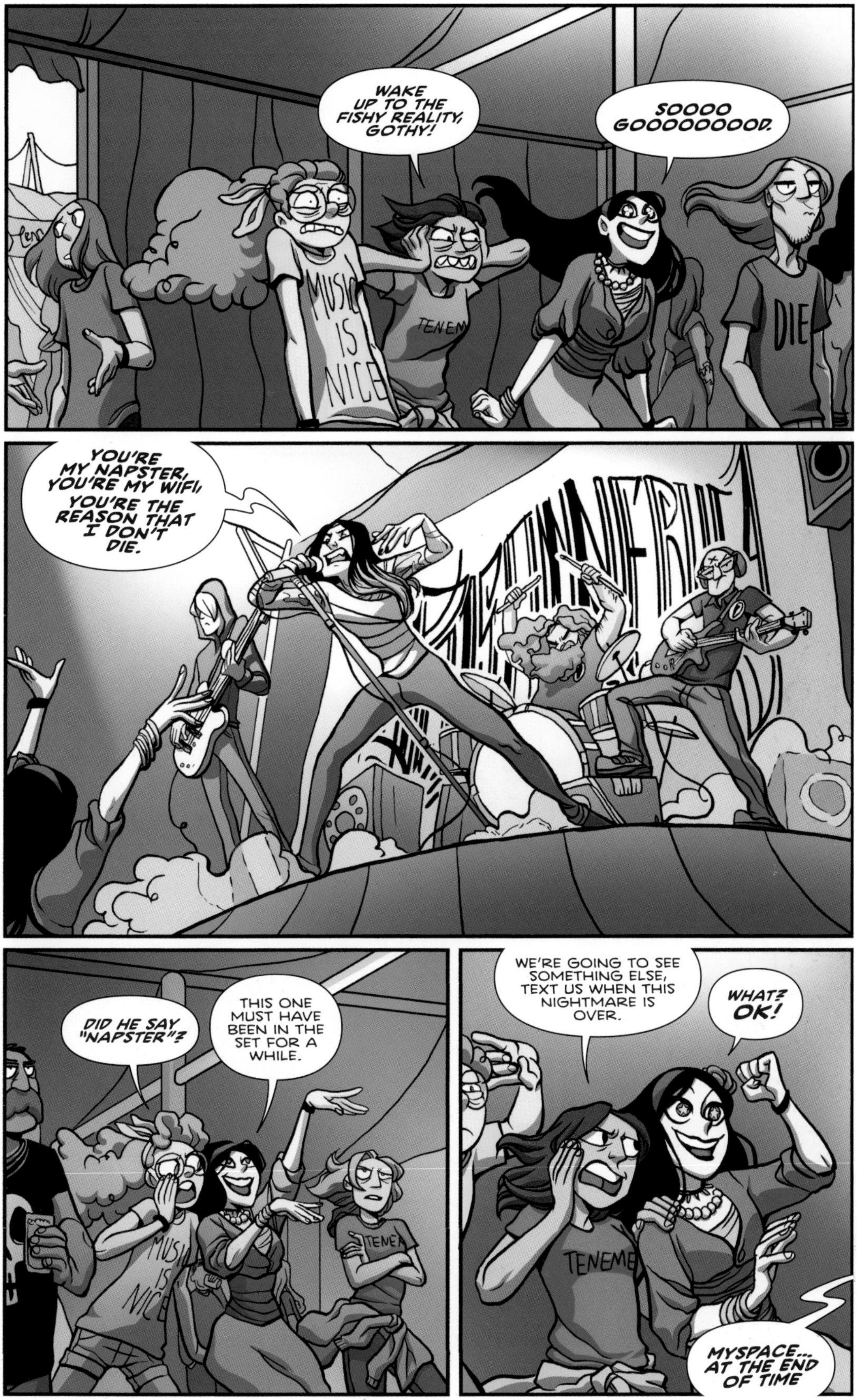
WAKE UP TO THE FISHY REALITY, GOTHY!
SOOOO GOOOOOOOOD.
MUSIC IS NICE
TENEM
DIE
YOU'RE MY NAPSTER, YOU'RE MY WIFI, YOU'RE THE REASON THAT I DON'T DIE.
DID HE SAY "NAPSTER"?
THIS ONE MUST HAVE BEEN IN THE SET FOR A WHILE.
WE'RE GOING TO SEE SOMETHING ELSE, TEXT US WHEN THIS NIGHTMARE IS OVER.
WHAT? OK!
TENEME
MYSPACE... AT THE END OF TIME

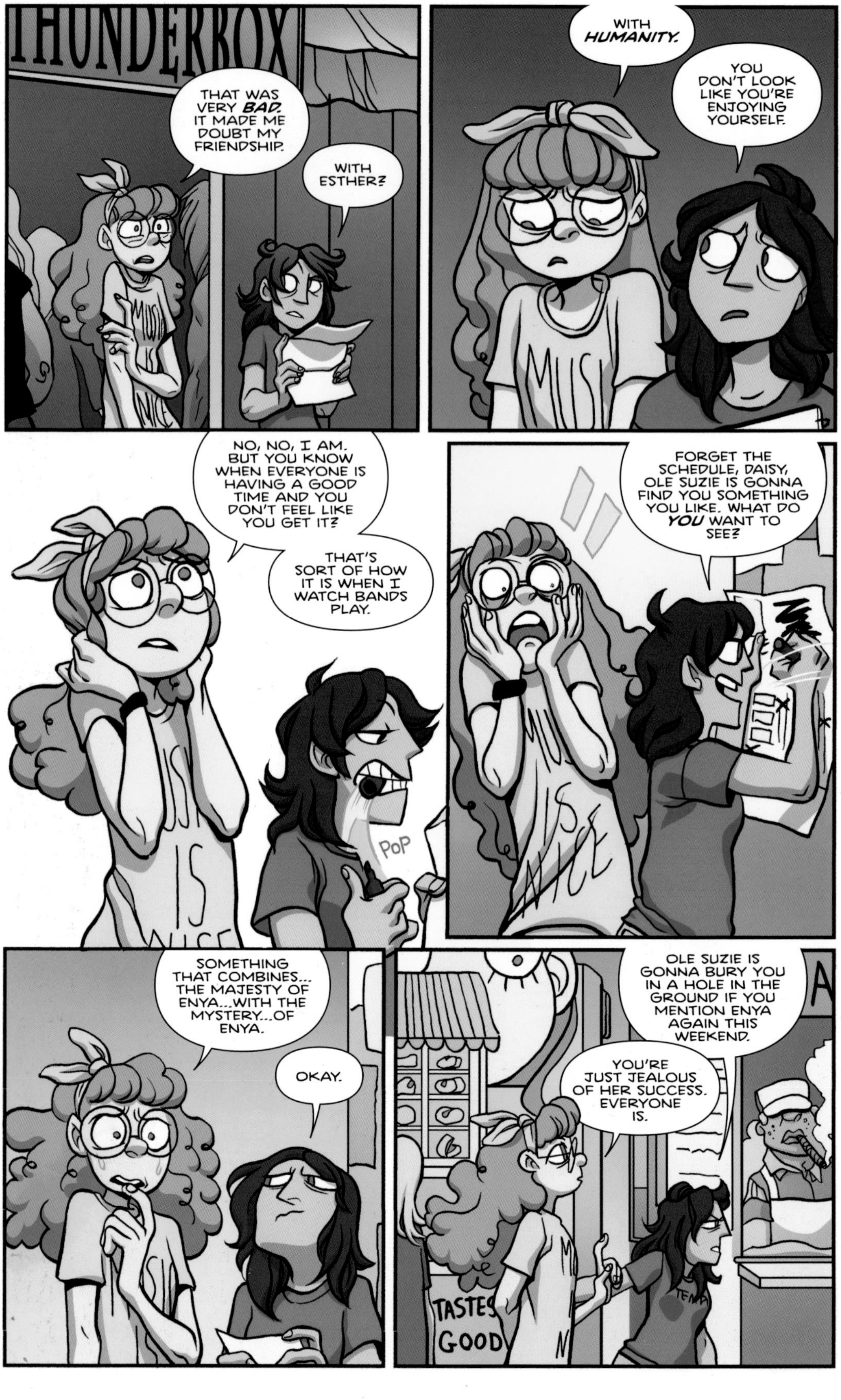
THUNDERBOX
THAT WAS VERY *BAD.* IT MADE ME DOUBT MY FRIENDSHIP.
WITH ESTHER?
WITH *HUMANITY.*
YOU DON'T LOOK LIKE YOU'RE ENJOYING YOURSELF.
NO, NO, I AM. BUT YOU KNOW WHEN EVERYONE IS HAVING A GOOD TIME AND YOU DON'T FEEL LIKE YOU GET IT?
THAT'S SORT OF HOW IT IS WHEN I WATCH BANDS PLAY.
POP
FORGET THE SCHEDULE, DAISY, OLE SUZIE IS GONNA FIND YOU SOMETHING YOU LIKE. WHAT DO *YOU* WANT TO SEE?
SOMETHING THAT COMBINES... THE MAJESTY OF ENYA...WITH THE MYSTERY...OF ENYA.
OKAY.
OLE SUZIE IS GONNA BURY YOU IN A HOLE IN THE GROUND IF YOU MENTION ENYA AGAIN THIS WEEKEND.
YOU'RE JUST JEALOUS OF HER SUCCESS. EVERYONE IS.
TASTES GOOD

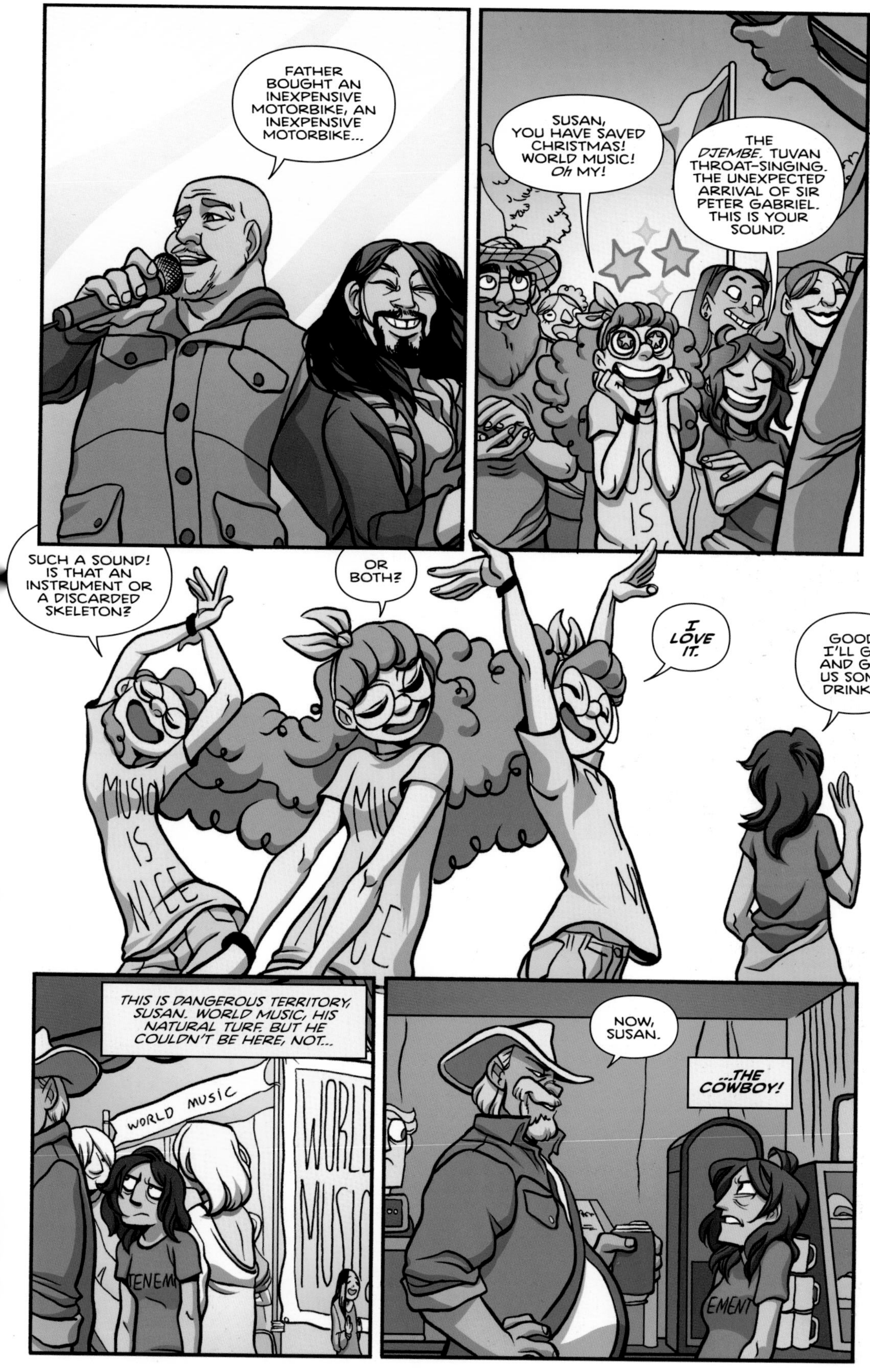
FATHER BOUGHT AN INEXPENSIVE MOTORBIKE, AN INEXPENSIVE MOTORBIKE...
SUSAN, YOU HAVE SAVED CHRISTMAS! WORLD MUSIC! *Oh* MY!
THE *DJEMBE*. TUVAN THROAT-SINGING. THE UNEXPECTED ARRIVAL OF SIR PETER GABRIEL. THIS IS YOUR SOUND.
SUCH A SOUND! IS THAT AN INSTRUMENT OR A DISCARDED SKELETON?
OR BOTH?
I LOVE IT.
GOOD. I'LL GO AND GET US SOME DRINKS.
MUSIC IS NICE
THIS IS DANGEROUS TERRITORY, SUSAN. WORLD MUSIC, HIS NATURAL TURF. BUT HE COULDN'T BE HERE, NOT...
WORLD MUSIC
WORLD MUSIC
TENEM
NOW, SUSAN.
...THE COWBOY!
EMENT

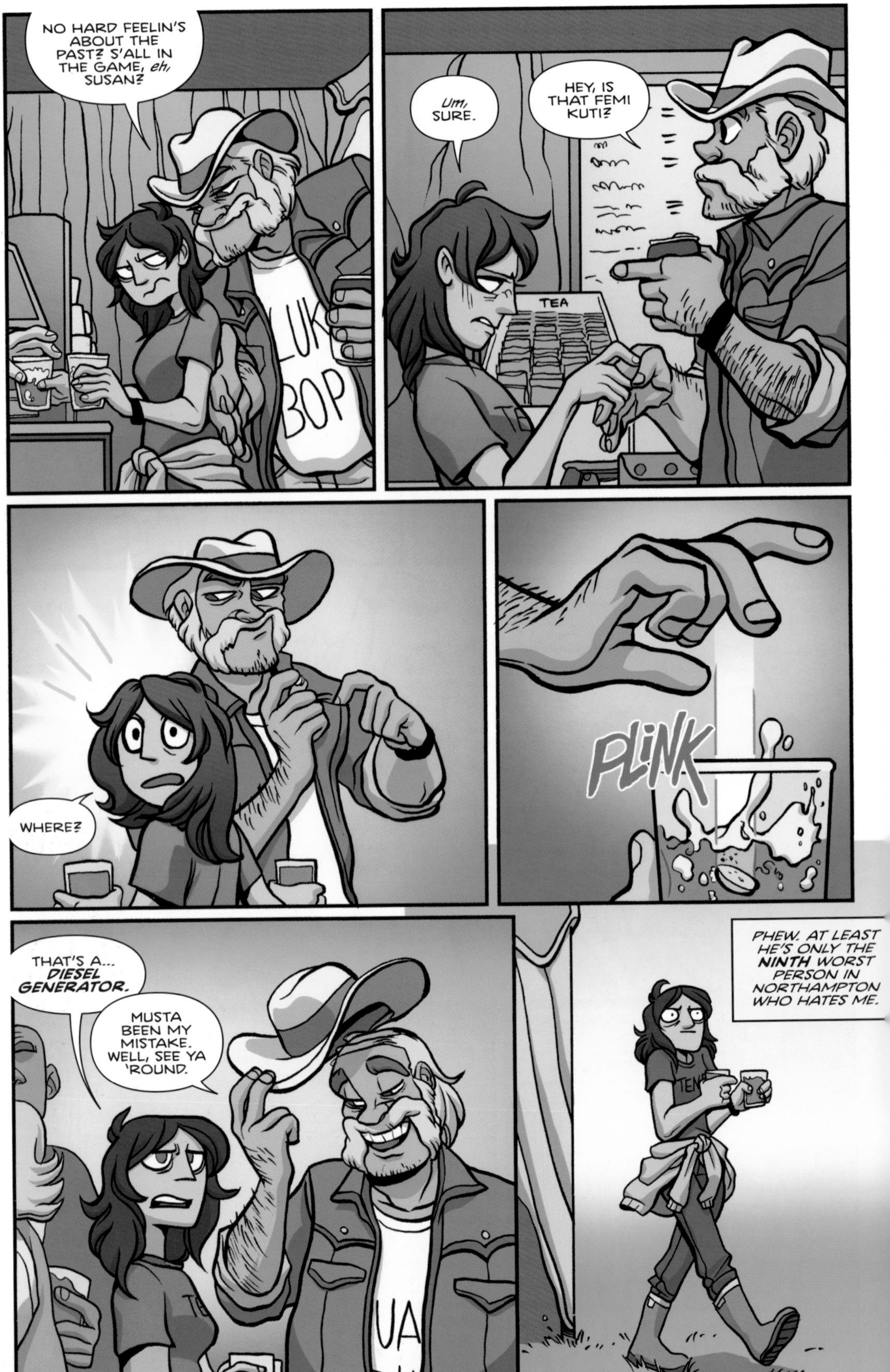

NO HARD FEELIN'S ABOUT THE PAST? S'ALL IN THE GAME, *eh,* SUSAN?
LUK BOP
Um, SURE.
HEY, IS THAT FEMI KUTI?
TEA
WHERE?
PLINK
THAT'S A... ***DIESEL GENERATOR.***
MUSTA BEEN MY MISTAKE. WELL, SEE YA 'ROUND.
*PHEW. AT LEAST HE'S ONLY THE **NINTH** WORST PERSON IN NORTHAMPTON WHO HATES ME.*

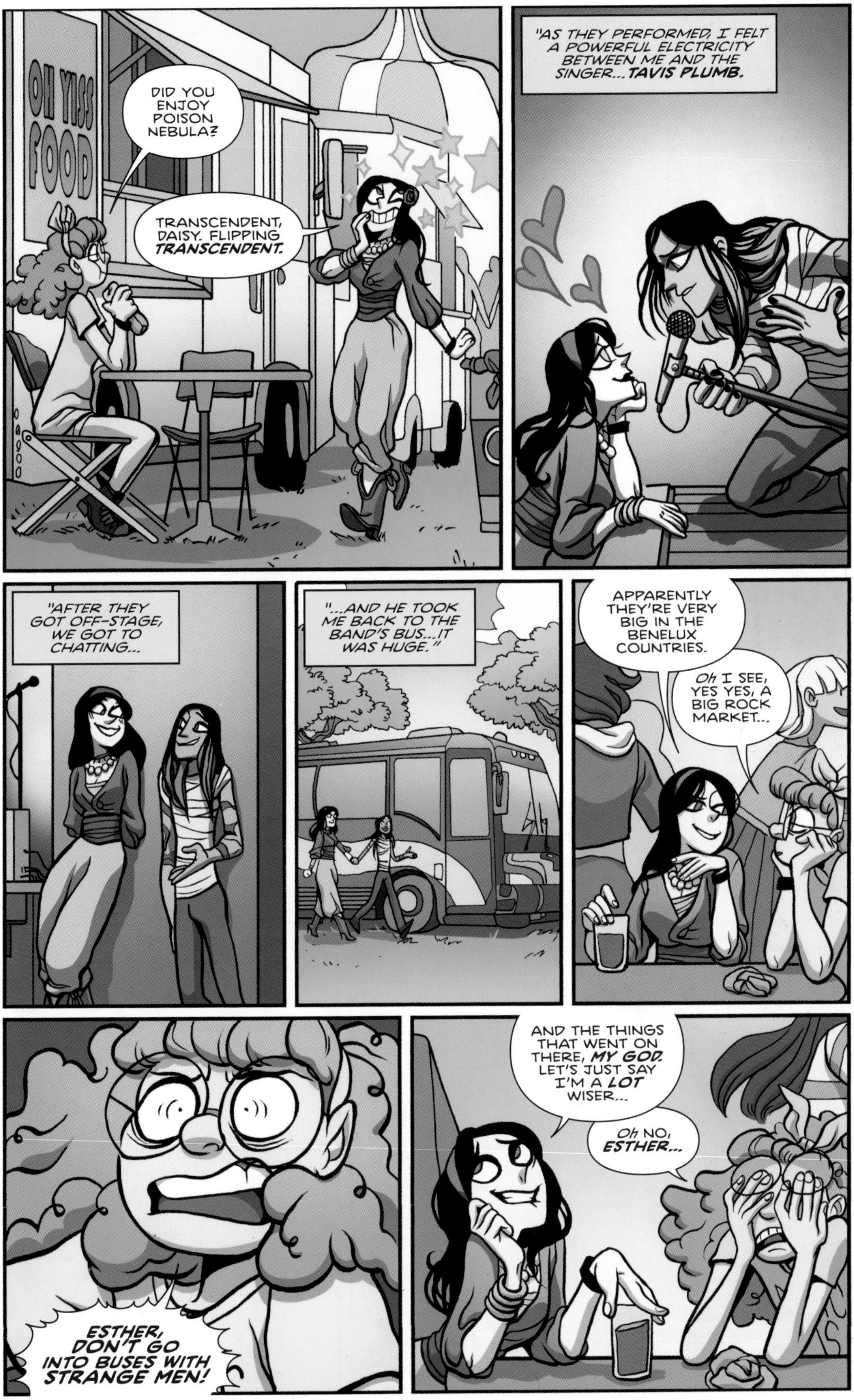

OH YISS FOOD
DID YOU ENJOY POISON NEBULA?
TRANSCENDENT, DAISY. FLIPPING TRANSCENDENT.
"AS THEY PERFORMED, I FELT A POWERFUL ELECTRICITY BETWEEN ME AND THE SINGER... TAVIS PLUMB.
"AFTER THEY GOT OFF-STAGE, WE GOT TO CHATTING...
"...AND HE TOOK ME BACK TO THE BAND'S BUS... IT WAS HUGE."
APPARENTLY THEY'RE VERY BIG IN THE BENELUX COUNTRIES.
Oh I SEE, YES YES, A BIG ROCK MARKET...
ESTHER, DON'T GO INTO BUSES WITH STRANGE MEN!
AND THE THINGS THAT WENT ON THERE, MY GOD. LET'S JUST SAY I'M A LOT WISER...
Oh NO, ESTHER...

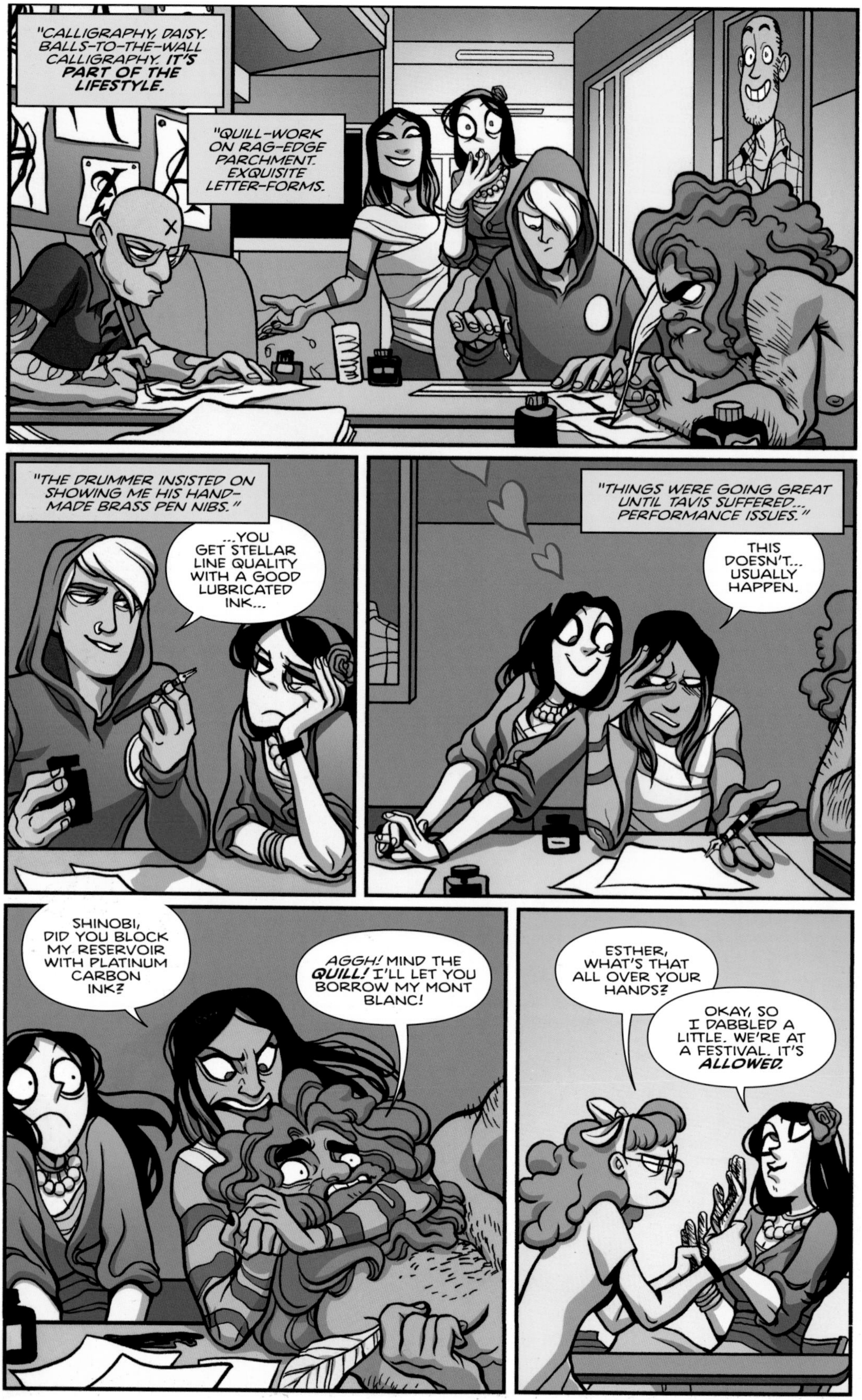
"CALLIGRAPHY, DAISY. BALLS-TO-THE-WALL CALLIGRAPHY. IT'S PART OF THE LIFESTYLE.
"QUILL-WORK ON RAG-EDGE PARCHMENT. EXQUISITE LETTER-FORMS.
"THE DRUMMER INSISTED ON SHOWING ME HIS HAND-MADE BRASS PEN NIBS."
...YOU GET STELLAR LINE QUALITY WITH A GOOD LUBRICATED INK...
"THINGS WERE GOING GREAT UNTIL TAVIS SUFFERED... PERFORMANCE ISSUES."
THIS DOESN'T... USUALLY HAPPEN.
SHINOBI, DID YOU BLOCK MY RESERVOIR WITH PLATINUM CARBON INK?
AGGH! MIND THE QUILL! I'LL LET YOU BORROW MY MONT BLANC!
ESTHER, WHAT'S THAT ALL OVER YOUR HANDS?
OKAY, SO I DABBLED A LITTLE. WE'RE AT A FESTIVAL. IT'S ALLOWED.

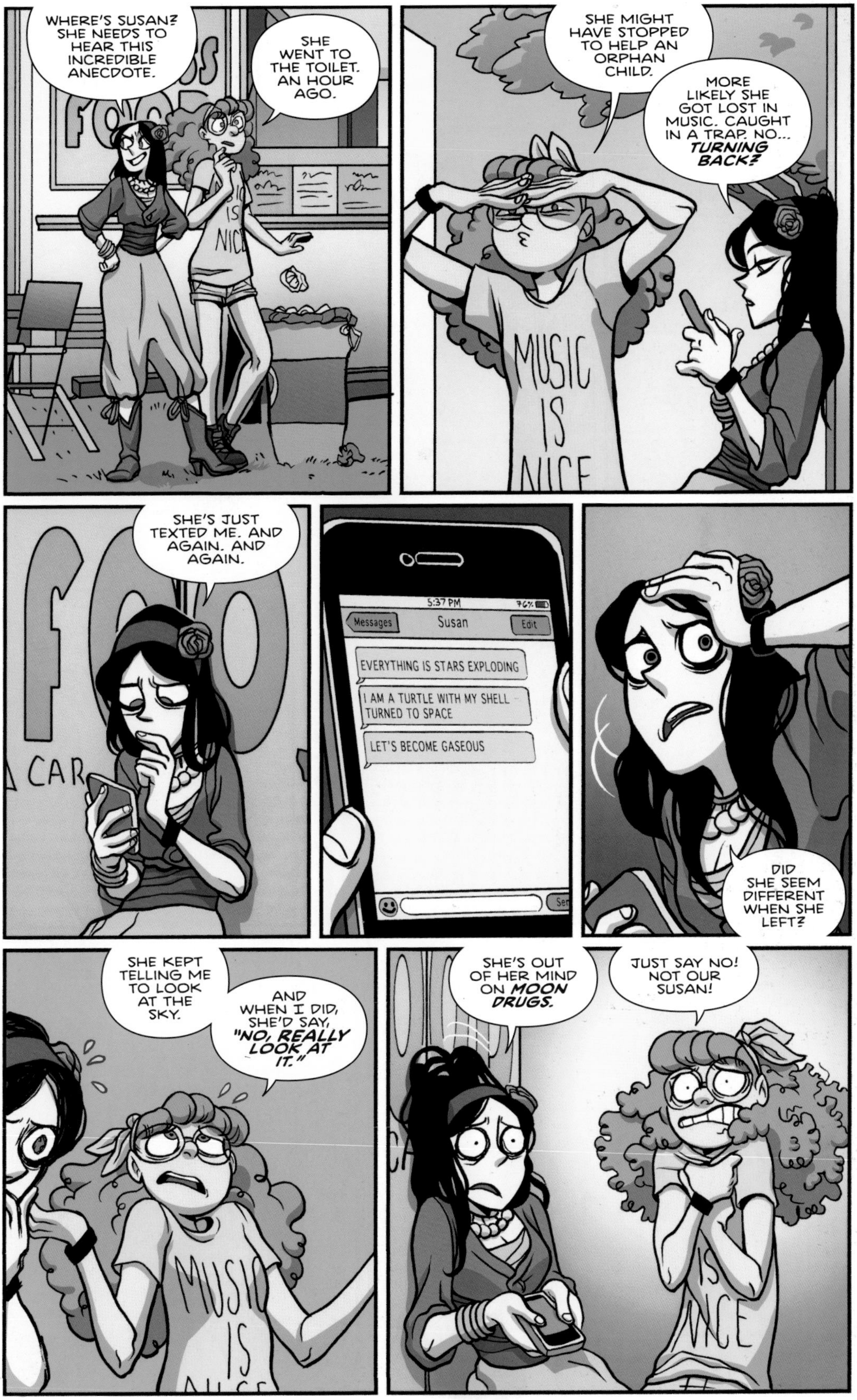

WHERE'S SUSAN? SHE NEEDS TO HEAR THIS INCREDIBLE ANECDOTE.
SHE WENT TO THE TOILET. AN HOUR AGO.
SHE MIGHT HAVE STOPPED TO HELP AN ORPHAN CHILD.
MORE LIKELY SHE GOT LOST IN MUSIC. CAUGHT IN A TRAP. NO... TURNING BACK?
MUSIC IS NICE
SHE'S JUST TEXTED ME. AND AGAIN. AND AGAIN.
5:37 PM
Messages
Susan
Edit
EVERYTHING IS STARS EXPLODING
I AM A TURTLE WITH MY SHELL TURNED TO SPACE
LET'S BECOME GASEOUS
DID SHE SEEM DIFFERENT WHEN SHE LEFT?
SHE KEPT TELLING ME TO LOOK AT THE SKY.
AND WHEN I DID, SHE'D SAY, "NO, REALLY LOOK AT IT."
SHE'S OUT OF HER MIND ON MOON DRUGS.
JUST SAY NO! NOT OUR SUSAN!

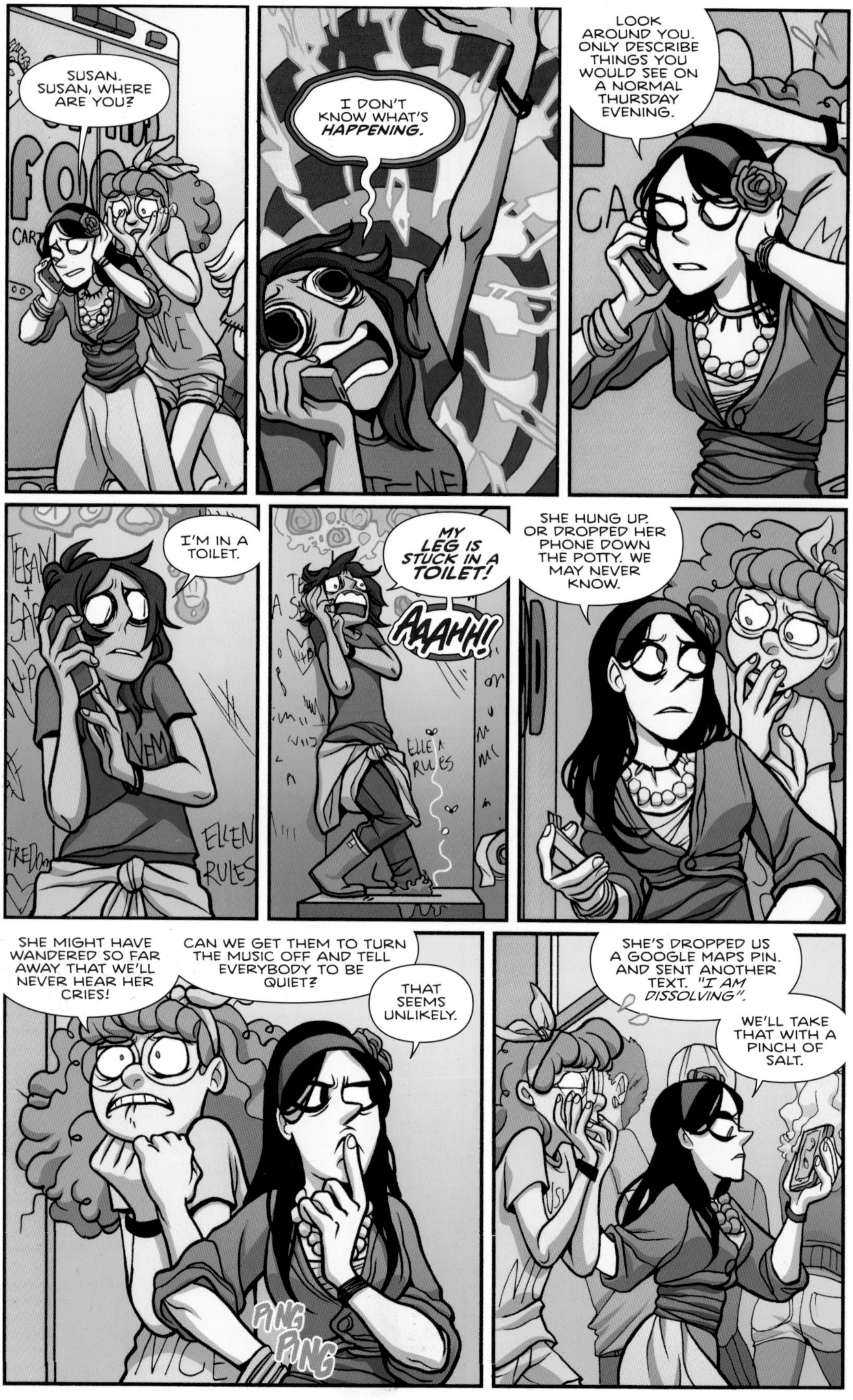
SUSAN. SUSAN, WHERE ARE YOU?
I DON'T KNOW WHAT'S *HAPPENING.*
LOOK AROUND YOU. ONLY DESCRIBE THINGS YOU WOULD SEE ON A NORMAL THURSDAY EVENING.
I'M IN A TOILET.
MY LEG IS STUCK IN A TOILET!
AAAHH!
SHE HUNG UP. OR DROPPED HER PHONE DOWN THE POTTY. WE MAY NEVER KNOW.
SHE MIGHT HAVE WANDERED SO FAR AWAY THAT WE'LL NEVER HEAR HER CRIES!
CAN WE GET THEM TO TURN THE MUSIC OFF AND TELL EVERYBODY TO BE QUIET?
THAT SEEMS UNLIKELY.
PING
PING
SHE'S DROPPED US A GOOGLE MAPS PIN. AND SENT ANOTHER TEXT. *"I AM DISSOLVING".*
WE'LL TAKE THAT WITH A PINCH OF SALT.

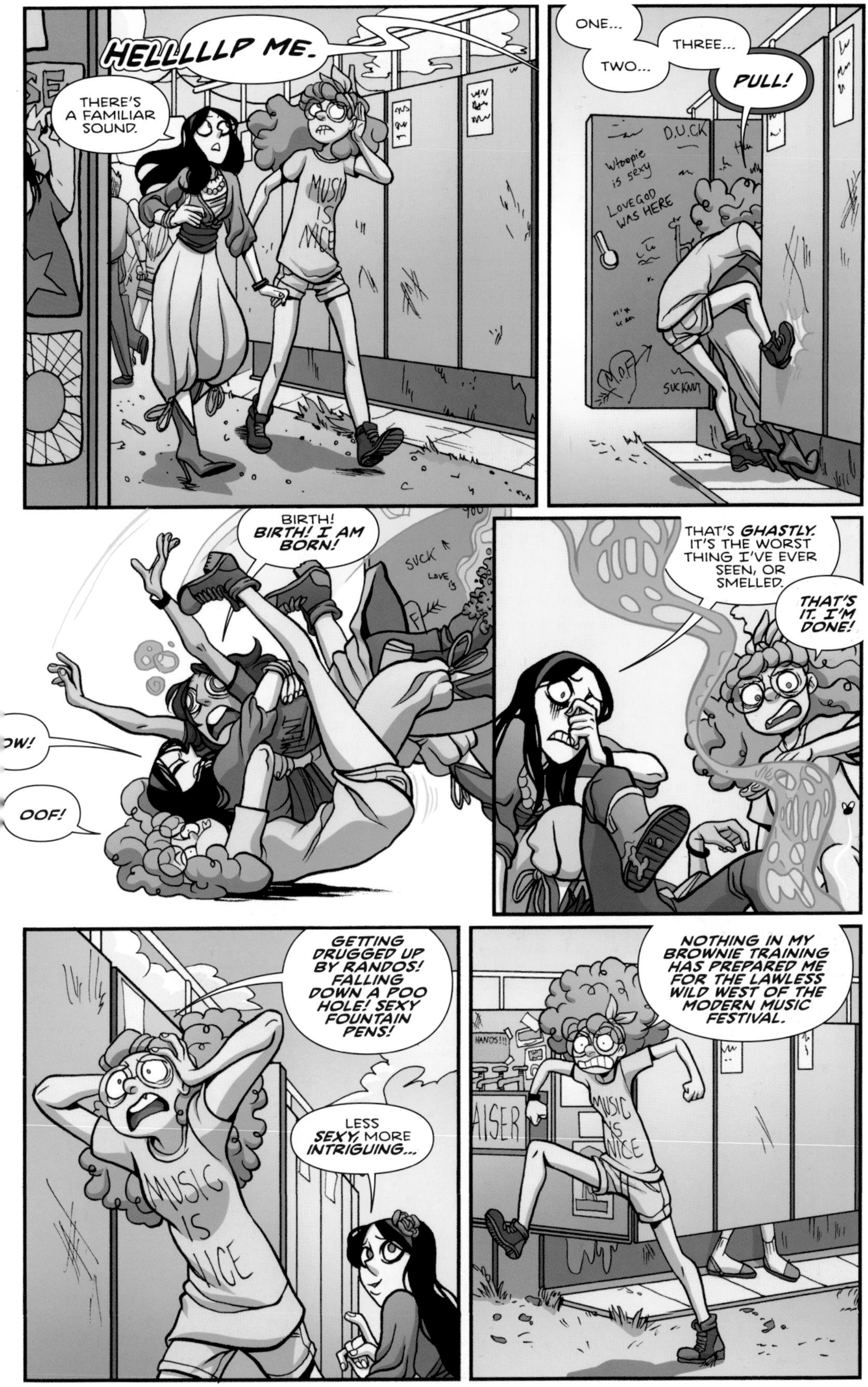
HELLLLLP ME.
THERE'S A FAMILIAR SOUND.
ONE...
TWO...
THREE...
PULL!
D.U.CK
Wroopie is sexy
LOVEGOD WAS HERE
SUCKNUT
BIRTH! BIRTH! I AM BORN!
OW!
OOF!
THAT'S GHASTLY. IT'S THE WORST THING I'VE EVER SEEN, OR SMELLED.
THAT'S IT. I'M DONE!
GETTING DRUGGED UP BY RANDOS! FALLING DOWN A POO HOLE! SEXY FOUNTAIN PENS!
LESS SEXY, MORE INTRIGUING...
MUSIC IS NICE
NOTHING IN MY BROWNIE TRAINING HAS PREPARED ME FOR THE LAWLESS WILD WEST OF THE MODERN MUSIC FESTIVAL.

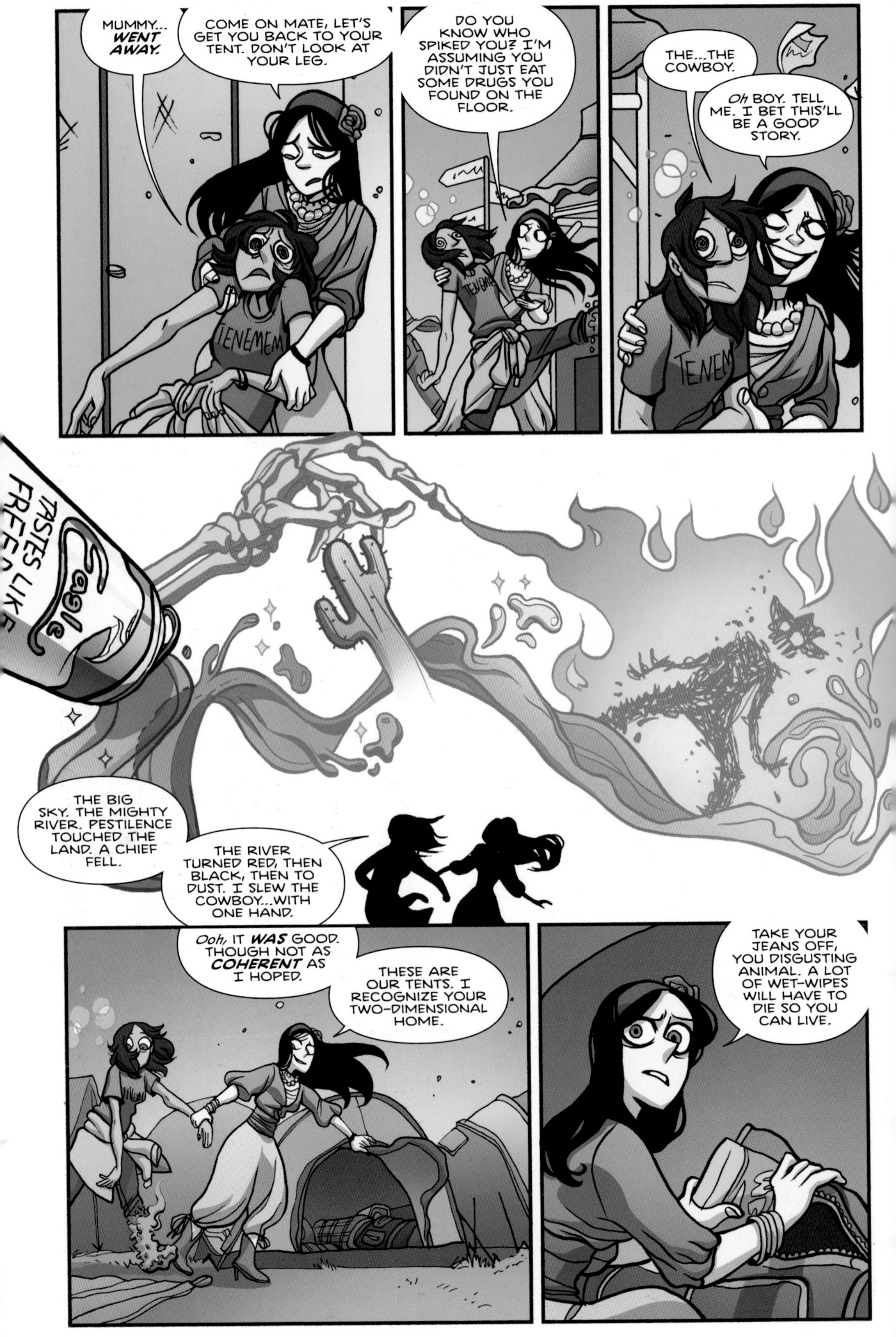

MUMMY... *WENT AWAY.*
COME ON MATE, LET'S GET YOU BACK TO YOUR TENT. DON'T LOOK AT YOUR LEG.
TENEMEM
DO YOU KNOW WHO SPIKED YOU? I'M ASSUMING YOU DIDN'T JUST EAT SOME DRUGS YOU FOUND ON THE FLOOR.
THE...THE COWBOY.
Oh BOY. TELL ME. I BET THIS'LL BE A GOOD STORY.
Eagle
TASTES LIKE FREED
THE BIG SKY. THE MIGHTY RIVER. PESTILENCE TOUCHED THE LAND. A CHIEF FELL.
THE RIVER TURNED RED, THEN BLACK, THEN TO DUST. I SLEW THE COWBOY...WITH ONE HAND.
Ooh, IT ***WAS*** GOOD. THOUGH NOT AS ***COHERENT*** AS I HOPED.
THESE ARE OUR TENTS. I RECOGNIZE YOUR TWO-DIMENSIONAL HOME.
TAKE YOUR JEANS OFF, YOU DISGUSTING ANIMAL. A LOT OF WET-WIPES WILL HAVE TO DIE SO YOU CAN LIVE.

WOULD YOU LIKE TO SIGN A PETITION TO BAN MICROBEADS IN SHAMPOO? STOP PLASTIC ENTERING THE FOOD CHAIN!

GREENPEACE

I DIDN'T EVEN **KNOW** ABOUT MICROBEADS. THINGS JUST GET **WORSE AND WORSE** HERE.

Peace & Healing fields

PEACE AND HEALING, THAT'S WHAT I NEED. PEACE...AND HEALING.

HELP ME! I NEED TO MEDITATE! MY CHAKRAS ARE ALL OVER THE PLACE!

I THINK THAT SPOT IS THE INTERSECTION OF TWO LEY LINES. GIVE IT A GO.

EGG SANDWICH... EGG SANDWICH... EGG SANDWICH.

MUSIC IS

FLINK FLINK

MOTHER EARTH, WHY DO YOU SCORN ME?

MUSIC IS

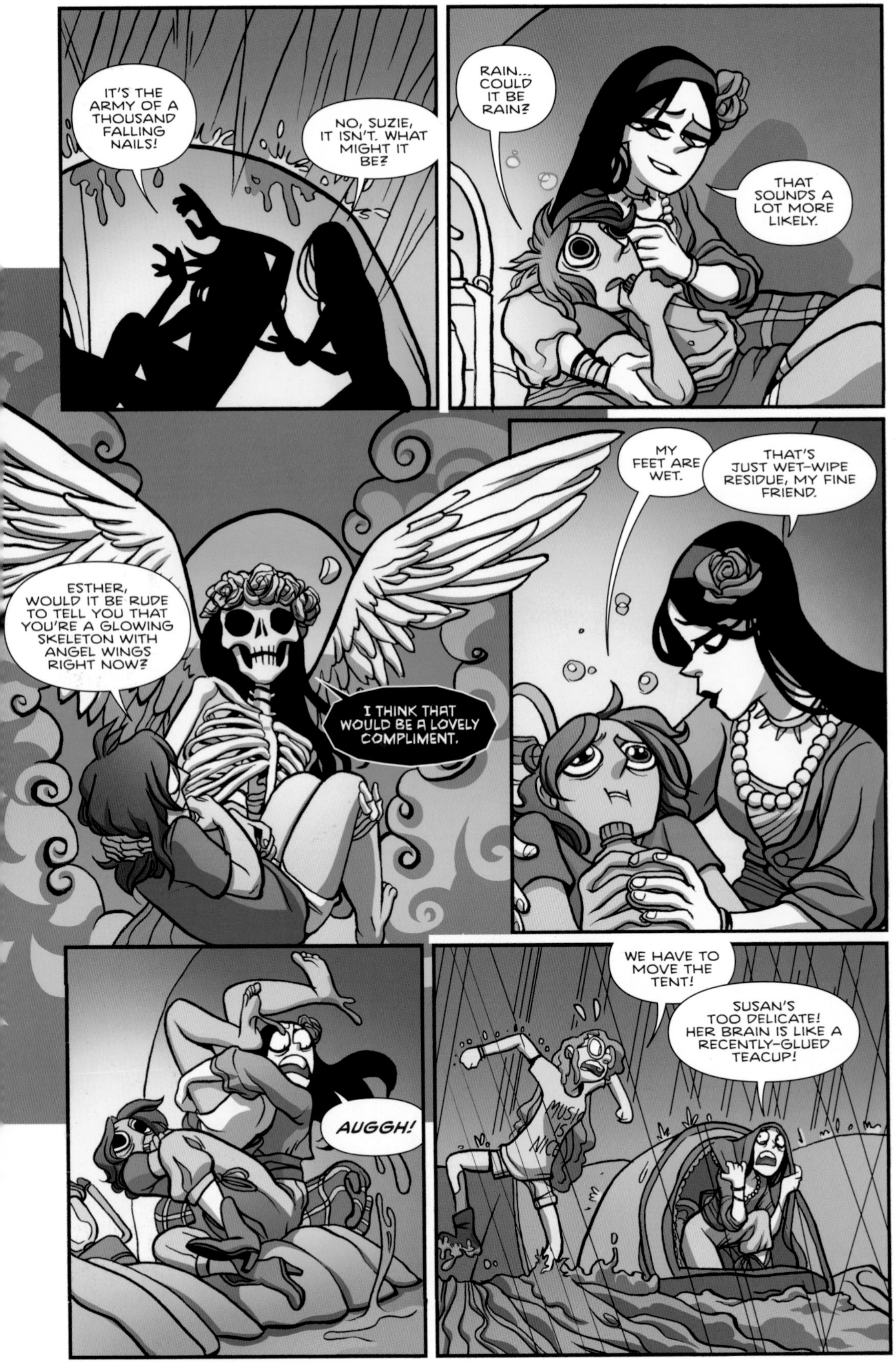
IT'S THE ARMY OF A THOUSAND FALLING NAILS!
NO, SUZIE, IT ISN'T. WHAT MIGHT IT BE?
RAIN... COULD IT BE RAIN?
THAT SOUNDS A LOT MORE LIKELY.
ESTHER, WOULD IT BE RUDE TO TELL YOU THAT YOU'RE A GLOWING SKELETON WITH ANGEL WINGS RIGHT NOW?
I THINK THAT WOULD BE A LOVELY COMPLIMENT.
MY FEET ARE WET.
THAT'S JUST WET-WIPE RESIDUE, MY FINE FRIEND.
AUGGH!
WE HAVE TO MOVE THE TENT!
SUSAN'S TOO DELICATE! HER BRAIN IS LIKE A RECENTLY-GLUED TEACUP!
MUSIC IS NICE

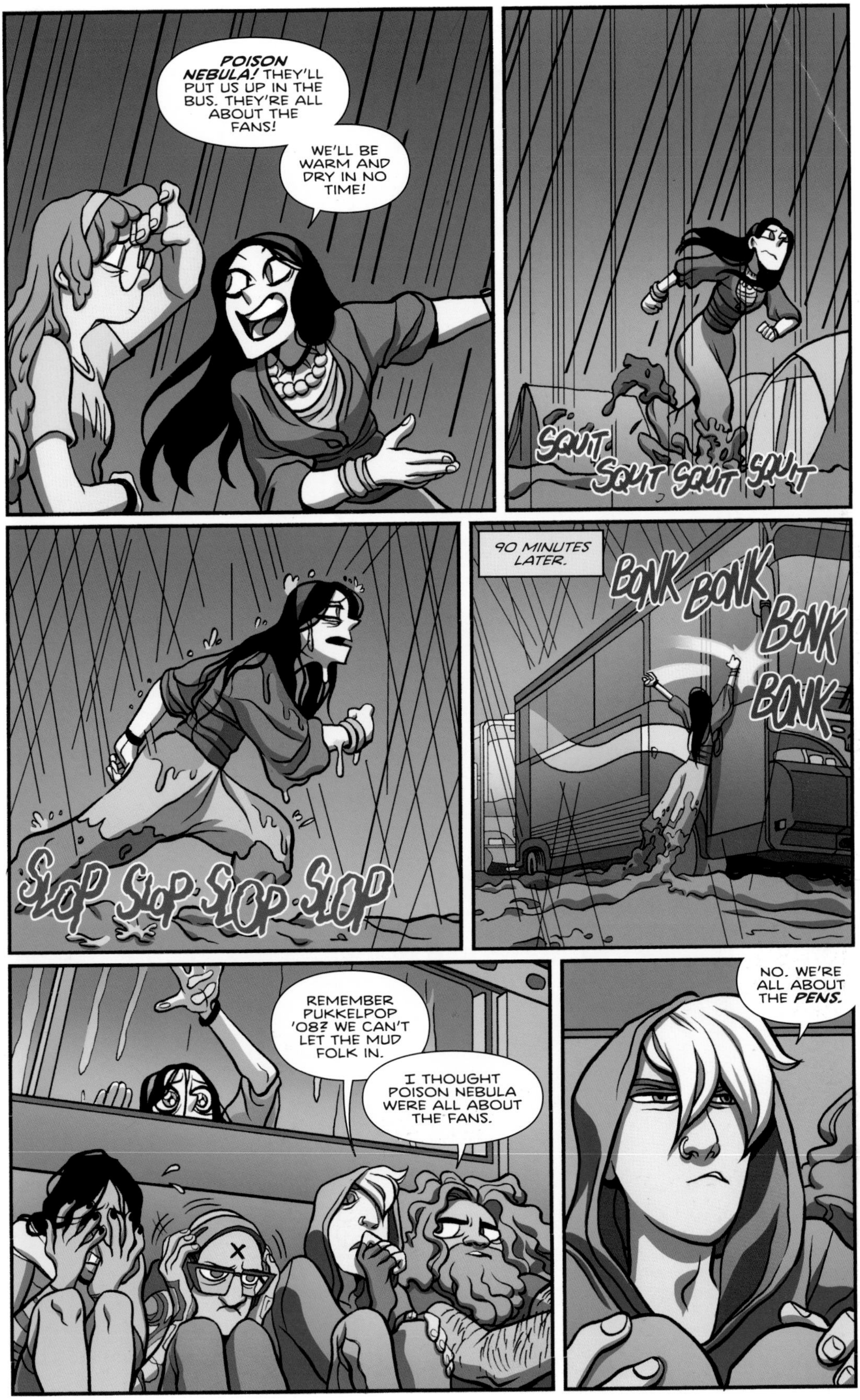
POISON NEBULA! THEY'LL PUT US UP IN THE BUS. THEY'RE ALL ABOUT THE FANS!
WE'LL BE WARM AND DRY IN NO TIME!
SQUIT SQUIT SQUIT SQUIT
SLOP SLOP SLOP SLOP
90 MINUTES LATER.
BONK BONK BONK BONK
REMEMBER PUKKELPOP '08? WE CAN'T LET THE MUD FOLK IN.
I THOUGHT POISON NEBULA WERE ALL ABOUT THE FANS.
NO. WE'RE ALL ABOUT THE PENS.

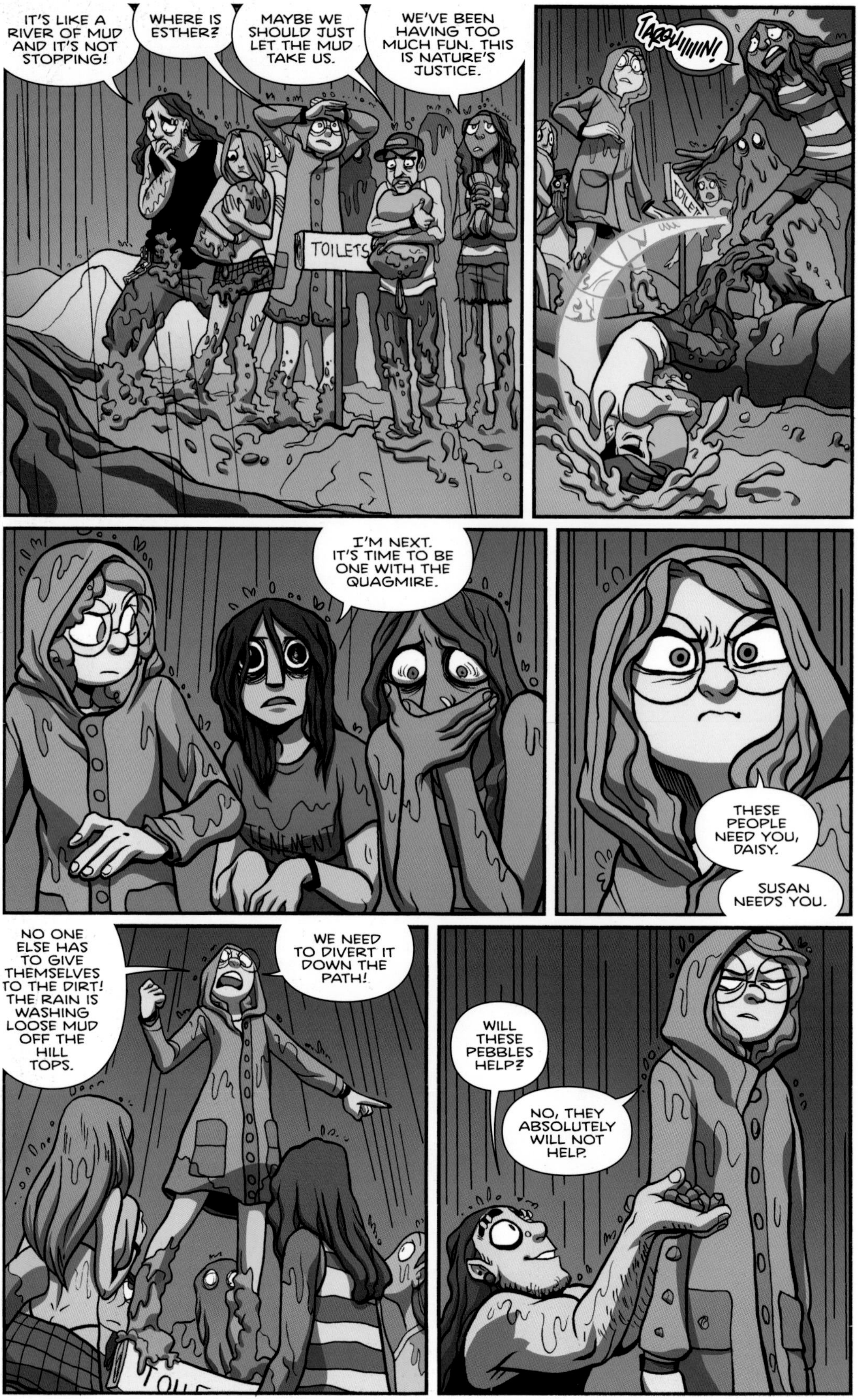
IT'S LIKE A RIVER OF MUD AND IT'S NOT STOPPING!
WHERE IS ESTHER?
MAYBE WE SHOULD JUST LET THE MUD TAKE US.
WE'VE BEEN HAVING TOO MUCH FUN. THIS IS NATURE'S JUSTICE.
TOILETS
TARGU!!!!!!N!
TOILETS
I'M NEXT. IT'S TIME TO BE ONE WITH THE QUAGMIRE.
TENEMENT
THESE PEOPLE NEED YOU, DAISY.
SUSAN NEEDS YOU.
NO ONE ELSE HAS TO GIVE THEMSELVES TO THE DIRT! THE RAIN IS WASHING LOOSE MUD OFF THE HILL TOPS.
WE NEED TO DIVERT IT DOWN THE PATH!
WILL THESE PEBBLES HELP?
NO, THEY ABSOLUTELY WILL NOT HELP.

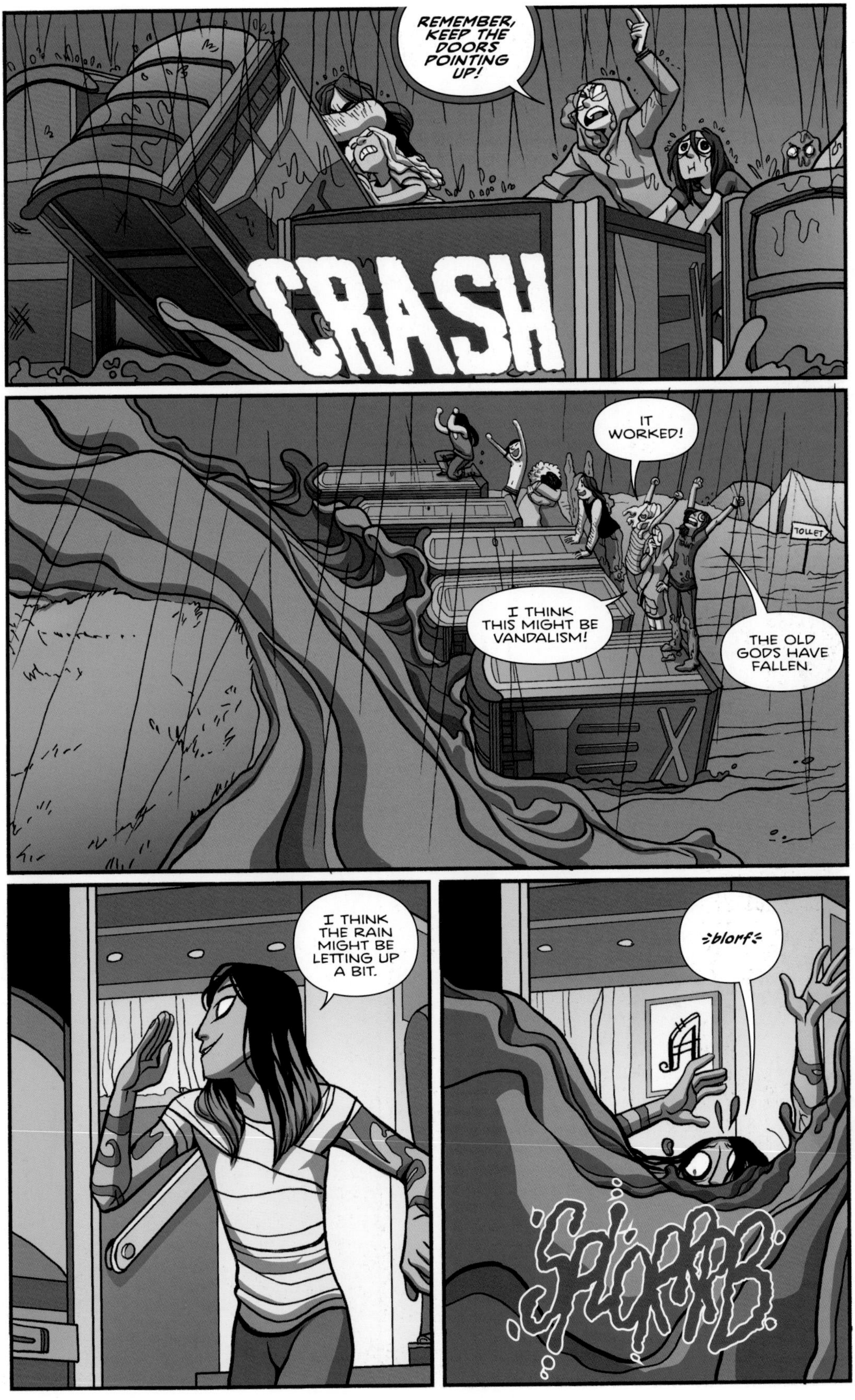
REMEMBER, KEEP THE DOORS POINTING UP!
CRASH
IT WORKED!
I THINK THIS MIGHT BE VANDALISM!
THE OLD GODS HAVE FALLEN.
TOILET
I THINK THE RAIN MIGHT BE LETTING UP A BIT.
blorf
SPLORRB

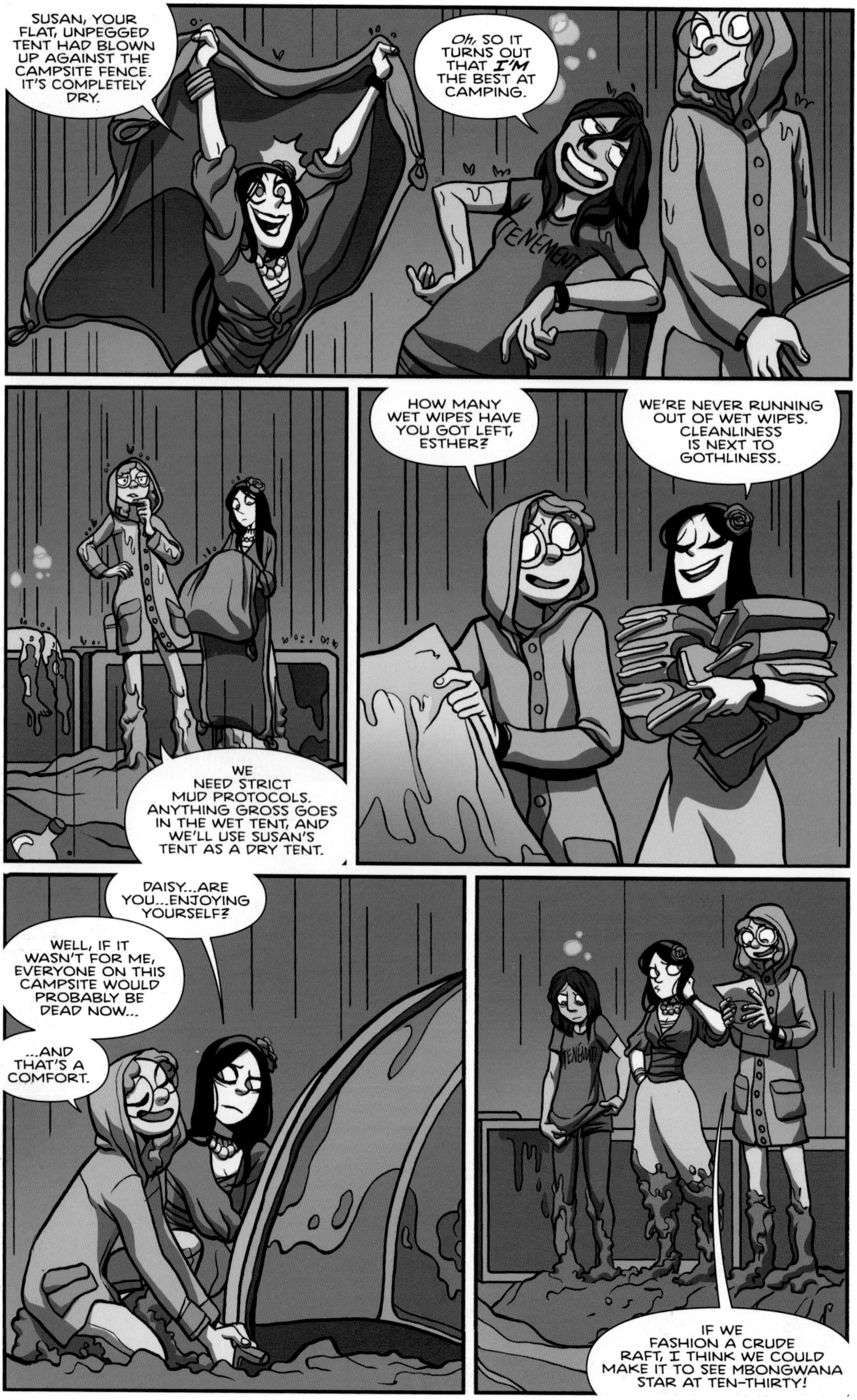
SUSAN, YOUR FLAT, UNPEGGED TENT HAD BLOWN UP AGAINST THE CAMPSITE FENCE. IT'S COMPLETELY DRY.
Oh, SO IT TURNS OUT THAT I'M THE BEST AT CAMPING.
TENEMENT
WE NEED STRICT MUD PROTOCOLS. ANYTHING GROSS GOES IN THE WET TENT, AND WE'LL USE SUSAN'S TENT AS A DRY TENT.
HOW MANY WET WIPES HAVE YOU GOT LEFT, ESTHER?
WE'RE NEVER RUNNING OUT OF WET WIPES. CLEANLINESS IS NEXT TO GOTHLINESS.
DAISY...ARE YOU...ENJOYING YOURSELF?
WELL, IF IT WASN'T FOR ME, EVERYONE ON THIS CAMPSITE WOULD PROBABLY BE DEAD NOW...
...AND THAT'S A COMFORT.
IF WE FASHION A CRUDE RAFT, I THINK WE COULD MAKE IT TO SEE MBONGWANA STAR AT TEN-THIRTY!

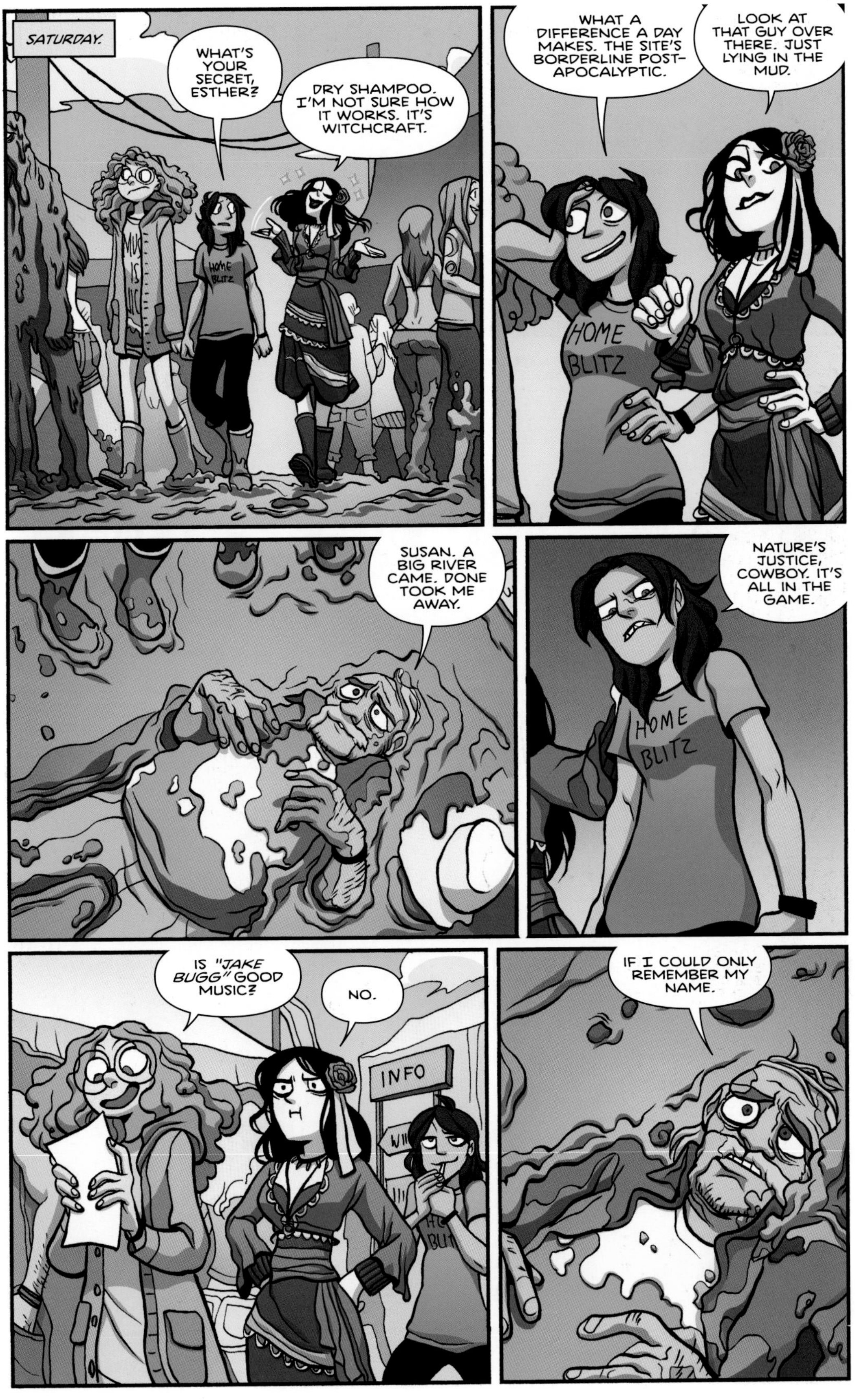
SATURDAY.
WHAT'S YOUR SECRET, ESTHER?
DRY SHAMPOO. I'M NOT SURE HOW IT WORKS. IT'S WITCHCRAFT.
WHAT A DIFFERENCE A DAY MAKES. THE SITE'S BORDERLINE POST-APOCALYPTIC.
LOOK AT THAT GUY OVER THERE. JUST LYING IN THE MUD.
SUSAN. A BIG RIVER CAME. DONE TOOK ME AWAY.
NATURE'S JUSTICE, COWBOY. IT'S ALL IN THE GAME.
IS "JAKE BUGG" GOOD MUSIC?
NO.
INFO
IF I COULD ONLY REMEMBER MY NAME.

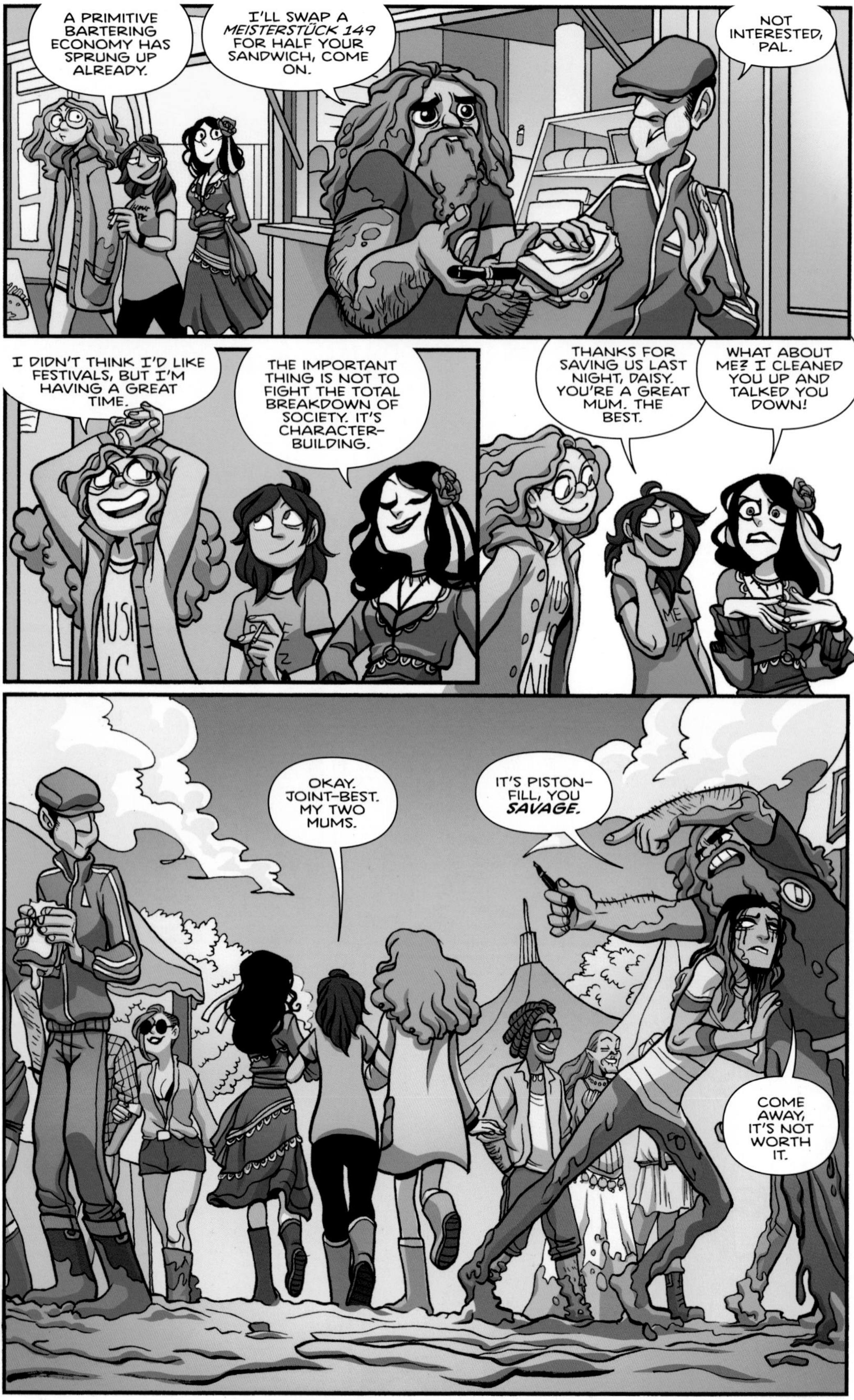
A PRIMITIVE BARTERING ECONOMY HAS SPRUNG UP ALREADY.
I'LL SWAP A *MEISTERSTÜCK 149* FOR HALF YOUR SANDWICH, COME ON.
NOT INTERESTED, PAL.
I DIDN'T THINK I'D LIKE FESTIVALS, BUT I'M HAVING A GREAT TIME.
THE IMPORTANT THING IS NOT TO FIGHT THE TOTAL BREAKDOWN OF SOCIETY. IT'S CHARACTER-BUILDING.
THANKS FOR SAVING US LAST NIGHT, DAISY. YOU'RE A GREAT MUM. THE BEST.
WHAT ABOUT ME? I CLEANED YOU UP AND TALKED YOU DOWN!
OKAY. JOINT-BEST. MY TWO MUMS.
IT'S PISTON-FILL, YOU ***SAVAGE.***
COME AWAY, IT'S NOT WORTH IT.

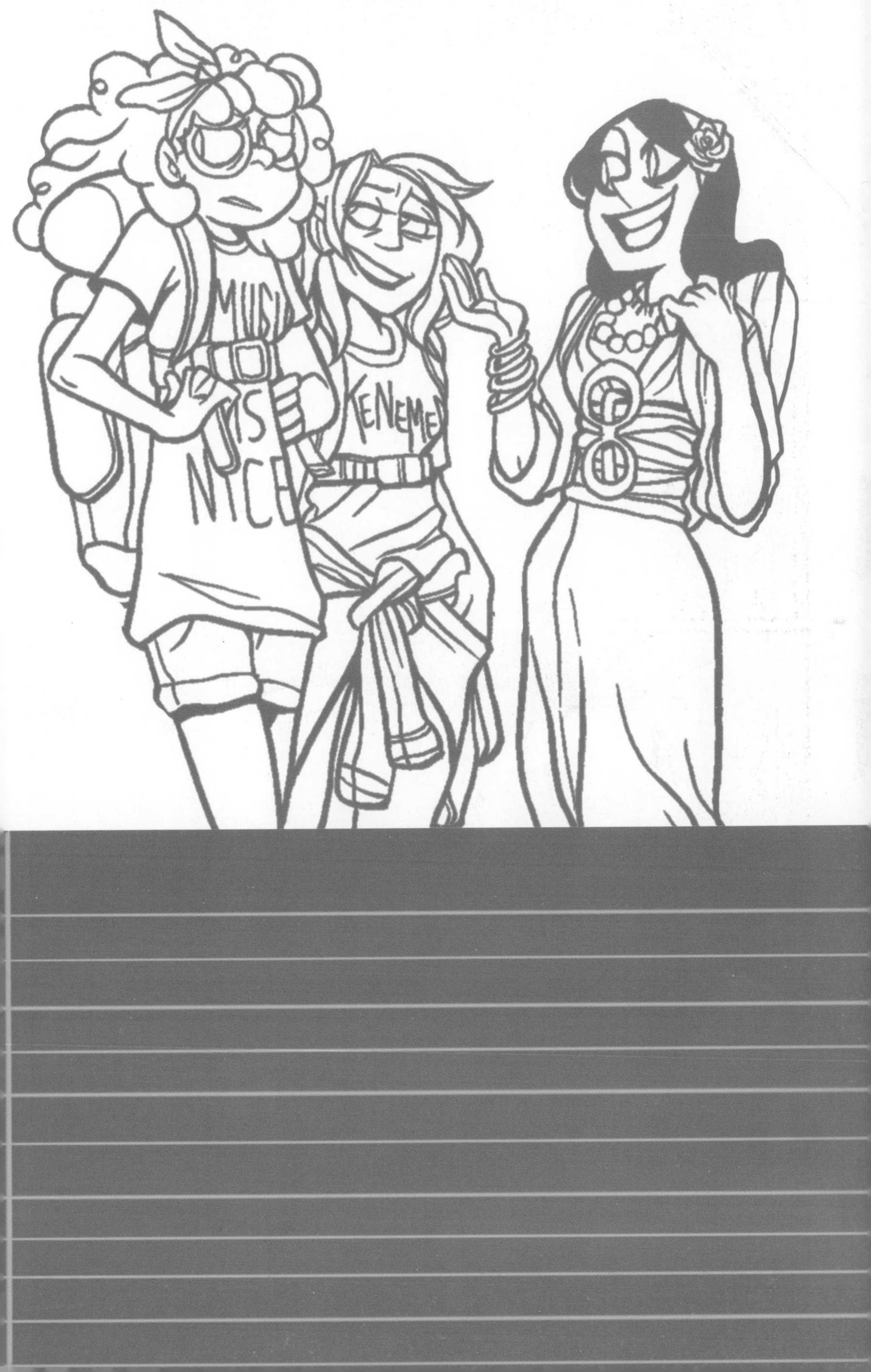
MUSI
IS
NICE
KENEME

CHAPTER TWENTY

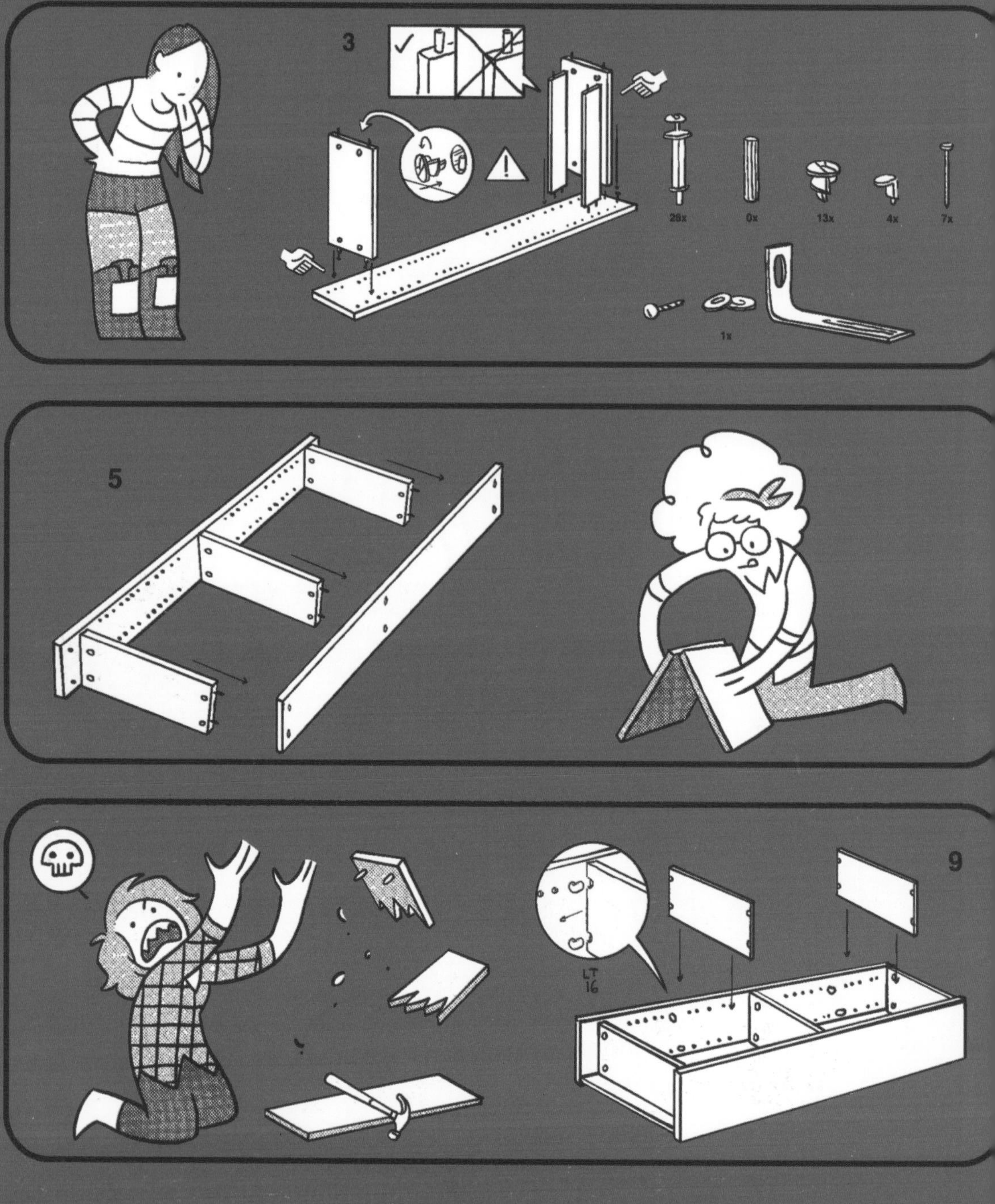
3
28x
0x
13x
4x
7x
1x
5
9
LT 16

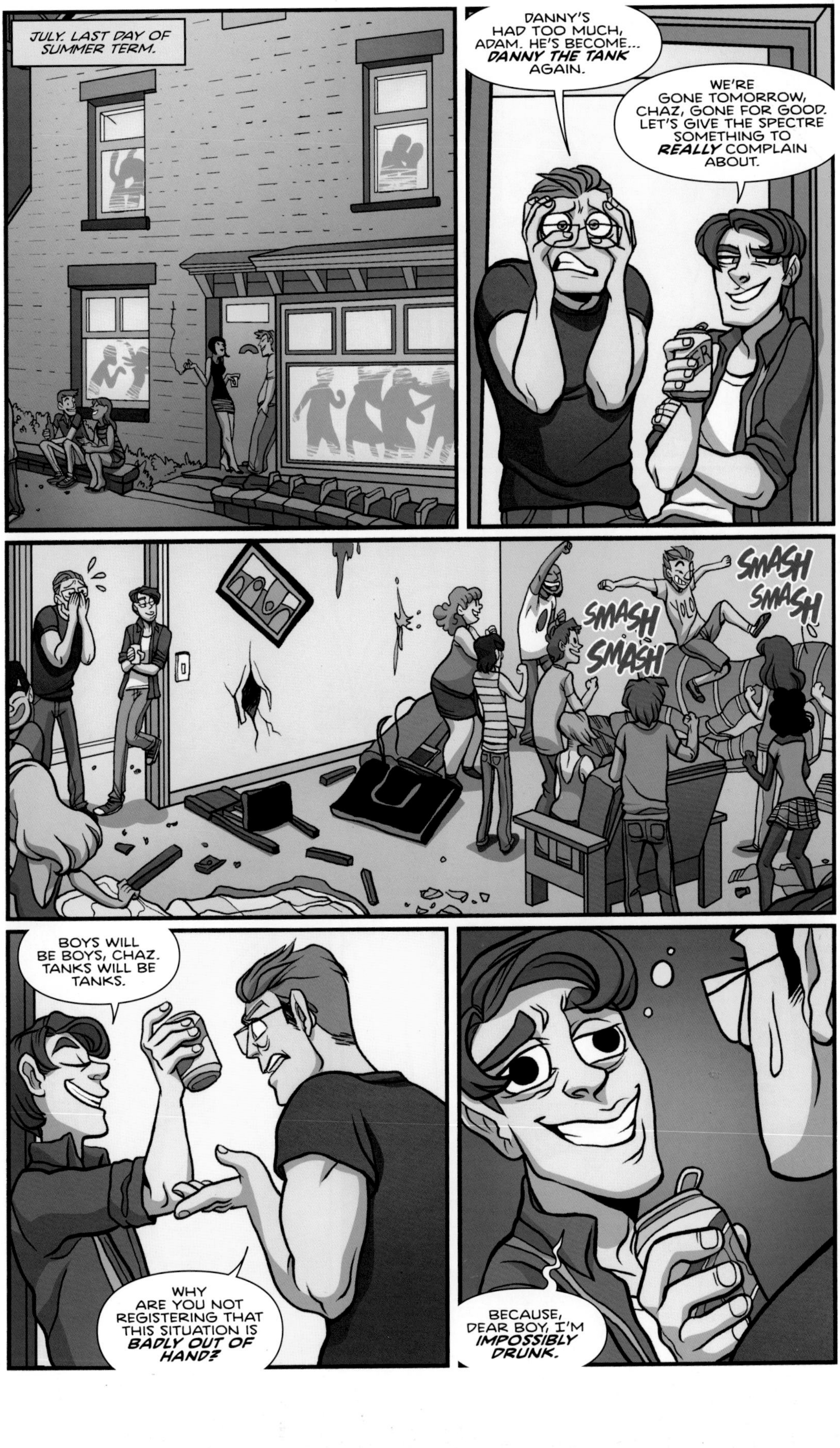

JULY. LAST DAY OF SUMMER TERM.
DANNY'S HAD TOO MUCH, ADAM. HE'S BECOME... **DANNY THE TANK** AGAIN.
WE'RE GONE TOMORROW, CHAZ, GONE FOR GOOD. LET'S GIVE THE SPECTRE SOMETHING TO **REALLY** COMPLAIN ABOUT.
SMASH SMASH
SMASH SMASH
YOLO
BOYS WILL BE BOYS, CHAZ. TANKS WILL BE TANKS.
WHY ARE YOU NOT REGISTERING THAT THIS SITUATION IS **BADLY OUT OF HAND?**
BECAUSE, DEAR BOY, I'M **IMPOSSIBLY DRUNK.**

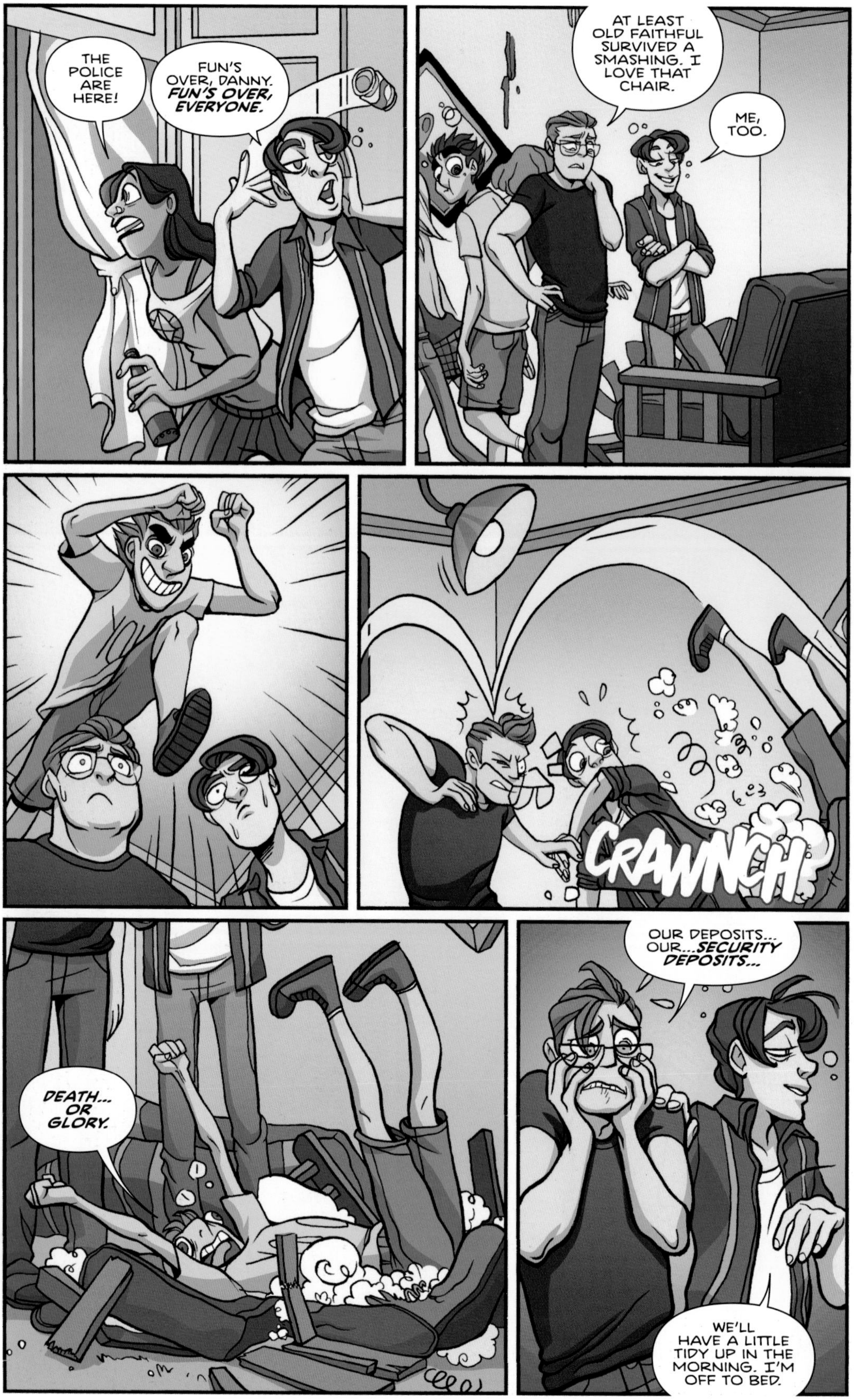
THE POLICE ARE HERE!
FUN'S OVER, DANNY. ***FUN'S OVER, EVERYONE.***
AT LEAST OLD FAITHFUL SURVIVED A SMASHING. I LOVE THAT CHAIR.
ME, TOO.
CRAWNCH
DEATH... OR GLORY.
OUR DEPOSITS... OUR...***SECURITY DEPOSITS...***
WE'LL HAVE A LITTLE TIDY UP IN THE MORNING. I'M OFF TO BED.

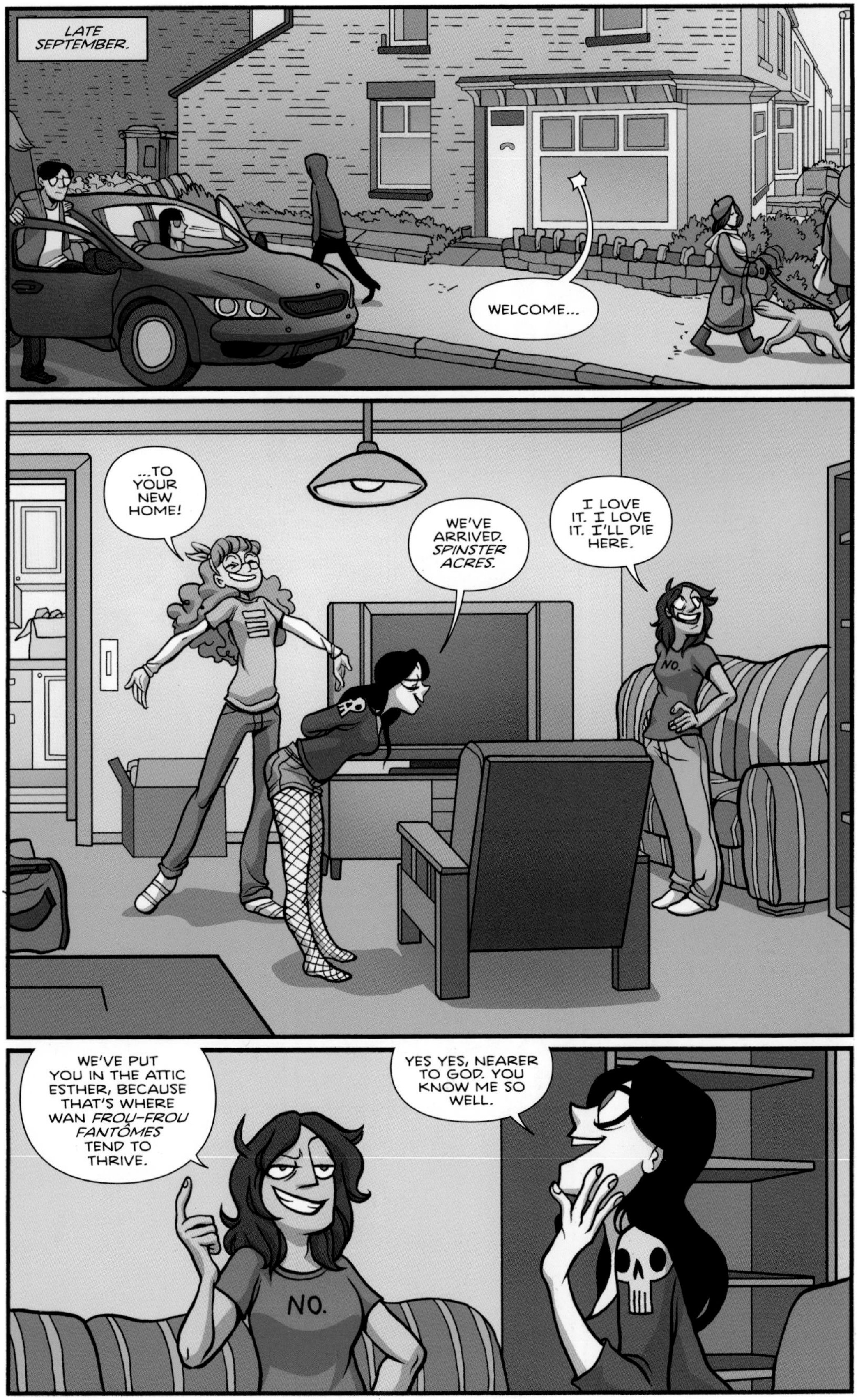

LATE SEPTEMBER.
WELCOME...
...TO YOUR NEW HOME!
WE'VE ARRIVED. *SPINSTER ACRES.*
I LOVE IT. I LOVE IT. I'LL DIE HERE.
NO.
WE'VE PUT YOU IN THE ATTIC ESTHER, BECAUSE THAT'S WHERE WAN *FROU-FROU FANTÔMES* TEND TO THRIVE.
YES YES, NEARER TO GOD. YOU KNOW ME SO WELL.
NO.

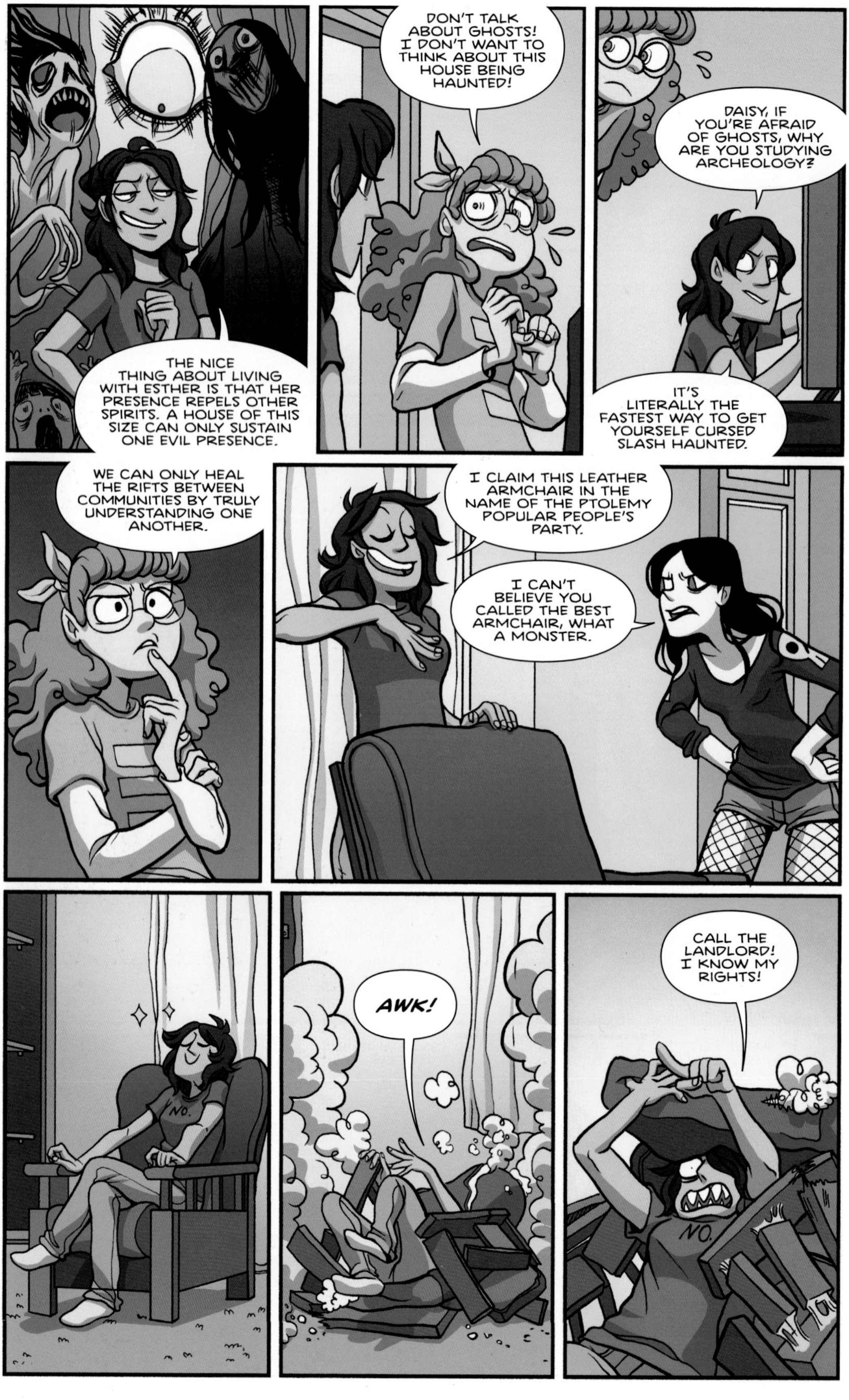
THE NICE THING ABOUT LIVING WITH ESTHER IS THAT HER PRESENCE REPELS OTHER SPIRITS. A HOUSE OF THIS SIZE CAN ONLY SUSTAIN ONE EVIL PRESENCE.
DON'T TALK ABOUT GHOSTS! I DON'T WANT TO THINK ABOUT THIS HOUSE BEING HAUNTED!
DAISY, IF YOU'RE AFRAID OF GHOSTS, WHY ARE YOU STUDYING ARCHEOLOGY?
IT'S LITERALLY THE FASTEST WAY TO GET YOURSELF CURSED SLASH HAUNTED.
WE CAN ONLY HEAL THE RIFTS BETWEEN COMMUNITIES BY TRULY UNDERSTANDING ONE ANOTHER.
I CLAIM THIS LEATHER ARMCHAIR IN THE NAME OF THE PTOLEMY POPULAR PEOPLE'S PARTY.
I CAN'T BELIEVE YOU CALLED THE BEST ARMCHAIR, WHAT A MONSTER.
NO.
AWK!
CALL THE LANDLORD! I KNOW MY RIGHTS!
NO.

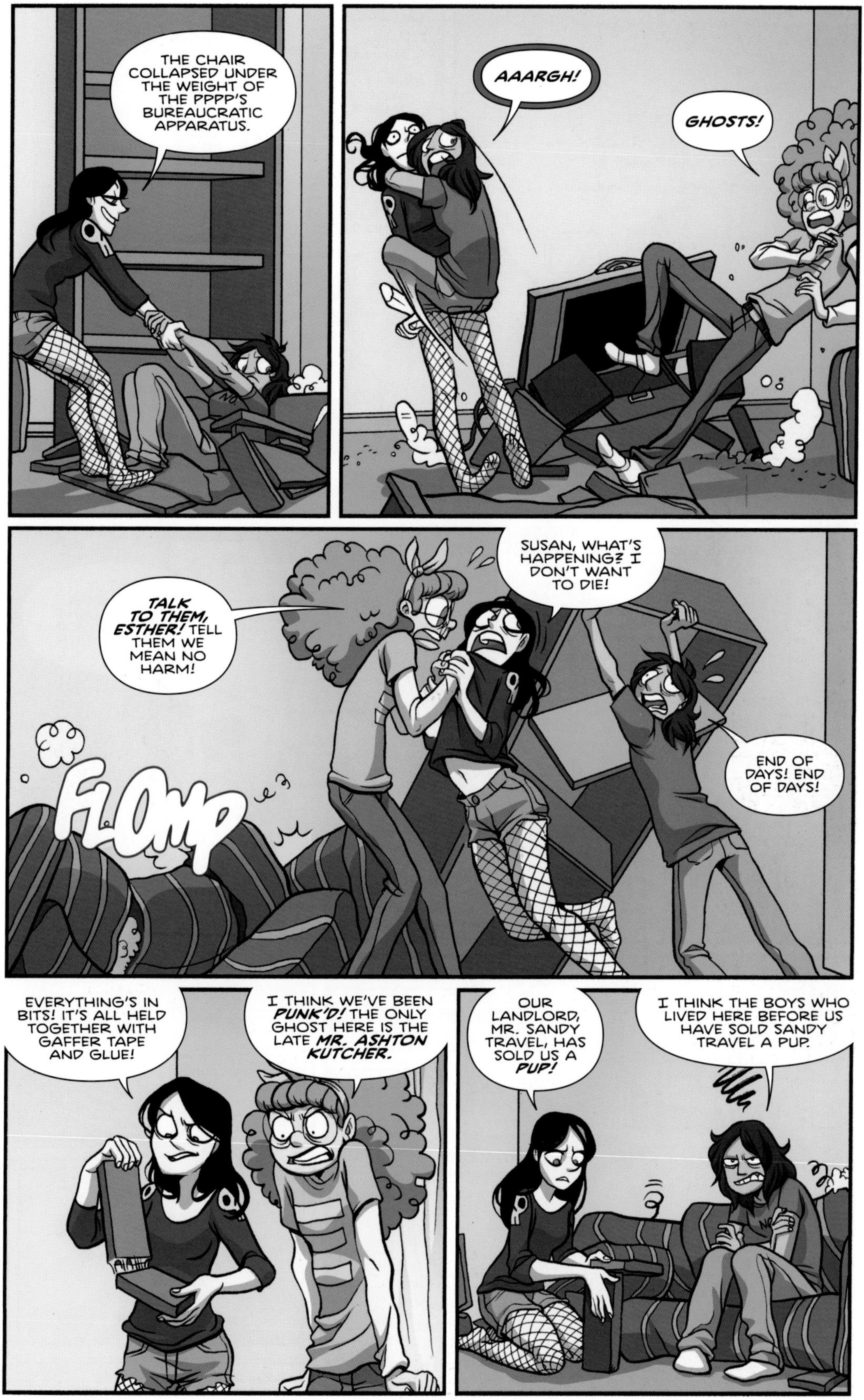
THE CHAIR COLLAPSED UNDER THE WEIGHT OF THE PPPP'S BUREAUCRATIC APPARATUS.
AAARGH!
GHOSTS!
TALK TO THEM, ESTHER! TELL THEM WE MEAN NO HARM!
SUSAN, WHAT'S HAPPENING? I DON'T WANT TO DIE!
END OF DAYS! END OF DAYS!
FLOMP
EVERYTHING'S IN BITS! IT'S ALL HELD TOGETHER WITH GAFFER TAPE AND GLUE!
I THINK WE'VE BEEN PUNK'D! THE ONLY GHOST HERE IS THE LATE MR. ASHTON KUTCHER.
OUR LANDLORD, MR. SANDY TRAVEL, HAS SOLD US A PUP!
I THINK THE BOYS WHO LIVED HERE BEFORE US HAVE SOLD SANDY TRAVEL A PUP.

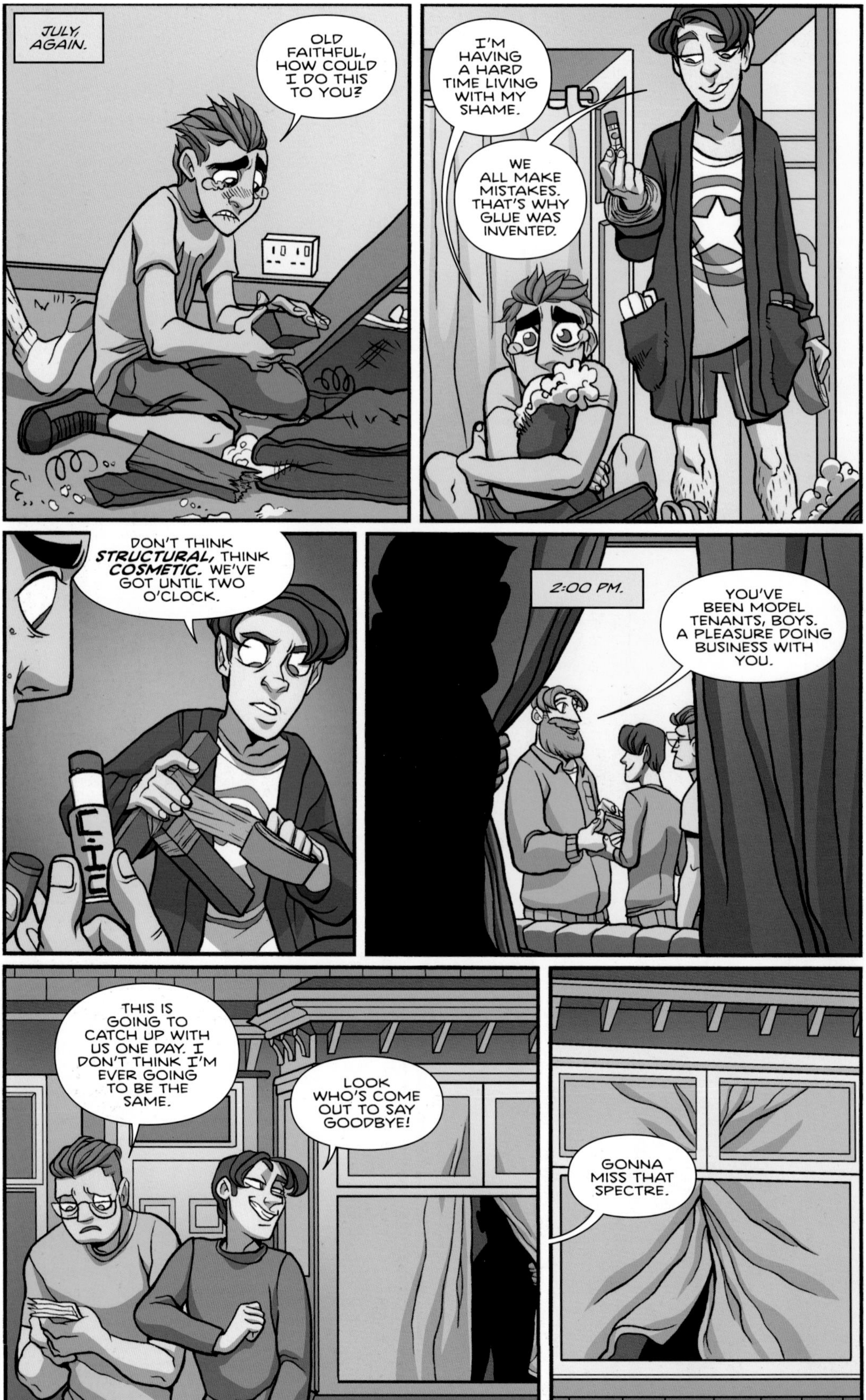
JULY, AGAIN.
OLD FAITHFUL, HOW COULD I DO THIS TO YOU?
I'M HAVING A HARD TIME LIVING WITH MY SHAME.
WE ALL MAKE MISTAKES. THAT'S WHY GLUE WAS INVENTED.
DON'T THINK STRUCTURAL, THINK COSMETIC. WE'VE GOT UNTIL TWO O'CLOCK.
2:00 PM.
YOU'VE BEEN MODEL TENANTS, BOYS. A PLEASURE DOING BUSINESS WITH YOU.
THIS IS GOING TO CATCH UP WITH US ONE DAY. I DON'T THINK I'M EVER GOING TO BE THE SAME.
LOOK WHO'S COME OUT TO SAY GOODBYE!
GONNA MISS THAT SPECTRE.

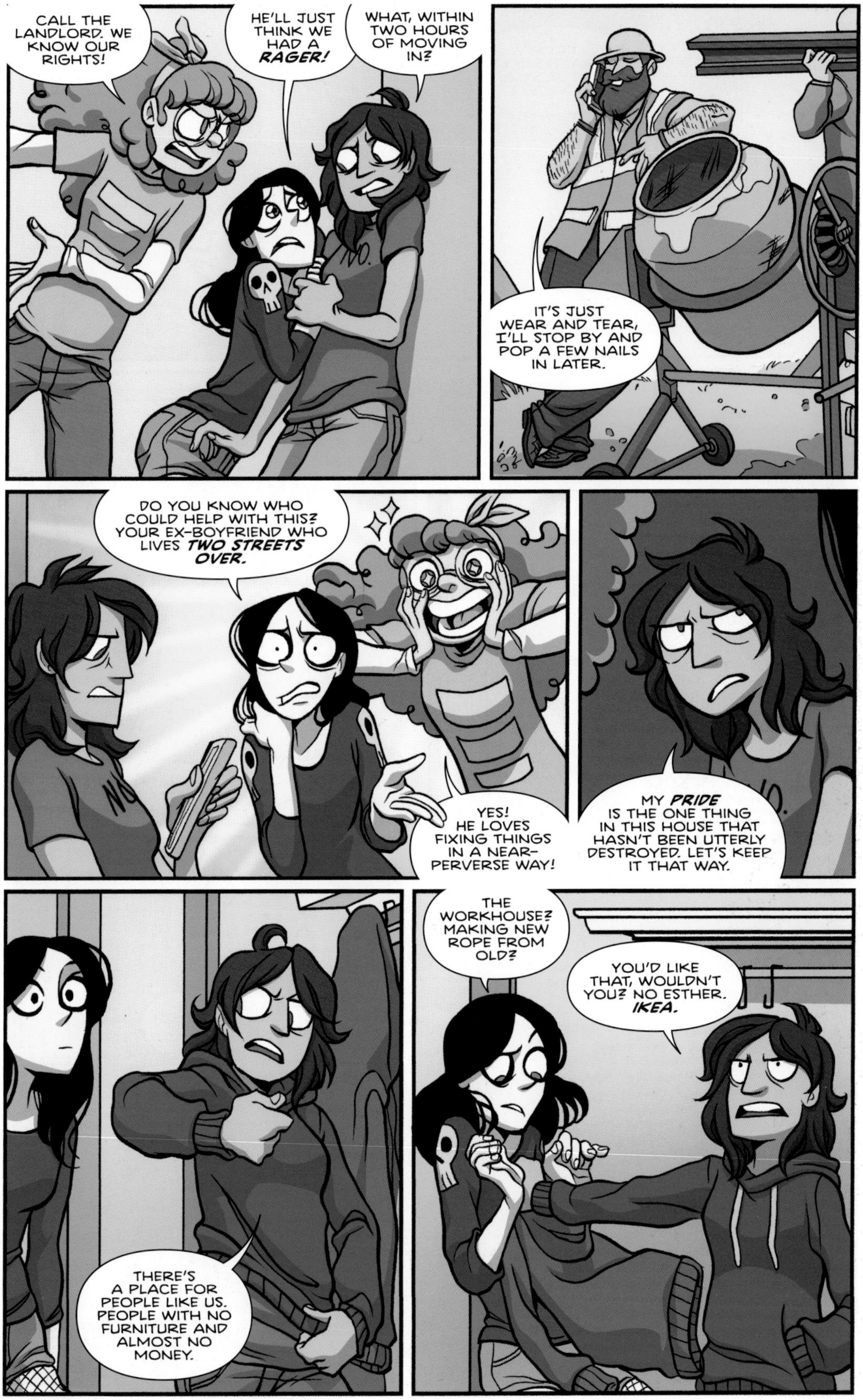
CALL THE LANDLORD. WE KNOW OUR RIGHTS!
HE'LL JUST THINK WE HAD A *RAGER!*
WHAT, WITHIN TWO HOURS OF MOVING IN?
IT'S JUST WEAR AND TEAR, I'LL STOP BY AND POP A FEW NAILS IN LATER.
DO YOU KNOW WHO COULD HELP WITH THIS? YOUR EX-BOYFRIEND WHO LIVES *TWO STREETS OVER.*
YES! HE LOVES FIXING THINGS IN A NEAR-PERVERSE WAY!
MY *PRIDE* IS THE ONE THING IN THIS HOUSE THAT HASN'T BEEN UTTERLY DESTROYED. LET'S KEEP IT THAT WAY.
THERE'S A PLACE FOR PEOPLE LIKE US. PEOPLE WITH NO FURNITURE AND ALMOST NO MONEY.
THE WORKHOUSE? MAKING NEW ROPE FROM OLD?
YOU'D LIKE THAT, WOULDN'T YOU? NO ESTHER. *IKEA.*

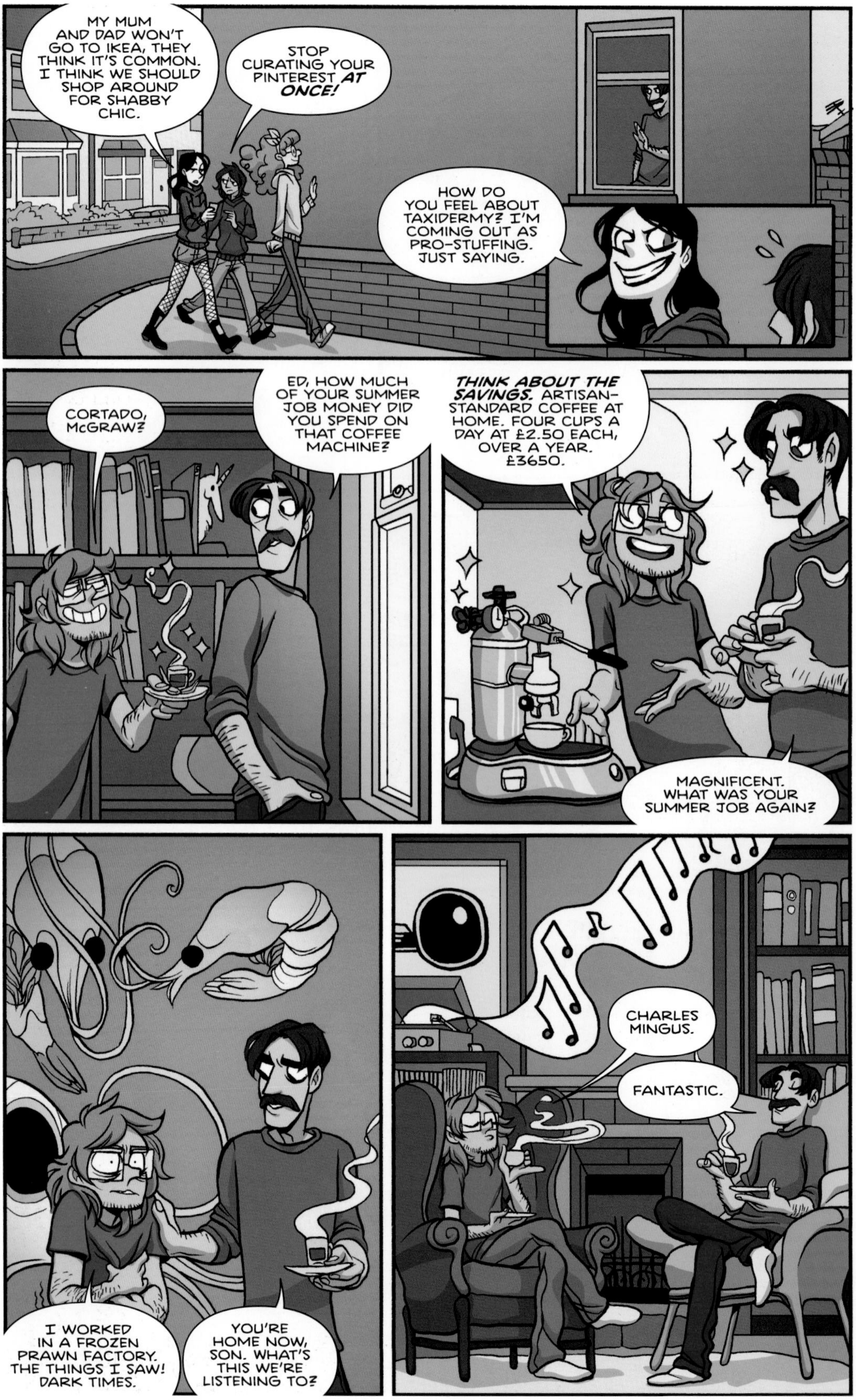
MY MUM AND DAD WON'T GO TO IKEA, THEY THINK IT'S COMMON. I THINK WE SHOULD SHOP AROUND FOR SHABBY CHIC.
STOP CURATING YOUR PINTEREST AT ONCE!
HOW DO YOU FEEL ABOUT TAXIDERMY? I'M COMING OUT AS PRO-STUFFING. JUST SAYING.
CORTADO, McGRAW?
ED, HOW MUCH OF YOUR SUMMER JOB MONEY DID YOU SPEND ON THAT COFFEE MACHINE?
THINK ABOUT THE SAVINGS. ARTISAN-STANDARD COFFEE AT HOME. FOUR CUPS A DAY AT £2.50 EACH, OVER A YEAR. £3650.
MAGNIFICENT. WHAT WAS YOUR SUMMER JOB AGAIN?
I WORKED IN A FROZEN PRAWN FACTORY. THE THINGS I SAW! DARK TIMES.
YOU'RE HOME NOW, SON. WHAT'S THIS WE'RE LISTENING TO?
CHARLES MINGUS.
FANTASTIC.

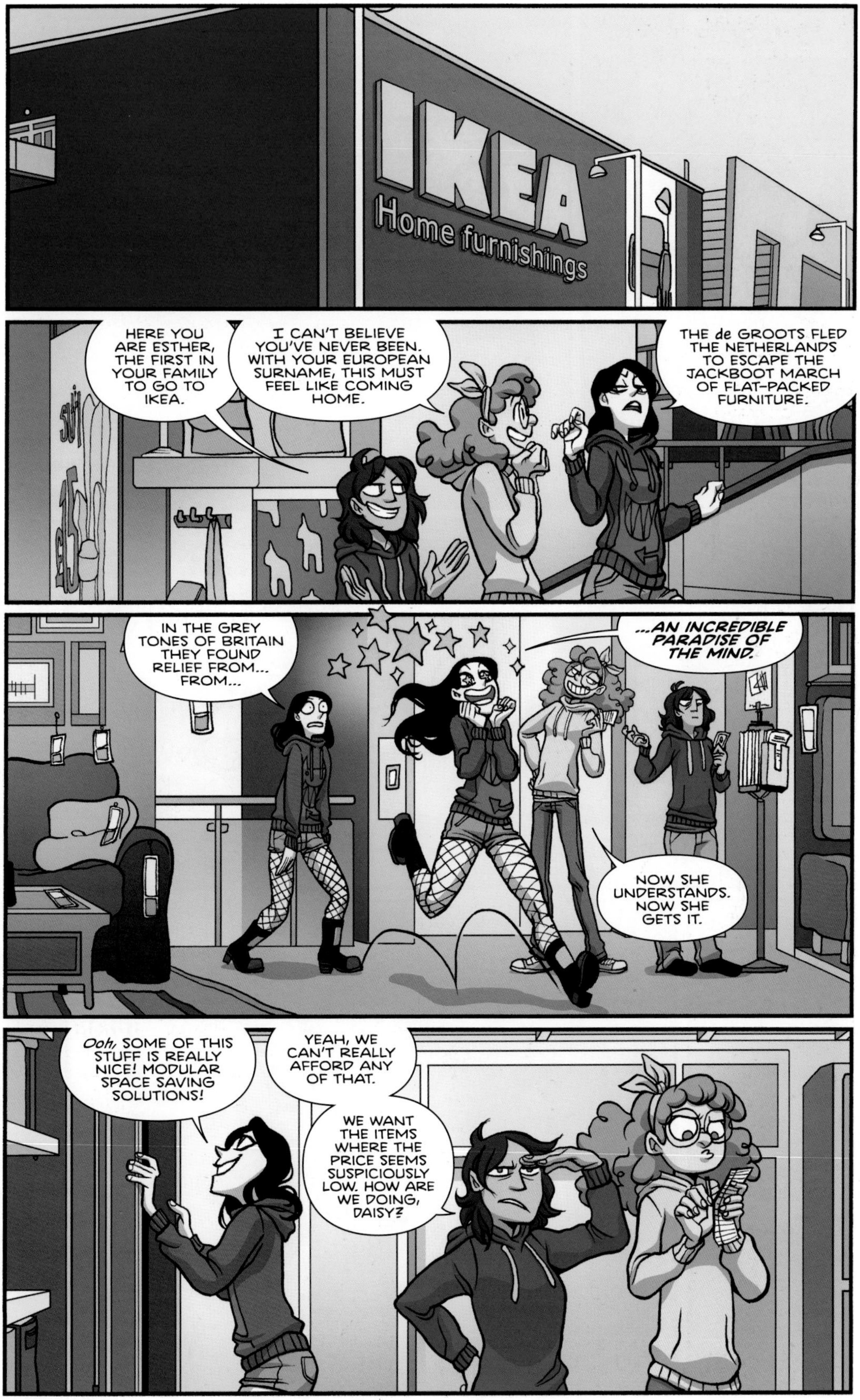
IKEA
Home furnishings
HERE YOU ARE ESTHER, THE FIRST IN YOUR FAMILY TO GO TO IKEA.
I CAN'T BELIEVE YOU'VE NEVER BEEN. WITH YOUR EUROPEAN SURNAME, THIS MUST FEEL LIKE COMING HOME.
THE de GROOTS FLED THE NETHERLANDS TO ESCAPE THE JACKBOOT MARCH OF FLAT-PACKED FURNITURE.
IN THE GREY TONES OF BRITAIN THEY FOUND RELIEF FROM... FROM...
...AN INCREDIBLE PARADISE OF THE MIND.
NOW SHE UNDERSTANDS. NOW SHE GETS IT.
Ooh, SOME OF THIS STUFF IS REALLY NICE! MODULAR SPACE SAVING SOLUTIONS!
YEAH, WE CAN'T REALLY AFFORD ANY OF THAT.
WE WANT THE ITEMS WHERE THE PRICE SEEMS SUSPICIOUSLY LOW. HOW ARE WE DOING, DAISY?

01 SJUKDOM mixing bowl £12

I THINK WE SHOULD... *DARE TO DREAM.*

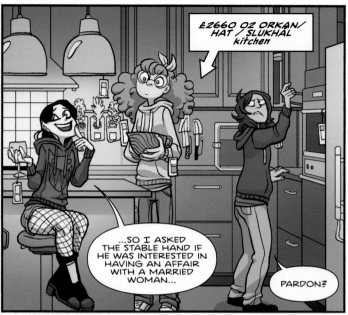

£2660 02 ORKAN/ HAT / SLUKHÅL kitchen

...SO I ASKED THE STABLE HAND IF HE WAS INTERESTED IN HAVING AN AFFAIR WITH A MARRIED WOMAN...

PARDON?

WE CAN NEVER SHOW OUR FACES AT THE GYMKHANA AGAIN AFTER YOUR FROLICS IN THE BARN!

I HAVE... *NEEDS.* NEEDS COLIN CAN'T SATISFY!

YOU'VE BOTH LOST YOUR MINDS.

03 EMALJÖGA sectional sofa £315

THAT SMELL...IS THAT...

...MANURE? AND THERE'S *HAY* IN THIS BED! ESTHER!

DON'T JUDGE HER! IT'S MEDICAL! YOU KNOW SHE CAN'T KEEP AWAY FROM THE PADDOCK!

04 STALLDRÄNG mattress £299

[Sjukdom = disease
Orkan/Hat/Slukhål = Hurricane / Hatred / Sinkhole
Emaljoga = Glass eye
Stalldräng = stable hand]

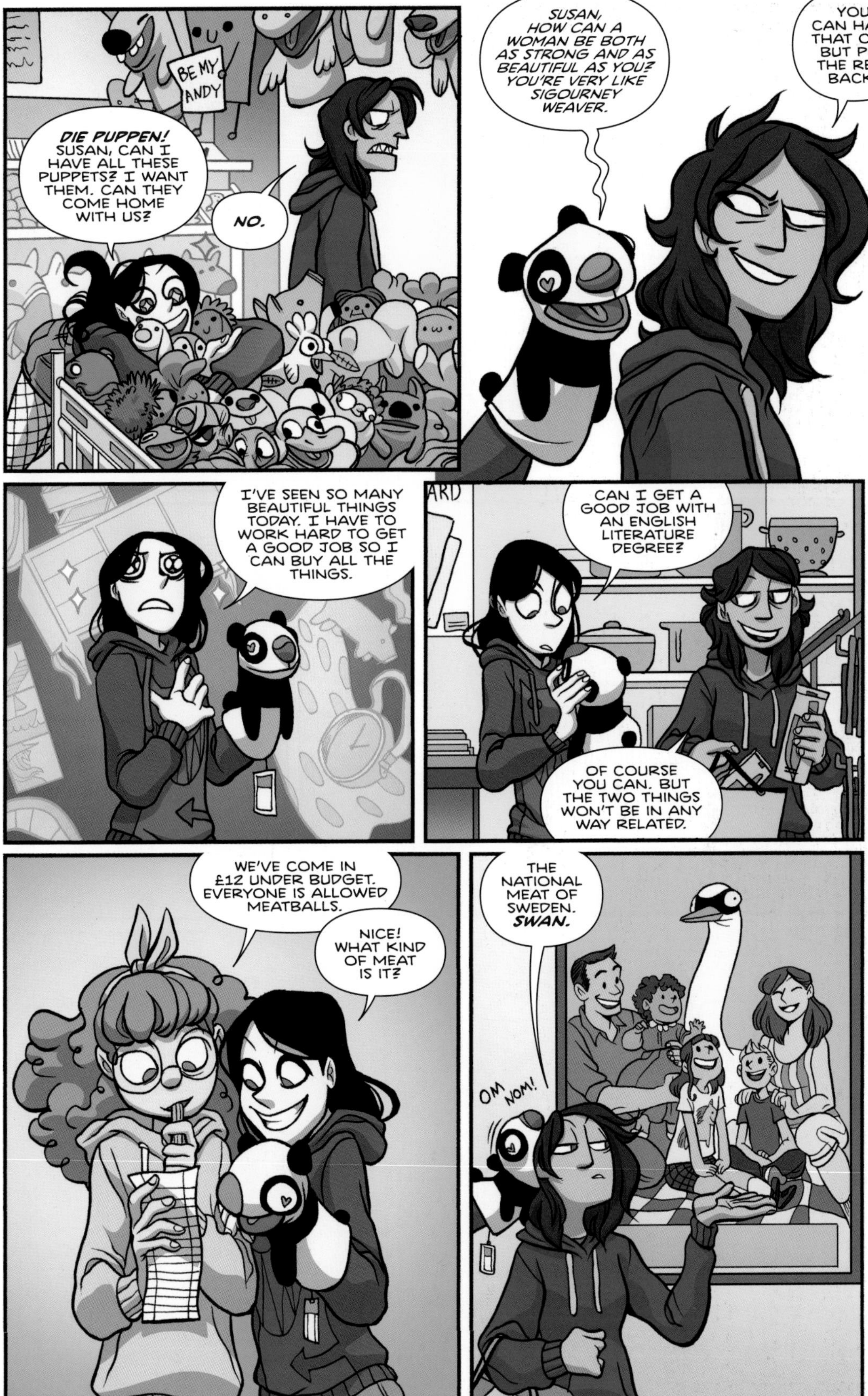
BE MY ANDY
DIE PUPPEN! SUSAN, CAN I HAVE ALL THESE PUPPETS? I WANT THEM. CAN THEY COME HOME WITH US?
NO.
SUSAN, HOW CAN A WOMAN BE BOTH AS STRONG AND AS BEAUTIFUL AS YOU? YOU'RE VERY LIKE SIGOURNEY WEAVER.
YOU CAN HAVE THAT ONE, BUT PUT THE REST BACK.
I'VE SEEN SO MANY BEAUTIFUL THINGS TODAY. I HAVE TO WORK HARD TO GET A GOOD JOB SO I CAN BUY ALL THE THINGS.
CAN I GET A GOOD JOB WITH AN ENGLISH LITERATURE DEGREE?
OF COURSE YOU CAN. BUT THE TWO THINGS WON'T BE IN ANY WAY RELATED.
WE'VE COME IN £12 UNDER BUDGET. EVERYONE IS ALLOWED MEATBALLS.
NICE! WHAT KIND OF MEAT IS IT?
THE NATIONAL MEAT OF SWEDEN. SWAN.
OM NOM!

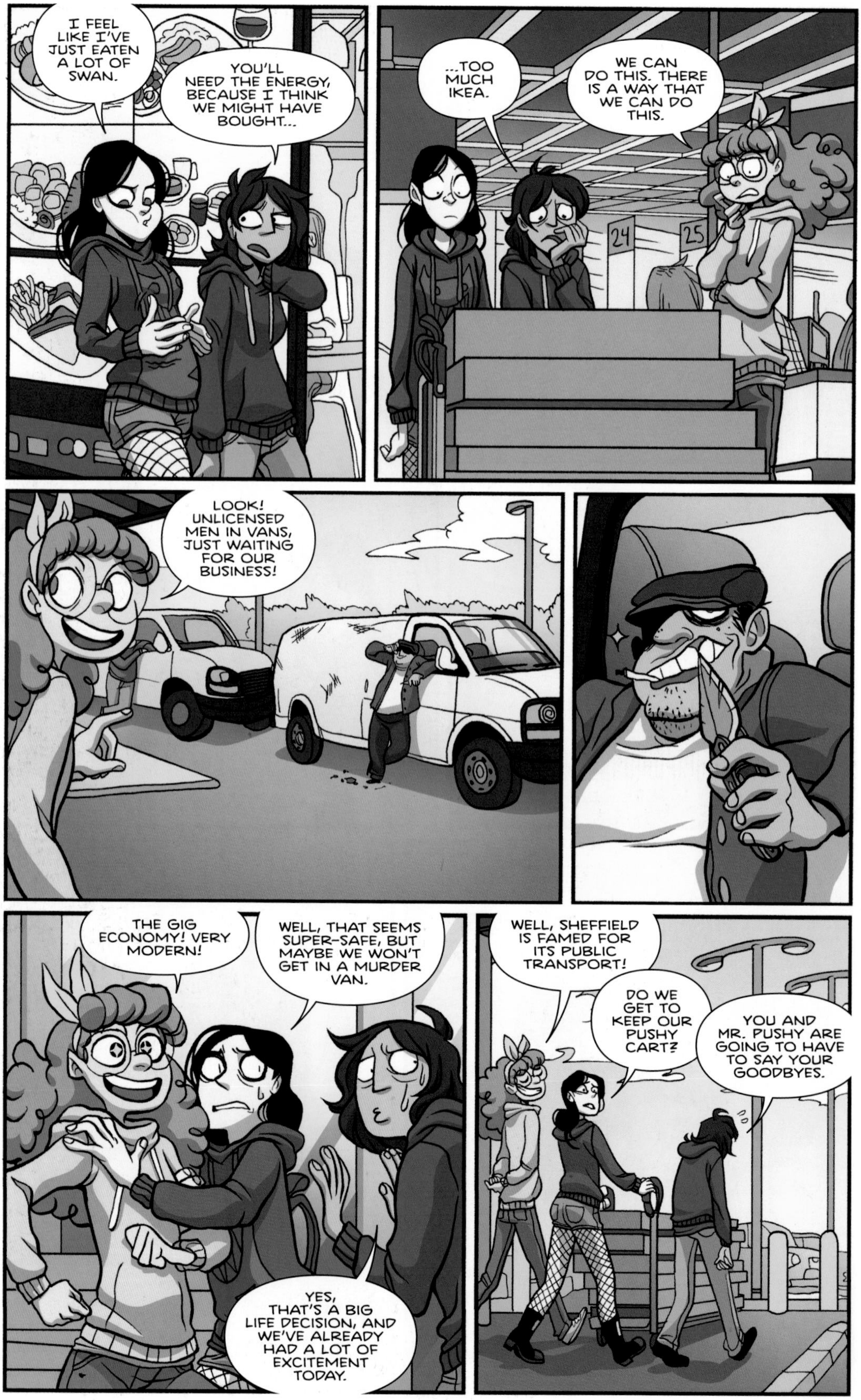
I FEEL LIKE I'VE JUST EATEN A LOT OF SWAN.
YOU'LL NEED THE ENERGY, BECAUSE I THINK WE MIGHT HAVE BOUGHT...
...TOO MUCH IKEA.
WE CAN DO THIS. THERE IS A WAY THAT WE CAN DO THIS.
24
25
LOOK! UNLICENSED MEN IN VANS, JUST WAITING FOR OUR BUSINESS!
THE GIG ECONOMY! VERY MODERN!
WELL, THAT SEEMS SUPER-SAFE, BUT MAYBE WE WON'T GET IN A MURDER VAN.
YES, THAT'S A BIG LIFE DECISION, AND WE'VE ALREADY HAD A LOT OF EXCITEMENT TODAY.
WELL, SHEFFIELD IS FAMED FOR ITS PUBLIC TRANSPORT!
DO WE GET TO KEEP OUR PUSHY CART?
YOU AND MR. PUSHY ARE GOING TO HAVE TO SAY YOUR GOODBYES.

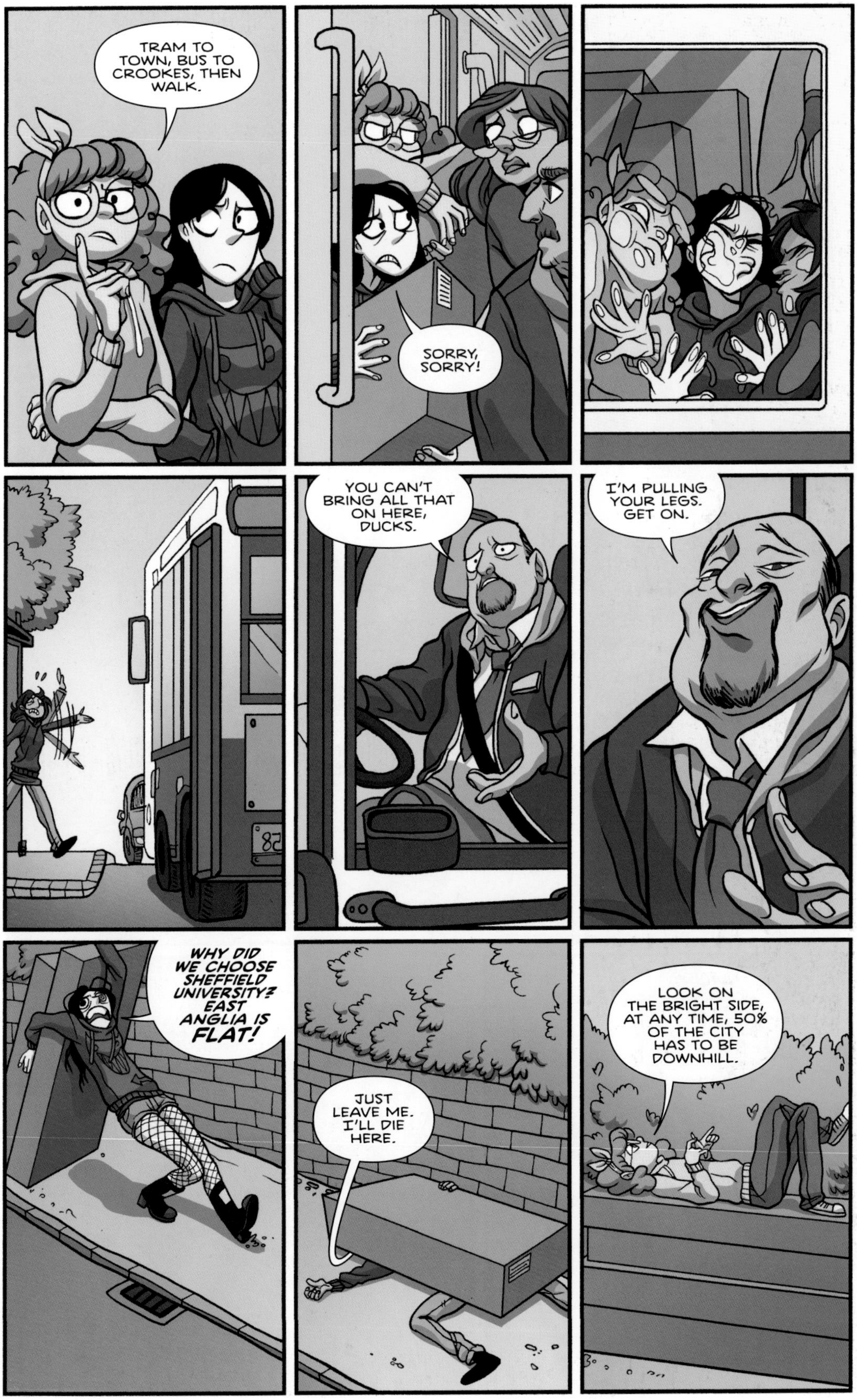
TRAM TO TOWN, BUS TO CROOKES, THEN WALK.
SORRY, SORRY!
YOU CAN'T BRING ALL THAT ON HERE, DUCKS.
I'M PULLING YOUR LEGS. GET ON.
WHY DID WE CHOOSE SHEFFIELD UNIVERSITY? EAST ANGLIA IS FLAT!
JUST LEAVE ME. I'LL DIE HERE.
LOOK ON THE BRIGHT SIDE, AT ANY TIME, 50% OF THE CITY HAS TO BE DOWNHILL.

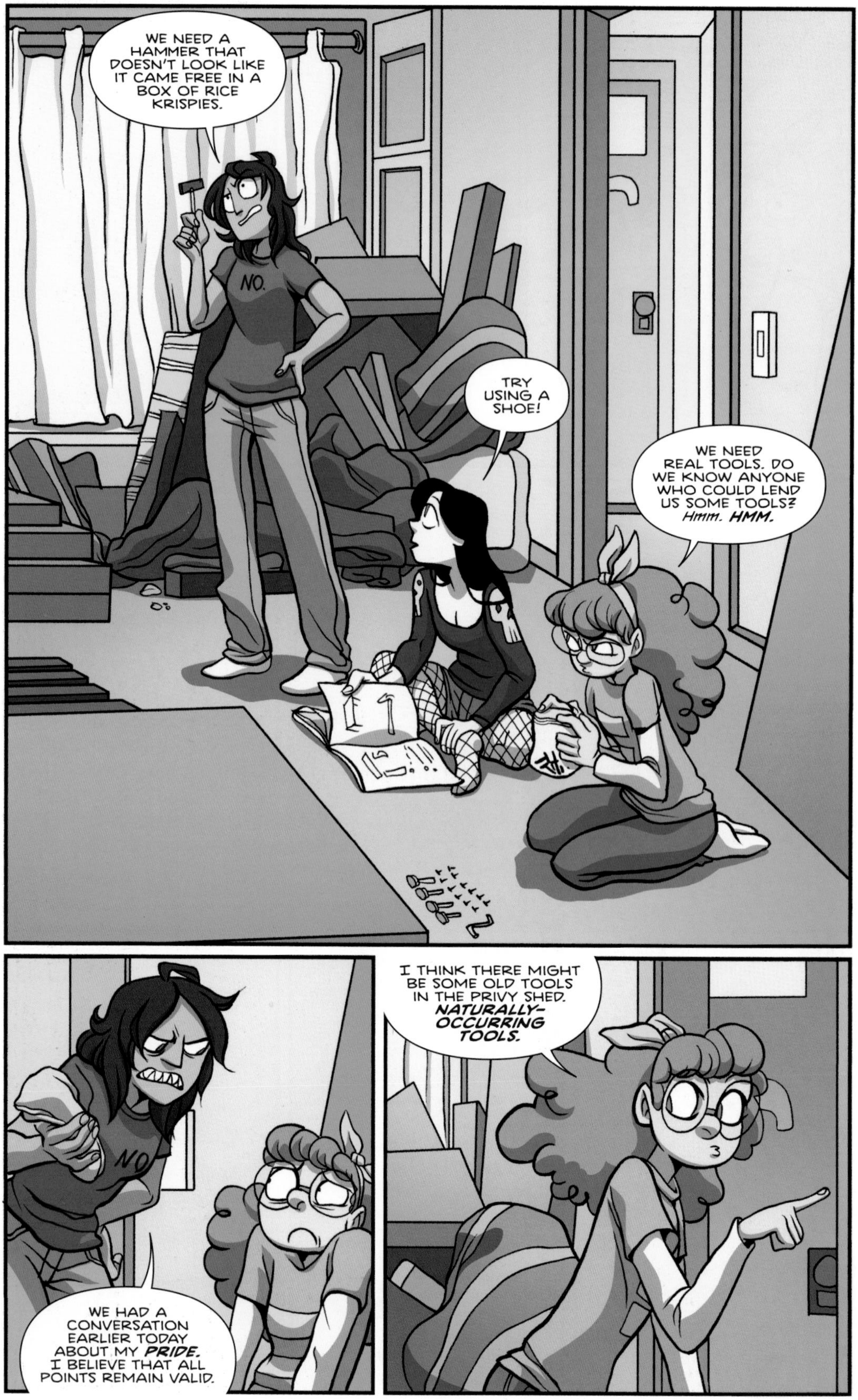
WE NEED A HAMMER THAT DOESN'T LOOK LIKE IT CAME FREE IN A BOX OF RICE KRISPIES.
NO.
TRY USING A SHOE!
WE NEED REAL TOOLS. DO WE KNOW ANYONE WHO COULD LEND US SOME TOOLS? *Hmm.* ***HMM.***
NO
WE HAD A CONVERSATION EARLIER TODAY ABOUT MY ***PRIDE.*** I BELIEVE THAT ALL POINTS REMAIN VALID.
I THINK THERE MIGHT BE SOME OLD TOOLS IN THE PRIVY SHED. ***NATURALLY-OCCURRING TOOLS.***

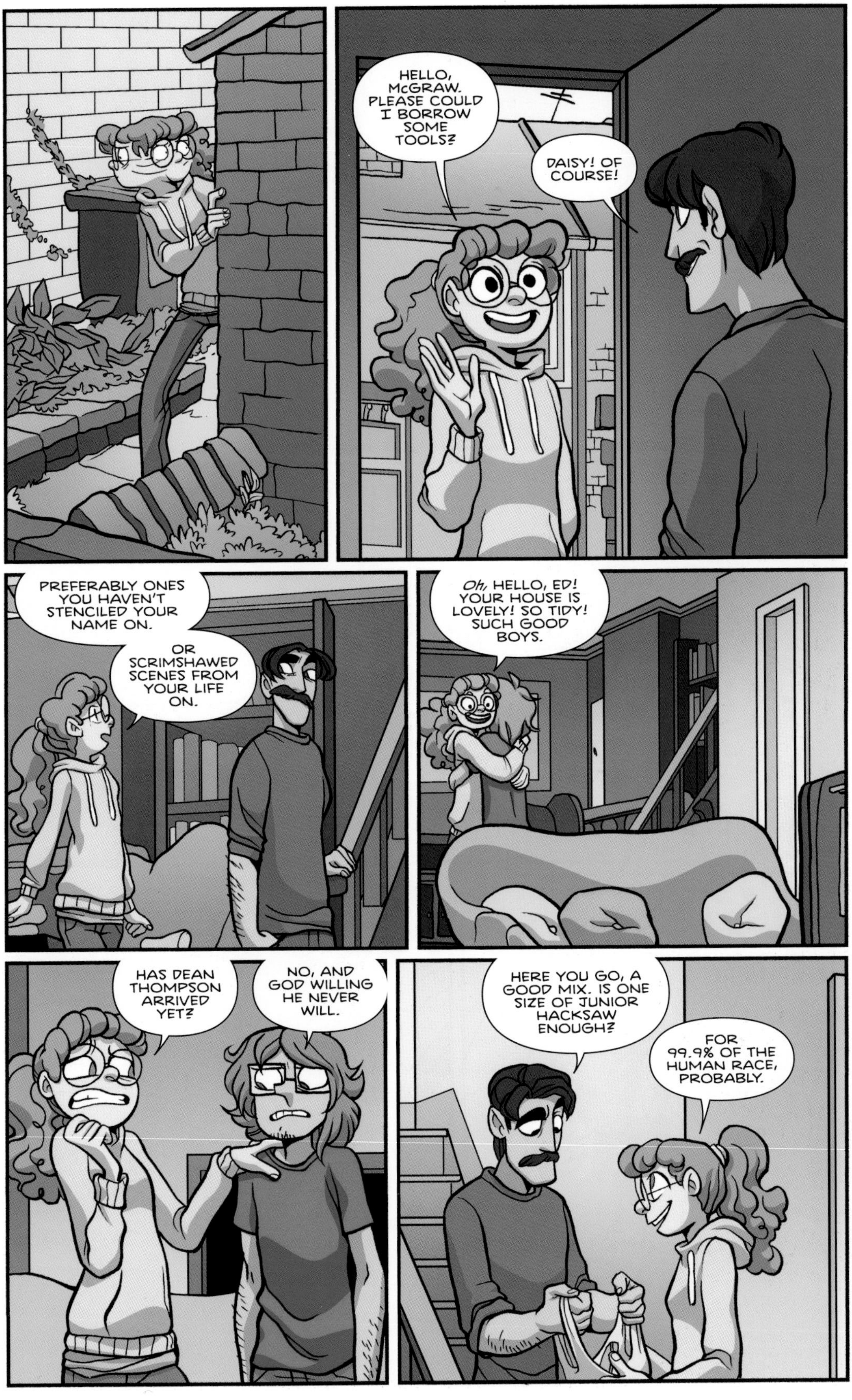
HELLO, McGRAW. PLEASE COULD I BORROW SOME TOOLS?
DAISY! OF COURSE!
PREFERABLY ONES YOU HAVEN'T STENCILED YOUR NAME ON.
OR SCRIMSHAWED SCENES FROM YOUR LIFE ON.
Oh, HELLO, ED! YOUR HOUSE IS LOVELY! SO TIDY! SUCH GOOD BOYS.
HAS DEAN THOMPSON ARRIVED YET?
NO, AND GOD WILLING HE NEVER WILL.
HERE YOU GO, A GOOD MIX. IS ONE SIZE OF JUNIOR HACKSAW ENOUGH?
FOR 99.9% OF THE HUMAN RACE, PROBABLY.

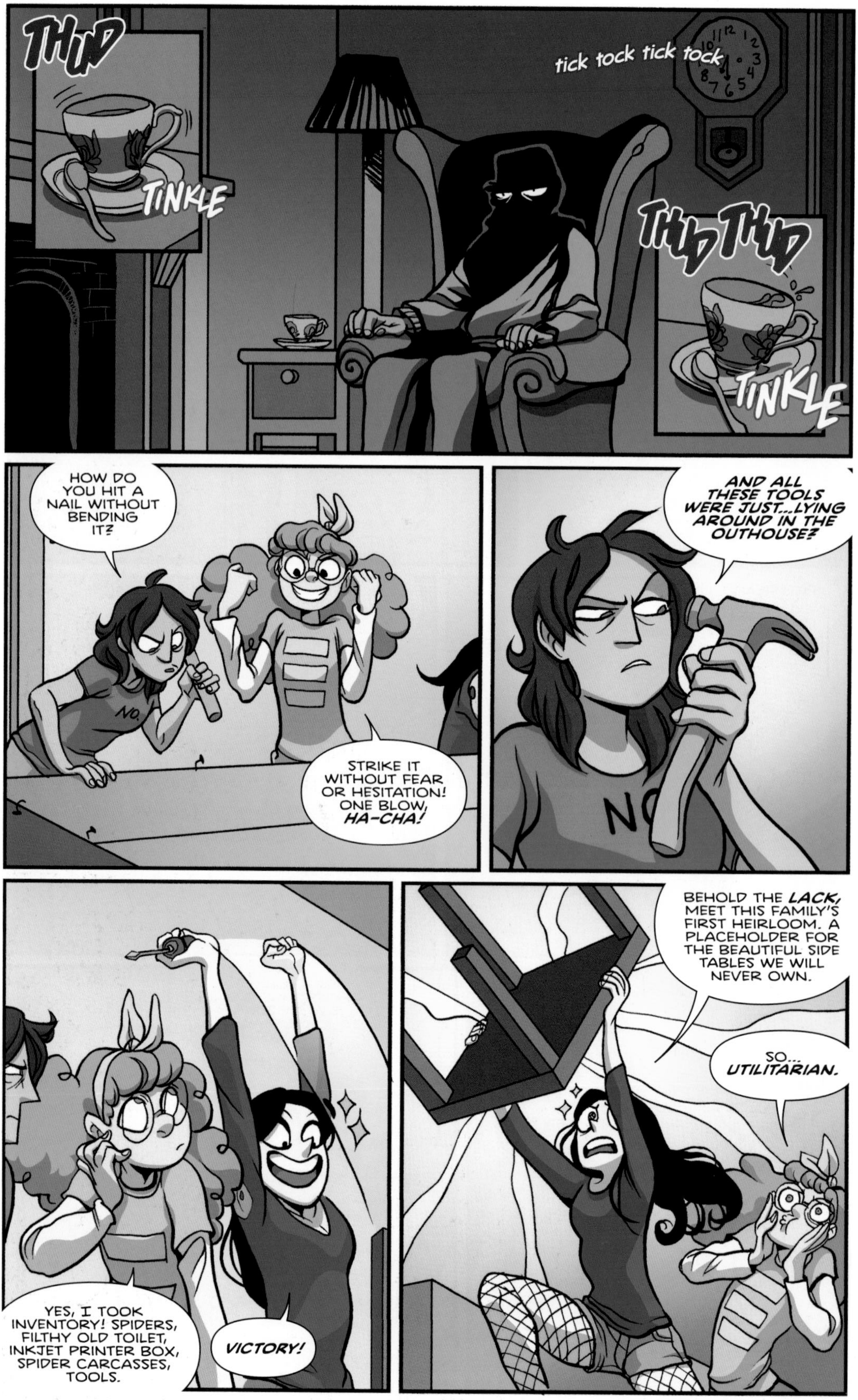
THUD
TINKLE
tick tock tick tock
THUD THUD
TINKLE
HOW DO YOU HIT A NAIL WITHOUT BENDING IT?
STRIKE IT WITHOUT FEAR OR HESITATION! ONE BLOW, *HA-CHA!*
AND ALL THESE TOOLS WERE JUST...LYING AROUND IN THE OUTHOUSE?
YES, I TOOK INVENTORY! SPIDERS, FILTHY OLD TOILET, INKJET PRINTER BOX, SPIDER CARCASSES, TOOLS.
VICTORY!
BEHOLD THE *LACK*, MEET THIS FAMILY'S FIRST HEIRLOOM. A PLACEHOLDER FOR THE BEAUTIFUL SIDE TABLES WE WILL NEVER OWN.
SO... *UTILITARIAN.*

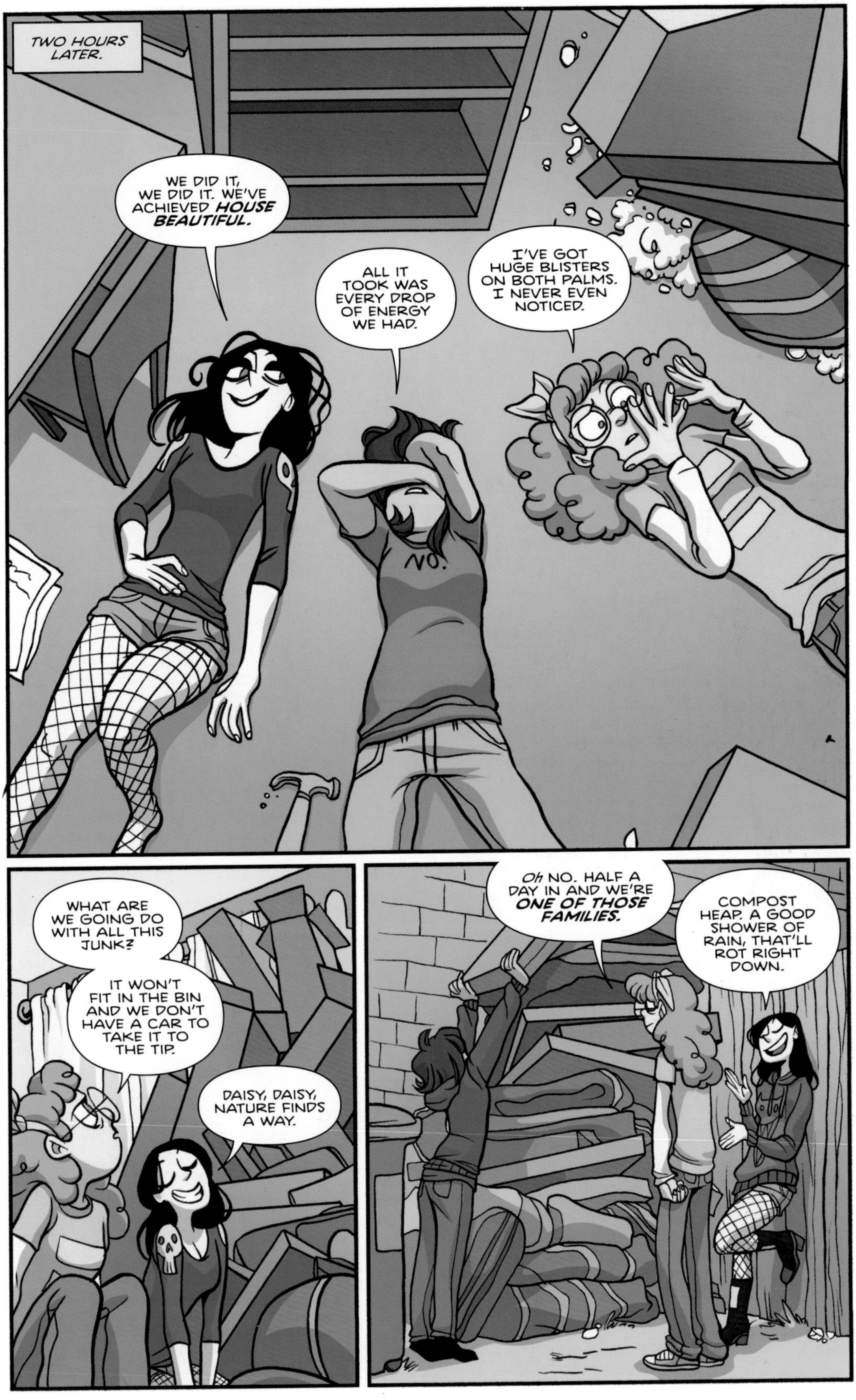

TWO HOURS LATER.
WE DID IT, WE DID IT. WE'VE ACHIEVED HOUSE BEAUTIFUL.
ALL IT TOOK WAS EVERY DROP OF ENERGY WE HAD.
I'VE GOT HUGE BLISTERS ON BOTH PALMS. I NEVER EVEN NOTICED.
NO.
WHAT ARE WE GOING DO WITH ALL THIS JUNK?
IT WON'T FIT IN THE BIN AND WE DON'T HAVE A CAR TO TAKE IT TO THE TIP.
DAISY, DAISY, NATURE FINDS A WAY.
OH NO. HALF A DAY IN AND WE'RE ONE OF THOSE FAMILIES.
COMPOST HEAP. A GOOD SHOWER OF RAIN, THAT'LL ROT RIGHT DOWN.

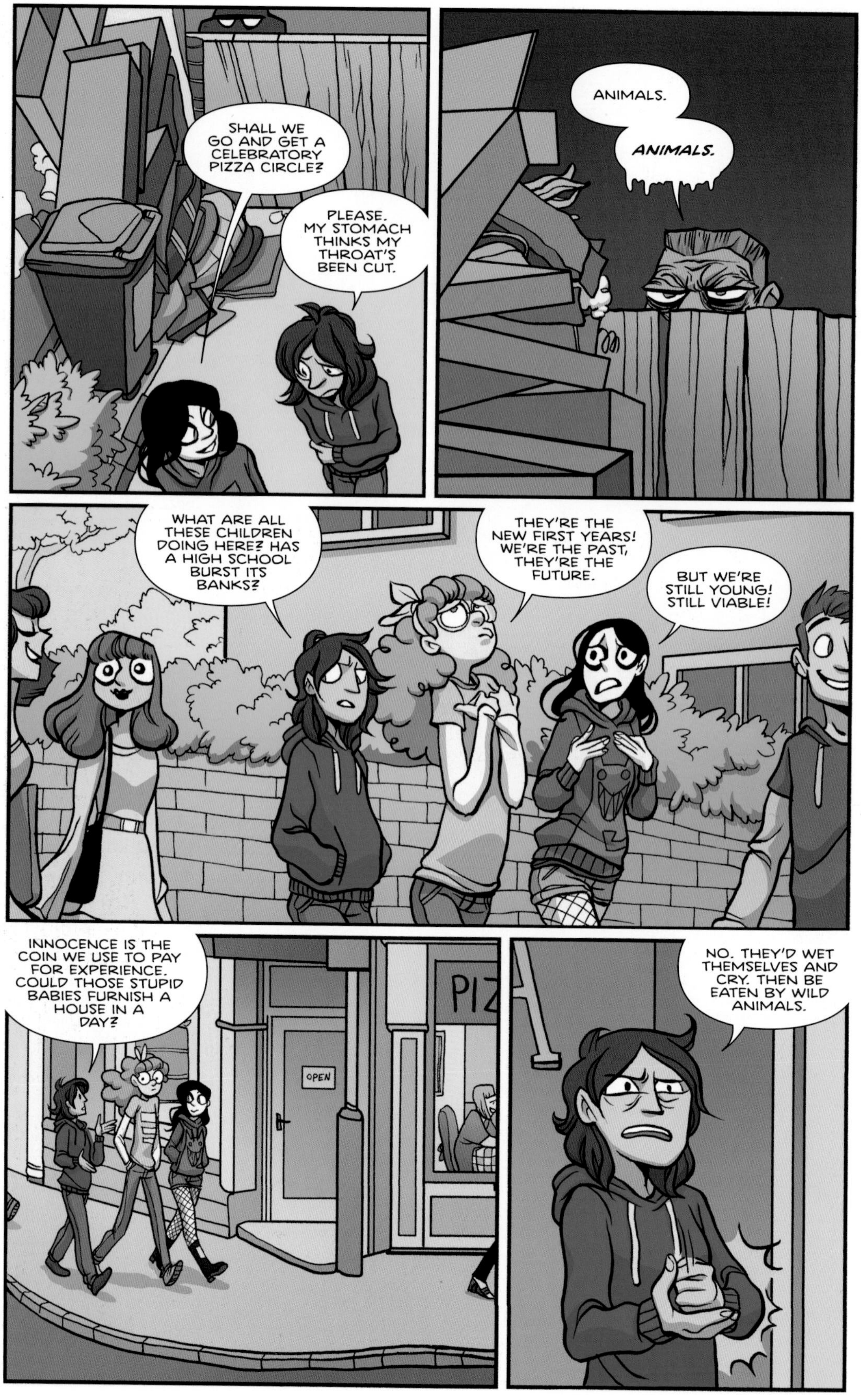
SHALL WE GO AND GET A CELEBRATORY PIZZA CIRCLE?
PLEASE. MY STOMACH THINKS MY THROAT'S BEEN CUT.
ANIMALS.
ANIMALS.
WHAT ARE ALL THESE CHILDREN DOING HERE? HAS A HIGH SCHOOL BURST ITS BANKS?
THEY'RE THE NEW FIRST YEARS! WE'RE THE PAST, THEY'RE THE FUTURE.
BUT WE'RE STILL YOUNG! STILL VIABLE!
INNOCENCE IS THE COIN WE USE TO PAY FOR EXPERIENCE. COULD THOSE STUPID BABIES FURNISH A HOUSE IN A DAY?
OPEN
PIZ
NO. THEY'D WET THEMSELVES AND CRY. THEN BE EATEN BY WILD ANIMALS.

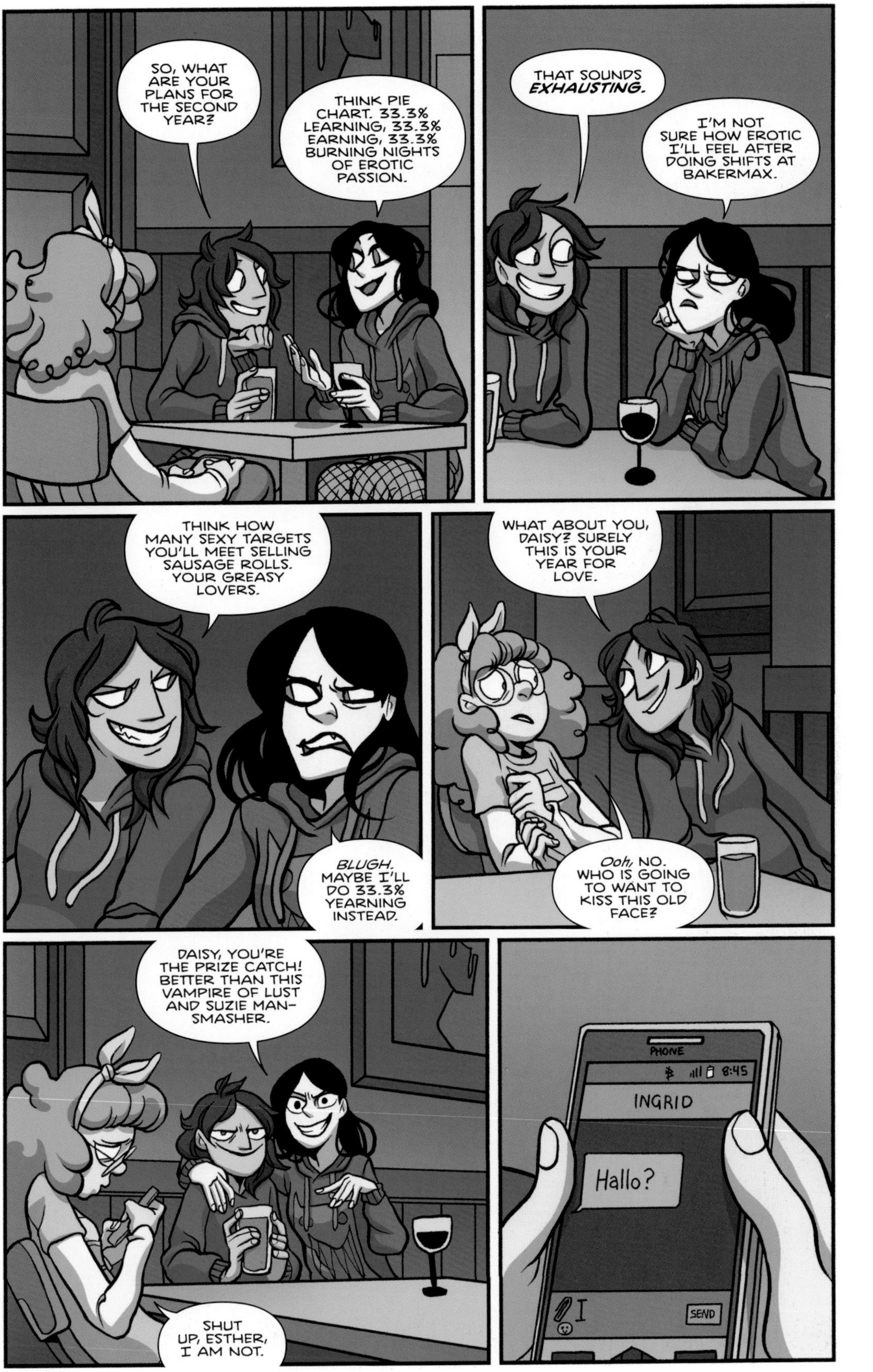
SO, WHAT ARE YOUR PLANS FOR THE SECOND YEAR?
THINK PIE CHART. 33.3% LEARNING, 33.3% EARNING, 33.3% BURNING NIGHTS OF EROTIC PASSION.
THAT SOUNDS *EXHAUSTING.*
I'M NOT SURE HOW EROTIC I'LL FEEL AFTER DOING SHIFTS AT BAKERMAX.
THINK HOW MANY SEXY TARGETS YOU'LL MEET SELLING SAUSAGE ROLLS. YOUR GREASY LOVERS.
BLUGH. MAYBE I'LL DO 33.3% YEARNING INSTEAD.
WHAT ABOUT YOU, DAISY? SURELY THIS IS YOUR YEAR FOR LOVE.
Ooh, NO. WHO IS GOING TO WANT TO KISS THIS OLD FACE?
DAISY, YOU'RE THE PRIZE CATCH! BETTER THAN THIS VAMPIRE OF LUST AND SUZIE MAN-SMASHER.
SHUT UP, ESTHER, I AM NOT.
PHONE
8:45
INGRID
Hallo?
SEND

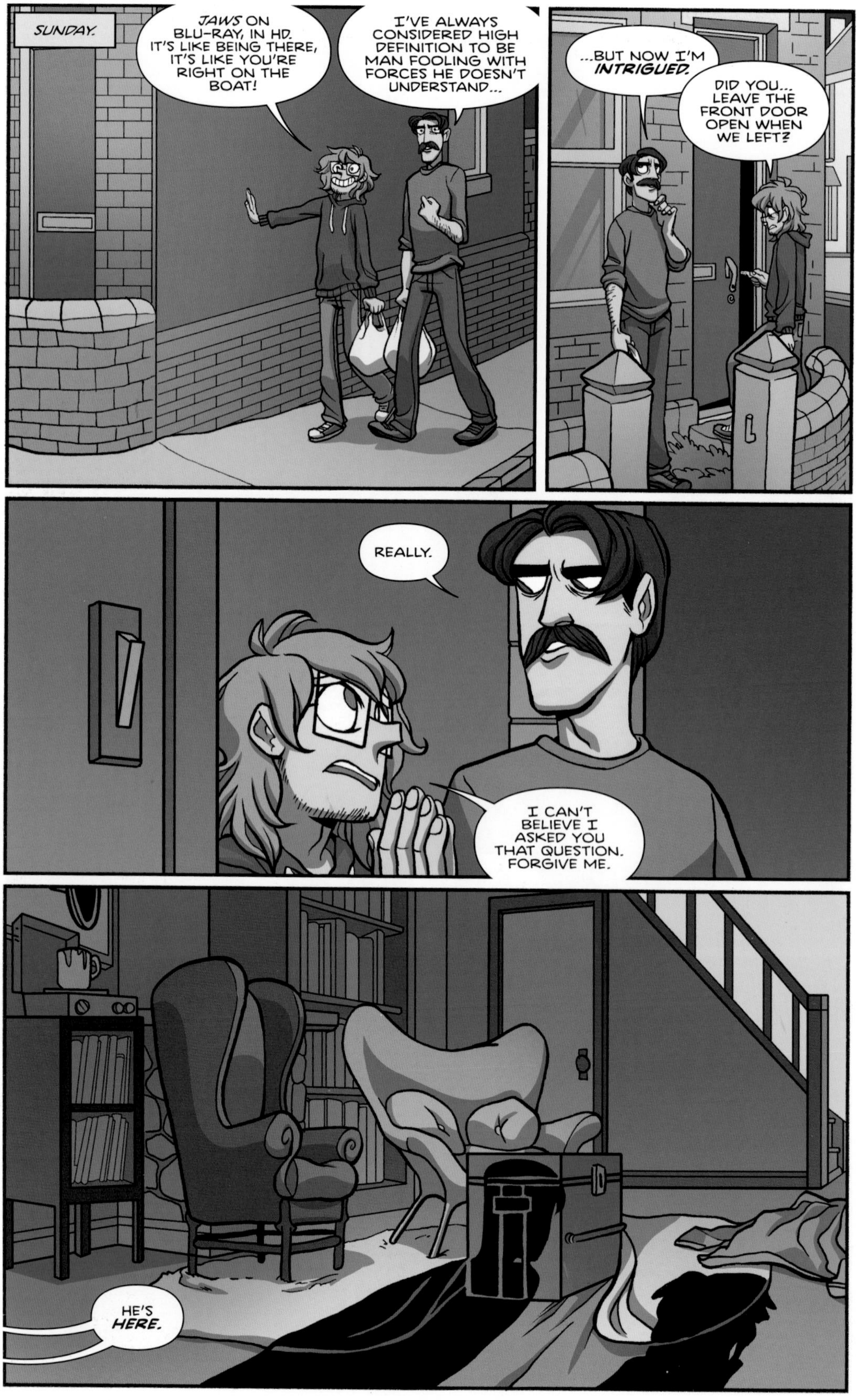
SUNDAY.
JAWS ON BLU-RAY, IN HD. IT'S LIKE BEING THERE, IT'S LIKE YOU'RE RIGHT ON THE BOAT!
I'VE ALWAYS CONSIDERED HIGH DEFINITION TO BE MAN FOOLING WITH FORCES HE DOESN'T UNDERSTAND...
...BUT NOW I'M INTRIGUED.
DID YOU... LEAVE THE FRONT DOOR OPEN WHEN WE LEFT?
REALLY.
I CAN'T BELIEVE I ASKED YOU THAT QUESTION. FORGIVE ME.
HE'S HERE.

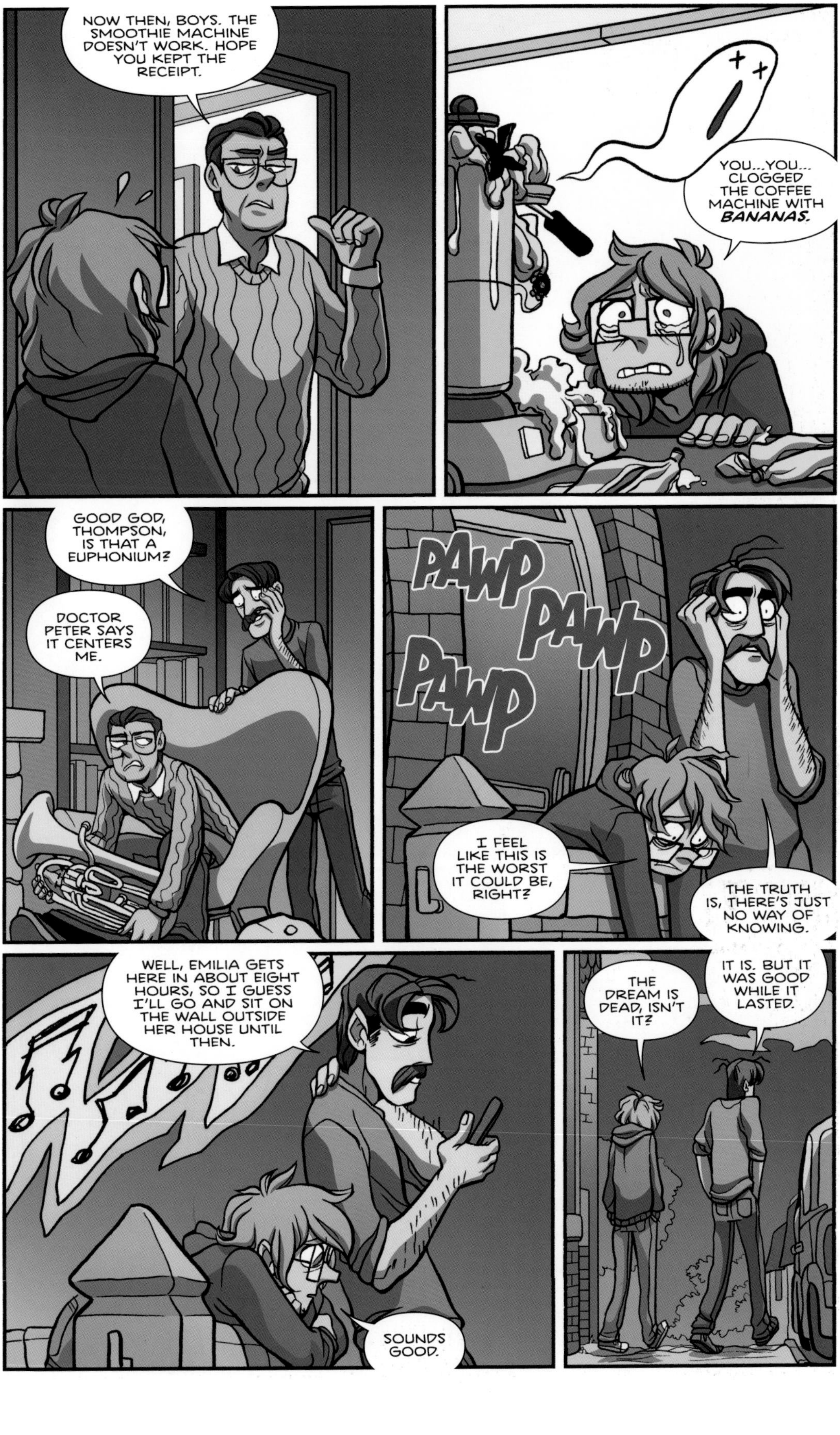
NOW THEN, BOYS. THE SMOOTHIE MACHINE DOESN'T WORK. HOPE YOU KEPT THE RECEIPT.
YOU...YOU... CLOGGED THE COFFEE MACHINE WITH BANANAS.
GOOD GOD, THOMPSON, IS THAT A EUPHONIUM?
DOCTOR PETER SAYS IT CENTERS ME.
PAWP PAWP PAWP
I FEEL LIKE THIS IS THE WORST IT COULD BE, RIGHT?
THE TRUTH IS, THERE'S JUST NO WAY OF KNOWING.
WELL, EMILIA GETS HERE IN ABOUT EIGHT HOURS, SO I GUESS I'LL GO AND SIT ON THE WALL OUTSIDE HER HOUSE UNTIL THEN.
SOUNDS GOOD.
THE DREAM IS DEAD, ISN'T IT?
IT IS. BUT IT WAS GOOD WHILE IT LASTED.

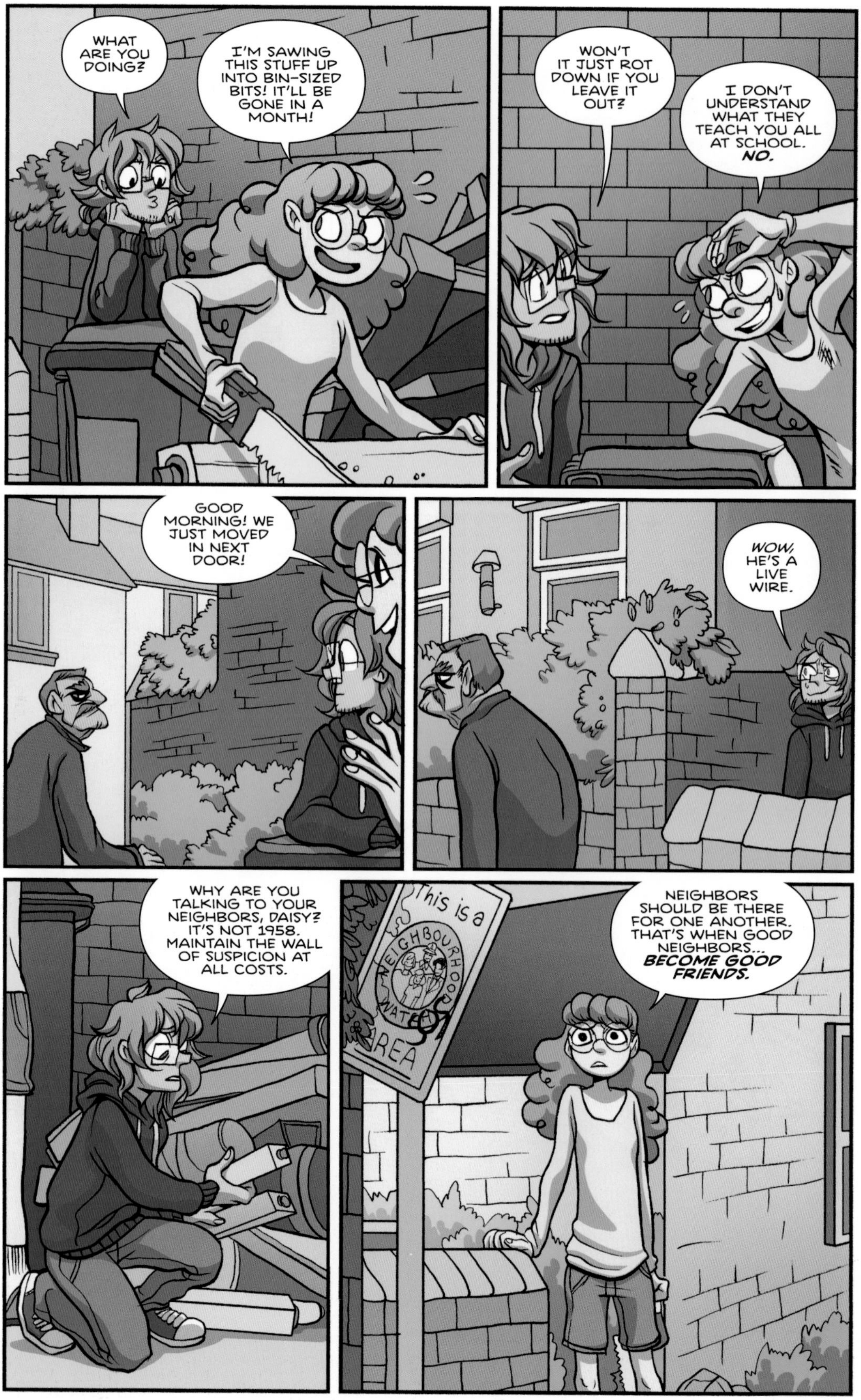
WHAT ARE YOU DOING?
I'M SAWING THIS STUFF UP INTO BIN-SIZED BITS! IT'LL BE GONE IN A MONTH!
WON'T IT JUST ROT DOWN IF YOU LEAVE IT OUT?
I DON'T UNDERSTAND WHAT THEY TEACH YOU ALL AT SCHOOL. ***NO.***
GOOD MORNING! WE JUST MOVED IN NEXT DOOR!
WOW, HE'S A LIVE WIRE.
WHY ARE YOU TALKING TO YOUR NEIGHBORS, DAISY? IT'S NOT 1958. MAINTAIN THE WALL OF SUSPICION AT ALL COSTS.
This is a NEIGHBOURHOOD WATCH AREA
NEIGHBORS SHOULD BE THERE FOR ONE ANOTHER. THAT'S WHEN GOOD NEIGHBORS... ***BECOME GOOD FRIENDS.***

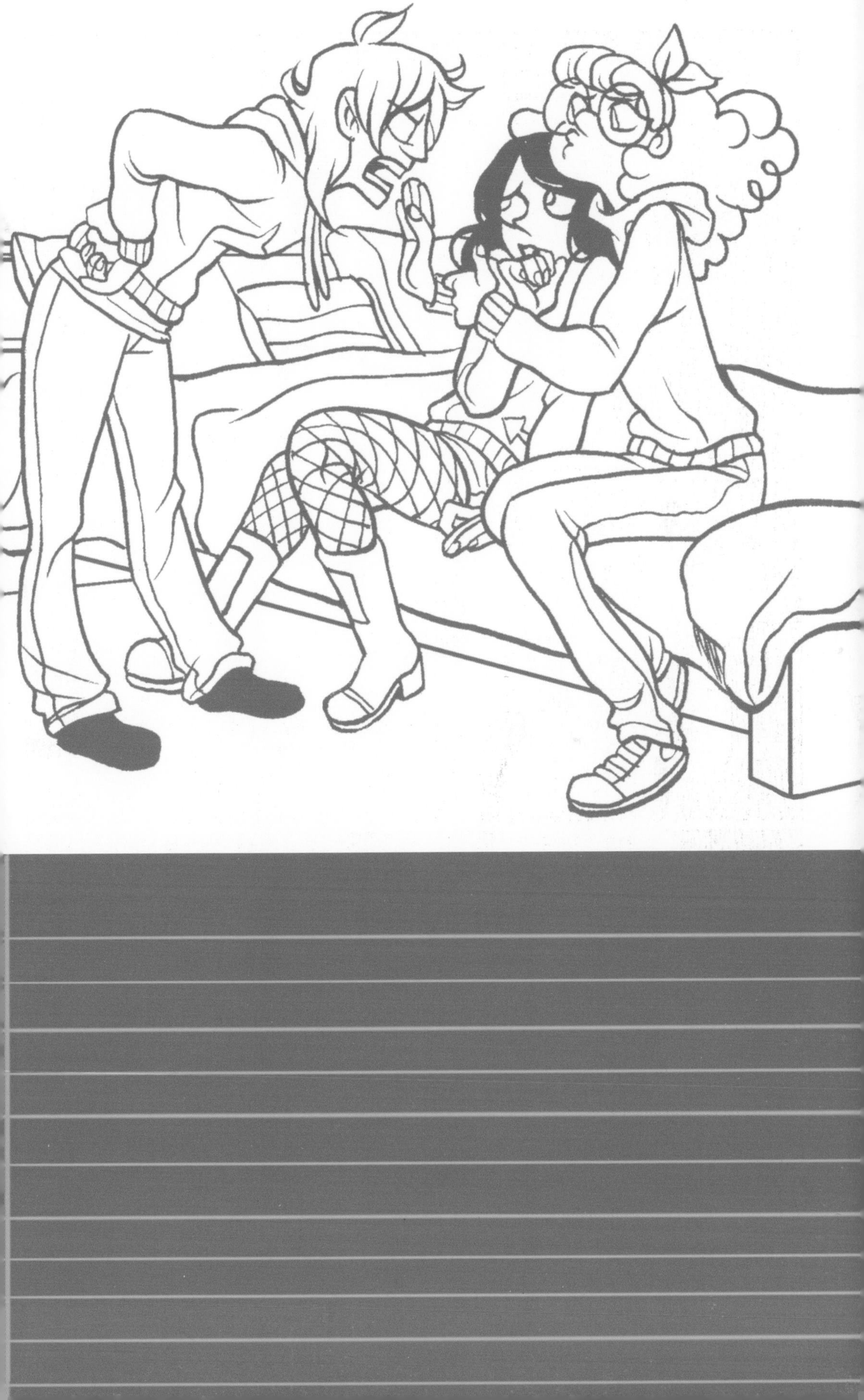

COVER

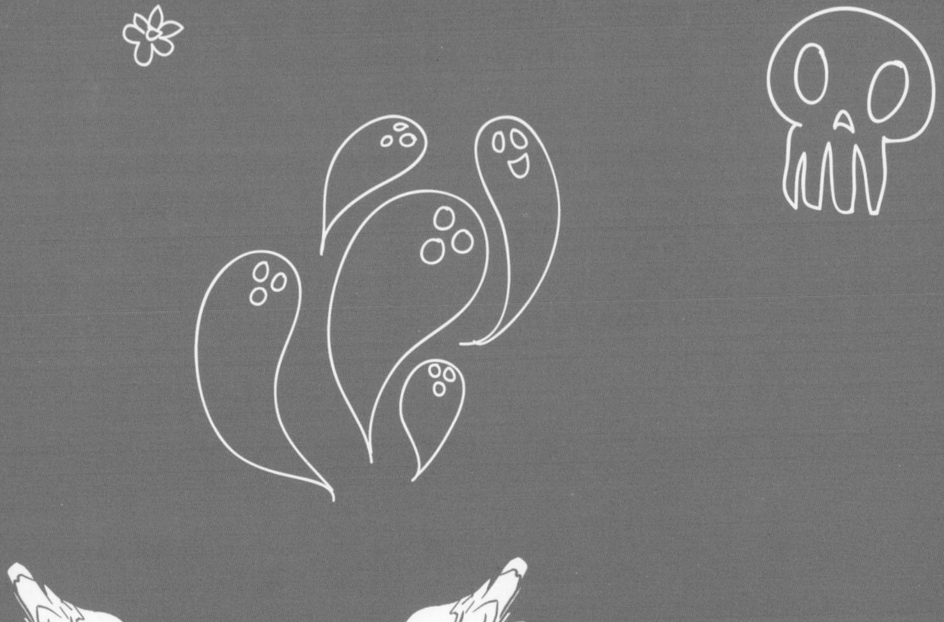

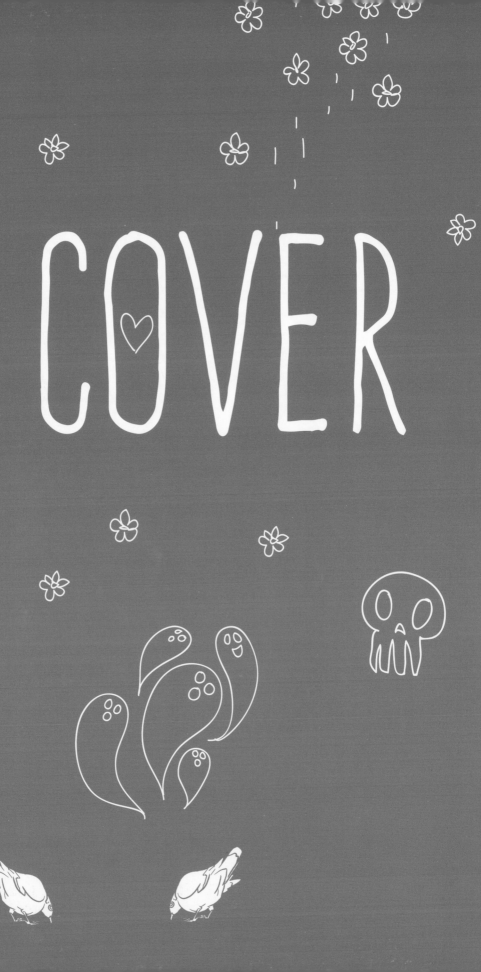

GALLERY

ISSUE #17 COVER
LISSA TREIMAN

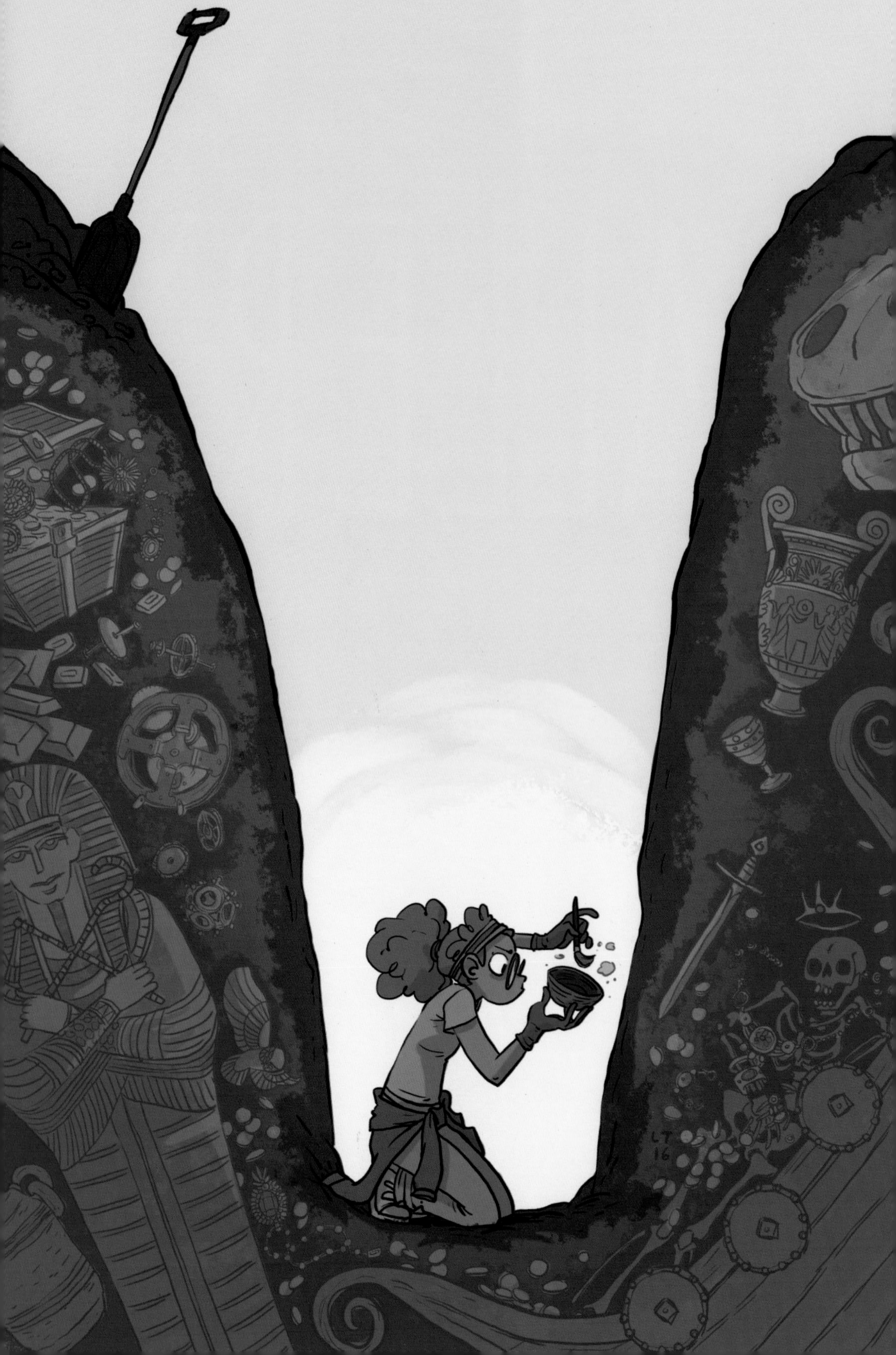

ISSUE #18 COVER
LISSA TREIMAN

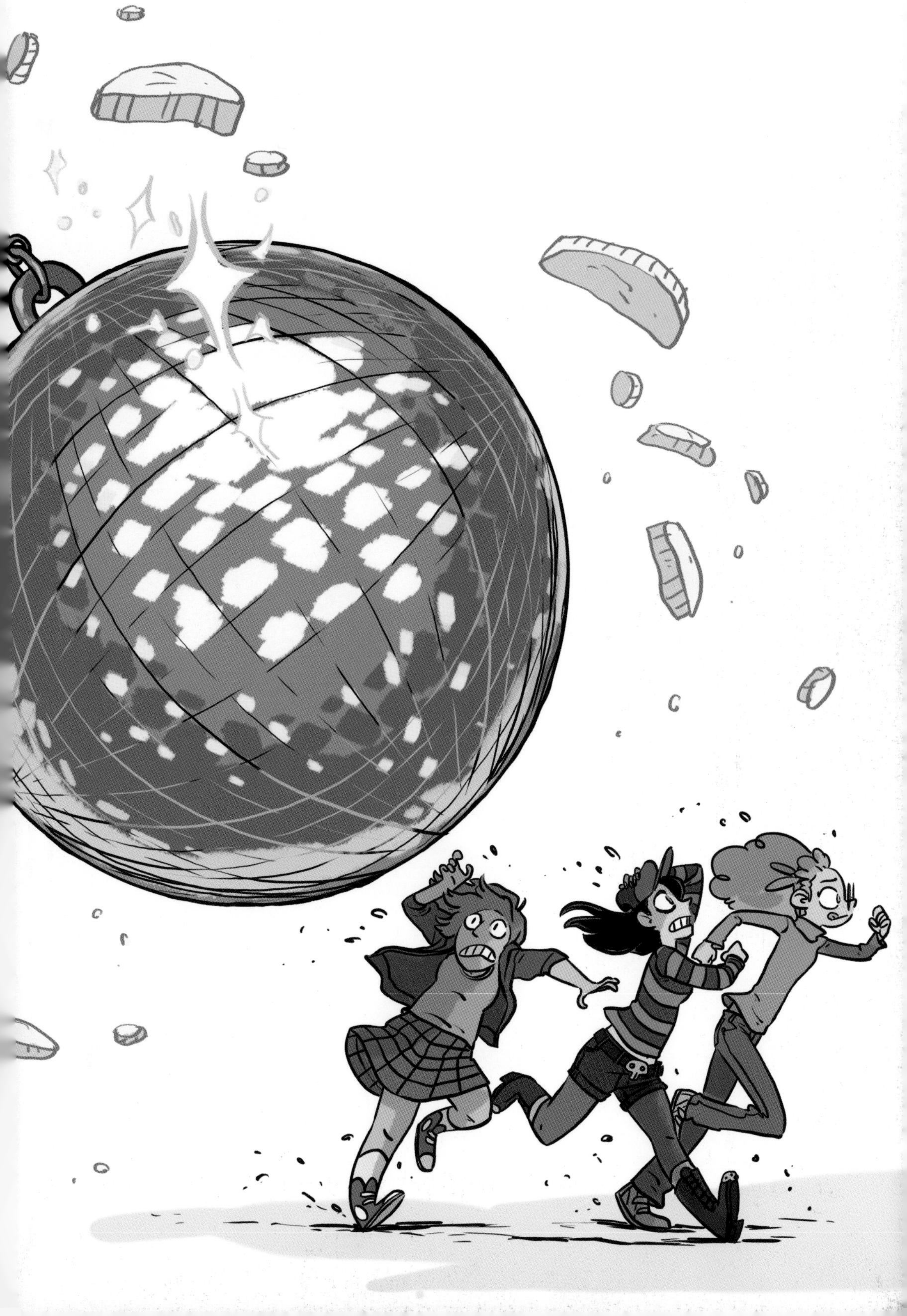

ISSUE #19 COVER
LISSA TREIMAN

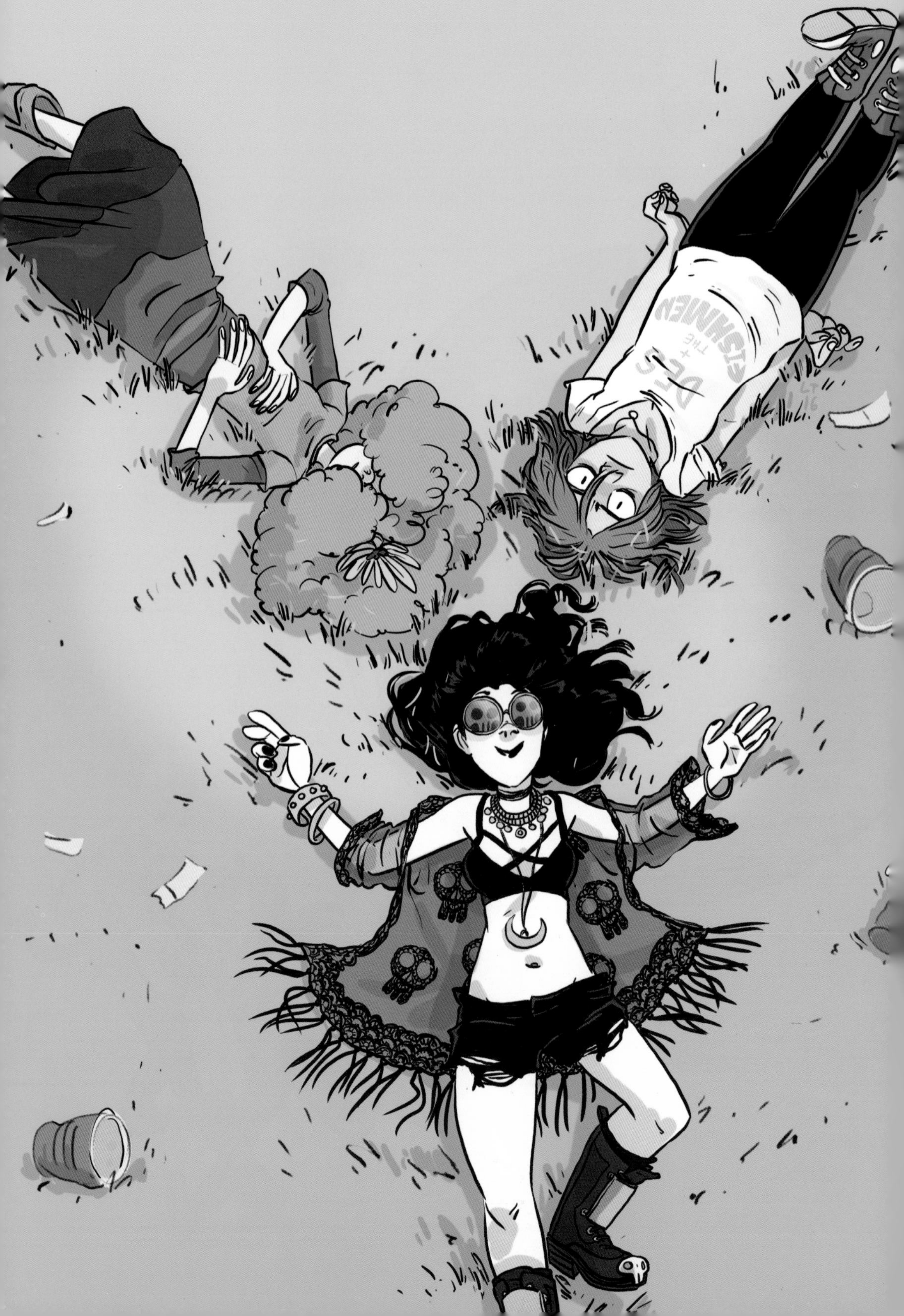

ISSUE #20 COVER
LISSA TREIMAN

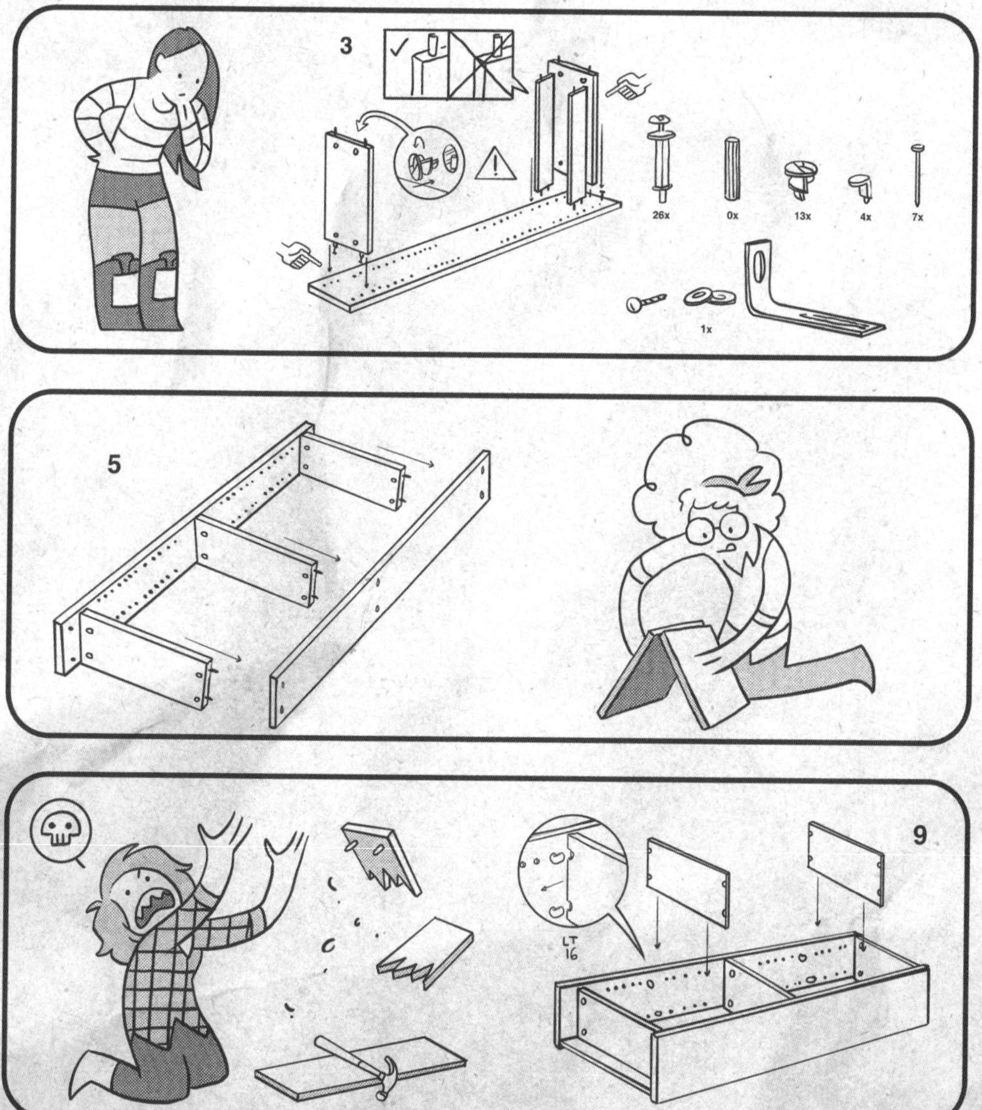

3
26x
0x
13x
4x
7x
1x
5
9
LT
16

SKETCH GALLERY

CHARACTER DESIGNS BY JOHN ALLISON

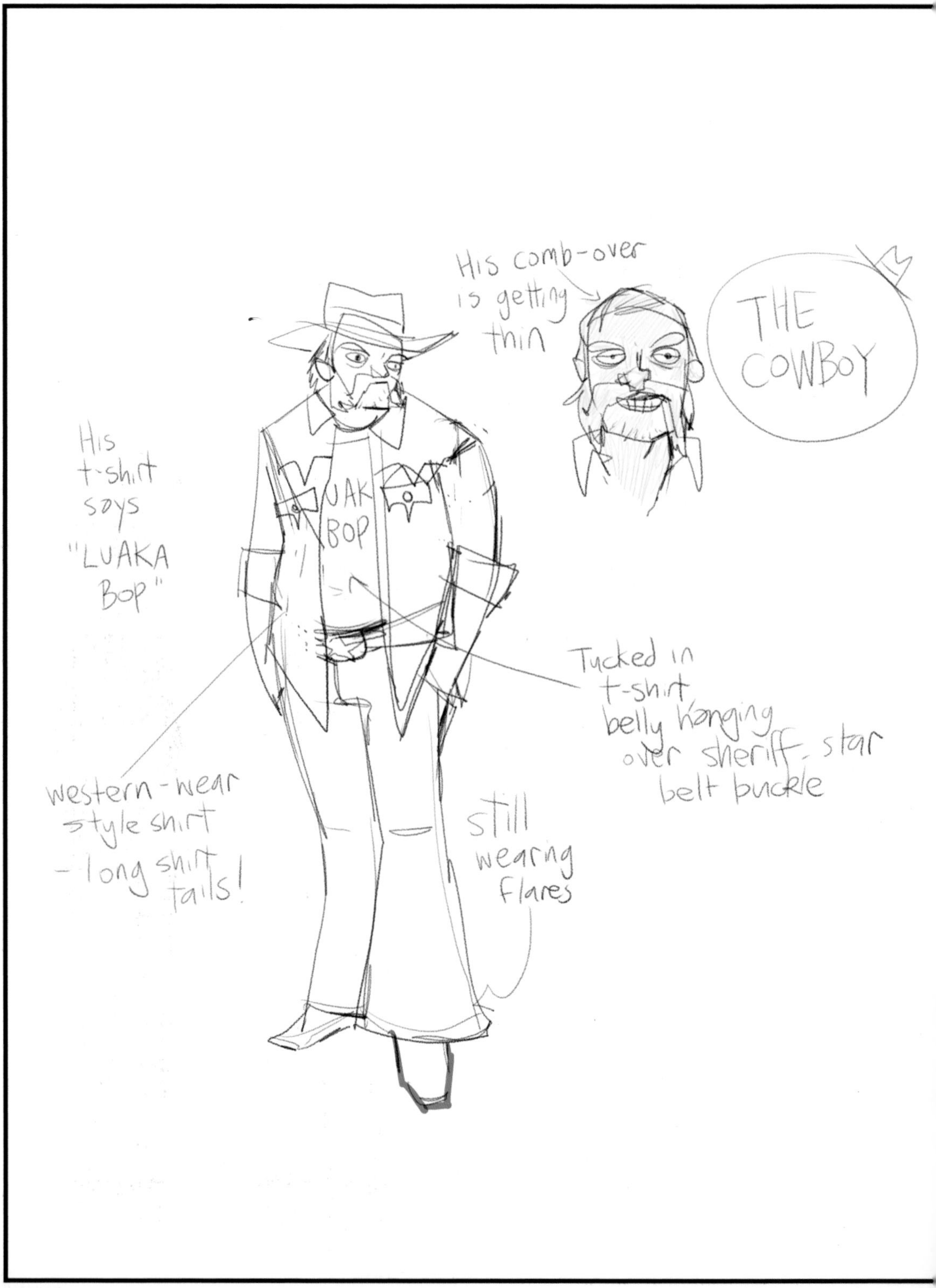
His comb-over is getting thin
THE COWBOY
His t-shirt says "LUAKA Bop"
UAK BOP
Tucked in t-shirt belly hanging over sheriff-star belt buckle
western-wear style shirt - long shirt tails!
still wearing flares

WEARS
EAR
PROTECTORS
ON STAGE

GHOSTLY
AND
MYSTERIOUS

TORTOISESHELL

TAVIS
PLUMB

TOO CHEERFUL
FOR METAL?

HOOD
ALWAYS
UP

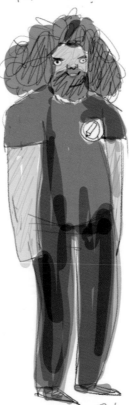

SHINOBI

NANDO

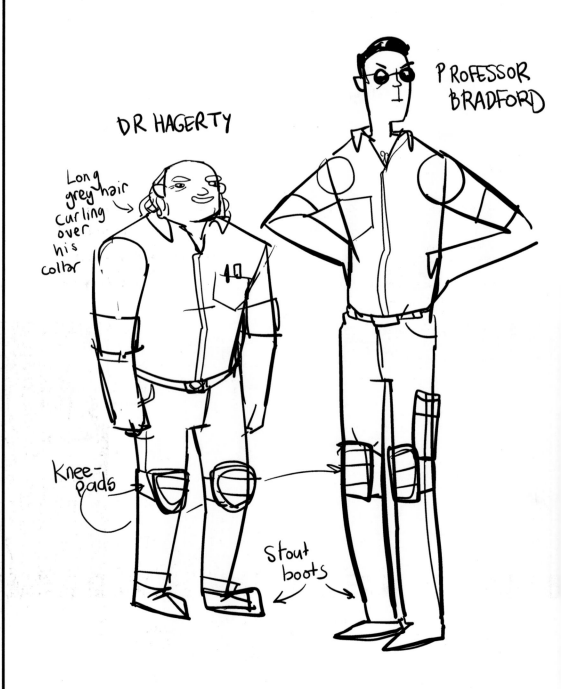

DR HAGERTY

PROFESSOR BRADFORD

Long grey hair curling over his collar

Knee-pads

Stout boots

ALSO FROM BOOM! BOX™

FOR THE LOVE OF IT

STEVENSON • ELLIS • WATTERS • ALLEN
LUMBERJANES
BEWARE THE KITTEN HOLY

LUMBERJANES

Noelle Stevenson | Grace Ellis | Shannon Watters | Brooke Allen

Vol. 1: Beware the Kitten Holy TP
$14.99 US • $18.99 CA • £10.99 UK | ISBN: 978-1-60886-687-8

Vol. 2: Friendship to the Max TP
$14.99 US • $18.99 CA • £10.99 UK | ISBN: 978-1-60886-737-0

Vol. 3: A Terrible Plan TP
$14.99 US • $18.99 CA • £10.99 UK | ISBN: 978-1-60886-803-2

Vol. 4: Out of Time TP
$14.99 US • $18.99 CA • £10.99 UK | ISBN: 978-1-60886-860-5

Allison + Treiman + Cogar
GIANT DAYS
VOLUME ONE

GIANT DAYS

John Allison | Lissa Treiman | Max Sarin

Vol. 1 TP
$9.99 US • $11.99 CA • £7.50 UK | ISBN: 978-1-60886-789-9

Vol. 2 TP
$14.99 US • $18.99 CA • £10.99 UK | ISBN: 978-1-60886-804-9

Vol. 3 TP
$14.99 US • $18.99 CA • £10.99 UK | ISBN: 978-1-60886-851-3

JONESY
HUMPHRIES • BOYLE • QUINN
VOLUME ONE

JONESY

Sam Humphries | Caitlin Rose Boyle

Vol. 1 TP
$9.99 US • $11.99 CA • £7.50 UK
ISBN: 978-1-60886-883-4

Hope Larson • Brittney Williams • Sarah Stern
GOLDIE VANCE
Volume One

GOLDIE VANCE

Hope Larson | Brittney Williams

Vol. 1 TP
$9.99 US • $11.99 CA • £7.50 UK
ISBN: 978-1-60886-898-8

TYSON HESSE'S
DIESEL
IGNITION

TYSON HESSE'S DIESEL: IGNITION

Available Now
$14.99 US • $18.99 CA • £10.99 UK
ISBN: 978-1-60886-907-7

ALSO AVAILABLE

HELP US! GREAT WARRIOR

Madeleine Flores
$19.99 US • $25.99 CA • £14.99 UK
ISBN: 978-1-60886-802-5

TEEN DOG

Jake Lawrence
$19.99 US • $25.99 CA • £14.99 UK
ISBN: 978-1-60886-729-5

THE MIDAS FLESH

Ryan North | Shelli Paroline | Braden Lamb

Vol. 1 TP
$14.99 US • $18.99 CA • £10.99 UK
ISBN 978-1-60886-455-3

Vol. 2 TP
$14.99 US • $18.99 CA • £10.99 UK
ISBN: 978-1-60886-727-1

POWER UP

Kate Leth | Matt Cummings
$19.99 US • $25.99 CA • £14.99 UK
ISBN: 978-1-60886-837-7

BOOM! BOX™ AVAILABLE AT YOUR LOCAL COMICS SHOP OR BOOKSTORE.

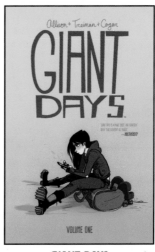

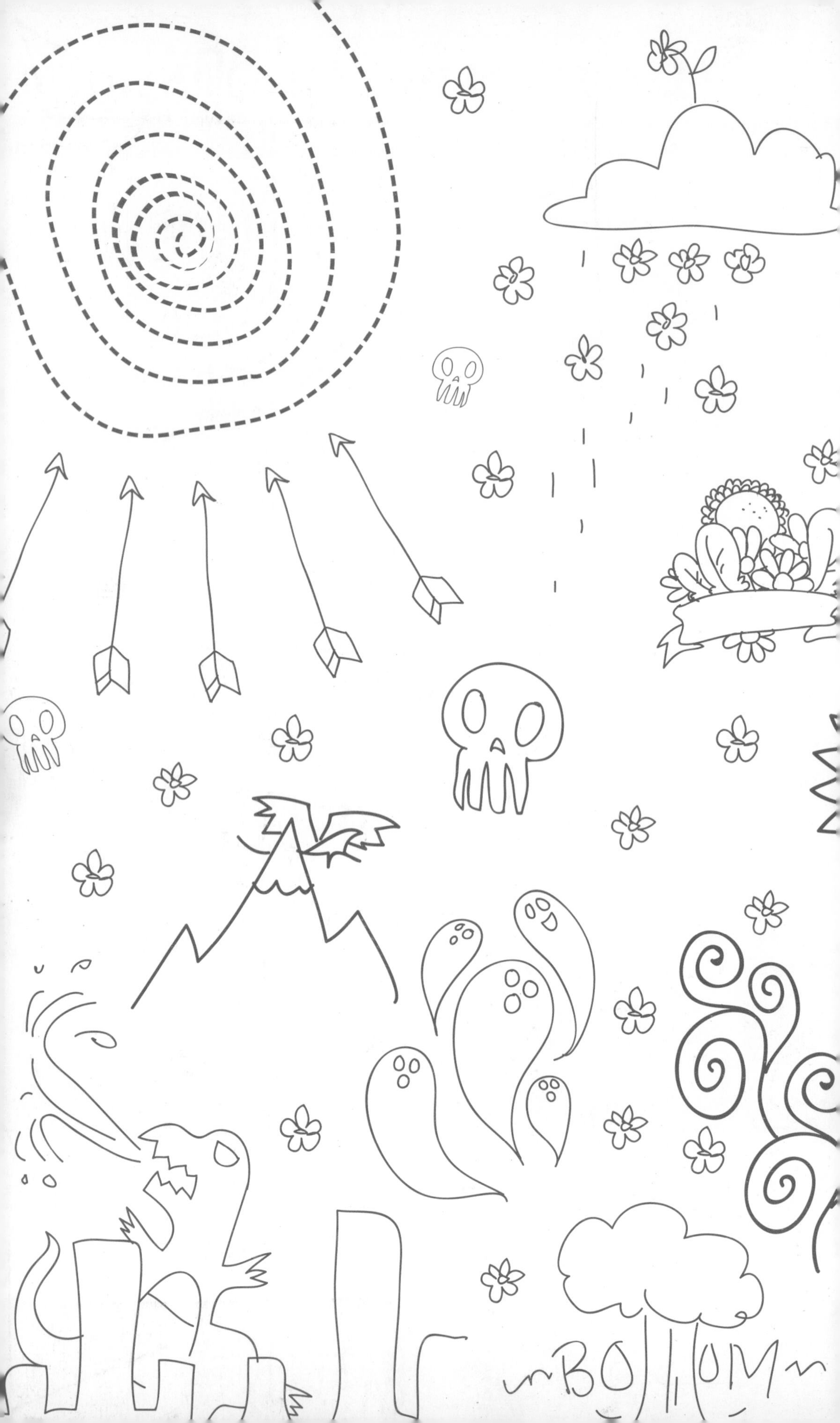